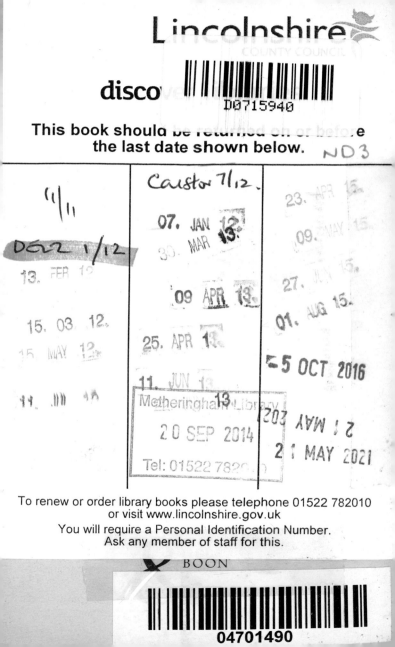

Lincolnshire

COUNTY COUNCIL

disco

D0715940

This book should be returned on or before the last date shown below.

ND3

To renew or order library books please telephone 01522 782010
or visit www.lincolnshire.gov.uk

You will require a Personal Identification Number.
Ask any member of staff for this.

BOON

"It only took us five minutes to get married, no reason why the divorce should take any longer."

"Glad you see it that way." He gave a sharp nod, and his hand went to the inside pocket of his suit. "Of course, I'll want to cover any inconvenience." He extracted a gold pen and a brown leather check book, flipping open the cover and glancing at her. "A million?"

Kaitlin blinked in confusion. "A million what?"

He breathed a sigh of obvious impatience. "Dollars," he stated. "Don't play coy, Kaitlin. You and I both know this is going to cost me."

Was he that desperate?

Wait a minute. *Was* he desperate?

Dear Reader,

I have a passion for historic buildings—big or small, opulent or plain. From the passageways of the Tower of London to the faded boards of a broken-down shed on a lonely prairie highway, I love to imagine who built a house, who walked its halls, who lived, who loved, and who might have died there all those years ago.

Billionaire Zach Harper is descended from pirates. His family castle, built on an island off the coast of New York, is a living museum and the centerpiece of his heritage. But when he accidentally marries architect Kaitlin Saville at a wild Vegas office party, everything is at risk.

I hope you enjoy Zach and Kaitlin's story. I modeled the Harper family castle after the real life Craigdarroch Castle in Victoria, British Columbia. If you're interested, there's a link to the castle on my website.

Happy reading!

Barbara

www.barbaradunlop.com

THE CEO'S ACCIDENTAL BRIDE

BY
BARBARA DUNLOP

Published in Great Britain 2011
by Mills & Boon, an imprint of Harlequin (UK) Limited,
Eton House, 18-24 Paradise Road, Richmond, Surrey TW9 1SR

© Barbara Dunlop 2011

ISBN: 978 0 263 88324 4

51-1111

Harlequin (UK) policy is to use papers that are natural, renewable and
recyclable products and made from wood grown in sustainable forests. The
logging and manufacturing processes conform to the legal environmental
regulations of the country of origin.

Printed and bound in Spain
by Blackprint CPI, Barcelona

Barbara Dunlop writes romantic stories while curled up in a log cabin in Canada's far north, where bears outnumber people and it snows six months of the year. Fortunately she has a brawny husband and two teenage children to haul firewood and clear the driveway while she sips cocoa and muses about her upcoming chapters. Barbara loves to hear from readers. You can contact her through her website at www.barbaradunlop.com.

For my fabulous editor, Kathryn Lye

One

Zach Harper was the last person Kaitlin Saville expected to see standing in the hallway outside her apartment door. The tall, dark-haired, steel-eyed man was the reason she was packing her belongings, the reason she was giving up her rent-controlled apartment, the person who was forcing her to leave New York City.

Facing him, she folded her arms across her dusty blue Mets T-shirt, hoping her red eyes had faded from her earlier crying jag and that no tear streaks remained on her cheeks.

"We have a problem," Zach stated, his voice crisp, and his expression detached. His left hand was clasped around a black leather briefcase.

He wore a Grant Hicks suit and a pressed, white shirt. His red tie was made of fine silk, and his cuff links were solid gold. As usual, his hair was freshly cut, face freshly shaved, and his shoes were polished to within an inch of their lives.

"*We* don't have anything," she told him, curling her toes into the cushy socks that covered her feet below the frayed hem of her faded jeans.

She was casual, not frumpy, she told herself. A woman had a right to be casual in her own home. Where Zach Harper had no right to be in her home at all. She started to close the door on him. But his hand shot out to brace it.

His hand was broad and tanned, with a strong wrist and tapered fingers. No rings, but a platinum Cartier watch with a diamond face. "I'm not joking, Kaitlin."

"And I'm not laughing." She couldn't give one whit about any problem the high-and-mighty Zach Harper might encounter during his charmed life. The man not only got her fired, but he also had her blackballed from every architectural firm in New York City.

He glanced past her shoulder. "Can I come in?"

She pretended to think about it for a moment. "No."

He might be master of his domain at Harper Transportation and at every major business function in Manhattan, but he did not have the right to see her messy place, especially the collection of lacy lingerie sitting under the window.

He clenched his jaw.

She set her own, standing her ground.

"It's personal," he persisted, hand shifting on the briefcase handle.

"We're not friends," she pointed out.

They were, in fact, enemies. Because that was what happened when one person ruined another person's life. It didn't matter that the first person was attractive, successful, intelligent and one heck of a good dancer. He'd lost all rights to...well, anything.

Zach squared his shoulders, then glanced both ways down the narrow corridor of the fifty-year-old building. The light was dim, the patterned carpets worn. Ten doors opened into this particular section of the fifth floor. Kaitlin's apartment was at the end, next to a steel exit door and a fire alarm protected by a glass cover.

"Fine," he told her. "We'll do it out here."

Oh, no, they wouldn't. They wouldn't do anything anywhere, ever again. She started to step back into the safety of her apartment.

"You remember that night in Vegas?" he asked.

His question stopped her cold.

She would never forget the Harper corporate party at the Bellagio three months ago. Along with the singers, dancers, jugglers and acrobats who had entertained the five-hundred-strong crowd of Harper Transportation's high-end clients, there was a flamboyant Elvis impersonator who'd coaxed her and Zach from the dance floor to participate in a mock wedding.

At the time, it had seemed funny, in keeping with the lighthearted mood of the party. Of course, her sense of humor had been aided that night by several cranberry martinis. In hindsight, the event simply felt humiliating.

"The paper we signed?" Zach continued in the face of her silence.

"I don't know what you're talking about," she lied to him.

In fact, she'd come across their mock wedding license just this morning. It was tucked into the lone, slim photo album that lived in her bottom dresser drawer beneath several pairs of blue jeans.

It was stupid to have kept the souvenir. But the glow from her evening on Zach's arm had taken a few days to fade away. And at the time she'd put the marriage license away, those happy minutes on the dance floor had seemed somehow magical.

It was a ridiculous fantasy.

The man had destroyed her life the very next week.

Now, he drew a bracing breath. "It's valid."

She frowned at him. "Valid for what?"

"Marriage."

Kaitlin didn't respond. Was Zach actually suggesting they'd signed a real marriage license?

"Is this a joke?" she asked.

"Am I laughing?"

He wasn't. But then he rarely laughed. He rarely joked, either. That night, she'd later learned, was quite the anomaly for him.

A cold feeling invaded her stomach.

"We're married, Kaitlin," he told her, steel eyes unflinching.

They were not married. It had been a lark. They'd been playacting up there on the stage.

"Elvis was licensed by the state of Nevada," said Zach.

"We were drunk," Kaitlin countered, refusing to believe such a preposterous claim.

"He filed a certificate."

"How do you know that?" Her brain was revving into overdrive, calculating the possibilities and the potential consequences.

"Because my lawyers tell me so." He gave a meaningful glance past her shoulder, into the apartment. "Can I please come in?"

She thought about her mystery novels covering the couch, the entertainment magazines that were sitting out on the coffee table, the credit card and bank statements in piles beside them, revealing her shopping habits for the past month. She remembered the telltale, half-eaten package of Sugar Bob's doughnuts sitting out on the counter. And, of course, there was the box of sexy underwear on full display in the afternoon sunshine.

But, if he was telling the truth, it wasn't something she could ignore.

She gritted her teeth and ordered herself to forget about his opinion. Who cared if he found out she had a weakness for Sugar Bob's? In a matter of days, he'd be out of her life. She'd leave everything she'd ever known, start all over in another city, maybe Chicago or Los Angeles.

Her throat involuntarily tightened at the thought, and her tears threatened to freshen.

Kaitlin hated being uprooted. She'd started over so many times already, leaving security and normalcy behind as she moved from one childhood foster home to another. She'd been in this small apartment since she started college. And it was the only place that had ever felt remotely like home.

"Kaitlin?" he prompted.

She swallowed to clear the thick emotions from her throat. "Sure," she told him with grim determination, stepping aside. "Come on in."

As she shut the door, Zach took in the disarray of packing boxes littering the apartment. There wasn't anywhere for him to sit down, and she didn't offer to clear a chair. He wouldn't be staying very long.

Though she tried to ignore it, her glance shifted involuntarily to the underwear box. Zach tracked her gaze, his resting on the mauve-and-white silk teddy her friend Lindsay had bought her for Christmas last year.

"Do you mind?" she snapped, marching over to pull the cardboard flaps shut.

"Not at all," he muttered, and she thought she heard a trace of amusement in his tone.

He was laughing at her. Perfect.

The cardboard flaps sprang back open again, and she felt the unwelcome heat of a blush. She turned to face him, placing her body between Zach and her underwear.

Behind him, she spied the open box of Sugar Bob's. Three of the doughnuts were missing, transferred from the white cardboard and cellophane container to her hips around nine this morning.

Zach didn't appear to have an ounce of fat on his well-toned body. She'd be willing to bet his breakfast had consisted of fruit, whole grains and lean protein. It was probably whipped up by his personal chef, ingredients imported from France, or maybe Australia.

He perched his briefcase on top of a stack of DVDs on her end table and snapped open the latches. "I've had my lawyers draw up our divorce papers."

"We need lawyers?" Kaitlin was still struggling to comprehend the idea of marriage.

To Zach.

Her brain wanted to go a hundred different directions with that inconceivable fact, but she firmly reined it in. He might be gorgeous, wealthy and intelligent, but he was also cold, calculating and dangerous. A woman would have to be crazy to marry him.

He swung open the lid of the briefcase. "In this instance, lawyers are a necessary evil."

Kaitlin reflexively bristled at the stereotype. Her best friend, Lindsay, wasn't the least bit evil.

For a second, she let herself imagine Lindsay's reaction to this news. Lindsay would be shocked, obviously. Would she be worried? Angry? Would she laugh?

The whole situation was pretty absurd.

Kaitlin anchored her loose auburn hair behind her ears, reflexively tugging one beaded jade earring as a nervous humor bubbled up inside her. She cocked her head and waited until she had Zach's attention. "I guess what happens in Vegas sometimes follows you home."

A muscle twitched in his cheek, and it definitely wasn't from amusement. She felt a perverse sense of satisfaction at having put him even slightly off balance.

"It would help if you took this seriously," he told her.

"We were married by Elvis." She clamped determinedly down on a spurt of nervous laughter.

Zach's gray eyes flashed.

"Come on, Zach," she cajoled. "You have to admit—"

He retrieved a manila envelope. "Just sign the papers, Kaitlin."

But she wasn't ready to give up the joke. "I guess this means no honeymoon?"

He stopped breathing for a beat, and there was something familiar about the way his gaze flicked to her lips.

She was struck by a sudden, vivid memory, instantly sobering her.

Had they kissed that night in Vegas?

Every once in a while, she had a fleeting image of his mouth on hers, the heat, the taste, the pressure of his full lips. She imagined that she could remember his arms around her waist, pulling her tight against his hard body, the two of them molding together as if they belonged.

In the past, she'd always chalked it up to a fevered dream, but now she wondered...

"Zach, did we—"

He cleared his throat. "Let's try to stay on track."

"Right." She nodded, determinedly pushing the hazy image out of her mind. If she'd kissed him even once, it was the worst mistake of her life. She detested him now, and the sooner he disappeared, the better.

She reached out her hand and accepted the envelope. "It only took us five minutes to get married, no reason why the divorce should take any longer."

"Glad you see it that way." He gave a sharp nod, and his hand went to the inside pocket of his suit. "Of course, I'll want to cover any inconvenience." He extracted a gold pen and a brown leather checkbook, flipped open the cover and glanced at her. "A million?"

Kaitlin blinked in confusion. "A million what?"

He breathed a sigh of obvious impatience. "Dollars," he stated. "Don't play coy, Kaitlin. You and I both know this is going to cost me."

Her jaw involuntarily dropped a notch.

Was he crazy?

He waited expectantly.

Was he desperate?

Wait a minute. *Was* he desperate?

She gave her brain a little shake. She and Zach were husband and wife. At least in the eyes of the law. Clearly, she was a problem for him. She doubted the high-and-mighty Zach Harper ran into too many problems. At least, none that he couldn't solve with that checkbook.

Huh.

Interesting.

This time, Kaitlin did chuckle, and tapped the stiff envelope against the tabletop. She certainly didn't want Zach's money, but she sure wouldn't say no to a little payback. What woman would?

This divorce didn't have to happen in the next five minutes. She'd be in New York for at least another couple of weeks. For once in his life, Mr. Harper could bloody well wait on someone else's convenience.

She took a breath, focused her thoughts and tried to channel

Lindsay. Lindsay was brilliant, and she'd know exactly what to do in this circumstance.

Then, the answer came to Kaitlin. She raised her brows in mock innocence. "Isn't New York a joint property state?"

Zach looked confused, but then his eyes hardened to flints.

He was angry. Too bad.

"I don't recall signing a prenup," she added for good measure.

"You want more money," he spoke in a flat tone.

All she really wanted was her career back.

"You got me fired," she pointed out, feeling the need to voice the rationale for her obstinacy.

"All I did was cancel a contract," he corrected.

"You had to know I'd be the scapegoat. Who in New York City is going to hire me now?"

His voice went staccato. "I did not like your renovation design."

"I was trying to bring your building out of the 1930s." The Harper Transportation building had infinite potential, but nobody had done anything to it for at least five decades.

He glared at her a moment longer. "Fine. Have it your way. I got you fired. I apologize. Now how much?"

He wasn't the least bit sorry for having her fired. He didn't care a single thing about her. The only reason he'd even remembered her name was because of the accidental marriage. And he'd probably had to look that up.

She squared her shoulders beneath the dusty T-shirt, determined to take this victory. "Give me one good reason why I should make your life easier?"

"Because you don't want to be married any more than I do."

He had a fair point there. The mere thought of being Zach Harper's wife sent a distinct shiver coursing its way up her spine.

It was distaste. At least she was pretty sure the feeling was distaste. With any other man, she might mistake it for arousal.

"Mrs. Zach Harper." She pretended to ponder, warming to

her stubborn stance as she purposely slowed to note her half-packed apartment. "Don't you have a roomy penthouse on Fifth Avenue?"

He clicked the end of his pen, slowly lowering it to his side. "Are you daring me to call your bluff?"

She cracked her first genuine smile in three months. He wouldn't do it. Not in a million years. "Yeah," she taunted boldly. "Go ahead. Call my buff."

He stepped closer, and an annoying buzz of awareness tickled its way through her stomach. They stared each other down.

"Or you could leave the divorce papers," she offered with mock sweetness. "I'll have my lawyer read them over next week."

"Two million," he offered.

"Next week," she retorted, trying not to show her shock at the exorbitant figure. "Summon up some patience, Zachary."

"You don't know what you're doing, *Katie*."

"I'm protecting my own interests," she told him.

And there was something to be said for that. Seriously. Who could guess what his lawyers had hidden in the divorce documents?

They were both silent. Horns honked and trucks rumbled by five floors below.

"I don't trust you, Zach," she informed him tartly. Which was completely true.

His expression hardening by the second, he stuffed the pen into his pocket, then deliberately tucked the checkbook away. He closed and latched the briefcase, and sharply straightened the sleeves of his jacket.

Seconds later, the door slammed shut behind him.

Zach slid into the passenger seat of the black Porsche Carrera idling at the curb outside Kaitlin's Yorkville apartment building and yanked the door shut behind him.

"Did she sign?" asked Dylan Gilby, as he slipped the gearshift into First.

Zach tugged the seat belt over his shoulder and clicked the latch into place. "Nope."

He normally prided himself on his negotiating skills. But there was something about Kaitlin that put him off his rhythm, and the meeting had been a colossal failure.

He didn't remember her being so stubborn. To be fair, he hadn't known her particularly well. They'd met a few times before the party, but it was only in passing while she was working on the renovation plans for his office building. He remembered her as smart, diligent, fun-loving and beautiful.

He had to admit, the beautiful part certainly still held true. Dressed to the nines in Vegas, she was the most stunning woman in a very big ballroom. Even today, in a faded baseball T-shirt and jeans, she was off the charts. No wonder he'd gone along with Elvis and said "I do." He was pretty sure, in that moment, he did.

"You offered her the money?" asked Dylan.

"Of course I offered her money." Zach had wanted to be fair. Well, and he'd also wanted the problem solved quickly and quietly. Money could usually be counted on to accomplish that.

"No go?" asked Dylan.

"She's calling her lawyer," Zach admitted with a grimace, cursing under his breath. Somehow, he'd played it all wrong. He'd blown his chance to end this neatly, and he had nobody to blame but himself.

Dylan flipped on his signal light and checked the rearview mirror on the busy street. He zipped into a tight space between a Mercedes and an old Toyota. "So, basically, you're screwed."

"Thank you for that insightful analysis," Zach growled at his friend. Harper Transportation could well be on the line here, and Dylan was cracking jokes?

"What are friends for?" joked Dylan.

"Procuring single malt." If ever there was a time that called for a bracing drink, this was it.

"I have to fly today," said Dylan. "And I get the feeling you'll need every brain cell functioning."

Zach braced his elbow against the armrest as the car angled its way through traffic on the rain-dampened street. He reviewed the conversation with Kaitlin like a postgame tape. Where had he messed it up?

"Maybe I should have offered her more," he ventured, thinking out loud. "Five million? Do people say no to five million?"

"You might have to tell her the truth," Dylan offered.

"Are you out of your mind?"

"Clinically, no."

"Tell her that she's inherited my grandmother's entire estate?"

Hand the woman control on a silver platter? Did Dylan want to guarantee Zach was ruined?

"She did, in fact, inherit your grandmother's estate," Dylan pointed out.

Zach felt his blood pressure rise. He was living a nightmare, and Dylan of all people should appreciate the outrageousness of the situation.

"I don't care what kind of paperwork was filed by the Electric Chapel of Love," Zach growled. "Kaitlin Saville is not my wife. She is not entitled to half of Harper Transportation, and I will die before—"

"Her lawyer may well disagree with you."

"If her lawyer has half a brain, he'll tell her to take the two million and run." At least Zach hoped that was what her lawyer would say.

The two of them were married. Yes. He'd have to own that particular mistake. But it couldn't possibly be a situation his grandmother had remotely contemplated when she wrote her will. There was the letter of the law, and then there was the spirit of the law. His grandmother had never intended for a stranger to inherit her estate.

He had no idea if New York was, in fact, a joint property state. But even if it was, he and Kaitlin had never lived together. They'd never had sex. They'd never even realized they were married. The very thought that she'd get half of his corporation was preposterous.

"Did you think about getting an annulment?" asked Dylan.

Zach nodded. He'd talked to his lawyers about that, but they weren't encouraging. "We never slept together," he told Dylan. "But she could lie and say that we did."

"Would she lie?"

"What do I know? I thought she'd take the two million." Zach glanced around, orienting himself as they approached an entrance to Central Park. "We going anywhere near McDougal's?"

"I'm not getting you drunk at three in the afternoon." Dylan shook his head in disgust as he took a quick left. The Porsche gripped the pavement, and they barely beat an oncoming taxi.

"Are you my nursemaid?" asked Zach.

"You need a plan, not a drink."

In Zach's opinion, that was definitely debatable.

They slowed to a stop for a red light at another intersection. Two taxi drivers honked and exchanged hand gestures, while a throng of people swelled out from the sidewalk in the light drizzle and made their way between the stopped cars.

"She thinks I got her fired," Zach admitted.

"Did you?"

"No."

Dylan sent him a skeptical look. "Is she delusional? Or did you do something that resembled getting her fired?"

"Fine." Zach shifted his feet on the floor of the Porsche. "I canceled the Hutton Quinn contract to renovate the office building. The plans weren't even close to what I wanted."

"And they fired her," Dylan confirmed with a nod of comprehension.

Zach held up his palms in defense. "Their staffing choices are none of my business."

Kaitlin's renovation plans had been flamboyant and exotic in a zany, postmodern way. They weren't at all in keeping with the Harper corporate image.

Harper Transportation had been a fixture in New York City for a hundred years. People depended on them for solid reliability and consistency. Their clients were serious, hardworking people who got the job done through boom times and down times.

"Then why do you feel guilty?" asked Dylan as they swung into an underground parking lot off Saint Street.

"I don't feel guilty." It was business. Nothing more and nothing less. Zach knew guilt had no part in the equation.

It was not as if he should have accepted inferior work because he'd once danced with Kaitlin, held her in his arms, kissed her mouth and wondered for a split second if he'd actually gone to heaven. Decisions that were based on a man's sex drive were the quickest road to financial ruin.

Dylan scoffed an exclamation of disbelief as he came parallel with the valet's kiosk. He shut off the car and set the parking break.

"What?" Zach demanded.

Dylan pointed at Zach. "I know that expression. I stole wine with you from my dad's cellar when we were fifteen, and I remember the day you felt up Rosalyn Myers."

The attendant opened the driver's door, and Dylan dropped the keys into the man's waiting palm.

Zach exited the car, as well. "I didn't steal anything from Kaitlin Saville, and I certainly never—" He clamped his jaw shut as he rounded the polished, low-slung hood of the Porsche. The very last element he needed to introduce into this conversation was Kaitlin Saville's breasts.

"Maybe that's your problem," said Dylan.

Zach coughed out an inarticulate exclamation.

"You married her," Dylan said, taking obvious satisfaction in pointing that fact out as they crossed the crowded parking lot. "You must have liked her. You said yourself you haven't slept with her. Maybe you're not so much angry as horny."

"I'm angry. Trust me. I can tell the difference." Zach's interest in Kaitlin was in getting rid of her. Anything else was completely out of the question.

"Angry at her or at yourself?"

"At *her*," said Zach. "I'm just the guy trying to fix the problem here. If she'd sign the damn papers, or if my grandmother hadn't—"

"It's not nice to be mad at your grandmother," Dylan admonished.

Zach wasn't exactly angry with Grandma Sadie. But he was definitely puzzled by her behavior. Why on earth would she put the family fortune at risk? "What was she *thinking?*"

Dylan stepped up onto the painted yellow curb. "That she wanted your poor wife to have some kind of power balance."

An unsettling thought entered Zach's brain. "Did my grandmother talk to you about her will?"

"No. But she was logical and intelligent."

Zach didn't disagree with that statement. Sadie Harper had been a very intelligent, organized and capable woman. Which only made her decision more puzzling.

After Zach's parents were killed in a boating accident when he was twenty, she'd been his only living relative. They'd grown very close the past fourteen years. She was ninety-one when she died, and had grown increasingly frail over the past year. She'd passed away only a month ago.

Zach thought he was ready.

He definitely wasn't.

He and Dylan headed into the elevator, and Dylan inserted his key card for the helipad on top of the forty-story building.

"She probably wanted to sweeten the deal," Dylan offered, with a grin. He leaned back against the rail, bracing his hands on either side as the doors slid shut. "With that kind of money on the table, you'll have a fighting chance at getting a decent woman to marry you."

"Your faith in me is inspiring."

"I'm just sayin'…"

"That I'm a loser?"

The elevator accelerated upward.

Dylan happily elaborated. "That there are certain things about your personality that might put women off."

"Such as?"

"You're grumpy, stubborn and demanding. You want to drink scotch in the middle of the day, and your ass isn't what it used to be."

"My ass is none of your business." Zach might be approaching thirty-five, but he worked out four times a week, and he could still do ten miles in under an hour.

"What about you?" he challenged.

"What about me?" Dylan asked.

"We're the same age, so your ass is in as much danger as mine. But I don't see you in a hurry to settle into a relationship."

"I'm a pilot." Dylan grinned again. "Pilots are sexy. We can be old and gray, and we'll still get the girls."

"Hey, I'm a multimillionaire," Zach defended.

"Who isn't?"

The elevator came smoothly to a halt, and the doors slid open to the small glass foyer of the helipad. One of Dylan's distinctive yellow-and-black Astral Air choppers sat waiting on the rooftop. A pilot by training, Dylan had built Astral Air from a niche division of his family's corporation to one of the biggest flight service companies in America.

Dylan gave a mock salute to a uniformed technician as he and Zach jogged to the chopper and climbed inside.

He checked a row of switches and plugged in the headset. "You want me to drop you at the office?"

"What are your plans?" asked Zach. He wasn't in a hurry to be alone with his own frustrations. He had a lot of thinking to do, but first he wanted to sleep on it, start fresh, maybe forget that he'd screwed up so badly with Kaitlin.

"I'm going up to the island," said Dylan. "Aunt Ginny's been asking about me, and I promised I'd drop in."

"Mind if I tag along?"

Dylan shot him a look of surprise. Aunt Ginny could most charitably be described as eccentric. Her memory was fading, and for some reason she'd decided Zach was a reprobate. She also liked to torture the family's Stradivarius violin and read her own poetry aloud.

"She has two new Pekingese," Dylan warned.

Zach didn't care. The island had always been a retreat for him. He needed to clear his head and then come up with a contingency plan.

"I hope your dad still stocks the thirty-year-old Glenlivet," he told Dylan.

"I think we can count on that." Dylan started the engine, and the chopper's rotor blades whined to life.

Two

A week later, Kaitlin met her best friend, law professor Lindsay Rubin, in the park behind Seamount College in midtown. The cherry trees were in full bloom, scenting the air, their petals drifting to the walkway as the two women headed toward the lily pad–covered duck pond. It was lunchtime on a Wednesday, and the benches were filled with students from the college, along with businesspeople from the surrounding streets. Moms and preschool kids picnicked on blankets that dotted the lush grass.

"I finished reviewing your papers," Lindsay said, swiping her shoulder-length blond hair over the shoulders of her classic navy blazer while they strolled their way down the concrete path.

Kaitlin and Lindsay's friendship went back to their freshman year at college. Social Services had finally stepped out of Kaitlin's life, and Lindsay had left her family in Chicago. On the same floor of the college dorms, they'd formed an instant bond.

They'd stayed close friends ever since, so Lindsay knew that Zach had ruined Kaitlin's career, and she applauded Kaitlin's desire for payback.

"Am I safe to sign?" asked Kaitlin. The sunshine was warm against her bare legs and twinkled brightly where it reflected off the rippling pond. "And how soon do I have to let him off the hook?"

Lindsay grinned in obvious delight. She pressed the manila envelope against Kaitlin's chest, and Kaitlin automatically snagged it.

"Oh, it's better than that," she said.

"Better than what?" Kaitlin was puzzled

Lindsay chuckled deep in her chest. "I mean, you can name your own ticket."

"My ticket to what?"

Why was Lindsay talking in riddles?

"Life," Lindsay elaborated in a singsong voice. "What do you want? A mansion? A jet? A billion dollars?"

"I told you, I said no to the money." Kaitlin hadn't changed her mind about the money. She didn't want what she hadn't earned. "And what do you mean a billion? He was talking about two million."

"It's more than just two million." Lindsay shook her head in what appeared to be amazement. "It's Sadie Harper herself."

Kaitlin lifted her hands, palms up, to signal her incomprehension. She assumed Sadie Harper must have something to do with Zach Harper, but that was as far as she got with the connection. What did the woman have to do with his money?

Lindsay lowered her voice, sounding decidedly conspiratorial as she moved closer to Kaitlin, her gaze darting dramatically around them. "Sadie was the matriarch of the Harper family. She died a month ago at the Harper house on Serenity Island."

The pathway split, and Lindsay eased Kaitlin toward the route that skirted the pond. Their high heels clicked against the smooth, sun-warmed concrete.

Kaitlin still didn't understand Lindsay's point.

"I read a copy of her will," said Lindsay. "You, my girl, are in it."

"How can I be in it?" This conversation was making less sense by the minute. Kaitlin didn't know Sadie Harper. Up until this minute, she'd never even heard of Sadie Harper.

"In fact," Lindsay continued, a lilt of delight in her voice, "*you* are the sole beneficiary."

Kaitlin instantly halted, turning to peer at Lindsay with narrowed eyes. Traffic zipped past on Liberty, engines roaring, horns honking. Cyclist and pedestrian traffic parted around them, some people shooting annoyed looks their way.

Lindsay tugged on Kaitlin's arm, moving them off to the side of the pathway. "She left her entire estate to Mrs. Zachary Harper."

"Get out," Kaitlin breathed.

"I am dead serious."

Kaitlin stepped farther aside to make room for a pair of cyclists skirting the edge of the path. "How did she even know about me?"

"She didn't." Lindsay gave her head a shake. "That's the beauty of it. Well, part of the beauty of it. The whole thing is truly very beautiful."

"Lindsay," Kaitlin prompted with impatience.

"The will holds her estate in trust until Zach gets married," said Lindsay. "But he's already married so, in the eyes of the law, you own fifty percent of Harper Transportation."

Kaitlin's knees went weak.

No wonder Zach had seemed desperate.

No wonder he was in such a hurry to get rid of her.

"So, what do you want?" Lindsay asked again, a giggle at the end of the question.

Speechless, Kaitlin shoved the envelope back at Lindsay, overwhelmed by the thought of what was at stake. She took a step away and shook her head in silent refusal.

"I don't want anything," she finally managed to reply.

"Don't be ridiculous," Lindsay cajoled.

"The wedding was a joke," Kaitlin reminded her. "It was a mistake. I didn't mean to marry him. And I sure don't deserve half his company."

"Then take the money instead," Lindsay offered reasonably.

As if that made it better. "I'm not taking his money, either."

Lindsay held up her palms in exasperation. "So, what do you want? What's the payback?"

Kaitlin thought about it for a moment. "I want him to sweat."

Lindsay chuckled and linked her arm with Kaitlin's, turning her to resume their walk. "Trust me, honey." She patted her on the shoulder. "He is definitely sweating."

"And I want a job," said Kaitlin with conviction. That was what she'd lost in this debacle. She needed her career back.

"I don't want free money," she told Lindsay, voice strengthening. "I want a chance to prove myself. I'm a good…no, I'm a *great* architect. And all I want is a fair shot at proving it."

The path met up with the sidewalk, and Lindsay tipped her head and stared up at the Harper Transportation sign on the pillar-adorned, ten-story concrete building across the street. "So, ask him for one," she suggested.

Kaitlin squinted at the massive blue lettering. She glanced to Lindsay, then again at the sign. Suddenly, the possibilities of the situation bloomed in her brain.

A slow smile grew on her face. "There's a reason I love you," she said to Lindsay, giving her arm a squeeze. "*That* is a brilliant plan."

And it was exactly what she'd do. She would make Zach Harper give her a job. She'd make him give her the job that should have been hers in the first place—developing designs for the renovation of his corporate headquarters.

She'd pick up right where she'd left off. In fact, she'd come up with an even better concept. Then, once she'd proven to him and to the world that she was a talented architect, she'd sign whatever papers he needed her to sign. He'd have his company back, and she'd have her life back. And, most importantly, she wouldn't have to leave New York City.

The light turned green, and she tugged on Lindsay's arm. "You're coming with me."

Lindsay hesitated, staying on the curb. "I have a class now."

"We'll be quick," Kaitlin promised.

"But—"

"Come on. I need you to spout some legalese to scare him."

"Trust me, he's already scared." But Lindsay started across the street.

"Then it'll be easy," Kaitlin assured her, stepping up on the opposite curb then mounting the short concrete staircase.

They made their way across the small serviceable lobby of the Harper Transportation building. Kaitlin had been in the building many times, so she knew Zach's office was on the top floor.

While they took the groaning elevator ride up twenty stories, she straightened her short black skirt and adjusted her sleeveless, jade-green sweater, anchoring the strap of her small handbag. She moistened her lips as they exited the elevator. Then she determinedly paced down the narrow hallway to Zach's receptionist.

"I'm here to see Zach Harper," Kaitlin announced with as much confidence as she could muster.

Her pulse had increased, and her palms were starting to dampen. She was suddenly afraid the plan wouldn't work. Like a drowning woman who'd been tossed a life vest, she was afraid her chance would float away before she could grab on to it.

"Do you have an appointment?" the young brunette woman asked politely, glancing from Kaitlin to Lindsay and back again. Kaitlin had seen the woman from a distance while working on the project for Hutton Quinn, but they'd never been introduced.

"No," Kaitlin admitted, realizing the odds were slim that Zach was available at that particular moment.

Lindsay stepped forward, standing two inches taller than Kaitlin, her voice telegraphing professionalism and importance. "Tell him it's a legal matter," she said to the receptionist. "Kaitlin Saville."

The woman's head came up, curiosity flaring briefly in her blue eyes. "Of course. One moment, please." She rose from her wheeled desk chair.

"Thanks," Kaitlin whispered to Lindsay, as the receptionist walked down the hallway that stretched behind her desk. "I knew you'd come in handy."

"I'll send you a bill," Lindsay responded in an undertone.

"No, you won't." Kaitlin knew her friend better than that. Lindsay had never charged her for anything in her life.

"Ten minutes from now, you'll be able to afford me," Lindsay joked.

"Send Zach the bill," Kaitlin suggested, a nervous sense of excitement forming in her belly. If this worked. If it actually worked...

"Will do," Lindsay promised.

The receptionist returned, a practiced, professional smile on her face. "Right this way, please."

She led them past a few closed doors to the end of the hallway where a set of double doors stood open on a big, bright, burgundy-carpeted room.

She gestured them inside, and Kaitlin entered first.

If she thought Zach had looked impressive standing in her apartment last week, it was nothing compared to what his office did for him. The fine surroundings reeked of power, and he was obviously in his element.

His big desk was walnut with inset cherry panels. A matching credenza and hutch were accented with cherry wood drawers, and a bookcase opposite showcased leather-bound volumes and nautical carvings. The desk chair was also leather, and high-backed with carved wood arms. Two guest chairs flanked the front of his desk, while a meeting table stood in an arched window alcove.

As Kaitlin crossed the thick carpet, Zach came to his feet. As usual, he wore a perfectly pressed, incredibly well-cut suit. His usual white shirt was crisp and bright. The necktie was gold this time, with a subtle silver thread that picked up the sunlight.

"Thank you, Amy." He nodded to the receptionist, who closed the doors as she left the room.

His gaze flicked to Lindsay and he quirked a questioning brow in her direction.

"My lawyer," Kaitlin explained to him. "Lindsay Rubin."

"Please sit down." Zach gestured to the leather guest chairs.

But Kaitlin chose to remain standing. "I'll sign your papers," she told him.

Zach's glance went back to Lindsay, then returned to Kaitlin. The barest hint of a smile twitched his full lips, and there was a definite flare of relief in his gray eyes.

"But I want two things," Kaitlin continued.

Though she knew she ought to enjoy this, she was far too nervous to get any pleasure out of watching him sweat.

This had to work.

It simply *had* to.

Zach's brow furrowed, and she could almost feel him calculating dollar figures inside his head.

"One—" she counted on her fingers, struggling to keep a quaver from forming in her voice "—our marriage stays secret." If people found out she was married to Zach, the professional credential of renovating his building would mean less than nothing. The entire city would chalk it up to their personal relationship.

"Two," she continued, "you give me a job. Renovation design director, or some similar title."

His eyes narrowed. "You want a job?"

"Yes," she confirmed.

He appeared genuinely puzzled. "Why?"

"I'll need an office and some support staff while I finish planning the renovations to your building. Since you already have those things available here…"

He was silent for a full three seconds. "I'm offering you money, not a job."

"I don't want your money."

"Kaitlin—"

She squared her shoulders. "This is not negotiable, Zach. I get free rein, carte blanche. I do your renovation, my way, and—"

He leaned forward, tenting his fingers on the polished desktop. "Not a hope in hell."

"Excuse me?"

They glared at each other for a drawn-out second while a thousand emotions skittered along her nervous system.

He was intimidating. He was also undeniably arousing. He was both her problem and her solution. And she was terrified this chance would somehow slip through her fingers.

Then Lindsay spoke up, her voice haughty and authoritarian as she stepped into the conversation. "You should know, Mr. Harper, that I've provided Ms. Saville with a copy of Sadie Harper's will, as filed with the probate court."

The room went to dead silent.

Nobody moved, and nobody breathed.

Kaitlin forced herself to straighten to her full height. She crossed her arms over her chest, letting his stunned expression boost her confidence.

"I'll divorce you, Zach," she told him. "I'll sign the entire company over to you. Just as soon as I have my career back."

His furious gaze settled on Kaitlin. His tone turned incredulous. "You're *blackmailing* me?"

Sweat prickled her hairline, anxiety peaking within her. "I'm making you a deal."

Several beats ticked by in thick silence, while her stomach churned with anxiety.

His expression barely changed. But finally, he gave a single, curt nod.

Her heart clunked deep in her chest, while a wave of relief washed coolly over her skin.

She'd done it.

She'd bought herself a second chance.

She doubted Zach would ever forgive her. But she couldn't let herself care about that. All that mattered was she was back on the job.

From beneath the stained concrete porch of the Harper Transportation building, Kaitlin stared at the rain pounding down on Liberty Street. It was the end of her first full day of work, and her nerves had given way to a cautious optimism.

Zach hadn't made her feel particularly welcome, but she did have a desk, a cubbyhole of a windowless office, with a drafting table and a bent filing cabinet. And, though other staff members seemed confused by the sudden change in the renovation project, one of the administrative assistants had introduced her around and offered to help out.

Kaitlin inhaled the moist May air. Fat raindrops were splashing on the concrete steps, forming puddles and rivulets on the pavement below. She glanced at the gray sky and gauged the distance to the subway staircase in the next block. She wished she'd checked the weather report this morning and tossed an umbrella into her bag.

"I trust you found everything you need?" Zach's deep voice held a mocking edge behind her.

Kaitlin twisted, taking in his towering height and strong profile against the backdrop of his historic building. She was forced to remind herself that she was in the driver's seat in this circumstance. She should make him nervous, not the other way around.

"Could you have found me a smaller office?" she asked, attempting to go on the offensive. He was obviously making some kind of a point by relegating her to a closet. It didn't take a genius to figure out he was attempting to put her in her place.

"Haven't you heard?" His mouth flexed in a cool half smile, confirming her suspicions. "We're renovating."

"I notice *your* office is plenty roomy," she persisted, hoping to give him at least a twinge of guilt.

"That's because I own the company." His expression hinted that he also owned a decent portion of the world.

She arched a meaningful brow in his direction, feeling a little more in control when his expression wavered. "So do I," she pointed out.

Her victory was short-lived.

"You want me to evict a vice president for you?" Left unsaid was the understanding that while he could easily give her special treatment, they both knew it would raise questions amongst the staff, potentially compromising her desire to keep their personal relationship a secret.

"You have nothing between the executive floor and a closet?" Of course, the last thing she wanted to do was call attention to herself. He had to treat her no better and no worse than any other employee. Right now, it certainly appeared he was treating her worse.

"Take your pick," Zach offered with a careless shrug. "I'll kick someone out."

Kaitlin hiked up her shoulder bag. "And they'll know it's me."

"You do own the company," he drawled.

She rolled her eyes. "Just treat me like you would anyone else."

"That seems unlikely." He nodded to a shiny, black late-model town car cruising up to the curb. "Can I give you a lift?"

She slid him an incredulous glance. He had to be kidding.

"Hop into the boss's car after my first day of work?" Right. That would work well to keep her under the radar.

"You afraid people will get the wrong idea?"

"I'm afraid they'll get the right idea."

His mouth quirked again. "I have some papers you need to sign."

The rain wasn't letting up, but she took a tentative step forward, muttering under her breath. "No divorce yet, Mr. Harper."

He stepped into the rain beside her, keeping pace, his voice going low as hers. "They're not divorce papers, Mrs. Harper."

The title on his lips gave her a jolt. She'd spent the day trying to forget about their circumstances and focus on getting started at her job. But she was beginning to realize forgetting their circumstances was going to be nearly impossible.

They were married, *married*.

She tipped her head, surreptitiously taking in his profile, the dark eyes, the furrowed brow and the small scar on his right cheekbone. She tried to imagine an intimate relationship, where they joked and touched and—

"Kaitlin?"

She gave herself a firm mental shake, telling herself to get control. "What kind of papers?"

He glanced around, obviously confirming a sufficient buffer of space between them and the other Harper employees heading out the doors. "Confirmation of my positions as the president and CEO."

"What are you now?"

"President and CEO." His gunmetal eyes were as dark and impenetrable as the storm clouds. He was not a man who easily gave away his emotions. "There's been a change in the company ownership," he explained.

It took a moment for the enormity of his words to sink in. Without her signature, his position in the company was in jeopardy. He couldn't do what he'd always done, and he couldn't be who he'd always been, without her consent on paper.

Something hard and cold slid though her stomach.

It wasn't right that she had this kind of power. All she wanted was to do her job. She didn't want to have to sift through her confusing feelings for Zach. And she sure didn't want to have to analyze the circumstances and decide if they were fair.

They weren't. But then neither was the alternative.

"Get in the car, Kaitlin," he told her. "We need to get this signed and settled."

She couldn't help but note the stream of employees exiting from the building. Even as they dashed down the rainy steps, most of them glanced curiously at Zach. Climbing into his car in full view of a dozen coworkers was out of the question.

She leaned slightly closer, muffling her voice. "Pick me up on Grove, past the bus stop."

He gave a subtle but unmistakable eye roll. "You don't think that's a bit cloak-and-dagger?"

"I'm trying to blend," she reminded him. Her plan to rescue her career would come to a screeching halt if people had any inkling that she had some leverage over Zach.

"You'll get soaked," he warned her.

A little water was the least of her worries.

Well, except for what it would do to her shoes. They'd been on sale, her only pair of Strantas. She loved what they did for her legs, and they looked great with anything black.

She braced herself, mentally plotting a path around the worst of the scattered puddles.

"Have a nice evening, Mr. Harper," she called loud enough for passersby to hear as she trotted down the stairs.

She made her way along the sidewalk, surging with the crowd toward the traffic light at the corner. When it turned green, she paced across the street, avoiding numerous black umbrellas in her path and hopping over the gurgle of water flowing against the opposite curb.

On the other side, she negotiated her way to the edge of the sidewalk, raking her wet hair back from her forehead and tucking it behind her ears. She swiped a few raindrops from her nose then extracted her cell phone, pressing the speed dial as she hustled toward the bus stop shelter.

"Kaitlin?" came Lindsay's breathless voice.

"What are you doing?"

"Riding the bike."

Kaitlin pictured Lindsay on the stationary bike crammed into the small living space of her loft. "I'm going to be late for dinner."

"What's going on?" Lindsay huffed.

As she wove her way through the wet crowd, Kaitlin lowered her voice to mock doom. "I'm about to get into a big black car with Zach Harper."

"Better send me the license plate number."

Kaitlin cracked a grin, comforted by Lindsay's familiar sense of humor. The two women had known each other so long, they were almost always on the same wavelength. "I'll text it to you."

A deep, classic-rock bass resonated in the background. A fixture whenever Lindsay exercised. "Why are you getting in his car?"

"He wants me to sign something."

"Better let me read it first."

"I will if it looks complicated," Kaitlin promised. "He says it's to reconfirm him as president and CEO." Not that she trusted everything Zach said. In fact, thus far, she trusted exactly nothing of what Zach said.

"It could be a trick," Lindsay warned.

Kaitlin grinned into the phone. "There is yet another reason I love you."

"I've got your back. Seriously, Katie, if you see the words *irreconcilable* or *absolute* I want you to run the other way."

"Will do." Kaitlin caught sight of the black car. "Oops. There he is. Gotta go."

"Call me when you're done. I want details. And dinner." There was a gasp in Lindsay's voice. "I definitely still want dinner."

"I'll call," Kaitlin agreed, folding her phone and tucking it into the pocket of her purse as Zach swung open the back door of his car and hopped out onto the sidewalk next to her.

He flipped up the collar of his gray overcoat and gestured her inside. She gathered her own wet coat around her and ducked to climb in.

"Lunatic," he muttered under his breath.

"Lucky for you we're not having children," she said over her shoulder as she settled into the seat.

"Lucky for me we're not buying plants." He firmly shut the door behind her before walking around the vehicle to get in behind the driver.

She shook the rainwater from her fingertips, smoothing her soaked jacket and frowning at her soggy bag. "Green and Stafford in Yorkville," she said to the driver, getting an unwelcome glimpse of herself in the side mirror.

"The penthouse, Henry," Zach corrected.

"You're not dropping me off?" She wasn't sure why his bad manners surprised her. Zach was all about his own convenience. His minions obviously didn't factor in on his radar.

"Henry will take you home later," he said.

Later? She raised her brow in a question.

"The papers are at my penthouse."

Of course they were. Having the papers available in the car would be far too simple. Resigned, she plunked her bag into her lap and gave up on trying to repair her look. She was a mess, and that was that.

"Don't you worry about inconveniencing me," she drawled. "It's not like I have a life."

Henry pulled into the snarl of traffic heading for Liberty and Wildon, while Zach sent her a speculative, sidelong glance. "Stroke of a pen gets you out of this any old time you want."

She determinedly shook her head. Much as she'd love to sever both their marital and business ties, if she let him off the hook, the man would fire her in the blink of an eye.

He leaned back in the leather seat, angling his body so that he faced her. "What if I promised you could keep your job?"

Rain rattled harder on the car's sunroof, while the wipers slapped their way across the windshield, blurring the view of the street.

Kaitlin made a half turn in the seat, meeting Zach's dark eyes. "That would require me trusting you."

"You can trust me," he assured her.

She coughed out a laugh. "You ruined my *life*."

He frowned. "I made you a very wealthy woman."

"I don't want to be a wealthy woman."

"I say again. You can get out of this anytime you want."

She made a show of glancing around the interior of the car. "Is there some way to exit this conversation?" she asked him. "Or does it just keep circling the drain?"

Horns honked in the lanes beside them as Henry inched his way through a left-hand turn. Kaitlin swiped at her damp, tangled hair, resisting an urge to slip off her soggy shoes and wiggle her toes into the thick carpet.

"You're going to find it very inconvenient being my business partner," Zach warned.

She cocked her head, watching him as she spoke. "Because you'll go out of your way to make it hell?"

He resettled himself in the butter-soft seat. "And here I thought I was being subtle."

"This is fifty pages long." Standing in the middle of Zach's penthouse living room, Kaitlin frowned as she leafed her way through the document.

"It deals with control of a multimillion-dollar corporation," he returned with what he hoped resembled patience. "We could hardly jot it down on a cocktail napkin."

Though he'd had a few days to come to terms with this bizarre twist in his life, Zach was still chafing at the circumstance. He didn't want to have to justify anything about Harper Transportation to Kaitlin, even temporarily. His grandma Sadie had complete faith in him—at least he'd always thought she'd had complete faith in him. He'd never had to explain anything about the company to her. He'd basically been running the show for over a decade.

But now there was Kaitlin. And she was underfoot. And she had questions. And he could only imagine what kind of monstrosity he'd be left with for an office building.

Dylan had pointed out yesterday that appeasing Kaitlin was better than losing half his company. Maybe it was. But barely.

"I'll need to have my lawyer look at this," Kaitlin announced, reaching down to pull open her oversize shoulder bag in order to deposit the document inside.

"Give it a read before you decide," Zach cajoled through half-gritted teeth. "It's not Greek." He pointed. "You and I sign page three, authorizing the board of directors. The board members have already signed page twenty, confirming my positions. The rest is…well, read it. You'll see."

She hesitated, peering at him with suspicion. But after a moment, she sighed, dropping her bag onto his sofa. "Fine. I'll take a look."

He tried not to cringe as her wet purse hit the white leather cushion of his new, designer Fendi.

"Your coat?" he offered instead, holding out his hands to accept it. The coat he'd hang safely in his hall closet before she had a chance to drape it over his ironwood table.

She slipped out of the dripping rain jacket, revealing a clingy, black-and-burgundy, knee-length dress. It had capped sleeves, a scooped neck and a pencil-straight skirt that flowed down to her shapely legs, which were clad in black stockings. Damp as they were, her high heels accentuated slim ankles and gorgeous calves.

Though they'd spoken briefly at the office this morning, she'd been wearing her coat at the time. He'd had no idea what was hidden beneath. Just as well he hadn't had *that* image inside his brain all day long.

"Thank you," she acknowledged, handing him the coat.

"I'm…uh…" He pointed in the general direction of the hallway and the kitchen, making his escape before she noticed he was ogling her body with his mouth hanging open.

In the kitchen, he found that his housekeeper had left a note informing him there was salad and a chicken dish in the fridge. She'd also left a bottle of Cabernet on the breakfast bar. Zach automatically reached for the corkscrew, breathing through the dueling emotions of frustration and arousal.

Sure, Kaitlin was an attractive woman. He knew that. He'd known that from the minute he met her. But there were attractive women everywhere. He didn't have to fixate on her.

He popped the cork.

No. No reason at all for him to fixate on her.

In fact, maybe he should get himself a date. A date would distract him. He'd been working too hard lately, that was all. A date with another, equally attractive woman would nip this fascination with Kaitlin in the bud.

He reached for the crystal glasses hanging from the rack below the cabinet.

Dylan had offered to introduce him to his newest helicopter pilot. He'd said she was attractive and athletic. She was a Yankees fan, but he could probably live with that. And she had a master's degree in art history. Who didn't like art history?

Before Zach realized what he'd done, he'd filled two glasses with wine.

"Oh, hell."

Then again, he supposed the woman deserved a drink. If she signed the papers, they'd toast the accomplishment. If she refused to sign, maybe the wine would loosen her up, and he could take another stab at convincing her.

He shrugged out of his suit jacket, moving farther down the

hallway to the master bedroom. There, he hung the jacket in his closet, shed his tie and glanced in the mirror above his dresser.

He definitely needed a shave. And his white shirt was wrinkled from being worn all day.

He glanced once at the jacket and considered putting it back on. But common sense prevailed. Instead, he unbuttoned his cuffs and rolled up the sleeves of his shirt. If this was a date, he'd shave and redress. But it wasn't a date. And his looks would be the last thing on Kaitlin's mind.

More comfortable, he returned to the kitchen and retrieved the wineglasses. He moved down the hallway to the living room. Inside the doorway, he paused.

Kaitlin seemed to have made herself at home. She'd kicked off her strappy shoes and curled her legs beneath her, knees bent and pressed together, stocking-clad feet pushing up against the arm of his sofa. Her hair was drying to a wild, glossy halo that framed her smooth skin. And her face was a study in concentration, red lips pursed, green eyes slightly squinted as she read her way through the pages.

She looked good in his living room, somehow settled and at home.

Funny, he'd seen her dressed up, dressed down, dancing with laughter and crackling with anger. But he'd never caught her unaware. And somehow he had the feeling this was the real woman, halfway between Vegas glitter and Saturday casual, her energy turned inward, mind working. He sensed a calm intelligence in her that he hadn't noticed before.

He must have moved, because she finally noticed him.

"Wine?" he offered, raising one of the glasses, walking forward, pretending he hadn't been staring.

"You're right," she told him, letting the papers drop into her lap, stretching an arm across the back of the sofa in an obviously unintended, sensual gesture.

"Never thought I'd hear you say that." But there was no bite to his words. He'd meant to mock her, but it came off as a gentle joke.

She flipped the document back to the first page and set it in front of her on the coffee table. "I'll sign it."

"Really?" Too late, he realized he sounded surprised. To cover, he handed her the glass of wine.

She accepted the glass and shrugged. "It's exactly what you said it was."

"How about that," he couldn't help but tease.

"Shocked the heck out of me," she returned, doing a double take, seeming to note he'd shed the jacket and tie.

He sat down on the other end of the couch. "Then, cheers." He lifted his glass.

She allowed a small smile, which made her prettier than ever. She leaned toward him, holding out her glass to clink it against his. The motion gave him a glimpse of her cleavage, and he was forced to drag his gaze away from her soft breasts.

They each took a sip.

Then her smile grew, and an impish dimple appeared in her right cheek. "Tough day at the office, dear?" She mimicked what was obviously a wifely voice of concern.

Something inside him responded warmly to the banter. "You know—" he paused for effect "—the usual."

"Is this weird?" she asked, eyes narrowing.

"Yes."

"Because it feels weird. I mean, on a scale of one to, well, weird, it's weird."

"Did that make sense inside your head?"

She took another drink, waving a dismissive hand. "I'm sure you got the gist of it."

"I did. And I agree. It's weird."

"We're married." She said the words in a tone of wonder.

"Yes, we are." Zach took a healthy swig from his own glass. He'd never been married. And even if he had, he couldn't help but doubt anything could prepare a man for this particular situation.

She paused, and then her voice went soft. "I'm not trying to ruin your life, you know."

He didn't like it that she seemed so vulnerable. It was better when she was acting tough and feisty. Then, it was easier to view her as a combatant. And he was beginning to admit fighting with Kaitlin was much safer than joking with her.

He struggled to put a hard note back in his voice. "I guess it was the blackmail scheme that had me confused."

Her green eyes were clear, open and honest. "I'm not looking to gain anything."

He made a show of skeptically raising his brows.

"I'm looking to set things right," she assured him.

He tried to sound doubtful. "Is that how this is playing out inside your head?"

"Once I've earned my way back into the good graces of my profession, you'll be home free. I want a career, Zach, not your company."

He had to admit, he believed her. He understood she was trying to make her own life better. Her methods weren't the most noble from where he was standing. But he did accept the fact that he was collateral damage.

She leaned forward and flipped to the signature page of the document. "Do you have a pen?"

"Sure." He rose and crossed to the small rosewood desk that held a telephone and a reading lamp.

"I'm meeting Lindsay for dinner," Kaitlin explained from behind him. "I don't want to be too late."

"I have a date," he lied, extracting a pen from the small desk drawer. He'd call Dylan and get the number of the pretty helicopter pilot just as soon as Kaitlin left.

"You're *cheating* on me?"

Her outburst surprised him, but when he turned, he saw the laughter lurking in her jade-green eyes.

"Yes," he answered easily, not about to rise to the bait. "I've been cheating on you since the wedding."

"Men," she huffed in pretend disgust, folding her arms across her chest, accenting her breasts.

Focusing beyond her lovely figure, he shrugged an apology on behalf of his gender as he crossed the room. "What can I say?"

She accepted the pen, bending her head to sign the papers. "Well, *I've* been faithful."

He waited for the punch line.

It didn't come.

"Seriously?" he asked.

She finished her signature with a flourish, declining to answer.

But he couldn't let it go. "You haven't had sex with anybody since Vegas?"

"What do you mean *since* Vegas." She sat up straight, handing the pen back in his direction. "Who do you think I had sex with in Vegas?"

He accepted it, feeling a twinge of remorse. "I didn't mean it that—"

"The only person I was with in Vegas was you and we didn't—" The amusement suddenly fled her eyes, replaced by uncertainty. "We, uh, didn't, did we?"

Okay, *this* was interesting. "You don't remember?" He might not have total recall of the entire night's events. But he knew they hadn't made love.

Then the vulnerability was back, and she slowly shook her head. "I barely remember the wedding."

He was tempted to string her along, but quickly changed his mind. The cursed vulnerability again. It made him want to protect her, not mess with her mind.

"We didn't," he assured her.

She tilted her head to one side. "Are you sure? Do *you* remember every minute?"

Their gazes locked for a couple of heartbeats.

"I'd remember that."

"So, you can't say for sure..."

"Has this been bothering you?" he asked.

"No."

"Because it sounds like—"

Suddenly, she snagged her bag and hooked it over her shoulder, coming to her feet. "It's not bothering me. If we did it, we did it."

"We *didn't*." Not that he hadn't wanted to. Not that he wouldn't love to. Not that he wasn't still—

Damn it. He had to stop going there.

"Because I'm not pregnant or anything," she said, slipping into her sexy shoes and straightening her clingy dress. The action pulled it tighter against her lithe body, and it was more than he could do not to let his gaze take a tour.

He summoned his strength. "Kaitlin. I think we need to leave Vegas back in Vegas."

"We tried."

That was true.

"But it didn't work," she pointed out.

"Blame Elvis," he drawled, fixing his gaze firmly on her face and telling himself to leave it right there.

Her smile grew. "You're funnier than you let on, you know?"

He gritted his teeth against her softening expression, those lips, those eyes, that tousled hair. It would be so easy to pull her into his arms and kiss her.

But for the first time in his life, he ignored the powerful urge.

"Thanks for signing the papers," he offered gruffly.

"Thanks for giving me a job."

The specter of her previous designs appeared inside his head. He didn't know what he'd do if she insisted on resurrecting them.

Now might not be the time. Then again, now might be the perfect time. They seemed to have come to a truce. Maybe he should take advantage of it.

"You know that building has been in my family for five generations," he declared.

"That doesn't mean it can't look good."

"There are a lot of different ways to make it look good." Classic ways. Functional ways. They were a transportation company, for goodness' sake, not an art museum.

He wished he could interest her in using the Hugo Rosche plans as a jumping-off point. Hugo had taken over after he'd canceled Hutton Quinn. Zach had paid a penalty to get out of the contract. But Hugo had left on good terms with a reference and several prospective clients set up by Zach. Hugo's plans made the most of the existing layout, and they'd only take about six months to implement.

"And I'm going to find the best one," she breezily promised. Her bravado frightened him.

"It's my heritage you're playing with, you know."

Her expression faltered for a split second, something close to pain flitting through her eyes. But she recovered instantly, and the confidence returned. "Then, you're a very lucky man, Zach Harper. Because I'm going to make your heritage a whole lot better."

Three

The following week, Kaitlin and Lindsay made their way into the bright pool of sunshine on the roof of the Harper Transportation building. The cement was solid beneath Kaitlin's feet, and the building seemed to fit seamlessly into its surroundings. Modern high-rises towered over on two sides, while across Liberty, they studied a row of dignified—if chipped—lion statues, and looked farther to the river.

The roof was square, blocked on one side by the service level and staircase. It was bordered by a three-foot-high concrete wall. Years of rain had stained it, but the mottled color evoked a certain nobility. Kaitlin couldn't help wonder what it would be like to work under the same roof as five generations of your ancestors.

Her mother had died when she was born. Her father was "unknown," not even a name on a birth certificate. And if nineteen-year-old Yvette Saville had had relatives somewhere nobody ever found them. All Kaitlin had of her own heritage was a single, frayed and blurry photo of her mother, and the address of the rooming house where Yvette had been living prior to Kaitlin's birth.

While her anger and frustration toward Zach had diminished as the days went by, she couldn't seem to fight off the spurt of jealousy that bubbled up when she thought about his heritage. He'd had such a safe and privileged upbringing. While she was on the outside looking in, he'd been wrapped in the loving embrace of his wealthy family, wanting for nothing, experiencing the finest life had to offer.

"Explain to me again why we couldn't go straight to Rundall's for lunch?" called Lindsay. She'd fallen behind in her higher heels and straight skirt.

"See that?" Kaitlin turned to walk backward, banishing her negative thoughts as she swept her arm, pointing toward the deep blue Hudson River. "If I can get a permit to add three stories, the view will be amazing."

A steady hum of traffic rose up to meet them, while barges slipped by against the tree-dotted New Jersey shoreline.

"Will that be expensive?" asked Lindsay, as she picked her way across the rough surface, steadying herself against a mechanical box, then an air-conditioning unit.

"Wildly," said Kaitlin, picturing the expanse of glass and the marble floors.

Lindsay flashed a wide grin as she came abreast of Kaitlin near the edge of the roof. "That's my girl. Not that Harper will ever notice. The man has more money than God."

"It would seem," Kaitlin agreed, thinking back to the fine art and antiques that decorated his huge penthouse apartment.

"I've been checking," said Lindsay in a conspiratorial tone, swiping back her stray blond hairs in the freshening breeze. "Did you know it started with the pirates?"

"What started with pirates?" Kaitlin peered over the edge to the busy street below. She wished she had a scaffolding so she could see exactly how the view would look if they went up three stories.

"The Harper family wealth," Lindsay said. "Yo ho ho and a bottle of rum. Pirates."

Kaitlin stretched up on her toes, shading her eyes against the brilliant sun. "I'm sure that's just a rumor."

New York City was full of colorful stories of countless founding families. Most of them were concocted by the families themselves to add social cachet and impress their friends. The Harpers could just as easily have been former potato farmers who arrived in the city from Idaho in 1910. Perhaps they'd sold something as mundane as farmland and crops to buy their first boat and start Harper Transportation.

"Of course it's a rumor," Lindsay pointed out. "It happened three hundred years ago. It's not like they have videotape."

Kaitlin cracked a smile at her friend's faux outrage. "Are you suggesting I've inherited tainted money?"

"I'm suggesting the man you're blackmailing was descended from thieves and murderers."

"Does that scare you?" Zach didn't scare Kaitlin anymore.

Well, not much. She was still intimidated by his angry glare. And she was definitely unsettled by the sexual awareness that bloomed to life whenever he strode by. It was becoming a regular part of her workday: email, coffee, drafting, Zach. Then boom, buzz, all she could think about was kissing him.

"Hell, no," Lindsay assured her. "I'm just sayin' you should watch out for his sword."

Kaitlin waggled her finger at Lindsay in admonishment. "That's a terrible joke."

Lindsay peered closer. "Are you blushing?"

"No," Kaitlin answered with a shake of her head, switching her attention to the steel gray barge plodding up the river.

"I didn't mean it the way it sounded."

"Sure you did."

Lindsay leaned forward to get a better view of Kaitlin's face. "You *are* blushing. What did I miss?"

"Nothing. I've barely seen him in three days."

Okay, so she'd seen him from afar, more than a few times. And he looked good from that distance—no frowns, no scowls. Her reaction to him was becoming almost comically predictable.

Her pulse rate would jump. Her skin would heat up. And she'd lose her train of thought.

"Are you falling for him?" asked Lindsay.

Kaitlin started to speak, but then stopped, unwilling to lie to Lindsay. "I'm admiring his features from afar," she admitted. "Along with half of the city."

Zach was an undeniably attractive man. So she found him good-looking? Big deal. So she occasionally found him charming? Another big deal.

He had breeding and education, and plenty of practice at dating and small talk. If she forgot about the fact that he'd tried to ruin her life, she could almost pretend he was a decent guy.

"He does make a hot pirate," Lindsay concurred with a saucy grin.

"Hot" definitely described the way he'd looked that night at his penthouse, his tie off, sleeves rolled up, a day's growth of beard shadowing his chin. He'd looked every inch the rakish pirate of his ancestors. And it had been more than sexy.

Lindsay was watching her closely. "Promise me you'll keep your head in the game."

Kaitlin tucked her loose hair firmly behind her ears, taking a quick check of her diamond stud earring. "My head is completely in the game," she assured Lindsay.

There wouldn't be a repeat of Vegas. Kaitlin had slipped up that night. She'd let down her guard, and Zach had turned on her within the week.

Apparently satisfied, Lindsay eased forward to peer over the edge. Taxis, buses and delivery trucks cruised past. Three city workers in hard hats set barriers up around an open manhole, while a police cruiser, lights flashing blue and red, pulled halfway up on the wide sidewalk.

"So, have you started unpacking yet?" asked Lindsay.

"Nope." Kaitlin watched two uniformed cops stride into a deli. She was more than happy to leave the topic of Zach behind. "I'm going to take advantage of having everything out of the way. Clean the carpets and paint the walls."

"Nesting?" asked Lindsay.

"Yes, I am." When she gave herself time to think about staying put in New York City, Kaitlin felt a surge of relief lighten her shoulders. She'd curled up in her window seat yesterday evening with a cup of cocoa, simply staring for an hour at the bustle of the neighborhood.

"You deserve a great place to call home," said Lindsay, warmth and caring evident in her tone.

Kaitlin smiled her agreement. "I may even buy that new rocker." She'd been admiring a big, overstuffed gliding rocker in the window of a local furniture store for a few months now. Something about it said home.

"You?" Lindsay teased. "A frivolous expenditure?"

Kaitlin nodded with conviction. With no means of support other than her part-time job, she'd been forced to be frugal during her college years. The habit was hard to break. But she was gainfully employed now, and she had good prospects. And she was determined to make herself a real home.

"First the rocker," she explained to Lindsay. "And then the Prestige espresso machine."

"I love hearing you talk like that." Lindsay laughed.

"It feels pretty good," Kaitlin admitted, then her voice caught on her age-old sensation of loneliness. "I *can* make it a real home."

Lindsay linked her arm and nudged up against her. "You've already made it a real home."

It didn't feel like a real home to Kaitlin. Then again, how would she know? Over her childhood years, most of her placements had been in group facilities instead of with families. The workers were mostly kind, but they came and went in shifts, and they often moved on to other jobs, replaced by new people, who were also nice, but also employees, not a family.

Lindsay gave her a squeeze, obviously recognizing that Kaitlin was getting emotional. "You ready for lunch?"

"Sure thing." There was no point in dwelling on the past. She was staying in New York City, and that was a great thing. The rocker would make a difference, she was sure of it. Maybe she'd get a cat, a calico or a black-and-white gerbil. A pet would make things that much more homey.

With one last look around, she followed Lindsay inside. They locked the rooftop door and took the aging elevator back to the third floor and Kaitlin's small office.

"There you are." Zach's greeting from inside the office sounded vaguely like an accusation.

"What are you doing here?" Kaitlin's guard immediately went up. She suspiciously scanned the room, the deck, the bookshelf, her computer, checking to see if anything had been disturbed. She'd put a password on her laptop, and she was keeping the preliminary renovation drawings under lock and key.

She'd made Zach promise to give her carte blanche on the project. But she still feared, given half a chance, he would try to micromanage it. She wasn't planning on giving him half a chance.

"I have something to show you," he announced from where he stood behind her tilted drafting table.

She saw that he'd rolled out a set of blue line drawings. She moved forward to get a better view. "Those aren't mine."

"They're something Hugo Rosche put together," he responded.

Kaitlin slipped between the desk and drafting table, while Lindsay waited in the doorway of the cramped office. Kaitlin stopped shoulder-to-shoulder with Zach, and he moved closer up against the wall.

"What's different than how it is now?" she asked, moving through the pages, noting that a few walls had been relocated. The lobby had been slightly expanded, and new windows were sketched in on the first floor.

"We'd also repaint, recarpet and get a decorator," said Zach.

She glanced up at him, searching his expression. "Is this a joke?"

He frowned at her.

"Because, I mean, if it's a joke, ha-ha." She dropped the pages back into place.

He looked affronted. "It's not a joke."

She gestured to the sheets of paper. "You're not seriously suggesting I use these."

"We don't need to make massive changes in order to improve the building," he insisted.

"I'm not a decorator, Zach. I'm an architect."

"Being an architect doesn't mean you need to tear down walls for the sake of tearing down walls."

She turned and propped her butt against the side of the desk, folding her arms over her chest and facing him head on. "Did you seriously think I'd fall for this?" Because if he had, he was delusional.

He lifted his chin. "I thought you'd at least consider it."

"I just considered it. I don't like it."

"Thank you so much for keeping such an open mind."

"Thank you so much for bringing me a fait accompli."

"I paid good money for these plans." He snagged the bottom of the sheets and began to roll them up. His voice rose, the offense clear in his tone. "And I paid good money for your original plans. And now I'm paying a third time for the same work."

Lindsay shifted forward, stepping fully into the room. "Would you prefer to fire Kaitlin and meet us in court?"

Zach's steel gaze shot her way.

He glared at her briefly, then returned his attention to Kaitlin. "I thought you could use them as a starting point."

Kaitlin shrugged. "Okay," she said easily.

His hands stilled. He drew back, eyes narrowing in suspicion. Then he paused and asked, "You will?"

She shrugged again. "Since they're virtually identical to the existing building, I've already used them as a starting point."

Lindsay coughed a surprised laugh.

Zach came back to life, snapping an elastic band around the paper roll, while Kaitlin hopped out of his way.

"It's my backup plan," Zach said to Dylan. It was Sunday afternoon, and the two men maneuvered their way through the crowded rotunda at Citi Field toward a Mets game. If there was one thing he'd learned from both his father and from Dylan's dad, it was that your contingencies had to have contingencies. Plans failed all the time. An intelligent man was prepared for failure.

Dylan counted on his fingers. "Plan A was to buy her off. Plan B was getting her to agree to the Hugo Rosche drawings. Low percentage on that one working, by the way." He skirted a trash can. "And now Plan C is to find her a new job?"

Zach didn't disagree on the Rosche drawings. It had been a long shot that she'd agree to use them. But finding her a new job could easily work. It was a well thought out strategy.

"She said it herself," he explained. "Her long-term goal is to get a good job. She wants her career back on track. And I don't blame her. Thing is, it doesn't have to be my building. It could be any building."

"She wants to stay in New York City," Dylan confirmed.

"New York City is a very big place. There are plenty of buildings to renovate."

"So, you invited her to the game, because...?"

That was another element of Zach's plan. "Because she was wearing a Mets T-shirt that day at her apartment. It turns out, she's a fan."

"And odds are she's never watched a game from a Sterling Suite," Dylan elaborated.

"I'm betting she hasn't," said Zach as he came to a stop near the escalator, glancing around for Kaitlin and Lindsay. "It works exceedingly well on Fortune 500 execs. Besides, my project is temporary. If I can find her a solid offer with a good firm, then she's got something permanent."

"And in order to accept the offer, she'll have to quit your project."

"Exactly." Zach couldn't help but smile at his own genius.

Dylan, on the other hand, had a skeptical expression on his face. "Good luck with that."

"Here she is," Zach announced in a loud voice, sending Dylan a quick warning glance.

The plan was perfectly sound. But it would take some finesse.

He wouldn't try to sell her on the idea of a new job right away. Today, he only wanted to smooth the path, get a little closer to her. He'd let her know he was interested in a good outcome for both of them. No reason they had to be at odds.

Next week, he'd make a few calls, talk to a few associates, field offers for her.

Kaitlin broke her way through the escalator lineup and angled toward them.

His mood lifted at the sight of her, and he recognized the danger in that hormonal reaction. It didn't mean he had a hope in hell of changing it. But it did mean he needed to be careful, keep his emotions in check and hold himself at a distance.

She was wearing a snug white T-shirt, faded formfitting blue jeans, scuffed white sneakers and a blue-and-orange Mets cap with a jaunty ponytail sticking out the back. He'd never had a girl-next-door thing, preferring glitz and glamour in his dates. But it didn't seem to matter what Kaitlin wore. She'd be his fantasy girl in a bathrobe.

Damn. He had to shut that image down right now.

Her friend Lindsay was a half pace behind her. She had topped a pair of black jeans with a white sleeveless blouse.

They came to a halt.

"Dylan," Zach said, resisting the urge to reach out and touch Kaitlin, "meet Kaitlin Saville and Lindsay Rubin."

"The lovely bride," Dylan teased Kaitlin, and Zach tensed at the edgy joke.

"The pirate," Lindsay countered with a low laugh, smoothly inserting herself between Dylan and Kaitlin, then shaking his hand.

"Zach's the pirate," Dylan informed her, a practiced smile masking his annoyance at what he considered an insulting label.

"I've been studying Zach's family history," Lindsay countered. "And I also came across yours."

"Why don't we head this way." Zach gestured toward the elevator. He didn't want an argument to mar the day. Plus, the game was about to start.

Kaitlin followed his lead, and she fell into step beside him.

"A pirate?" she asked him in what sounded like a teasing voice.

That was encouraging.

"So I'm told," he admitted.

"Well, that explains a lot."

Before Zach could ask her to elaborate, Lindsay's voice interrupted from behind. "It seems Caldwell Gilby cut a swath through the Spanish Main, plundering gold, ammunition and rum."

Zach could well imagine Dylan's affronted expression. The sparks were about to fly. But he had to admit, he kind of liked Lindsay's audacity.

"You can't trust everything you read on the internet," Dylan returned dryly.

Kaitlin leaned a little closer to Zach, voice lowering. "Is this going to end badly?"

"Depends," he answered, listening for the next volley.

"I read it in the *Oxford Historic Encyclopedia* at the NYU Library," came Lindsay's tart retort.

"It could end badly," Zach acknowledged.

While he'd long since accepted the fact that his family's wealth had its roots in some pretty unsavory characters, Dylan had always chosen to pretend his ancestor fought against the pirate Lyndall Harper, and on the side of justice.

The two men had zigzagged across the Atlantic for years, lobbing cannonballs at each other. They'd fought, that much was true. But neither was on the right side of the law.

The suite level elevator doors had opened, so they walked inside.

"Caldwell had letters of authority from King George," said Dylan, turning to face the glowing red numbers.

"Forged and backdated in 1804," Lindsay retorted without missing a bead.

"Have you ever seen the originals?" Dylan asked. "Because I've seen the originals."

Kaitlin merely grinned at Zach from beneath her ball cap. "My money's on Lindsay."

He took in her fresh face, ruby lips, dark lashes and that enticing little dimple. He caught the scent of coconut, and for a split second he imagined her in a bright bikini, flowers in her hair, on a tropical beach.

"Is it a bet?" she asked, interrupting his thoughts.

"Sorry?" He shook himself back to reality.

"Ten bucks says Lindsay wins." She held out her hand to seal the deal.

Zach took her small, soft hand in his, shaking slowly, drawing out the touch, his attraction to her buzzing through ever nerve cell in his body. "You're on."

The elevator came smoothly to a stop, and they made their way along the wide, carpeted hallway to the luxury suite. For many years, the Harpers and the Gilbys had shared a corporate suite for Mets games. Dylan's father used them the most often, but they had proven a valuable corporate tool for all of them in wooing challenging clients.

"Wow." The exclamation whooshed out of Kaitlin as she crossed through the arched entrance and into the big, balconied room. It comfortably held twenty. A waiter was setting out snacks on the countertop bar, next to an ice-filled pail of imported beer and a couple of bottles of fine wine.

"Will you look at this." Like an excited kid, she beelined across to the open glass doors and out onto the breezy, tiered balcony, where two short rows of private seats awaited them.

Happy to leave Dylan and Lindsay to their escalating debate, Zach followed Kaitlin out.

"So this is how the other half lives," she said, bracing her hands on the painted metal rail, and gazing out over home plate. Rows of fan-filled seats cascaded below them, and a hum of excitement wafted through the air.

"It works well for entertaining clients." Zach heard a trace of apology in his voice, and he realized he wanted her to know it wasn't all about self-indulgence.

"At Shea Stadium, we used to sit over there." She pointed to the blue seats high behind third.

"Was that when you were a kid?"

She shook her head. "It was when we were in college." And a wistful tone came into her voice. "My first live game was sophomore year."

"So, you were a late bloomer?" He shifted to watch her profile, wondering what had prompted the sadness.

"As a kid, I watched as many as I could on TV." She abruptly turned to face the suite, and her tone went back to normal. "You got any beer in there?"

"No live games as a kid?" he persisted, seeing an opening to get to know her on a more personal level.

"Not a lot of money when I was a kid." She sounded defiant. He could tell he was being dared to probe further.

He opened his mouth to ask, but a cheer came up from the crowd as the players jogged onto the field.

Kaitlin clapped her hands. And by the time the din had abated, Zach decided to leave it alone. He patted one of the balcony chairs in the front row. "Have a seat. I'll bring you a beer." Two stairs up, he twisted back. "You want chips or something?"

"Hot dog?" she asked.

He couldn't help but grin at the simple request. "One hot dog, coming up."

Back inside the suite, while Dylan explained some of the finer points of King George's Letters of Authority, the waiter quickly organized hot dogs and beer.

In no time, Zach was settled next to Kaitlin, and the game was under way.

As the Mets went up to bat, they ate their loaded hot dogs. Between bites, she unselfconsciously cheered for the hits and groaned at the strikes. Zach found himself watching her more than he watched the players.

After the final bite of her hot dog, she licked a dab of mustard from the pad of her thumb. The gesture was both subconscious and sexy. Somehow, it looked remarkably like a kiss.

"That was delicious," she said, grinning around the tip of her thumb. "Thanks."

He tried to remember the last time he'd dated a woman who enjoyed the simple pleasure of a hot dog. Lobster, maybe, caviar, certainly, and expensive champagne was always a winner. But the finer things had mattered to his dates, his money had always mattered.

Then he remembered Kaitlin owned half his fortune. And he remembered they weren't on a date.

"So…" She adjusted her position, crossing one leg over the opposite knee, and adjusted her cap, apparently remembering the same things as him. "Why did you invite me here?"

He feigned innocence. "What do you mean?"

She gestured to the opulence behind them. "The suite. The baseball game. Imported beer. What's up?"

"We're working together."

"And…" She waited.

"And I thought we should get to know each other." Sure, he had another objective. But it was perfectly rational for the two of them to get to know each other. The renovations would take months. They'd be in each other's lives for quite some time to come.

"I'm not signing the divorce papers," she warned him.

"Did I ask?" There was no need for her to get paranoid.

"And I'm not changing the renovation designs, either."

"You could at least let me look at them."

"No way," she determinedly stated.

He tried feigning nonchalance. "Okay. Then let's talk about you."

She came alert. "What about me?"

"What are your plans? I mean long-term. Not just this single project."

The crack of a bat against the ball resonated through the stadium, and she turned to face forward while a runner sprinted to first. "That's no secret," she answered, gaze focused on the game. "A successful career in architecture. In New York City."

He took a sip of the cold beer, concentrating on getting this conversation just right. "I'd like to help you."

Her mouth quirked into a rueful smile. "You are helping. Reluctantly, we both know. But you *are* helping."

"I mean in addition to the Harper renovation project. I know people. I have contacts."

"I'm sure you do." She kept her attention fixed on the game while the opposing pitcher threw a strike, retiring the batter, and the Mets headed out to the field.

"Let me use them," Zach offered.

She turned then to paste him with a skeptical stare. "Use your contacts? To help *me?*"

"Yes," he assured her with a nod.

She thought about it for a few minutes while the pitcher warmed up. Zach was tempted to prompt her, but he'd messed up so many conversations with her already, he decided silence was the safer route.

"I read where you're going to the chamber of commerce dinner next Friday," she finally ventured, turning to watch him.

"The resurgence of global trade in northern Europe," he confirmed. They'd asked him to speak. He'd prefer to sit in the back and enjoy the single malt, but having a profile at these things was always good for business.

"Are you taking anyone?" she asked, gaze darting back to the action on the field.

"You mean a date?"

She nodded. "It's a dinner. I assume it would be partly social. It seems to me it would be acceptable to bring a date."

"Yes, it's acceptable. And no, I don't have one."

Another batter cracked a high fly ball. They watched the trajectory until it was caught out in center field.

"Will you take me?"

Zach rocked back and turned. A reflexive rush of excitement hit his body as he studied her profile. "You're asking me for a date?"

But she rolled her eyes and adjusted her cap. "I'm asking you to get me in the door, Zach, not dance with me. You said you wanted to help. And there will be people there who are good for my career."

"Right." He shifted in his seat, assuring himself he wasn't disappointed. It was a lie, of course. But he definitely wasn't stupid.

Dating Kaitlin would be a huge mistake. Dancing with her was out of the question. What if it was as great as he'd remembered? What then?

She drew a satisfied sigh, her shoulders relaxing. "And, before Friday, if you wouldn't mind telling at least five people that you've hired me back. Influential people. It would be great for me if word got around."

He had no right to be disappointed. This was business for her. It was business for him, too. Introducing her around at the chamber dinner played right into Plan C. She was right. There would be influential people there, a myriad of corporate executives, many of whom would have contacts in the architectural world. If he was lucky, really lucky, she'd find a job right there at the dinner.

Still, he struggled to keep his voice neutral as he told her, "Sure. No problem."

"You did offer to help," she pointed out.

"I said sure."

"Are you annoyed?" she asked.

"I'm being blackmailed," he reminded her. Was he supposed to be thrilled about it?

"Every marriage has its complications," she returned on an irreverent grin.

Just then, the Mets pitcher struck out the third batter with the bases loaded, and Kaitlin jumped from her seat to cheer.

Zach watched her in the sunlight and struggled very hard to feel annoyed. But then she punched a fist in the air, and her T-shirt rode up, revealing a strip of smooth skin above her waistband. And annoyance was the last thing he was feeling toward his accidental wife.

The chamber dinner was a dream come true for Kaitlin. The people she met were friendly and professional, and she came away feeling as if she'd met the who's who of the Manhattan business world. Zach had certainly stuck to his pledge of helping her. He'd introduced her to dozens of potential contacts, left her in interesting conversations, but seemed to magically appear whenever she felt alone or out of place.

It was nearly midnight when they finally climbed aboard his thirty-foot yacht for the return trip to Manhattan. Like the suite at the baseball game, the yacht clearly showed Zach had the means and the desire to enjoy the finer things in life. Lindsay was right, Kaitlin could spend as much as she needed on the renovations, and he'd barely notice.

The chamber dinner had been held at an island marina just off the coast of southern Manhattan. Most people had traveled by water taxi but a few, like Zach, had brought their own transportation.

"This is a nice ride," she acknowledged one more time, as they settled into a grouping of comfortable, white, cushioned furniture. The sitting area, on a teak wood deck, was positioned next to a covered hot tub near the stern of the boat, protected from the wind by a glass wall at midship, but providing an incredible view over the aft rail.

Kaitlin chose a soft armchair, while Zach took a love seat at a right angle to her, facing the stern. The pilot powered up the engine, and they glided smoothly out into the bay.

"It's slower than a helicopter," said Zach. "But I like it out here at night."

Kaitlin tipped her head and gazed at the twinkling skyline. A three-quarter moon was rising, and a few stars were visible beyond the city's glow. "You have a helicopter?"

"Dylan has the helicopters. My company owns ships."

Kaitlin had liked Dylan, even if Lindsay hadn't seemed to warm up to him. Then again, there were few things Lindsay enjoyed more than a rollicking debate, and Dylan had played right into her hand. Kaitlin was convinced Lindsay missed being in a courtroom. Lindsay had worked for a year as a litigator, and Kaitlin had always wondered about her choice to take the teaching position.

"Tell me more about the pirates," she said to Zach. She'd never met anyone with such a colorful family history.

"You want a drink or anything?" he asked.

She shook her head, slipping off her shoes and bending her knees to tuck her feet beneath her in the shimmering black cocktail dress. "One more glass of champagne, and I'll start singing karaoke."

"Champagne it is." He started to rise, his devilish smile showing straight white teeth in the muted deck light.

"Don't you dare," she warned, with a waggle of her finger. "Trust me. You do not want me to sing."

He rocked back into his seat and loosened his tie. He ran a hand, spread-fingered, through his thick hair and crossed one ankle over the opposite knee. In the buffeting breeze, with the faint traces of fatigue around his dark eyes, he looked disheveled and compellingly sexy.

"Back to the pirates," she prompted in an effort to distract herself from her burgeoning desire. "Is it all true?"

He shrugged easily. "Depends on what you've heard."

"I heard that your ancestor was a pirate, arch enemy of Dylan's ancestor, and the two of them formed a truce nearly three hundred years ago on what is now Serenity Island. I heard the nexus of your fortune is stolen treasure."

Criminal or not, she still found herself envious of his detailed family history. Zach would know details of his parents, his grandparents, his aunts and uncles, and every ancestor back three hundred years. Kaitlin would give anything to be able to go back even one generation.

"Well, it's all true," said Zach. "At least as far as we can tell. Dylan's in denial."

Kaitlin laughed lightly, remembering the argument at the baseball game. "It sure sounded like it."

Zach removed his tie and tossed it on the love-seat cushion beside him. "Dylan wants to pretend his family was pure of heart. I think he must have more scruples than me."

"You're unscrupulous?" she couldn't resist asking.

"Some would say."

"Would they be right?"

He looked her square in the eyes. "Like I'm going to answer that."

She couldn't tell if he was still teasing. And maybe that was deliberate. "Are you trying to keep me off balance?" she asked, watching his expression closely.

"You're not exactly on my side."

"I thought we'd formed a truce." She certainly felt as if they'd formed a truce tonight.

"I'm appeasing you," he told her. His tone and dark eyes were soft, but the words revealed his continued caution.

"And I'm trying to build you a masterpiece," she responded tartly.

He sighed, and seemed to relax ever so slightly. "You're trying to build yourself a masterpiece."

She had to concede that one. Her primary motivation in this was her own reputation. Of course, it was all his fault she was forced into this position.

"You make a fair point," she admitted.

"So, who's unscrupulous now?"

"I'm not unscrupulous. Just practical." She had no one in this world to depend on but herself.

Orphans learned that fact very quickly in life. If she didn't have a career, if she couldn't provide for herself, nobody would do it for her. Since she was old enough to understand, she'd feared poverty and loneliness.

She was sure the view was quite different from where Zach was sitting on millions of dollars worth of New York real estate. He had a successful company, money to burn and a lineage that went back to the dawn of statehood.

"So, what have you decided?" he asked.

"About what?" Was there anything left outstanding on their deal? She thought they were both quite clear at this point.

"My building. You've been working at it for a couple of weeks now. Tell me what you have in mind."

Kaitlin instantly saw through his ploy. No wonder he'd

behaved so well this evening. He'd been lulling her into a false send of security.

She came to her feet, keeping a close eye on him, backing toward the rail. The teak deck was cool and smooth beneath her bare feet. "Oh, no, you don't. I'm not opening myself up for a fight over the details."

He rose with her. "You'll need my input at some point. It might as well be—"

"Uh-uh." The breeze brushed the filmy, scalloped-hem dress against her legs and whipped the strands of hair that had worked their way loose from her updo. "No input. *My* project."

He widened his stance. "I'll have to approve the final designs."

The waves rolled higher, and she braced herself against the rail. "What part of carte blanche didn't you understand?"

He took a few steps forward. "The part where I sign the check."

"*We* sign the check."

He came even closer, all pretense of geniality gone from his expression. He was all business, all intimidation. "Right. And 'we' had best be happy with both the plans and the price tag."

"There is no limit on this project's budget."

He came to a halt, putting a hand on the rail, half trapping her. "I won't let you bankrupt my company."

She struggled not to react to his nearness. "Like I could possibly bankrupt Harper Transportation. You give me too much credit."

The boat lunged into a trough, and he swayed closer. "You want to see the balance sheets?"

"I want to see a new Manhattan skyline."

"It's talk like that that scares me, Kaitlin."

Her scare him?

He was the one unsettling her.

His intense expression brought her heart rate up. His lips were full, chin determined, eyes intense, and his hard, rangy body was far too close for her comfort. Sweat prickled at her hairline, formed between her breasts, gathered behind her knees, and was then cooled by the evening breeze.

His arms were only inches away. He could capture her at any moment, kiss her, ravage her.

She swallowed against her out-of-control arousal.

Any second now, she'd be throwing herself in his arms. Maybe talking about the renovation was the lesser of all evils.

"I was planning more light." Her voice came out sexy, husky, and she couldn't seem to do a thing about it. "More glass. A higher lobby. Bigger offices."

Had he moved closer?

"Bigger offices mean fewer offices," he pointed out.

She didn't disagree.

"Do you know the cost of space in midtown Manhattan?" His rebuke sounded like a caress.

"Do you know the soft value of impressing your future clients?" she returned, her brain struggling hard to grasp every coherent thought.

Had *she* moved closer? Her nose picked up his scent, and it was sensually compelling. She swore she could feel the heat of his body through his dress shirt.

"Do you think the makers of tractor parts and kitchen appliances care what my lobby looks like?" His breath puffed against her lips.

"Yes."

They stared at each other in silence, inhaling and exhaling for long seconds. The rumble of the yacht's motor filled the space around them.

Something dangerous flared in Zach's intense gray eyes. It was darkly sensual and completely compelling.

Her body answered with a rush of heat and a flare of longing that sent a throbbing message to every corner of her being.

She struggled through the muddle of emotions clouding her brain. "The people who make tractor parts also have tickets to Lincoln Center. They do care about your lobby."

"It's a building, not a piece of art." The yacht lurched, and his hand brushed against hers. She nearly groaned out loud.

"It can be both," she rasped.

Things could do double duty.

Look at Zach. He was both an adversary and a—

What? What was she saying?

He could be her lover?

"Kaitlin?" His voice was strangled, while his gaze flared with certain desire. His full lips parted, his head tipping toward hers.

The boat rolled on a fresh set of waves, and she gripped the rail, transfixed by the sight of his body closing in on hers.

She flashed back to Vegas.

He'd kissed her there.

How could she have ever doubted it?

Elvis had pronounced them husband and wife, and Zach had thrown his arms around her, kissing her thoroughly and endlessly. It was only the cheers from the crowd that had finally penetrated their haze and forced them to pull apart. It was a miracle they hadn't slept together that night.

Why hadn't they slept together that night?

She remembered getting into the elevator with a couple of her female coworkers, then stumbling into her room and dropping, fully dressed, onto the plush, king-size bed.

No Zach.

But he was here now.

And they were alone.

And she remembered. She wished she didn't. But she remembered his lips on hers, his arms around her, the strength of his embrace, the taste of his mouth, the sensual explosions that burst along her skin.

She wanted it again, wanted it so very, very much.

She gave in to her desire and leaned ever so slightly forward. His mouth instantly rushed to hers. His free arm snaked around her, pressing against the small of her back, pulling her tight as the deck surged beneath them.

She pressed forward, arms twining around his neck. Her lips softened, parted. He murmured her name, and his hand splayed farther down her spine. His tongue invaded, and the taste of him combined with the scent of the salt air, the undulation of the boat and heat of his hands brought a moan from her very core.

He shifted so that his back was to the rail. His free hand caressed her cheek, brushed through her hair, moved down to her neck, her shoulder. He pushed off the strap of her dress, then his lips followed, tasting their way along her bare, sensitized skin.

His kisses, his passion, made her gasp. She tangled her fingers through his hair, pushing her body tightly against his, shifting her thighs as his leg slipped between them. His hand cupped her breast through the flimsy fabric of her dress, while his lips found hers again, and she bent backward with the exquisite pressure of his hot kiss.

The boat lurched again, and they lost their balance, stumbling a few steps sideways.

Zach was quick to steady her, clasping her tightly to him, lips next to her ear.

"You okay?" His voice was hollow.

"I'm—" She drew a shaky breath.

Was she okay? What on earth had she just done? One minute they were arguing over office sizes, the next they were practically attacking each other.

He held her tight. Neither spoke as they drew deep breaths.

Finally, he stroked her messy hair. "Are you thinking what I'm thinking?"

"That we've both gone completely insane?"

He chuckled low. "That's pretty close."

"We can't do this."

"No kidding."

"You need to let go of me."

"I know." He didn't move.

"I'm blackmailing you. You're trying to outflank, outmaneuver and outthink me along the way. And then we're getting divorced."

"As long as we're both clear on the process."

The flutter in her stomach told her there was way more to it than that. But she had to fight it. She couldn't let herself be attracted to this man. She certainly couldn't let herself kiss him, or worse.

They were adversaries. And this was her one chance to get her life back. And she couldn't let any lingering sexual desire mess that up.

"You need to let me go, Zach."

Four

After a long, sleepless night, and a lengthy heart-to-heart with Lindsay as they drove up the coast of Long Island, Kaitlin watched her friend browse through a tray of misshapen silver coins in a small beachfront antique shop.

"I never thought I'd hear myself say this." Lindsay selected one plastic-wrapped item and read the provenance typed neatly on the attached card. "But, as your lawyer, I must strongly advise you not to sleep with your husband."

"I am *not* sleeping with my husband," Kaitlin reminded her. And she had absolutely no intention of going there. Desire and action were two completely different things.

Two women checking out a painting in the next aisle slid their curious gazes to Kaitlin, and their expressions shifted from smirks to bemusement.

Kaitlin leaned a little closer to Lindsay and whispered, "Okay, that just sounds stupid when I say it out loud."

"He's playing you," said Lindsay, dropping the first coin and switching to another, turning it over to read.

"Neither of us meant for it to happen," Kaitlin pointed out. Zach's shock and regret had seemed as genuine as hers.

Lindsay glanced up from the coin, arching her a skeptical look. "Are you sure about that?"

"I'm sure," Kaitlin returned with conviction. They'd both sworn not to let it happen again. It was as much her fault as his.

"And what were you doing right before you kissed him?" Lindsay gave up on the coin rack and meandered her way across the shop floor.

Kaitlin followed, only half paying attention to the merchandise. Lindsay was the one who'd suggested driving up the coast to visit antique stores. They'd never done it before, but Kaitlin was game for anything that would distract her.

"We were on deck," she told Lindsay. "Fantastic boat, by the way."

"You mentioned that. So, were you eating? Drinking? Stargazing?"

"Arguing art versus architecture." Kaitlin took her mind back to the first minutes of the return trip. "He wanted to see my designs."

"I rest my case." Lindsay lingered in front of a glass case displaying some more gold coins. "Aha. This is what I was looking for."

"What case?" asked Kaitlin. What was Lindsay resting?

Lindsay fluttered a dismissive hand, attention on the coins. "The case against Zach." Then she tapped her index finger against the glass in answer to a clerk's unspoken question. "I'd like to see that one."

"I don't follow," said Kaitlin.

"The coin is from the *Blue Glacier*."

"Yes, it is," the clerk confirmed with an enthusiastic smile, unlocking the case and extracting a plastic-covered, gold, oblong coin.

"You were resting your case," Kaitlin prompted.

Lindsay inspected the coin, holding it up to the sunlight and turning it one way, then the other. "You were arguing with Zach about art versus architecture. Which side were you on, by the way?"

"Zach's afraid my renovation plans will be impractical," explained Kaitlin. "I told him architecture could be both beautiful and functional. He's stone-cold on the side of function."

"Not hard to tell that from his building." Lindsay put down her purse and slipped the coin under a big magnifying glass on a stand on the countertop.

"When did you become interested in coins?" asked Kaitlin. Lindsay was going through quite a procedure here.

"The two of you were fighting," Lindsay continued while she peered critically at the coin. "I'm assuming you were winning since, aside from holding all the trump cards, you were right." She straightened. "Then suddenly, poof, he's kissing you."

The clerk eyed Kaitlin with obvious interest, while Lindsay gave Kaitlin a knowing look. "Do you think there's a slim possibility it was a distraction? Do you think, maybe, out of desperation to seize control of the project, your *husband* might be trying to emotionally manipulate you?"

Kaitlin blinked. Manipulate her?

"You know," Lindsay continued, "if you gave away the fact you thought he was hot—"

"I never told him he was hot."

"There are other ways to give yourself away besides talking. And you *do* think he's hot."

The clerk's attention was ping-ponging between the two women.

Kaitlin realized she probably *had* given herself away. On numerous occasions. And while they were arguing on the boat, her attraction to Zach must have been written all over her face.

But what about Zach? Had he felt nothing? Could he actually be that good an actor? Had he pounced on an opportunity?

Humiliation washed over her. Lindsay was right.

"Darn it," Kaitlin hissed under her breath. "He was *faking?*"

Lindsay patted her arm in sympathy, her tone going gentle. "That'd be my guess."

Kaitlin scrunched her eyes shut.

"I'll take this one," Lindsay told the clerk. Then she wrapped a bracing arm around Kaitlin's shoulders. "Seriously, Katie. I hate to be the one to say this. But what are the odds he's falling for you?"

Lindsay was right. She was so, so right. Kaitlin had been taken in by a smooth-talking man with an agenda. He didn't want her. He wanted her architectural designs, so he could shoot holes in them, talk her out of them, save himself a bundle of money. His interests were definitely not Kaitlin's interests.

How could she have been so naive?

She clamped her jaw and took a bracing breath.

Then she opened her eyes. "You're right."

"Sorry."

"Don't sweat it. I'm fine," Kaitlin huffed. She caught a glimpse of the hefty price tag on the coin and seized the opportunity to turn the attention from herself. "You know that's two thousand dollars?"

"It's a bargain," said the clerk, punching keys on the cash register.

But Lindsay wasn't so easily distracted. "I think he's trapped. I think he's panicking. And I think *he* thinks you'll be more malleable if you fall for him."

"How long have you been interested in antique coins?" Kaitlin repeated. Notwithstanding her desire to change the subject, it really *was* a lot of money.

"I'm not interested in coins," Lindsay replied. "I'm interested in pirates."

Oh, this was priceless. "You're fixating on Dylan Gilby?"

"Wrong. I'm fixating on *Caldwell* Gilby. I'm proving that smug, superior Dylan does, indeed, owe his wealth to the ill-gotten gains of his pirate ancestor."

"The *Blue Glacier was* sunk by pirates," the clerk offered as she accepted Lindsay's credit card to pay for the purchase.

"By the *Black Fern*," Lindsay confirmed in a knowledgeable and meaningful tone. "Captained by dear ol' Caldwell Gilby."

The clerk carefully slid the coin in a velvet pouch embossed with the store's logo. "The captain of the *Blue Glacier* tried to scuttle the ship against a reef rather than give up his cargo. But the pirates got most of it anyway. A few of the coins were recovered from the wreck in 1976." The clerk handed Lindsay the pouch. "You've made a good purchase."

As they turned for the door to exit the pretty little shop, Lindsay held up the pouch in front of Kaitlin's face. "Exhibit A."

Kaitlin searched her friend's expression. "You have got to get back in the courtroom."

"Weren't we talking about you?" asked Lindsay. "Kissing your husband?"

"I don't think so." Kaitlin was going to wallow through that one in private.

Lindsay dropped the coin into her purse and sobered. "I don't want you getting hurt in all this."

Kaitlin refused to accept that. "I'm not about to get hurt. I kissed him. Nothing more." That was, of course, the under-statement of the century.

Still, they'd come to their senses before anything serious had happened. Or maybe Kaitlin was the one who'd come to her senses. Zach hadn't been emotionally involved on any level. Even now, he was probably biding his time, waiting for the next opportunity to manipulate her all over again.

"He's only after one thing," Lindsay declared with au-thority.

Kaitlin struggled to find the black humor. "And it's not even the usual thing."

Lindsay gave Kaitlin's shoulder another squeeze. "Just don't let your heart get caught in the crossfire."

"My heart is perfectly safe. I'm fighting for my career." Kaitlin wouldn't get tripped up again. She couldn't afford it. She was fighting against someone who was even less principled than she'd ever imagined.

Dylan showed his disagreement, backing away from Zach's office desk. "I am *not* stealing corporate secrets for you."

Zach exhaled his frustration. "They're my corporate secrets. You're not stealing them, because I *own* them."

"That's the Harper family style," Dylan sniffed in disdain. "Not the Gilbys'."

"Will you get off your moral high horse." It was all well and good for Dylan to protect his family name, but it had gotten completely out of hand the past few weeks.

"I have principles. So, sue me."

"I give you the key to my car." Zach ignored Dylan's protests and began to lay out a simple, straightforward plan.

Dylan folded his arms belligerently across the front of his business suit. "So I can break in to it."

"So you can *unlock* it. There is no breaking required."

"And steal Kaitlin's laptop."

"Her briefcase is probably a better bet," Zach suggested. "I suspect the laptop has a password. You photocopy the drawings. You put them back. You lock my trunk, and you're done."

"It's stealing, Zach. Plain and simple."

"It's photocopying, Dylan. Even Kaitlin's pit bull of a lawyer—"

"Lindsay."

Zach rapped his knuckles on his desktop. "Even Lindsay would have to admit that intellectual property created by Kaitlin while she was on the Harper Transportation payroll belongs to the company. And the company belongs to me."

"And to her."

Zach, exasperated, threw up his hands. "Whose side are you on?"

"This doesn't feel right."

Zach glared at his lifelong friend, searching for the argument that would bring Dylan around to logic. He couldn't help but wish a few of Caldwell's more disreputable genes had trickled down through the generations.

It wasn't as if they were knocking over a bank. It was nothing more than a frat prank. And he owned the damn designs. And while they might technically be half hers, they were also half his—morally, they were all his—and he had a corporation to protect. A corporation that employed thousands of people, all of them depending on Zach to make good decisions for Harper Transportation.

"I need to know she won't ruin me," he said to Dylan. "We know she's out for revenge. And think about it, Dylan. If she was only worried we'd disagree on the aesthetics of the renovation, she'd flaunt the drawings in my face. She's up to something."

Dylan stared in silence for a long minute, and Zach could almost feel him working through the elements of the situation.

"Up to what?" he finally asked, and Zach knew he had him.

"Up to spending Harper Transportation into a hole we can't climb out of then walking away and letting me sink."

"You think she'd—"

"I *don't know* what she'd do. That's my point. I don't know anything about this woman except that she blames me for everything that's wrong in her life."

Even as he said the words to Dylan, Zach was forced to silently acknowledge they weren't strictly true. He knew more than that about Kaitlin. He knew she was beautiful, feisty and funny. He knew her kisses made him forget they were enemies. And he knew he wanted her more than he'd ever wanted any woman in his life.

But that only meant he had to be tougher, even more determined to win. His feelings for her were a handicap, and he had to get past them.

"If it was you," Zach told Dylan in complete honesty, "if someone was after you, I'd lie, cheat and steal to save you."

Dylan hesitated. "That's not fair."

"How is it not fair?"

"You'd lie, cheat and steal at the drop of a hat."

Zach couldn't help but grin. It was a joke. Dylan had no basis for the accusation, and they both knew it.

Zach rounded the desk, knowing Dylan was on board. "That's because I'm a pirate at heart."

"And I am not."

Zach clapped Dylan on the shoulder. "But I'm working on you."

"That's what scares me."

"You may be a lot of things," said Zach, "but scared isn't one of them."

Dylan shook his head in both disgust and capitulation. "Give me your damn car keys," he grumbled. "And you owe me one."

Zach extracted his spare key from his pocket and handed them to Dylan. "I'll pay it back anytime you want. We'll be at Boondocks in an hour. The valet parking is off Forty-fourth."

Dylan glanced down at the silver key in his palm. "How did it come to this?"

"Lately, I ask myself that every morning."

Dylan quirked a half smile. "Maybe if you'd get yourself back on the straight and narrow."

"I am on the straight and narrow. Now get out there and steal for me."

Dylan on side, Zach cleared his evening's schedule and exited his office, making his way to the third floor. He had been making a point by putting Kaitlin in such a cramped space. It occurred to him that Dylan might be right. His moral compass could, in fact, be slipping.

He wasn't particularly proud of this next plan. But he didn't see any other way to get the information. And the situation was getting critical. Finding Kaitlin a new job wasn't going as smoothly as he'd expected. There was the real possibility he'd have to implement her renovation plans, and he couldn't afford to be blindsided by whatever extravagant and ungainly design she'd dreamed up.

He arrived at her office as she was locking the door at the end of the workday. She had both her laptop and a burgundy leather briefcase in her hands.

"You busy for dinner?" he asked without preamble.

She turned in surprise, her gaze darting up and down the hall, obviously worried about who might see them talking.

"Why?" Suspicion was clear in her tone.

"I'm attending a business event," he offered levelly.

"On your yacht?"

He tried to interpret her expression. Were her words a rebuke or a joke? Was she nervous at the thought of being alone with him again? If so, could it be because she was still attracted to him?

They'd pledged to keep their hands off each other, but she could be wavering. He was definitely wavering. He'd been wavering as soon as the words were out of his mouth.

"At Boondocks," he answered, shelving his physical desire for the moment. "I thought you might like to meet Ray Lambert."

Her green eyes widened. Ah, now he had her attention.

Ray Lambert was president of the New York Architectural Association. Zach had done his homework on this. He'd planned an introduction so valuable, it would be impossible for Kaitlin to say no to dinner.

"You're meeting Ray Lambert?" she asked cautiously.

"For dinner. Him and his wife."

Now her tone was definitely wary as she tried to gauge his motives. "And you're willing to take me along?"

Zach gave a careless shrug. "If you don't want to—"

"No, I want to." Her brow furrowed. "I'm just trying to figure out your angle."

He couldn't help but admire the way her brain was working through this. She was smart. But he was smarter. At least in this instance. With anybody but Ray Lambert, the plan would likely have failed.

"My angle is meeting your conditions for returning my company to me," Zach told her. It was true. It wasn't the whole truth, but it was part of the truth. "You want a career in this town, Ray's a good guy to meet."

She tilted her head to an unconsciously sexy angle. "No strings attached?"

His gaze automatically dropped to her luscious lips and his primal brain engaged. He didn't intend to lower his voice to a sexy timbre, nor did he plan to ease his body forward, but it all happened anyway. "What kind of strings did you have in mind?"

"You promised," she reminded him, looking trapped and worried.

"So did you."

"I'm not doing anything."

"I'm not doing anything, either," he lied. He was thinking plenty, and his body was telegraphing his desire. "Your imagination's filling in the blanks."

"You're looking at me," she accused.

"You're looking back," he countered.

"Zach."

"Katie." It was a stupid move, and not at all in keeping with his grand plan for tonight, but he reached forward and brushed his knuckles up against hers. It was a subtle touch, but it had the impact of a lightning bolt.

It obviously hit her, too. And he couldn't stop the surge of male satisfaction that overtook his body.

Her cheeks flushed, her irises deepened to emeralds. Her voice went sultry. "This isn't a date."

"Don't trust yourself?" he dared.

"I don't trust *you*."

"Smart move," he conceded, admiring her intelligence all over again as he pulled back from his brinkmanship.

He knew Harper Transportation had to be his primary concern. And he needed to get his hands on her drawings by fair means or foul. His company, his employees, his family legacy, all depended on it.

"Are you trying to make me say no?" she asked him.

"I honestly don't know what I'm trying to do." The confession was out of him before he could censor it.

Complicated didn't begin to describe his feelings for Kaitlin. He desperately wanted to kiss her. He craved the feel of her body against his. Given half a chance, he knew he'd tear off her clothes and make love to her until neither of them could move.

And then the power balance would be completely in her favor, and Harper Transportation wouldn't stand a chance.

He forced himself to back off farther, putting a buffer of space between them.

"Ray Lambert?" she confirmed, apparently willing to put up with Zach for the introduction.

He gave her a nod. Despite the detour into their inconvenient attraction to one another, his plan had worked. As he'd known it would. The intellectual evaluation of another person's emotions was an astonishingly effective tool for manipulation. And, apparently, it was a gift he had.

Her expression relaxed ever so slightly, causing a stab of guilt in his gut.

"You know, you're either nicer than I thought," she told him, "or more devious than I can understand."

"I'm much nicer than you think," Zach lied.

"Can you pick me up at home?"

He knew if he let her go home, she'd ditch the briefcase. That wasn't part of the plan. So, he made a show of glancing at his watch. "No time for that. We'll have to leave from here."

Her hesitation showed in the purse of her lips.

"I can pick you up at the bus stop again," he offered, knowing that would eliminate one of her hesitations.

It was her turn to glance at her watch. "Five minutes?"

He agreed. Then he watched until she got on the elevator. He wasn't going to risk her stowing the briefcase back in her office either.

At the opulent Boondocks restaurant, Kaitlin and Zach settled into a curved booth with Ray Lambert and his wife, Susan. The restaurant was on two levels, the upper overlooking the atrium that served as both an entrance and a lounge. Palm trees and exotic plants blooming from both floor and wall pots added to the fresh ambiance that included high ceilings, huge windows overlooking the park and natural wood and rattan screens to provide privacy between the tables.

Kaitlin had used the walk to the bus stop to call Lindsay and regain her equilibrium. Thank goodness some semblance of sanity had kept her from kissing Zach right there in the Harper building hallway.

She'd been inches, mere seconds, from throwing herself in his arms all over again and falling completely under his sensual spell. She was a fool, an undisciplined fool.

In desperation, she'd confessed to Lindsay and begged for a pep talk, needing to put some emotional armor around herself before the dinner started. As usual, Lindsay had shocked her back to reality, then used humor to put her on an even keel.

"Have we by any chance met in the past?" Ray asked Kaitlin as the two shook hands over a table set with silver, crystal and crisp white linen. Zach had slid partway around the booth seat and settled next to Susan, while Ray was directly across from Kaitlin.

"Once," she answered Ray. "Three years ago, at the NYAA conference. I was one of probably six hundred people who came through the receiving line."

He smiled at her. "That must have been it. I'm pretty good with faces."

Lindsay just hoped he wasn't remembering her ignominious firing from Hutton Quinn. Though, if he was, he didn't give anything away.

"Anyone else interested in the '97 Esme Cabernet?" Susan pointed to the wine list that was open in front of her.

Kaitlin was grateful for the change in topic.

"One of her favorites," Ray explained with a benevolent smile toward his wife. "You won't be disappointed."

Zach glanced to Kaitlin, obviously looking for her reaction.

She nodded agreeably, proud of the way her hormones were staying under control. This was a business dinner, nothing more. And it was going to stay that way. "I'd love to try it," she told Susan.

Susan smiled and closed the wine list.

A waiter immediately appeared beside their table.

While Ray ordered the wine, Kaitlin's attention caught on a couple crossing the foyer below. They were heading for the curved staircase, and even from this distance she could recognize Lindsay and Dylan.

She straightened to get a better view as they started up the stairs. What could they possibly be doing here?

Kaitlin couldn't miss Lindsay's red face. Her friend was furious.

"What the—" Though Kaitlin clamped her jaw on the unladylike exclamation, Zach swiveled to stare at her confusion. Then he followed the direction of her gaze.

Lindsay and Dylan had made it to the top of the stairs and bore down on the table. As they did, Zach sat bolt upright, obviously observing the fury on Lindsay's face.

The waiter left with the wine order just as Lindsay and Dylan arrived. They presented themselves, and Lindsay's quick gaze noted Ray and Susan. She schooled her features.

"I'm so sorry to interrupt." She smiled at Kaitlin, and her glance went meaningfully to the briefcase she held in her hand, moving it into clear view.

Burgundy.

It was Kaitlin's.

What was she doing with Kaitlin's briefcase?

"We just wanted to say hi," Lindsay continued, her voice full of forced cheer. "I met up with Dylan in the *garage*."

Kaitlin felt Zach stiffen beside her, while Dylan blushed.

Dylan? The garage? Her briefcase?

She felt her jaw drop open.

"We're going to get a table now," Lindsay announced smoothly, giving Kaitlin a soft squeeze on the shoulder. "Enjoy your dinner. But maybe we could talk later?" She hooked her arm into Dylan's and pasted him to her side.

Kaitlin couldn't help herself. She turned to gape at Zach in astonishment. Her briefcase had been in his trunk. How did Lindsay end up with it? And what was Dylan's connection?

Zach's face remained impassive as he focused beyond Kaitlin to Dylan. "We'll talk to you *later*."

Lindsay made a half turn to address Ray and Susan. "I'm really sorry to have interrupted. I hope you all enjoy your dinner."

Then she gave Kaitlin one ominous glance before propelling Dylan farther into the restaurant.

Kaitlin's immediate reaction was to follow them. But before she could rise from her seat, Zach's hand clamped down on her thigh, holding her firmly in place.

The action was shocking, the sensation electric.

"That was Dylan Gilby," he smoothly informed Ray and Susan. "Astral Air."

Kaitlin reached down to surreptitiously remove Zach's hand, but her strength was no match for his.

"I've met his father," Ray acknowledged. If he'd noticed anything strange in the conversation, he was too professional to let on.

"Dylan and I grew up together," Zach elaborated, filling the silence even while Kaitlin tried to work her leg free.

"Ah, here's the wine," Susan announced, looking pleased by the arrival of the steward.

As soon as Ray's and Susan's attention was distracted by the uncorking process, Zach leaned over. "Stay still," he hissed into Kaitlin's ear.

"What did you *do?*" Kaitlin demanded in an undertone.

"We'll talk later," he huffed.

"Bet on it."

"Stop struggling."

"Let go of me."

"Not until I'm sure you'll stay put."

"We first discovered this one in Marseille," said Ray, lifting his glass with a flourish for the ceremonial tasting.

Kaitlin quickly redirected her attention. She tried not to squirm against Zach's grip. His hand was dry and warm, slightly callused, definitely not painful, but absolutely impossible to ignore.

She wasn't wearing stockings today, and his hand was on her bare leg. His pinky finger had come to rest slightly north of her midthigh hemline. And his fingertips had curled into her sensitive inner thigh.

Now that her anger had settled to a hum, a new sensation pulsed its way through her system.

The touch of Zach's hand was turning her on.

Ray nodded his approval on the wine, and the steward filled the other three glasses before topping up Ray's.

When the wine was ready, Ray raised his glass for a toast. "A pleasure to meet you, Kaitlin. And congratulations on your contract with Harper Transportation. It's an important building."

"We're lucky to have her," Zach responded courteously.

Kaitlin thanked them both, clinked her glass against each of theirs, avoiding eye contact with Zach, then took a healthy swallow. The wine was incredibly delicious. More importantly, it contained a measure of alcohol to take the edge off her frustration.

Another waiter arrived with four large, leather-bound dinner menus, which he handed around to the table's occupants.

Zach accepted his with one hand, still not relinquishing his hold on Kaitlin.

She opened hers, trying to concentrate on the dishes and descriptions in front of her, but the neat script blurred on the page.

Had his hand moved?

Was it higher now?

Ever so slightly, and ever so slowly, but completely unmistakably his fingertips were brushing their way up the inside of her thigh.

Her muscles contracted in reaction. She could feel her skin heat, and her breathing deepened.

"The pumpkin soup to start?" he asked her, voice low and completely casual in her ear.

She opened her mouth, but she couldn't seem to form any words. She could barely sit still. Her toes curled and her fingers gripped tightly around the leather menu.

"Maybe the arugula salad?" he continued.

How could he do that? How could he sit there and behave as

if everything was normal, when she was practically jumping out of her skin?

"I'm going with the yellowfin tuna," Susan chirped.

Ray and Susan both looked to Kaitlin with questions on their faces.

Zach's hand slipped higher, and she very nearly moaned.

"Kaitlin?" he prompted.

She knew she should slap his hand away. She should call him right here, right now, on his unacceptable behavior. It would serve him right.

He'd be embarrassed in front of Ray Lambert. But then so would she. She'd be mortified if Ray—if *anyone*—knew what Zach was doing under the tablecloth.

"Arugula," she blurted out.

"The risotto is delicious," Susan offered helpfully.

Kaitlin tried to smile her thanks. But she wasn't sure if it quite came off, since she was gritting her teeth against Zach's sensual onslaught.

She balanced the heavy menu against the tabletop, holding it with one hand. Then she dropped the other to her lap, covering Zach's. "Stop," she hissed under her breath. "Please." The word came out on a desperate squeak.

His hand stilled. But then he turned it, meeting hers, and his thumb began a slow caress of her palm.

A new wave of desire flowed through her.

She could pull away anytime she wanted. But she didn't want to pull away. Lord help her, she wanted to savor the sensation, feel the raw energy pulse through her body. And when his hand turned back, and the caress resumed on her thigh, she didn't complain.

"The salmon," he said decisively, closing his menu and setting it aside.

Susan pulled her menu against her chest, speaking over the top. "The dill sauce is to die for."

Ray gave his wife's shoulder a quick, friendly caress. "It's beyond me why she doesn't weigh three hundred pounds."

"I have a great metabolism," Susan said, adding a self-deprecating laugh. "I don't do nearly enough exercise to deserve all those desserts."

Zach turned to Kaitlin, his fingertips still working magic as he spoke. "And what do you want?"

The double entendre boomed around them both.

Her gaze was drawn to the depths of his eyes, knowing there was no disguising her naked longing. "Risotto," she managed to say.

"And for dessert?" He pressed more firmly against her inner thigh, his palm sliding boldly against her sensitized skin.

"I'll decide later."

He gave a slow, satisfied smile, and a gleam of attraction turned his gray eyes to silver.

Just as she was tumbling completely and hopelessly under his spell, Lindsay's words came back to haunt her. *Do you think there's a slim possibility it was a distraction?*

Oh, no.

He was doing it, again.

And she was falling for it, willingly, and *all over again.*

Humiliation was like ice water to her hormones. She steeled her wayward desire, letting anger replace her lust.

"No dessert," she told him sternly, dropping her hand to her thigh and firmly removing his.

"Crème brûlée," said Susan. "Definitely crème brûlée for me."

Zach's gaze slid to Kaitlin for a split second. But then he obviously decided to give up. Distraction was not going to work for him this time. His behavior was reprehensible, and her lapse in judgment was thoroughly unprofessional. What would it take for her to learn?

Thankfully, Susan launched into a story about a recent business trip to Greece.

Kaitlin forced herself to listen, responding with what she hoped were friendly and intelligent answers to Ray's and Susan's questions, then asking about their trip to London and their new ski chalet in Banff, as appetizers, dinner and then dessert were served.

Zach didn't touch her again, luckily for him. Because by the time the crème brûlée was finished, the check arrived, and Ray and Susan said their good-nights, Kaitlin's mood had migrated to full-on rage.

As the waiter cleared the last of the dishes, smoothing the white linen tablecloth, Lindsay and Dylan appeared.

Lindsay plunked herself next to Zach, the briefcase between them, while Dylan sat much more reluctantly across from Kaitlin.

"They stole your briefcase," Lindsay said without preamble. "They *stole* your briefcase."

Kaitlin had presumed that was what happened. She immediately turned an accusing glare on Zach. There was no need to voice the question, so she waited silently for his explanation.

"It was in my trunk," he pointed out in his own defense. "*My* trunk."

Lindsay opened her mouth, but Dylan jumped in before she could speak. His blue eyes glittered at Zach. "Seems there are some finer points of the law you may not have taken into account here."

"They're *my* drawings," Zach stated.

The waiter reappeared, and conversation ceased. "May I offer anyone some coffee?"

"A shot of cognac in mine," said Lindsay.

"All around," Zach added gruffly, making a circle motion with his index finger.

Kaitlin wasn't inclined to argue.

"They are *my* drawings." Her words to Zach were stern as the man walked away.

"I paid you to make them," he countered.

"You *both* paid her to make them," Lindsay pointed out in an imperious tone.

"I wouldn't argue with her," Dylan muttered darkly.

Lindsay shot him a warning look.

He didn't seem the least bit intimidated by her professorial demeanor as he stared levelly back. "I had a math teacher like you once."

"Didn't seem to do you any good," she retorted.

"You stole my briefcase!" Kaitlin felt compelled to bring everyone back to the main point. "Was this entire dinner a ruse?"

She shook her head to clear it. "Of *course* it was a ruse. You're despicable, Zach. If I hadn't told Lindsay you'd invited me here. And if she didn't have a very suspicious nature—"

"A *correctly* suspicious nature," Lindsay pointed out to both men.

"—you'd have gotten away with it."

"I was planning to put it back," Dylan defended.

"I need to see the designs," said Zach, not a trace of apology in his tone. "My company, your company, pretend all you like, but I'm the guy signing the check. And I'm the guy left picking up the pieces once your game is over."

"That *game* happens to be my life." She wasn't playing around here. If she didn't fix her career, she didn't have a job. If she didn't have a job, there was nobody to pay rent, nobody to buy food.

He brought his hand down on the table. "And whatever's left when the dust clears happens to be mine."

Sick to death of the contest of wills, Kaitlin capitulated.

She waved a hand toward her briefcase. "Fine. Go ahead. There's nothing you can do to change them anyway. You don't like 'em, complain all you want. I will ignore you."

Zach wasted no time in snagging the briefcase from the bench seat between him and Lindsay. He snapped open the clasps, lifted the lid and extracted the folded plans. He awkwardly spread them out on the round table.

Just then, the waiter arrived and glanced around for a place to set the coffee.

Zach ignored him, and the man signaled for a folding tray stand.

Kaitlin accepted a coffee. She took her cup in her hand, sipping it while she sat back to wait for Zach's reaction.

She suspected he'd be angry. Her designs called for some

pretty fundamental and expensive changes to his building. But a small part of her couldn't help but hope he'd surprise her.

Maybe he had better taste than she thought. Maybe he'd recognize her genius. Maybe he'd—

"Are you out of your ever-lovin' mind?" His gray eyes all but glowed in anger.

Five

In the restaurant's parking garage, Lindsay twisted the key in the ignition of her silver Audi Coupe and pushed the shifter into Reverse. They peeled out of the narrow parking spot and into the driving lane.

"I suppose that could have been worse," Kaitlin admitted as they zipped toward the exit from the underground.

Zach had hated the renovation designs. No big surprise there. But since they were in a public place, he couldn't very well yell at her. So, that was a plus. And she wouldn't change them. He could gripe as much as he liked about a modern lobby not being in keeping with his corporate image, but they both knew it was about money.

Lindsay pressed a folded bill into the parking lot attendant's hand. "He *stole* your briefcase."

"I knew not seeing them was making him crazy," said Kaitlin, still getting over the shock at this turn of events. "But I sure didn't think he'd go that far."

Lindsay flipped on her signal, watching the traffic on the

busy street. "All that righteous indignation, the insistence on principles."

"I know," Kaitlin added rapidly in agreement. "The lectures, the protestations, and then wham." She smacked her hands together. "He steals the drawings right out from under my nose."

"I'm not a pirate," Lindsay mocked as she quickly took the corner, into a small space in traffic. "Nobody in my family was ever a pirate."

Kaitlin turned to stare at her friend. "What?"

"*We* have morals and principles."

"Are you talking about Zach?"

"Zach didn't steal your drawings."

"He sure did," said Kaitlin.

"Dylan was the guy with the briefcase in his hands."

"Only because Zach asked him to get it. Dylan's just being loyal."

"Ha!" Lindsay coughed out a laugh.

"Linds?" Kaitlin searched her friend's profile.

Lindsay changed lanes on the brightly lit street, setting up for a left turn. "What?"

"I say again. Do you think you're getting a little obsessed with Dylan Gilby?"

"The man's a thief and a reprobate."

"Maybe. But Zach's our problem."

Lindsay didn't answer. She adjusted her rearview mirror then changed the radio station.

"I think Zach'll leave it alone now," she said. "I mean, he's seen the drawings. He gave it his best—"

"You're changing the subject."

"Hmm?"

Kaitlin gaped at her friend in astonishment. All this fighting was a ruse. "You've got a thing for Dylan."

"I've got a thing for proving he's a pirate," Lindsay stated primly, sitting up straight in the driver's seat, flipping on the windshield wipers. "It's an intellectual exercise."

"Intellectual, my ass."

"It's a matter of principle. Plus, the semester just ended, and I'm a little bored."

Despite all the angst of the evening, Kaitlin couldn't help but laugh. "I think it's a matter of libido."

"He's incredibly annoying," said Lindsay.

"But he is kind of cute." Kaitlin rotated her neck, trying to relieve the stress.

"Maybe," Lindsay allowed, braking as a bus pulled onto the street. "In a squeaky-clean-veneer, bad-boy-underneath kind of way."

"Is that a bad kind of way?" The few times Kaitlin had met Dylan at the office, she'd mostly found him charming. He had a twinkle in his blue eyes, could make a joke of almost anything and, if it hadn't been her briefcase in question, she might have admired his loyalty to Zach for stealing it.

Lindsay gave a self-conscious grin, rubbing her palms briskly along the curve of the steering wheel. "Fine. You caught me. I confess."

Grinning at the irony, Kaitlin continued. "His best friend's locked in an epic struggle with your best friend. You've called into question the integrity of his entire family. And you practically arrested him for stealing my briefcase. But other than that, I can see the two of you really going somewhere with this."

Lindsay shook back her hair. "I'm only window-shopping. Besides, there's nothing wrong with a little libido mixed in with an intellectual exercise."

Kaitlin couldn't help laughing. It was a relief to let the anger go. "Zach groped me under the table during dinner. How's that for libido?"

Lindsay sobered, glancing swiftly at Kaitlin before returning her attention to the road. "Seriously?"

"I guess he's still trying to distract me."

They pulled into a parking spot in front of Kaitlin's apartment building, and Lindsay set the parking brake, shifting in her seat. "Tell me that's not why you showed him the plans."

"It wasn't *that* distracting." Well, in fact he was entirely *that* distracting. But the distraction was irrelevant to her decision. "I showed him the plans to shut him up."

"You're sure?"

"I'm sure." *Mostly.*

Lindsay gave a wry grin. "Poor Zach. Part of me can't wait to see what he tries next."

And part of Kaitlin couldn't help hoping it involved seduction.

In his office Monday morning, Zach was forced to struggle to keep from fantasizing about Kaitlin. He was angry with her over the lavish designs, and he needed to stay that way in order to keep his priorities straight. Thinking about her smooth legs, her lithe body and those sensuous, kissable lips was only asking for trouble. Well, more trouble. More trouble than he'd ever had in his life.

"—to the tune of ten million dollars," Esmond Carson was saying from one of the burgundy guest chairs across from Zach's office desk.

At the mention of the number, Zach's brain rocked back to attention. "What?" he asked bluntly.

Esmond flipped through the thick file folder on his lap. The gray-haired man was nearing sixty-five. He'd been a trusted lawyer and advisor of Zach's grandmother Sadie for over thirty years. "Rent, food, teacher salaries, transportation. All of the costs are overstated in the financial reports. The foundation has a huge stack of bills in arrears. The bank account has maxed out its overdraft. That's how the mess came to my attention."

Zach couldn't believe what he was hearing. How had things gotten so out of hand? "Who *did* this?"

"Near as we can tell, it was a man named Lawrence Wellington. He was the regional manager for the city. And he disappeared the day after Sadie passed away. My guess is that he knew the embezzlement would come to light as soon as you took over."

"He stole ten million dollars?"

"That's what it looks like."

"You've called the police?"

Esmond closed the file folder, his demeanor calm, expression impassive. "We could report it."

"Damn right we're reporting it." Zach's hand went to his desk phone. Someone had stolen from his grandmother. Worse, they'd stolen from his grandmother's charitable trust. Sadie was passionate about helping inner-city kids.

"We're having him arrested and charged," Zach finished, lifting the receiver and raising it to his ear.

"That might not be your best option."

Zach paused, hand over the telephone buttons. He lifted his brows in a silent question.

"It would generate a lot of publicity," said Esmond.

"And?" Who cared? It wasn't as if they had any obligation to protect the reputation of a criminal.

"It'll be a media circus. The charity, your grandmother's name, all potentially dragged through the mud. Donors will get nervous, revenue could drop, projects might be canceled. No one and no company wants their name linked with criminal behavior, no matter how noble the charity."

"You think it would go that way?" asked Zach, weighing the possibilities in his mind, realizing Esmond had a valid point.

"I know a good private investigative firm," said Esmond. "We'll look for the guy, of course. And if there's any benefit in pressing charges, we'll press them. But my guess is we won't find him. From the records I've reviewed, Lawrence Wellington was a very shrewd operator. He'll be long gone. Sadie's money's long gone."

Zach hissed out a swearword, dropping the receiver and sliding back in his tall chair.

The two men sat in silence, midmorning sunshine streaming in the big windows, muted office sounds coming through the door, the familiar hum of traffic on Liberty Street below.

"What would Sadie want?" Esmond mused quietly.

That one was easy. "Sadie would want us to help the kids." Zach's grandmother would want them to swiftly and quietly help the kids.

Esmond agreed. "Are you in a position to write a check? I can pull this out of the fire if you can cover the losses."

What a question.

Like every other transportation company in the world, Harper's cash flow had been brutalized these past few years. He had ships sitting idle in port, others in dry dock racking up huge repair bills, customers delaying payment because of their own downturns, creditors tightening terms, and Kaitlin out there designing the Taj Mahal instead of a functional office building.

"Sure," he told Esmond. "I'll write you a check."

He put Esmond in touch with his finance director, asked Amy to have Kaitlin come to his office, then swiveled his chair to stare out at the cityscape, hoping against hope his grandmother wasn't watching over him at this particular moment. In the three short months since her death, it felt as if the entire company was coming off the rails.

Not entirely his fault, of course. But the measure of a business manager wasn't how he performed when things were going well, it was how he performed under stress. And the biggest stress of his present world was on her way up to see him right now.

A few minutes later, he heard the door open and knew it had to be Kaitlin. Amy would have announced anyone else.

"You can close it behind you," he told her without turning.

"That's okay," she said, her footsteps crossing the carpet toward his desk.

He turned his chair, coming to his feet, in no mood to be ignored. He strode around the end of the big desk. "You can close the door behind you," he repeated with emphasis.

"Zach, we—"

He breezed past her and firmly closed it himself.

"I'd prefer you didn't do that." Her voice faded off as he turned and met her head-on.

She wore a slim, charcoal-gray skirt, topped with a white-and-gold silk blouse. The skirt accented her slender waist, and was short enough to show off her shapely legs, while the blouse clung softly to her firm breasts. The top buttons were undone, showing a hint of cleavage and framing her slender neck. A twisted gold necklace dangled between her breasts, while matching earrings swung from her small ears beneath a casual updo.

His gut tightened predictably at the sight of her, and he took the few steps back to the middle of the room.

Did she have to look like a goddess every day in the office? Had the woman never heard of business suits or, better yet, sweatpants? Could she not show up in loafers instead of three-inch, strappy heels that would haunt his dreams?

"I would prefer..." She started for the door.

He snagged her arm.

She glanced pointedly down to his grip. "Are you going to manhandle me again?"

Manhandling her did begin to describe what he wanted to do. He'd gone home Friday night with his muscles stretched taut as steel. He'd tossed and turned, prayed for anger, got arousal, and when he finally slept, there she was, sexy, beckoning, but always out of reach.

He searched her expression. "Am I frightening you?"

"No."

"I'm making you angry?"

"Yes."

"Deal with it." He wouldn't scare her, but he truly didn't care if she got mad.

She set her jaw. "I am."

"Because you're making me angry, too." That wasn't the only thing she was making him. But it was the only one he'd own up to—both out loud and inside his head.

"Poor baby," she cooed.

"You're taunting me?" *That* was what she wanted to do here? He could barely believe it.

"I'm keeping the upper hand," she corrected him, crossing her arms, accentuating her breasts, increasing his view of her cleavage.

He coughed out a laugh of surprise, covering up the surge of arousal. "You think you have the upper hand?"

"I *know* I have the upper hand. And there's nothing you can say or do to make me—"

He took a step forward. He was at the end of his rope here. The woman needed to wake up to reality.

Her eyes went wide, and her lips parted ever so slightly.

"Make you what?" he breathed.

"Zach." Her tone held a warning, even as her expression turned to confusion and vulnerability.

His attention locked in on her, and her alone.

"Make you what?" he persisted.

She didn't answer. But the tip of her tongue flicked out, moistening her lips.

He closed his throat on an involuntary groan, and his world shrank further.

He shifted closer, fixated on her lips.

His thigh brushed hers.

Her lips softened, and her breathing deepened.

He inhaled the exotic perfume, daring to lift his hand, stroking the back of his knuckles against her soft cheek.

She didn't stop him. Instead, her eyelids fluttered closed, and she leaned into his caress. His desire kicked into action. And he tipped his head, leaning in without conscious thought to press his lips against hers.

They were soft, pliable, hot and delicious. Sensation instantaneously exploded inside his brain. He was back on the yacht, the ocean breeze surrounding them, her taste overpowering his senses, the stars a backdrop to their midnight passion.

His arms went around her, and hers around him. Their bodies came flush, the sensation achingly familiar. She molded to him, fitting tight in all the right places.

He moved her backward, pressing her against the office wall. His hands slipped down, cupping her tight little bottom, resisting an urge to drag her sharply against his hardening body. He was on fire for her.

His hands went to her hair, stroking through the softness, cradling her gorgeous face while he peppered kisses, tracing a line over her tiny ear, down the curve of her neck, along her shoulders, to the edge of her soft silk blouse.

Her fingers twined in his hairline. Her lips parted farther, her tongue finding his, her perfect breasts pushing tightly against his chest, beading so that he could feel them. She stretched up, coming onto her toes, fusing her mouth with his, and slid her hands beneath his jacket.

Those small hands were hot through the cotton of his shirt. He wanted to rip it off, strip her bare, hold her naked body against his own and finish what they kept starting.

But a jangling phone penetrated his brain. Sounds from the outer office came back into focus. He heard Amy's voice. Someone answered, and he came to the abrupt realization of where they were.

He forced himself to stop, cradled Kaitlin's head against his shoulder, breathing deeply, all anger toward her having evaporated.

"We did it again," he breathed.

She stiffened, pulling away. "This is why I didn't want the door closed."

He let her go, pretending it wasn't the hardest thing he'd ever done. Then he forced a note of sarcasm into his voice, refusing to let her see just how badly she made him lose control. "You don't trust yourself?"

"I don't trust *you*," she told him for at least the third time.

Fair enough. He didn't trust himself, either.

But it wasn't all him. It definitely hadn't all been him.

She straightened her blouse and smoothed her hair. "What is it you needed to see me about?"

Zach forced himself to turn away. Looking at her was only asking for more trouble.

"Can we sit?" He gestured to two padded chairs at angles to each other in front of his floor-to-ceiling windows.

Without a word, she crossed to one of them and sat down, fixing her focus on a point on the skyline outside, folding her hands primly in front of her.

Zach's hormones were still raging, but he inhaled a couple

of bracing breaths, taking a seat and focusing his own attention on a seascape painting on the wall past Kaitlin's right ear.

"I just spoke to my grandmother's lawyer," he explained, composing and discarding a number of approaches on the fly. He had to convince her to pull back on the renovations. It was more important than ever, and he couldn't afford to screw this conversation up.

Kaitlin's attention moved to his face, her lips pursing, green eyes narrowing. "What do you mean by that?"

He gave up and met her gaze. She was so damn gorgeous, feisty, challenging. Even now, he wanted to take her back into his arms and change the mood between them. "Just what I said."

"What happened?" She jerked forward in her chair. "Am I out of the will? Did you find a loophole? Are you firing me?" Then she jumped to her feet. "If you're firing me, you should have said something before…" She gestured with a sweeping arm, across the office to the spot where they'd kissed. "Before…"

Zach stood with her. "I am *not* firing you. Now, will you sit back down."

She watched him warily. "Then what's this about?"

"Sit down, and I'll tell you." He gestured to her chair and waited.

She glared at him but finally sat.

He followed suit, refocusing. This wasn't going well. It was not going well at all. "A problem has come to light with my grandmother's charitable trust."

Kaitlin's features remained schooled and neutral.

"There's been some money—a lot of money—embezzled from the bank account by a former employee."

He paused to see if she'd react, but she waited in silence.

Zach leaned slightly forward, his feet braced apart on the carpet in front of him, choosing his words carefully. "Therefore, I am going to have to shift some cash from Harper Transportation to the trust fund, or some of her projects will collapse, like the after-school tutoring programs and hot lunches."

Kaitlin finally spoke. "Do you need me to sign some-thing?"

Zach shook his head.

"Then what?"

"Harper Transportation's cash flow will be tight for the next year or so." He mentally braced himself. "So we may need to talk seriously about scaling back on the renovation—"

"Oh, no, you don't." She emphatically crossed her arms.

"Let me—"

"You mess with my emotions."

"I'm not messing with anything," he protested.

"Try to put me off balance," she accused.

"I'm offering you honesty and reason." He was. He was giving her the bald truth of the matter.

"One minute we're kissing—" she snapped her fingers in the air "—next, you're asking for concessions."

His anger trickled back. "The two were *not* related."

"Well, it won't work this time, Mr. Zachary Harper." She tossed her pretty hair, tone going to a scoff. "Embezzlement from dear ol' granny's charitable fund, my ass."

"You think I'm *lying?*"

"Yes."

What was the matter with her? He had documentation. It was the easiest thing in the world to prove.

"I'll show you the account statements," he offered. "The bank records."

"You can show me anything you want, Zach. Any high-school kid with a laptop and a printer in his basement can fake financial statements."

"You doubt the integrity of my accountants?"

"I doubt the integrity of *you*." She came to her feet again, color high, chin raised, shoulders squared, looking entirely ready for battle.

Once again, he rose with her.

Though her hair was in an updo, she swiped her hands behind her ears, tugging at both gold earrings. "You've tried evasion, coercion, outright threats, theft, seduction and now emotional manipulation."

He clenched his jaw, biting back an angry retort.

"Good grief, Zach. Granny, a charity and hungry kids? I'm surprised you didn't add a dying puppy to the mix." She tapped her index finger against her chest. "I am renovating, and I am doing it my way. And for that, you get half a corporation and a divorce decree. It's a bargain, and you should quit trying to change the terms."

Zach fumed, but bit back his words. He knew that anything he said would make things worse. A contingency strategy was his only hope. And he was all out of frickin' contingency strategies.

Having apparently said her piece, Kaitlin squared her shoulders. She put her sculpted nose in the air and turned on her heel to leave.

As the door shut firmly behind her, Zach unclenched his fists. He closed his eyes for a long second. Then he dropped into his chair.

The woman was past impossible.

She was suspicious. She was determined. And she was oh, so sexy.

She was going to bring down a three-hundred-year-old dynasty, and he had no idea how to stop her.

"Plan C is a bust," he informed Dylan, spinning the near empty glass of single malt on the polished, corner table at McDougals.

Dylan dropped into the padded leather chair opposite, nodding to Zach's drink. "Well, at least you waited until five."

"I'm lucky I made it past noon." How could one woman be so frustrating? Her renovation plans went way beyond repairing her reputation. What she was planning to do to his building was just plain punitive.

Dylan signaled a waiter.

"I talked to a couple dozen more people today," said Zach. "Nothing's changed. I can get her an entry-level job, easy. But nothing that comes close to the opportunity she has at Harper Transportation."

The waiter quickly took Dylan's order and left.

Dylan shrugged in capitulation. "So, give it up. Let her go for it. You'll have a weird, incredibly expensive building. And you'll live with it."

"She's adding three stories," Zach reminded Dylan. "Knocking out nearly five floors for the lobby. Did you see the marble pillars? The saltwater fish tank?"

Dylan gave a shrug. "I thought they were a nice touch."

"I bailed out Sadie's charity today."

"Why?"

"Some jackass embezzled ten million dollars. My cash flow just tanked completely. So, tell me, Dylan, do I sell off a ship or slow down repairs?"

Dylan's expression and tone immediately turned serious. "You need a loan?"

"No." Zach gave a firm shake of his head. "More debt is not the answer."

"Another partner? You want to sell me some shares?"

"And be a minor partner in my own company? I don't think so. Anyway, I'm not mixing business with friendship." Zach appreciated the offer. But this problem was his to solve.

"Fair enough," Dylan agreed. "What are your options?"

"Nothing." Zach took a drink. He needed Kaitlin to scale back on the renovation. Short of that, his options were very limited.

Selling a ship was a stupid idea. So was slowing down repairs. He'd need the entire fleet up and running so they could capitalize on any rise in demand. A company the size of Harper Transportation had to have serious cash flow to keep going. More ships, more cash flow. Fewer ships would result in a downward spiral that could prove fatal.

"Always the optimist," said Dylan, accepting his own glass of Glenlivet from the waiter.

Zach tossed back a swallow. "Kaitlin is going to bankrupt me, and there's absolutely nothing I can do to stop her."

Dylan's voice went serious again. "What exactly do you need her to do?"

Zach spun the glass again. "Come to her senses."

"Zach. Seriously. Quit wallowing in self-pity."

Zach took a bracing breath. "Okay. Right. I need her to scale back. Build me a reasonable quality, standard office building. No marble pillars. No fountains. No palm trees. And no mahogany arch. And especially no two-thousand-gallon saltwater aquarium."

Dylan thought about it for a moment. "So, make her want to do just that."

"How?" Zach demanded. "I've tried everything from bribery to reason. It's like trying to use a rowboat to turn the *Queen Mary* around."

Dylan was quiet for a few more minutes. Zach tried to focus his thoughts. He tried to get past the emotions clouding his brain and think rationally. But it didn't seem to be working.

"What about Sadie?" asked Dylan.

"What about her?" Zach didn't follow.

"Sadie left Kaitlin the company."

"And?" How was that a plus in Zach's present circumstances?

"And Kaitlin would have to be downright callous not to care about what Sadie would want."

"You think I should convince Kaitlin to respect Sadie's wishes?" That would be an awful lot easier if Sadie had actually left wishes. But her only wish seemed to be for Zach's wife to control him.

Dylan lifted his glass in a toast, ice cube clinking against the crystal. "That's exactly what I think you should do."

"What wishes? Where wishes? Sadie left no wishes, Dylan."

"Would she want a flashy, avant-garde showpiece?"

"Of course not." Zach's grandmother Sadie was all about heritage and tradition. She had been the guardian of the Harper family history Zach's entire life, and she had an abiding respect for everyone that went before her.

"Then help Kaitlin learn that," Dylan suggested.

Zach couldn't see that happening. "She's already accused me of emotionally manipulating her."

"Did you?"

"No." Zach paused. "Well, I made a couple of passes at her. But it wasn't manipulation. It was plain old lust."

"Better stop doing that." Dylan drank.

"No kidding." Though, if Zach was realistic, it was probably a whole lot easier said than done.

Zach still couldn't see Dylan's plan working. "I doubt she'll listen to me long enough to learn about Sadie. And, even if she does, she'll assume I'm lying." At this point, there was no way Kaitlin would believe anything Zach said.

"Don't tell her about Sadie."

"Then how…" Zach tapped his index finger impatiently against the table.

Dylan gave a secretive little smile and polished off his drink. "Show her Sadie."

Zach gave his head a shake of incomprehension, holding his hands palms up.

"Take her to the island," said Dylan. "Show her Sadie's handiwork. Then ask her to design something for the office building that respects your grandmother. Kaitlin seems pretty smart. She'll get it."

Zach stilled. It wasn't a half-bad idea. In fact, it was a brilliant idea.

He let out a chopped laugh. "And you claim to be honest and principled."

"I'm not suggesting you lie to her."

"But you are frighteningly devious."

"Yeah," Dylan agreed. "And I've got your back."

Six

"He's after something," Kaitlin said as Lindsay plunked a large take-out pizza from Agapitos on Kaitlin's small, dining room table. "A guy doesn't make an offer like that for no reason."

Lindsay returned to the foyer, kicked off her shoes and dropped her purse, refastening her ponytail.

It was Sunday afternoon. The Mets game was starting on the sports channel, and both women were dressed in casual sweatpants, loose T-shirts and cozy socks.

"No argument from me," she said as she followed Kaitlin into the compact kitchen area of the apartment. "My point is only that you should say yes."

Kaitlin pulled open the door to her freezer and extracted a bag of ice cubes. "And play into his hands?"

Lindsay's voice turned dreamy. "A private island? Mansions? All that delicious pirate history? I don't care what he's up to, we're going to have one hell of a weekend."

Kaitlin paused, blender lid in her hand, and stared at Lindsay. "We?"

The announcer's voice called a long fly ball, and both

women turned to watch the television in the living room. The hit was caught deep in center field, and they both groaned their disappointment before turning back to the drink making.

Lindsay hopped up on one of the two wooden stools in front of the small breakfast bar, pushed aside the weekend newspaper and leaned on her elbows. "You're not going to Serenity Island without me."

"I'm not going to Serenity Island at all." Kaitlin dumped a dozen ice cubes into the blender. There was no way in the world she'd spend an entire weekend with Zach.

"It's the chance of a lifetime," Lindsay insisted.

"Only for those of us with a pirate fetish." Kaitlin added mango, pineapple, iced tea, mint and vodka to the ice cubes, mixing up their secret recipe for mango madness. It was a Sunday tradition, along with the take-out pizza and a baseball game.

"It's not a fetish," Lindsay informed her tartly. "It's more of an obsession."

Kaitlin hit the button on the blender, filling the apartment with the grinding noise. "You want to sleep with a pirate," she called above the din. "That's a fetish. Look it up."

Lindsay's grin was unrepentant. "First off, I have to prove he's a pirate."

With the mixture blended, Kaitlin hit the off switch and poured it into two tall glasses. Lindsay shifted back to her feet, headed for a cupboard and grabbed a couple of stoneware plates and put a slice of pizza on each of them.

"Here's something," Kaitlin began as they made their way back to the living room. "Put on that red-and-gold dress, and the Vishashi shoes, then tell him you'll sleep with him if he admits he's a pirate." She stepped to one side so that Lindsay could go around and take her usual spot on the couch beside the window.

"That's not ethical," said Lindsay with a note of censure.

Kaitlin scoffed out a laugh. "As opposed to arriving on his island to gather evidence against him?"

"It's not like I'm going to break into his house," Lindsay offered reasonably.

"You're definitely not going to break into his house, since we're *not going*."

"Spoilsport."

Kaitlin settled on the couch and snagged one of the plates of pizza, gaze resting on the baseball game while she took a bite of the hot pepperoni and gooey cheese. She sighed as the comfort food hit her psyche. "I don't want to think about it anymore."

"Going to Serenity Island?"

"Zach. The renovation. The arguments. The kisses. Everything. I'm tired. I just want to sit here, watch the game and dull my senses with fat and carbs."

"That seems like a big waste of time." But Lindsay took a bite of the Agapitos, extrathick, stuffed-crust pizza and stared at the action on the television screen in silence.

Though Kaitlin tried to concentrate on the players, her mind kept switching back to Zach and his possible motives for the invitation. "I wish I had your capacity for mental chess games," she ventured out loud.

"How exactly did he ask you?" asked Lindsay, shifting at her end of the couch so she was facing Kaitlin, obviously warming up for a good discussion.

Kaitlin thought back to the moment in her office. "He was polite—excruciatingly polite—and I think a little nervous. He said he wanted me to learn about his family, get a better understanding of his grandmother."

"Any kisses, caresses, groping…?"

Kaitlin made a gesture that threatened to toss her pizza at Lindsay. "Just words."

"Were you disappointed?"

"No."

"Are you lying?"

"Only a little." Zach was one incredibly sexy man and, for better or worse, he turned Kaitlin on like there was no tomorrow. She couldn't stop it. She could barely fight the urge to act on it. Which was why visiting Serenity Island was one very, very bad idea.

There was a full count on the batter, and they both turned to watch Campbell swing and miss.

Kaitlin took a generous gulp of the mango madness. Then she gestured with her glass. "I know he's trying to outsmart me."

"Good thing we're onto him," Lindsay said.

"He gets me alone, he'll try seducing me. I know he thinks it's to his advantage." And it probably was. She couldn't think straight when he kissed her. Heck, she couldn't think straight when he looked at her.

"So turn the tables on him."

"Huh?"

"Seduce him back."

Kaitlin nearly choked on her pizza. Seduce Zach? *Seduce* Zach? Why not just jump off the top of his building and be done with it? "Are you kidding me?"

"Two can play at that game, baby." Lindsay gave a sage nod. "Women have been getting their own way through sex for thousands of years."

"You want me to *sleep* with him?"

Zach was every woman's fantasy. He was rich, great-looking, smart and funny. He'd had women fawning over him since he was a teenager. He'd likely seen and done it all. It was laughable to think Kaitlin could hold her own in bed with Zach.

"He is your husband," Lindsay pointed out.

"He's not that kind of a husband."

"Okay. Forget that," said Lindsay. "But look at it this way. If we don't go to the island, he'll try something else. If we go, he thinks he's winning. But we're onto him, and we'll be waiting for his next move."

Kaitlin had to admit, Lindsay's logic had some merit. Trouble was, the thought of Zach's next move triggered a flare of desire that curled her toes.

They flew to Serenity Island in one of Dylan's Astral Air helicopters. It was the first time Kaitlin had flown anywhere. Vacations weren't part of her foster care upbringing, and airplane tickets were not something she considered one of the necessities of life.

Their first stop after landing on the island was Dylan's parents' house. It was adjacent to the private helipad. The Gilby garage was home to a small fleet of golf carts that Kaitlin and Lindsay were informed were the only motor vehicles on the island.

David and Darcie Gilby were away in Chicago on business, but their various housekeepers and caretakers were in residence, along with Dylan's aunt Ginny, who greeted the four of them in the foyer in a bright red, 1950s swing dress with a multistrand pearl necklace and clip-on earrings.

"Young people," she cried, taking both of Dylan's hands in her own. "So nice of you to bring company."

Ginny was a very attractive woman for what must have been her age. Her face was wrinkled, but her short white hair was perfectly styled with flip curls at the ends, and her makeup was flawless. Two little white puff-ball dogs trotted across the floor, nails clicking on the hardwood until they stopped beside her.

"Hello, Auntie," said Dylan, giving the woman a kiss on her powdered cheek. "How are you?"

"And which one of these lovely young ladies is yours?" asked Ginny, sizing up both Kaitlin and Lindsay, taking in their faces, hair and clothing as if they were in a pageant and she was the judge.

"We're just friends," said Dylan.

One of the dogs gave a sharp bark.

"Nonsense." Ginny winked at Kaitlin. "This young man's a catch." She moved closer, voice lowering as if she was confiding a secret. "He has money, you know."

Kaitlin couldn't help but grin.

"Now this one—" Ginny made a half turn and shook a wrinkled finger in Zach's direction "—he's always been a hoodlum."

"Hello, Aunt Ginny," said Zach, with what was obvious patience.

"Caught him in the linen closet with Patty Kostalnik."

"Ginny," Zach protested.

"Did you now?" Kaitlin asked the older woman, her inflection making her interest obvious.

"Or was it that Pansy girl?" Ginny screwed up her wrinkled face. "Never liked that one. She used to steal my crème de menthe. It was May, because the apple trees were blooming."

Kaitlin slid a glance to Zach, enjoying his embarrassment.

He shook his head as if to deny the accusation.

"Kaitlin and Lindsay are staying at Zach's for a few days," Dylan told his aunt Ginny.

"Nonsense," Ginny retorted. "You need a wife, young man." She moved between Kaitlin and Lindsay and took each of them by an arm. "They need to stay here so you can woo them. Which one do you want?"

"They're staying with Zach," Dylan repeated.

Ginny clicked her tongue in admonishment. "You've got to learn to stand up for yourself. Don't let Zachary take them both." She looked to Kaitlin. "You want him?"

Kaitlin felt herself blush. "I'm afraid I'm already—"

She turned to Lindsay, her voice a bark of demand. "What about you?"

"Sure," said Lindsay with a mischievous grin. "Like you say, Dylan's a good catch."

Ginny beamed, while Zach chuckled, and a look of horror came over Dylan's face.

Ginny drew Lindsay off to one side. "Right this way to the kitchen, young lady. You can help me with the pie."

Dylan watched as they left the foyer and proceeded down a long hallway.

"You're not going with them?" asked Zach, still obviously controlling his laughter.

"She got herself into it," said Dylan with a fatalistic shake of his head. "The woman's on her own."

"That Pansy girl?" Kaitlin asked Zach, not ready to let him off the hook for that one.

"I was fifteen, and she was two years older."

"Uh-huh?" Kaitlin waited for more details.

"She taught me how to kiss," Zach admitted.

"And...?"

"And nothing. You jealous?"

Kaitlin frowned, sensing he was about to turn the tables. "Not me."

"Right this way," Dylan interrupted, pointing through an archway and ushering them from the foyer farther into house.

Kaitlin was happy to leave the conversation behind, and she was more than impressed by the house.

Only a few years old, the large and luxurious Gilby home was perched on a cliff overlooking the ocean and the distant coast of Connecticut. The west wall of the great room was two stories high and made completely of glass. Hardwood floors gleamed beneath open-beam ceilings, and a sweeping staircase curled toward a second-story overtop of the kitchen area where Lindsay had disappeared.

After Kaitlin had a chance to look around, they moved out onto a huge deck dotted with tables and comfortable furniture groupings. Large potted plants were placed around the perimeter, and a retractable roof was halfway shut, providing shade on half the deck and sunshine on the other.

"You must entertain a lot," Kaitlin said to Dylan, taking in the wet bar and two huge gas barbecues.

He nodded in answer to her question. "There's a great big party room downstairs. Plenty of extra bedrooms. And do you see those green roofs below the ridge?"

Kaitlin moved to the rail, leaning out to gaze along the steep side of a mountain. "I see them."

"Those are guest cottages. There's a service road that loops around the back. My mom loves to have guests here."

Kaitlin glanced straight down to see a kidney-shaped swimming pool with a couple of hot tubs beside it on a terra-cotta patio. The swimming area was surrounded by an emerald lawn. And, beyond the Gilbys' place, farther toward what looked like a sandy beach, and in the opposite direction of the cottages, she spied a stone spire and a jagged roofline that stuck up above the trees.

She pointed. "What's that down there?"

"That's Zach's place," Dylan replied.

Kaitlin glanced back at Zach in surprise. "You live in a castle?"

"It's made of stone," he replied, walking closer to the rail to join her. "And it's drafty and cavernous. I guess you could call it a castle. You know, if you wanted to sound pompous and have people laugh at you."

"It's a castle," she cooed, delighted at the thought of exploring it. "When was it built?"

"It's been around for a few generations," Zach offered without elaboration.

"Early 1700s," said Dylan. "The Harpers believe in honoring their roots."

Kaitlin's delight was replaced by an unexpected pang of jealousy deep in her chest. How many generations was that? Was there nothing not perfect about Zach's charmed life?

"I can't wait to see it," she said in what came out as a small voice.

Zach glanced sharply at her expression.

"The Harpers restore and preserve," Dylan explained. "The Gilbys prefer to bulldoze and start fresh."

"Philistines," Lindsay proclaimed as she breezed out onto the deck. In blue jeans and a green blouse, she somehow looked completely relaxed and at home.

Kaitlin, on the other hand, was now feeling awkward and jumpy. "How's the pie coming?" she asked, turning away from Zach's scrutiny.

Though she couldn't control her reflexive reactions, she had long since learned not to wallow in self-pity about her upbringing. It was what it was. She couldn't change it. She could only make the best of here and now. Well, maybe not exactly here and now. She only wanted to make it through the weekend.

"We're all invited, or should I say 'commanded' to stay for dinner," said Lindsay.

"That's Auntie," said Dylan, with a stern look for Lindsay. "You know she'll be fitting you for a wedding dress over dessert."

Lindsay fought with her unruly blond hair in the swirling wind, making a show of glancing around the deck and into the great room. "No problem," she informed him. "I could easily live here."

Dylan rolled his eyes at her irreverence.

"I've got nothing against living off the avails of pirating," she added with a jaunty waggle of her head. Then she tugged at the gold chain around her neck and pulled a gold medallion from below her blouse, swinging it in front of Dylan.

With a start, Kaitlin recognized it as the coin her friend had purchased from the antique shop. Lindsay was wearing it around her *neck?*

"What's that?" he demanded.

"Booty from your ancestor's plundering."

"It is not." But Dylan took a closer look.

"From the *Blue Glacier*," she informed him in triumph.

"Okay. That's it." Dylan captured her arm and tugged her back across the deck. "Come here."

Kaitlin watched Dylan hustle Lindsay through the open doors into the great room. "Where's he taking her?" she asked Zach with curiosity.

"My guess is that he's showing her the Letters of Authority."

Kaitlin shook her head in amazement over their willingness to engage in this particular contest. "Lindsay spent two thousand dollars on that coin from the *Blue Glacier*," Kaitlin told Zach. "Apparently, it was sunk by the *Black Fern* and Captain Caldwell Gilby."

"I know the story," said Zach.

"So, when do I get my ten bucks?"

He gave her a look of confusion.

"The bet at the baseball game," she reminded him. "Lindsay has unrefutable evidence that Dylan is descended from pirates. I believe that means she'll win the argument. And I believe that means you owe me ten dollars."

"Signed by King George..." Dylan's voice wafted through the open doors.

"Here we go," Zach muttered in a dire tone.

"It's still not legal," Lindsay retorted.

"Maybe not today."

Curiosity getting the better of her, Kaitlin settled to watch the debate through the open doorway.

Lindsay and Dylan were turned in profile. They were both obviously focused on something hanging on the wall.

"Forget the fact that Caldwell Gilby plundered in international waters," said Lindsay. "Just because a corrupt regime gives you permission to commit a crime—"

"One point to me," Kaitlin murmured to Zach.

"You're calling the British monarchy a corrupt regime?" Dylan demanded.

"That one's mine," said Zach, leaning back on the deck rail and crossing one ankle over the other.

"Your great, great, great, however many grandfathers held people at gunpoint—"

"Go, Lindsay," Kaitlin muttered, holding out her hand for the ten.

"I suspect it was swordpoint, maybe musketpoint," said Dylan.

"*Held* them at gunpoint," Lindsay stressed. "And took things that didn't belong to him."

Kaitlin gave Zach a smirk and tapped her index finger against her chest. Dylan didn't know who he was up against.

But Lindsay wasn't finished yet. "He sank their ships. He killed people. You don't need to be a lawyer to know he was a thief and a murderer."

"Oh, hand it over," Kaitlin demanded.

Dylan suddenly smacked Lindsay smartly on the rear.

She jumped. "Hey!"

"You crossed the line," he told her.

Kaitlin's jaw dropped. She sucked in a breath, waiting for Lindsay to react.

This was going to be bad.

Oh, it was going to be very, very bad.

Dylan said something else, but Kaitlin didn't hear the words.

In response, Lindsay leaned closer. It looked as if she was answering.

Kaitlin stayed still and waited. But the shouting didn't start, and the insults didn't fly.

Instead, Dylan reached out and stroked Lindsay's cheek. Then he butted his shoulder against hers and left it resting there.

For some reason, she didn't pull away.

Suddenly, Zach grasped Kaitlin's arm and turned her away.

"Huh?" was all she could manage to say.

"They don't need an audience," said Zach.

"But…" She couldn't help but glance once more over her shoulder. "I don't…" She turned back to stare at Zach. "Why didn't she kill him?"

"Because they're flirting, not fighting." Zach leaned on the rail, gazing into the setting sun. "Just like you and me."

The breath whooshed out of Kaitlin's chest. "We are not—"

"Oh, we so are."

"So far, so good?" asked Dylan, parking himself next to Zach at the rail of the deck after dinner. Lights shone from the windows of the Gilby house. The pool was illuminated in the yard below. And the twinkle of lights from Zach's house was visible in the distance.

"I think so." Zach motioned to the three women inside, where Ginny was playing right into his plan. "She's showing them photographs from when she and Sadie were girls."

"I dropped a hint to Lindsay," said Dylan, taking credit. "She immediately asked Ginny if there were any pictures."

"Good thought," Zach acknowledged. Ginny and Sadie had grown up together on Serenity Island. And though Ginny's short-term memory was spotty, she seemed to remember plenty of stories from decades back. She was in a perfect position to give Kaitlin some insight into his grandmother. And it had the added advantage of coming from a third party. Kaitlin couldn't accuse Zach of trying to manipulate her.

The thought that Zach could execute a master plan through the eccentric Aunt Ginny was laughable. Though, he supposed, that was exactly what they were doing.

"Lindsay's a fairly easy mark," Dylan added. "Mention a pirate, and off she goes like a heat-seeking missile."

"I notice you're protesting a bit too much about the pirates," Zach pointed out. Sure, Dylan was sensitive about his background, but Zach had never seen him pushed to anger over it.

"It sure makes her mad," Dylan mused.

"Our ancestors were not Boy Scouts," Zach felt compelled to restate.

"And the British monarchy was not a corrupt regime."

"There were a lot of beheadings."

Dylan shrugged. "Different time, different place."

"Yeah? Well, good luck getting Lindsay into bed with that argument."

Dylan's expression turned thoughtful. "Don't you worry about me. Lindsay likes a challenge. And I'm a challenge."

"That's your grand scheme?"

Dylan quirked his brows in self-confidence. "That's my grand scheme."

Zach had to admit, it was ingenious.

"Now let's talk about yours."

"Zachary?" came Ginny's imperious voice as she appeared in the doorway.

Zach glanced up.

"Over here," she commanded.

Dylan snickered as Zach pushed back to cross the deck.

Ginny beckoned him closer with a crooked finger.

"I need your help," she whispered, glancing into the great room.

"Sure." He bent his head to listen.

"We're going downstairs for some dancing." Ginny had always been a huge music fan, particularly of the big bands. And dancing had always been an important part of social functions on the island.

"No problem." He nodded.

"You ask the redhead, Miss Kaitlin." She gave Zach a conspiratorial nod. "I have a good feeling about the other one and Dylan."

"Lindsay," Zach prompted.

"He seems to have a particular interest in her rear end."

"*Ginny.*"

She gave a short cackle. "I'm not naive."

"I never thought you were."

"You young people didn't invent premarital sex, you know."

Okay, Zach wasn't going anywhere near that conversation. "Dancing," he responded decisively and carried on into the house.

"Kaitlin," he called as he approached the two women huddled together on one of the sofas, their noses in one album and another dozen stacked on a table in front of them.

She glanced up.

"Downstairs," he instructed, pointing the way. "We're going to dance."

She blinked back at him in incomprehension.

He grinned at her surprise and strode closer, linking her arm and swooping her to her feet.

"Ginny's matchmaking," he whispered as they made their way to the wide, curved staircase. "I've been instructed to snag you as a partner so Dylan will ask Lindsay."

"She's very sweet," Kaitlin disclosed, sorting her feet out underneath herself.

"They're a family of plotters," said Zach.

"Yeah? Well, you're a fine one to talk."

Zach couldn't disagree.

They reached the bottom of the stairs, and the huge party room widened out in front of them.

"Wow," said Kaitlin, stepping across the polished, hardwood floor, moving between the pillars to gaze at the bank of glass doors that opened to the patio, the pool and the manicured lawn.

She tipped her head back to take in the high ceiling with its twinkling star lights. She put her arms out, twirled around and grinned like a six-year-old.

Not that she looked anything remotely like a child.

She wore sexy, high-heeled sandals and a pair of snug black pants. They were topped with a metallic thread tank that shimmered under the lights. While she moved, she reached up, raking her loose hair back with her fingers. It shone, and she shone, and he couldn't wait to hold her in his arms.

A member of the staff was working the sound system, and strains of "Stardust" came up to flow around them from a dozen speakers.

Ginny, Dylan and Lindsay arrived, laughing and joking as they spilled onto the polished floor.

"You need a partner, Auntie," Dylan declared, snagging her hand. It was obvious to Zach that Dylan knew exactly what his aunt was up to.

"Oh, don't you be silly," a blushing Ginny said, then slapped his hand away. "I'm far too old to dance."

Zach moved toward Kaitlin. She was definitely the one he'd be dancing with tonight. He took her easily into his arms, and moved them both to the music, swirling them away from the others.

"It's been a while since we did this," he murmured, as her body settled tentatively against his.

"And the last time didn't end so well," she pointed out. But she picked up the rhythm and ever so slowly relaxed into his lead as he stepped them toward the bank of windows.

"It could have ended better," he agreed. It could have ended with her in his bed. It should have ended that way.

He pulled back and glanced down at her beautiful face. Why hadn't it ended that way?

"Ginny said she was your grandmother's best friend when they were girls."

Zach nodded his concurrence. "Back then, my grandmother Sadie was the caretaker's daughter."

Kaitlin relaxed a little more. "Ginny said Sadie grew up here, married here and died here. All on this island."

Zach chuckled at the misleading description of Sadie's life. "They did let her off once in a while."

"Those are some really deep roots."

"I guess they are."

"Yours are even deeper."

"I suppose," he told her absently, more interested in paying attention to the way she molded against him than in talking about his family history.

She'd relaxed completely now. Her head was tucked against his shoulder, one arm around his back, their hands clasped and drawn inward, while her legs brushed his with every step.

As the song moved on, she eased closer. Their thighs met snugly together, her smooth belly and soft breasts plastered against him. Her heat seeped into his body, and he could smell the subtle scent of her perfume. It had to be her regular brand, because he remembered it from Vegas, from the yacht, from his office.

The song ended, but the sound of Count Basie immediately came up. "It Could Happen to You." Ginny obviously wasn't giving Dylan any opportunity to escape her planned romantic web with Lindsay.

Fine with Zach. Wild horses couldn't pull him away from Kaitlin.

"I was thinking—" he began.

"Shh," she interrupted.

"What?"

"Can you please not talk for a minute?"

"Sure?" But curiosity quickly got the better of him. "Why not?"

Her voice was low and sweet. "I'm pretending you're someone else."

"Ouch," he said gently, ignoring the sting of her words. Because she had pressed even closer, closing her eyes and giving herself up to his motion.

"I'm pretending I'm someone else, too." She sighed. "Just for a minute, Zach. Just for this song? I want to shut out the world and make believe I belong here."

His chest tightened.

He gathered her closer still and brushed a gentle kiss on the top of her head.

You do belong here, he silently thought.

Seven

Kaitlin had never in her life seen anything quite so magnificent as the Harper castle. And it truly was a castle. Made of weathered limestone, it had had both chimneys and turrets. It was three full stories. And there looked to be what she could only imagine was an extensive attic network beneath the steep-pitched roofs.

Inside, wood panels gleamed, while ornate, suspended chandeliers bounced light into every nook and cranny. It was furnished throughout with antiques. Rich draperies hung from high valences and thick carpets muted footfalls and gave a welcoming warmth to the cavernous rooms.

Each of three wings had a showpiece staircase that wound up through the three stories and beyond. The biggest staircase began on the main floor in the entry rotunda. From the rotunda, Zach had shown them through the great hall, a beautiful library, plus drawing and dining rooms. The kitchen was fitted with modern appliances, but stayed true to its roots through wood and stonework and the gleaming array of antique copper pots and implements hanging from ceiling racks.

Last night, Kaitlin and Lindsay had each been appointed a

guest suite on the second floor. Zach's suite was on the third, while Sadie had converted the old servants' quarters to a private bedroom, bath and sitting room on the main floor. Zach told them that the bathrooms had been added in the early 1900s and updated every few decades since.

Five staff members lived in the castle year-round: a grounds-keeper, maintenance man, a cook and two personal maids to Sadie. Although the workload had obviously eased since Sadie's death, Kaitlin learned Zach kept them all on. They seemed very welcoming of company.

"Did you ever get lost in here?" Kaitlin asked Zach in the morning, as he showed her through a passageway that led to the north wing. Lindsay had left right after breakfast to swim in the pool at the Gilby house and, Kaitlin suspected, to flirt with Dylan.

"I must have as a little kid," he told her, pushing open the door that led to the pale blue sitting room that had belonged to Sadie. "But I don't ever remember being lost."

Kaitlin stepped inside the pretty room and gazed around with interest. "Can I get your cell phone number in case I have to call for help?"

"Sure," he answered easily from the doorway. "But you can orient yourself by the staircases. The carpets are blue in the main wing, burgundy in the north and gold in the east."

Sadie's sitting room housed a pale purple settee, several ornately carved tables and armchairs and a china cabinet with an amazing array of figurines, while a grand piano stood on a raised dais in the corner.

The morning sunshine streamed in through many narrow windows. Some were made of stained glass, and Kaitlin felt as if she should tiptoe through the hush.

She ran her fingers across the rich fabric coverings and the smooth wood surfaces, wandering toward the piano. "How old are these things?"

"I haven't a clue," said Zach.

She touched middle C, and the tone reverberated through the room.

"Sadie used to play," he told her. "Ginny still does sometimes."

"I learned 'Ode to Joy' on the clarinet in high school." That about summed up Kaitlin's musical experience.

She made her way to a china cabinet, peering through the glass to see figurines of cats and horses and several dozen exquisitely painted teacups. "Do you think she'd mind me looking around like this?"

"She's the reason you're here," he replied.

Kaitlin suddenly realized Zach was still standing in the doorway. She turned in time to catch a strange expression on his face.

"Something wrong?" she asked, glancing behind her, suddenly self-conscious. Perhaps he didn't want her snooping through this room after all.

"Nothing." His response was definitely short.

"Zach?" She moved closer, confused.

He blinked a couple of times, drew a deep breath. Then he braced his hand on the door frame.

"What is it?" she asked.

"I haven't come in here." He paused. "Not since..."

Kaitlin's chest squeezed around her heart. "Since your grandmother died?"

He nodded in answer.

"We can leave." She moved briskly toward the door, feeling guilty for having done something that obviously upset him.

He shaped his lips in a smile and stepped decisively into the room, stopping her forward progress. "No. Sadie put my wife in her will. It's right that you should learn about her."

For the first time, it occurred to Kaitlin that in addition to being blindsided by the news of their Vegas marriage, Zach had likely been blindsided by the will itself.

"You didn't expect your wife to inherit, did you?" she asked, watching him closely.

He paused, gazing frankly into Kaitlin's eyes. "That would be an understatement."

"Was Sadie angry with you?"

"No."

"Are you sure?"

"I'm sure."

"Maybe you didn't visit her enough."

He shook his head and moved farther into the room.

Kaitlin pivoted to watch as he walked toward the windows. "Seriously. Would she have liked you to come home more often?"

"I'm sure she would have."

"Well, maybe that's—"

"She left you a few hundred million because I didn't show up here enough?" He turned back to face her, folding his arms over his chest.

Kaitlin took a step back, blinking in shock. "Dollars?"

"It wasn't like I never came home," Zach defended.

"Okay, I'm going to forget you said that." Kaitlin knew Harper International was a very big company, but hundreds of millions? All those zeros were going to make her hyperventilate.

"She did want me to get married," Zach admitted, half musing to himself.

But Kaitlin's mind was still on the hundreds of millions of dollars. It was a massive, overwhelming responsibility. How on earth did Zach handle it?

He swept his arm, gesturing around the room. "As you can probably tell, the Harper family history was important to Sadie."

"The responsibility would freak me out," Kaitlin confessed.

"The family history?"

"The millions, billions, whatever, corporation."

"I thought we were talking about my grandmother."

Right. Kaitlin pushed the company's value to the back of her mind. It was a moot point anyway. Her involvement would be short-lived.

"What did you do to make her mad?" she asked again, knowing there had to be more than he was letting on. Zach was right, Sadie wouldn't have cut him out of her will because he didn't visit often enough.

His lips thinned as he drew an exasperated sigh. "She wasn't mad."

Kaitlin crossed her arms over her own chest, cocking her head and peering dubiously up at him.

"Fine," he finally conceded. "She was impatient for me to have children. My best guess is that she was trying to speed things up by bribing potential wives."

"That would do it," said Kaitlin with conviction, admiring Sadie's moxie. She could only imagine the lineup that would have formed around the block if Zach had been single and word got out about the will.

"I'm not sure I want the kind of woman who's attracted by money," he stated.

"She was obviously trying," Kaitlin said, defending Sadie's actions. "It was *you* who wasn't cooperating."

He rolled his eyes heavenward.

"Seriously, Zach." Kaitlin couldn't help but tease him. "I think you should step up and give your grandmother her dying wish. Get married and have a new generation of little Harper pirates."

He didn't miss a beat. "Are you volunteering for the job?"

Nice try. But he wasn't putting her on the defensive.

She smoothly tucked her hair behind her ears and took a half step in his direction, bringing them less than a foot apart. "You want me to call your bluff?"

"Go ahead."

"Sure, Zach. I'm your wife, so let's have children."

He stepped in, bring them even closer. "And you claim you're not flirting."

"I'm not flirting," she denied.

"We're talking about sex." His deep voice hummed along her nervous system, messing with her concentration.

"We're talking about babies," she corrected.

"My mistake. I thought you were making a pass at me."

She inched farther forward, stretching up to face him. "If I make a pass at you, Zachary, you'll know it."

He leaned in. "This feels like a pass, Katie."

"You wish."

"I do." He didn't laugh. Didn't back off. Didn't even flinch.

They breathed in unison for a long minute. His gaze dropped to her mouth, and the urge to surrender became more powerful with each passing second.

He seemed to guess what she was thinking. "We won't stop this time," he warned.

She knew that.

If he kissed her, they'd tear off their clothes right here in Sadie's sitting room.

Sadie's sitting room.

Kaitlin cringed and drew away.

Zach's expression faltered, but she forced herself to ignore it, pretending to be absorbed in the furniture and the decorations, moving farther from him to peer through the door into Sadie's bedroom.

It took her a minute before she thought she could speak. "Sadie seems like she was an incredible person."

"She was," said Zach, his tone giving away nothing.

Maybe Kaitlin had imagined the power of the moment. "Do you miss her?"

"Every day." There was a vacant sound to his voice that made Kaitlin turn.

She caught his unguarded expression, and a lump formed in her throat.

For all his flaws, Zach had obviously loved his grand-mother.

"Back then," Ginny informed Kaitlin and Lindsay from where she lay on a deck lounger, head propped up, beside the Gilbys' pool, "Sadie was a pistol."

While Lindsay was chuckling at Ginny's stories of growing up on Serenity Island, Kaitlin had been struggling to match the seemingly meticulous, traditional Sadie who'd been in charge of the Harper castle for so many years, with the lively young girl who'd apparently run wild with Ginny.

Both Kaitlin and Lindsay were swimming in the pool. Right now, their arms were folded over the painted edge, kicking to keep their balance while Ginny shared entertaining stories. The water was refreshing in the late afternoon heat. A breeze had come up off the ocean, and dozens of birds flitted in the surrounding trees and flower gardens.

Kaitlin was beginning to think Serenity Island was paradise.

"It wasn't like it is now," Ginny continued, gesturing widely with her half-full glass of iced tea. "None of these helicopters and the like. When you were on the island, you were here until the next supply ship."

"Did you like living here?" asked Lindsay, stretching out and scissor-kicking through the water.

"We constantly plotted ways to get off," said Ginny, with a conspiratorial chuckle. "Probably ten kids in all back then, what with the families and the staff. We were seventeen. Sadie convinced my daddy that I needed to learn French. *Mais oui*. Then I convinced him I couldn't possibly go to Paris without Sadie."

"You went to Paris?" Lindsay sighed, then pushed off the pool wall and floated backward in her magenta bikini. "I love Paris."

Kaitlin had never been to Paris. Truth was, she'd never left New York State. Shelter, food and education were the top of her priority list. Anything else would have to come after that. Though, someday, she'd like to see Europe, or maybe California, even Florida.

"We took one year of our high school in France," said Ginny, draining the glass of iced tea. "Came home very sophisticated, you know."

One of the staff members immediately arrived with another pitcher of iced tea, refilling Ginny's glass. She offered some to Kaitlin and Lindsay, filling up a fresh glass for each of them. They thanked the woman and set their glasses on the pool deck in easy reach.

Kaitlin had spent several hot hours today prowling through the castle. The dusty attic rooms were particularly hot and stuffy.

Now she was grateful for the cool water of the pool and the refreshing glass of iced tea.

Ginny waited until the young woman left the pool deck and exited back into the main house.

Then she sat up straighter, leaning toward Kaitlin and Lindsay. "Zachary's grandfather, Milton Harper, took one look at Sadie in those diaphanous Parisian dresses and, boom, she was pregnant."

Kaitlin tried to hide her surprise at learning such an intimate detail. Back in the 1950s, it must have caused quite a scandal.

Lindsay quickly returned to the pool edge next to Kaitlin. "They had to get married?" she asked.

Ginny pointed a finger at Lindsay. "I'm not recommending it to you," she cautioned. "You girls want to know how to catch a man nowadays?"

"Not necessar—"

Lindsay elbowed Kaitlin in the ribs. "How?"

"Withhold sex," Ginny told them with a sage nod. "They can get it any old place they want out there—" she waved a hand toward the ocean, apparently including the world in general in her statement "—but you say no, and he'll keep coming back, sniffing around."

"Auntie," came Dylan's warning voice. But it held more than a trace of humor as he strode across the deck in a pair of blue jeans and a plain T-shirt. "I don't think that's the advice I want you giving our lady guests."

Ginny harrumphed as he leaned down to give her a kiss on the cheek.

"You're cramping my style," he admonished her with good humor.

Ginny looked to Lindsay again, gesturing to her grandnephew. "This one's a catch."

"I'll try not to sleep with him," Lindsay promised. Then she covered her chuckle with a sip from her glass.

"You'll do more than try, young lady." Ginny, on the other hand, seemed completely serious. "I like you. Don't mess this up."

Lindsay sobered. "Yes, ma'am." But as she spoke, Kaitlin caught the smoldering look that passed between her and Dylan.

For all her plain-spoken, sage wisdom, Ginny had just made a fatal error with those two. She might as well have dared them to sleep together.

"Help me up, dear." Ginny reached for Dylan, and he grasped her hand, supporting her elbow, and gently brought her to her feet.

It took her a moment to get stabilized, and Dylan kept hold of her.

"Now that you're here," she said to him, "I thought I might call Sadie—" Then she stopped herself, a fleeting look of confusion entering her aging eyes. "Silly me. I meant the rose garden. I think I'd like to visit Sadie's rose garden."

Dylan slid a look of regret in Lindsay's direction. But there was no impatience in his voice when he spoke. "I'd be happy to drive you down," he told Ginny.

Kaitlin hopped out of the pool, adjusting her mint-green bikini bottom and making sure the straps had stayed in place. "I'll do it," she offered to both Ginny and Dylan.

She'd love to tour Sadie's rose garden. There was a picture of it in its heyday on the wall of one of the drawing rooms in the castle. She'd driven one of the little golf carts between the houses that afternoon, and it was very easy.

"Thank you, dear," said Ginny as Kaitlin scrubbed the towel over her wet hair. "You're a good girl. You should go ahead and sleep with Zachary."

Kaitlin stopped drying and blinked at the old woman in shock.

"Those Harper men aren't the marrying kind," Ginny elaborated.

"Zach already married Kaitlin," Lindsay offered. Then she froze halfway out of the pool. "I mean…"

"Are you pregnant?" asked Ginny, her gaze taking a critical look at Kaitlin's flat stomach.

Kaitlin quickly shook her head. "I'm not pregnant."

"I'm sorry," Lindsay squeaked in horror.

"Well, I don't know how you trapped him," said Ginny matter-of-factly. "Sadie and I have despaired that he'd even give any woman a second glance."

Kaitlin looked to Dylan for assistance. Did the situation require further explanation? Would Ginny forget the entire conversation by morning?

But he was too busy struggling to control his laughter to be of any help.

"We're, uh, not sure it's going to work out," Kaitlin explained, feeling as though she needed to say something.

"Well, how long have you been married?" asked Ginny, slipping a thin wrap over her shoulders, obviously oblivious to the undercurrents rippling through the conversation.

Kaitlin hesitated. "Um, a few months."

"Then you've already had sex," Ginny cackled with salacious delight.

"Who's had sex?" Zach's voice startled Kaitlin as he appeared from between two of the pool cabanas and came to join the group. His curious gaze darted from one person to another.

"You and Kaitlin," said Dylan.

"What?" He took in Kaitlin's bathing suit–clad body, his intense gaze making goose bumps rise on her skin and heating her to the core.

"Ginny and I are going to the rose garden," she announced, swiftly wrapping the big towel around her body. There was no reason she had to remain here. Dylan could bring Zach up to speed.

She and Ginny headed for the cabana that held her clothes.

Sadie's rose garden had obviously been a spectacular showpiece in its day. Some sections of the formal gardens had been kept up over the years by the castle staff, but it was obviously too much work to keep it all from overgrowing.

As Kaitlin and Ginny had made their way through the connected stone patios, beside gazebos, along stone trails and past the family's beautifully preserved chapel, Ginny shared stories of fabulous weekend-long garden parties, and of the dignitaries that had visited the island over the years.

Kaitlin got a picture of a carefree young Sadie growing into a serious, responsible young woman, with an abiding respect for the heritage of the family she'd married into. All signs pointed to Sadie and Milton being very much in love, despite the pregnancy and their hurried wedding.

Ginny clipped flowers as she talked, and Kaitlin ended up carrying a huge armful of the roses—yellow, white, red and pink. They were fragrant and gorgeous.

At the end of their walk, Ginny pleaded exhaustion and asked Kaitlin to take the roses up to the family cemetery and lay them on Sadie's grave.

Kaitlin had easily agreed. She'd delivered Ginny to the Gilby house and into the care of the staff there. Then she'd followed Ginny's directions and driven one of the golf carts up the hill to the family cemetery.

Visiting the graveyard was a surreal experience.

Isolated and windswept, it was perched on the highest point of the island, at the end of a rocky goat track that was almost more than the cart could navigate. She had stopped at the end of the trail to discover a small, rolling meadow dotted with Harper and Gilby headstones, and some that she guessed were for other island residents, maybe the ships' crews or staff dating all the way back to the pirates Lyndall and Caldwell.

Wandering her way through the tall, blowing grass, reading the inscriptions on the headstones, she could almost hear the voices of the past generations.

Both of the pirates had married, and they'd had several children between them. Kaitlin tried to imagine what it must have been like for Emma Cinder to marry Lyndall Harper in the 1700s. Did her family know he was a pirate when they agreed to let her marry him? Had he kidnapped her, snatched her away from a loving family? Did she love him, and was she happy here in what must have been an unbelievably isolated outpost? The castle wouldn't have existed, never mind the pool, the golf carts or the indoor plumbing.

While she read the dates on the old stones, Kaitlin couldn't help but picture Zach in pirate regalia, sword in his hand, treasure chest at his feet. Had Lyndall been anything like him—stubborn, loyal, protective? Had Emma fallen in love with Lyndall and followed him here? Perhaps against her family's wishes?

As she wandered from headstone to headstone, Kaitlin tried to piece together the family histories. Some of the lives were long, while some were tragically short. Clipped messages of love and loss were etched into each stone.

A mother and an infant had died on the same day in 1857. A tragic number of the children hadn't even made it to ten years old. There were few names other than Harper and Gilby, leading Kaitlin to speculate the daughters had married and moved off the island.

Most of the young women who'd married the Harper and Gilby men had given them children, then died as grandmothers and were buried here. In one case, Claudia Harper married Jonathan Gilby. But they didn't have any children. And that seemed as close as the families came to intermingling.

Then Kaitlin came to two new headstones—clean, polished, white marble set at the edge of the cemetery. They were Drake and Annabelle Harper. Both had died June 17, 1998. They could only be Zach's parents.

Though the roses were for Sadie, Kaitlin placed a white rose on each of Zach's parents' graves. Then she lowered herself onto the rough grass, gazing across the tombstones to the faraway ocean, trying to imagine how it would feel to belong in a place like this.

She turned her memory to the single picture of her mother, and to the sad rooming house where Yvette had ended up. Kaitlin drew up her knees, wrapping her arms around them, telling herself it was all going to be okay. She *would* nail the perfect renovation for the Harper building. Then she'd find herself a permanent job. She'd stay in New York, and Lindsay would be there with her.

She'd finally build herself a home, and things would be better than ever. Starting right now. She might not have roots. But she had prospects. She had ideas. And she wasn't afraid to work hard.

A raindrop splashed on her hand.

She blinked, raised her head and glanced over her shoulder to find that billowing, dark storm clouds had moved in behind her, changing the daylight to a kind of funny twilight.

She reluctantly came to her feet and dusted off the rear end of her shorts, smoothing her white blouse as droplets sprinkled on her hair and her clothes. With one last, longing look at the family cemetery, she made her way back to the electric golf cart at the head of the trail.

Her clothes damp now, she climbed onto the narrow, vinyl bench seat, pressed her foot down on the brake, turned the key to the on position and pushed on the gas pedal.

She pushed down harder, then harder still, but nothing happened. The cart didn't move forward like it should have.

She rechecked the key, turned it to off then back to on again. Then she went through the entire procedure a second time. Still, nothing happened. She didn't move.

Rain was coming down harder now, and the clouds had blocked the last vestige of the blue sky. The wind was picking up, whipping the fat raindrops sideways through the open cart.

Kaitlin whacked her palm against the steering wheel in frustration. The timing could not have been worse.

It might be a dead battery, or it might be a malfunction. Either way, she was well and truly stuck. She retrieved her cell phone, speed dialing Lindsay's number.

The call went immediately to voice mail.

Kaitlin left a message, hoping Lindsay wasn't holed up somewhere in Dylan's arms.

Okay, so she really didn't hope that. If Lindsay truly wanted to fulfill her pirate fantasy, then Kaitlin hoped that was exactly where she was. But she hoped it wasn't a long fantasy. And she truly wished she'd jotted down Zach's cell phone number when they'd joked about it this morning. She might not be lost in his castle, but she could certainly use his help.

She glanced around the wind- and rain-swept meadow, the tombstones jutting shadows in the gloom. She told herself there were still a couple of hours until dark, so there was plenty time for Lindsay to get her message. And how long could a person possibly frolic in bed with a pirate?

Okay. Bad question.

Thunder rumbled above Kaitlin, and a burst of wind gusted sideways, splattering the raindrops against her face.

Then again, maybe Ginny would wake up from her nap and tell them Kaitlin had gone to the cemetery. Assuming Ginny remembered that Kaitlin had gone to the cemetery. Would Ginny recall that?

Kaitlin peered once again at the tombstones on the horizon. She wasn't wild about sitting here in a graveyard in the middle of a thunderstorm. Not that she was afraid of ghosts. And if any of Zach's ancestors were ghosts, she had a feeling they'd be friendly. Still, there was a horror-movie aspect to the situation that made her jumpy.

The rain beat down harder, gusting in from all sides, and soaking everything inside the cart. Her shorts grew wet. Her bare legs became streaked with rivulets of water through the dust from the meadow. And her socks and running shoes were soaking up raindrops at an alarming rate.

She rubbed the goose bumps on her bare arms, wishing she'd put on something more than a sleeveless blouse. Too bad she hadn't tossed a sweater in the backseat.

Lightning flashed directly above her, and a clap of thunder rumbled ominously through the dark sky. It occurred to her that the golf cart was made of metal, and that she was sitting on the highest point on the island.

She wasn't exactly a Boy Scout, but she did know that that particular combination could be dangerous. Fine, she'd walk already.

There was still plenty of light to see the trail. It was all downhill, and it couldn't be more than forty-five minutes, an hour tops, to get back to Dylan's house.

* * *

"What do you mean, she's not here?" Zach studied a disheveled Dylan, then Lindsay. He didn't need to know what they'd been doing. Though it was completely obvious to anyone what they'd been doing. "Where would she be?" he demanded.

He'd checked the rose garden over an hour ago. He'd also combed through the entire castle, including the attic rooms and the staff quarters. And he'd just confirmed that Aunt Ginny was napping in her room. So the two of them weren't together.

"Maybe she went to the beach?" Lindsay ventured, ineffectually smoothing her messy hair.

"When was the last time you saw her?" asked Zach.

Dylan and Lindsay exchanged guilty looks.

"Never mind." What they'd been doing for the past three hours was none of his business. And they certainly weren't Kaitlin's babysitters.

"She can't be far," Dylan said. "We're on an island."

Zach agreed. There were only so many places she could be without having flown away on a chopper or taken a boat. And she didn't do either of those things.

There was the chance that she'd fallen off a cliff.

He instantly shut that thought down. Kaitlin wasn't foolish. He was sure she was fine. He watched the rain pounding against the dark window. It seemed unlikely she'd stay outside in this. So maybe she was already back at the castle. He could call—

Wait a minute.

"You've got her cell number," he said to Lindsay.

"Right." Lindsay reached for her pockets. Then she glanced around, looking puzzled.

After a few seconds, Dylan stepped in. "I'll check the pool house."

Zach shook his head in disgust. He did not want to know the details of their tryst. He pulled out his own phone. "Just tell me her number."

Lindsay rattled it off, and Zach programmed it into his phone then dialed.

It rang several times before Kaitlin came on the line. "Hello?"

Her voice was shaky, and the wind was obviously blowing across the mouthpiece.

She was still out in the storm.

"You okay?" he found himself shouting, telling himself not to worry.

"Zach?"

"Where are you?"

"Uh…"

"Kaitlin?" Not worrying was going to be a whole lot easier once he figured out what was going on.

"I think I'm about halfway down the cemetery trail," she said.

"You're *driving* in this?" What was the matter with her?

"Not driving, I'm walking."

"What?" He couldn't help the shock in his exclamation.

"I think the cart's battery died," she explained.

Okay. That made sense. "Are you okay?"

"Mostly. Yeah, I think so. I fell."

Zach immediately headed for the garage. "I'm on my way."

Dylan and Lindsay came at his heels.

"Thanks," said Kaitlin, relief obvious in her voice.

"What were you doing up there?" he couldn't help but ask.

"Where is she?" Lindsay blustered, but Zach ignored the question, keeping his focus on Kaitlin.

"The roses," said Kaitlin, sounding breathless. "Ginny asked me to put the roses on Sadie's grave."

"Are you sure you're not hurt badly?" Adrenaline was humming through his system, heart rate automatically increasing as he moved into action.

The wind howled across the phone.

"Kaitlin?"

"I might be bleeding a little."

Zach's heart sank.

"I tripped," she continued. "I'm pretty wet, and it's dark. I can't exactly see, but my leg stings."

Zach hit the garage door button, while Dylan pulled the cover off a golf cart.

"I want you to stop walking," Zach instructed. "Wherever you are, stay put and wait for me. What can you see?"

"Trees." Was there a trace of laughter in her voice?

"How far do you think you've come?" He tried to zero in. "Is the trail rocky or dirt?"

"It's mud now."

"Good." That meant she was past the halfway point. "You want me to stay on the line with you?" he asked as he climbed onto the cart.

"I should save my battery."

"Makes sense. Give me ten minutes."

"I'll be right here."

Zach signed off and turned on the cart.

"Where is she?" Lindsay repeated.

"She was at the cemetery. Cart battery died. She's walking back."

Lindsay asked something else, but Zach was already pulling out of the garage, zipping past the helipad and turning up the mountain road. The mud was slick on the road, and the rain gusted in from all sides.

He knew he shouldn't worry. She was fine. She'd be wet and cold, but they could fix those problems in no time. But he'd feel a whole lot better once she was safe in his—

He stopped himself.

In his arms?

What the hell did that mean?

Safe *inside* was what he'd meant. Obviously. He wanted her warm and dry, just like he'd want any other human being inside and warm and dry on a night like this.

Still, it was a long ten minutes before his headlights found her.

She was soaked to the skin. Her legs were splattered in mud, her hair was dripping and her white blouse was plastered to her body.

As the cart came to a skidding stop, he could see she was shivering. He wished he'd thought to bring a blanket to wrap around her for the ride home.

Before he could jump out to help her, she climbed gingerly into the cart. So instead, he stripped off his shirt, draping it around her wet shoulders and tugging it closed at the front.

"Thanks," she breathed, settling on the seat next to him, wrapping her arms around her body.

He grabbed a flashlight from its holder behind the seat and shone it on her bare legs. "Where are you hurt?" He inspected methodically up and down.

She turned her ankle, and he saw a gash on the inside of her calf, blood mixing with the mud and rainwater.

"It doesn't look too bad," she ventured bravely.

But Zach's gut clenched at the sight, knowing it had to be painful. The sooner they got her home and cleaned up, the better.

He ditched the flashlight, turned the cart on and wrapped his arm around her shoulders, pulling her against his body in an attempt to warm her up.

"What happened?" he asked as they straightened onto the road, going back downhill.

"Ginny wanted to put the roses on Sadie's grave. But she was too tired after the tour of the garden." Kaitlin paused. "It's really nice up there at the cemetery."

"I guess." Though the last thing Zach cared about at the moment was the aesthetics of the cemetery.

Then again, Kaitlin was fine. She was cold, and she needed a bandage. But she was with him now, and she was fine. He reflexively squeezed her shoulders.

"I'm soaking your shirt," she told him.

"Don't worry about it."

"I feel stupid."

"You're not stupid. It was nice of you to help Aunt Ginny." It really was. It was very nice of her to traipse up to the cemetery to place the roses for Ginny.

"The other cart's still back there," she told him in a worried voice. "It wouldn't start. Did I do something wrong?"

"The battery life's not that long on these things."

She shivered. "Will it be hard to go and bring it back?"

"Not hard at all," he assured her. "But we'll wait until the rain stops before we do that."

The rain was pounding down harder now, the lightning strikes and thunder claps coming closer together. The cart bounced over ruts and rocks, the illumination from the headlights mostly absorbed by the pitch-dark.

"Thanks for rescuing me," she said.

Something tightened in Zach's chest, but he ignored the sensation. She was his guest. And there were real dangers on the island. The cliffs for instance. He was relieved that she was safe. It was perfectly natural.

"It was nothing," he told her.

"I was getting scared," she confessed.

"Of what?"

"I'm here on a mysterious pirate island, in a graveyard, in the dark, in a storm." Her tone went melodramatic. "The whole thing was starting to feel like a horror movie."

Zach couldn't help but smile at her joke. "In that case, I guess I did rescue you." He maneuvered around a tight curve, picking up her lightening mood. "And you probably owe me. Maybe you could be my slave for life?"

"Ha!" She knocked her head sideways against his shoulder, her teeth chattering around her words. "Nice try, Harper. First you'd command I stop blackmailing you. Then you'd make me divorce you. Then you'd fire me and kick me out of your life."

Zach didn't respond. That wasn't even close to what he'd had in mind.

Eight

In Kaitlin's guest bathroom, the claw-footed bathtub and homemade lilac candles were completely nineteenth century. While the limitless hot water and thick terry robe were pure twenty-first.

She was finally warm again.

Zach had brought Kaitlin straight to her room in the castle, where someone had laid out a tray of fruit and scones. He'd called Dylan on the way to let them know everything was fine. Half a scone and a few grapes were all she could manage before climbing directly into the tub, while Zach had disappeared into some other part of the castle.

Now the second floor was shrouded in silence. One of the staff members had obviously been in her room while she bathed, because the bed was turned down, her nightgown laid out and the heavy, ornate drapes were drawn across the boxed windows. She guessed they expected her to sleep, but Kaitlin was more curious than tired.

On her initial tour of the castle, she'd discovered the family portrait gallery that ran between the guest bedrooms and the main staircase on the second floor. She'd glanced briefly this morning at the paintings hanging there. But now that she'd read the family tombstones, she couldn't wait to put faces to the names of Zach's ancestors.

She opened her bedroom door a crack, peeping into the high-ceilinged, rectangular room. There was no one around, so she retightened the belt on the thick, white robe and tiptoed barefoot over the richly patterned carpet.

Chandeliers shone brightly, suspended from the arched, stone ceiling at intervals along the gallery. Smaller lights illuminated individual paintings, beginning with Lyndall Harper himself at one end. He looked maybe forty-five, a jeweled sword hilt in his hand, blade pointing to the floor. She couldn't help but wonder how many battles the sword had seen. Had he used it to vanquish enemies, maybe kill innocent people before stealing their treasure and taking their ships?

Of course he had.

He was a pirate.

She returned her attention to his face, shocked when she realized how much he looked like Zach. A few years older, a few pounds heavier, and there were a few more scars to his name. But the family resemblance was strong, eerily strong.

She left the painting and moved along the wall, counting down the generations to the portrait of Zach's father at the opposite end. She guessed Zach had yet to be immortalized. Maybe he'd refused to sit still long enough for his image to be painted.

She smiled at the thought.

She'd counted twelve generations between Lyndall and Zach. The paintings on this wall were all men. But she'd noticed the ladies' portraits were hung on the opposite side of the room.

She walked her way back, studying Lyndall all over again. The main staircase of the grand hall was behind him in the painting, so he'd definitely been the one to build the castle. It was strange to stand on a spot in a room, then see that same place depicted nearly three hundred years earlier. She shivered at the notion of the pirate Lyndall walking this same floor.

"Scary, isn't it?" came Zach's voice, his footfalls muted against the carpet.

For some reason, his voice didn't startle her.

"He looks just like you." She twisted, squinting from one man to the other.

"Want to see something even stranger?" He cocked his head and moved toward the wall of ladies' portraits.

Kaitlin followed him across the room.

"Emma Cinder." He nodded to the painting. "She was Lyndall's wife."

The woman sat prim and straight at a scarred wooden table, her long red hair twisted into a crown of braids. She was sewing a sampler, wearing green robes over a thin, champagne-colored, low-cut blouse with a lace fringe that barely covered her nipples. Her red lips were pursed above a delicate chin. Her cheeks were flushed. And her deep green eyes were surrounded by thick, dark lashes.

"Wow," said Kaitlin. "You don't think ten-times great-grandma when you see her."

Zach chuckled. "Look closer."

Kaitlin squinted. "What am I looking for?"

"The auburn hair, the green eyes, those full, bow-shaped lips, the curve of her chin."

Kaitlin glanced up at him in confusion.

He smoothed his hand over her damp hair. "She looks a lot like you."

"She does not." But Kaitlin's gaze moved back to the painting, peering closer.

"She sure does."

"Okay, maybe a little bit," she admitted. Their eyes were approximately the same shape, and the hair color was the same. But there were probably thousands of women in New York with green eyes and long, auburn hair.

"Maybe a lot," said Zach.

"Where was she from?" Kaitlin's curiosity was even stronger now than it had been in the cemetery. What could have brought Emma to Serenity Island with Lyndall?

"She was from London," said Zach. "A seamstress I was told. The daughter of a tavern owner."

"And she married a pirate?" Kaitlin had to admit, Lyndall was a pretty good-looking pirate. But still…

"He kidnapped her."

"No way."

Zach leaned down to Kaitlin's ear, lowering his voice to an ominous tone. "Tossed her on board his ship and, I'm assuming, had his way with her all the way across the Atlantic."

Kaitlin itched to reach up and touch the portrait. "And then they got married?"

"Then they got married."

"Do you think she was happy here? With him?" For some reason, it was important to Kaitlin to believe Emma had been happy.

"It's hard to say. I've read a few letters that she got from her family back in England. They're chatty, newsy, but they're not offering to come rescue her. So I guess she must have been okay."

"Poor thing," said Kaitlin.

"He built her a castle. And they had four children. Look here." Zach gently grasped Kaitlin's shoulders and turned her to guide her back to the men's portrait wall.

She liked it that he was touching her. There was something comforting about his broad hands firmly holding her shoulders. He'd kept his arm around her the whole ride back from the cemetery, his body offering what warmth he could in the whipping wind. And that had been comforting, too.

"Their eldest son, Nelson," said Zach, gesturing to the portrait with one hand, leaving the other gently resting on her shoulder.

"What about the rest of the children?"

"Sadie has their portraits scattered in different rooms. The other two sons died while they were still children, and the daughter went back to a convent in London."

"I saw the boys' tombstones," said Kaitlin. "Harold and William?"

"Good memory." Zach brushed her damp hair back from her face, and for some reason, she was suddenly reminded of what she was wearing.

She was naked under the white robe, her skin glowing warm, getting warmer by the minute. She realized the lapels had gaped open, and she realized the opening had Zach's attention.

Their silence charged itself with electricity.

She knew she should pull the robe closed again, but her hands stayed fast by her sides.

Zach made a half turn toward her.

His hand slowly moved from her shoulder to her neck, his fingertips brushing against her sensitive skin.

"Sometimes I think they had it easy." Zach's voice was a deep, powerful hum.

"Who?" she managed to breathe. Every fiber of her attention was on the insubstantial brush of his hand.

His other hand came up to close on the lapel of her robe. "The pirates," he answered. "They ravage first, and ask questions later."

He tugged on the robe, pulling her to him, and his mouth came down on hers. It was hot, firm, open and determined.

She swayed from the intense sensation, but his arm went around her waist to hold her steady as the kiss went on and on.

He tugged the sash of the robe, releasing the knot, so it fell open. His free hand slipped inside, encircling her waist again, pulling her bare breasts against the texture of his shirt.

Her arms were lost in the big sleeves, too tangled to be of any use. But she breathed his name, parted her lips, welcomed his tongue into the depths of her mouth.

His wide hand braced her rib cage, thumb brushing the tender skin beneath her breast. Her nipples peaked, a tingle rushing to their delicate skin. Her thighs relaxed, reflexively easing apart, and he moved between them, the denim of his pants sending shock waves through her body.

He deftly avoided the portrait as he pressed her against the smooth stone of the wall. His hand cupped her breast. His lips found her ear, her neck, the tip of her shoulder, as he pushed the robe off. It pooled at her feet, and she was completely naked.

He drew back for a split second, gazing down, drinking in the picture of her body.

"Gorgeous," he breathed, lips back to hers, hands stroking her spine, down over her buttocks, to the back of her thighs. Then up over her hips, her belly, her breasts. She gasped as he stroked his fingertips across her nipples, the sensation near painful, yet exquisite.

His hands traced her arms, twining his fingers with hers, then holding them up, braced against the wall while his mouth made its moves on her body. He pressed hot, openmouthed kisses from her lips to her neck, found her breasts, drawing each nipple into the heat, suckling until she thought her legs would give way beneath her.

She groaned his name in a plea.

He was back to her mouth, his hands moving down, covering her breasts, taking over from his lips, thumbs stroking across her wet nipples.

She tangled her hands in his hair, pushing his mouth harder against hers, kissing deeper, mind blank to everything but his taste and touch. One of his hands moved lower, stroking over her belly, toying with her silky hair, sliding forward.

She wrapped her arms around him, anchoring her body more tightly against him, saving her failing legs, burying her face in the crook of his neck and tonguing the salt taste from his skin.

His fingers slipped inside her, and a lightning bolt electrified her brain. She cried out his name, an urgency blinding her. She fumbled with the button on his jeans, dragging down the zipper.

He cupped her bottom, lifting her, spreading her legs, bracing her against the cool wall.

A small semblance of sanity remained.

"Protection?" she gasped.

"Got it."

One arm braced her bottom, while his hand cupped her chin.

He kissed her deeply, their bodies pressed together, her nerves screaming almost unbearably for completion.

"Now," she moaned. "Please, now."

It took him a second, and then he was inside her, his heat sliding home in a satisfying rush that made her bones turn to liquid and the air whoosh out of her lungs.

Her hands fisted and her toes curled as she surrendered herself to the rhythm of his urgent lovemaking. Her head tipped back, the high ceiling spinning above her. Lightning lit up the high windows, while thunder vibrated the stone walls of the castle.

She arched against him, struggling to get closer. Her breaths came in gasps, while the pulsating buzz that started at her center radiated out to overwhelm her entire body.

She cried his name again, and he answered with a guttural groan. Then the storm, the castle and their bodies throbbed together as one.

When the universe righted itself, Kaitlin slowly realized what they'd just done.

Bad enough that they'd made love with each other. But they weren't locked up in some safe, private bedroom. She was naked, in an open room of the castle, where five other people worked and lived. Any one of them could have walked up the staircase at any moment.

She let out a pained groan.

"You okay?" Zach gasped, glancing between them and around them.

"Somebody could have seen us," she whispered.

He tightened his hold on her. "Nobody would do that."

"Not on *purpose*."

"The staff are very discreet."

"Well, apparently we're not."

"God, you feel good."

She couldn't help stealing another glance toward the staircase. "I'm completely naked."

He chuckled low. "We just gave in, broke all our promises, consummated our marriage, and you're worried because somebody *might* have seen us?"

"Yes," she admitted in a small voice. She hadn't really had time to think about the consummation angle. More that they had, foolishly, given in to their physical attraction.

"You're delightful," he told her.

"That sounded patronizing."

"Did it?" His voice dropped to a sensual hush, and his mouth moved in on hers. "Because patronizing is the last thing I'm feeling right now."

His kiss was long and deep and thorough. And by the time he drew back, the pulse of arousal was starting all over in her body. She wanted him. Still.

"Again?" he asked, nibbling at her ear, his palm sliding up her rib cage toward her breast.

"Not here." She didn't want to risk it again.

"Okay by me." He gently eased himself from her body, flicked the button to close his pants, then lifted her solidly into the cradle of his arms and headed for the staircase to his bedroom.

"My robe," she protested.

"You won't need it."

Zach held Kaitlin naked in his arms, inhaling the coconut scent of her hair, reveling in the silk of her smooth skin beneath his fingertips. A sheet half covered them, but his quilts had long since been shoved off the king-size bed.

"This is gorgeous," she breathed, one hand wrapped around the ornately carved bedpost, as she gazed up at the scrollwork on his high ceiling.

"*This* is gorgeous," he corrected, stroking his way across her smooth belly to the curve of her hip bone.

She looked great in his bed, her shimmering, auburn hair splayed across his pillowcase, her ivory skin glowing against his gold silk sheets.

"I never knew people lived like this." She captured his hand that had wandered to her thigh, giving his palm a lingering kiss.

"It took me a while to figure out some people didn't," he admitted.

She released his hand and came up on one elbow. "Were you by any chance a spoiled child?"

"I wouldn't call it spoiled." He couldn't stop touching her, so he ran his palm over the curve of her hip, tracing down her shapely thigh to the tender skin behind her knee. "But I was about five before I realized everybody didn't have their own castle."

Kaitlin's eyes clouded, and she went silent.

He wanted to prompt her, but he forced himself to stay silent.

She finally spoke in a small voice. "I was about five when I realized most people had parents."

Her words shocked him to the core, and his hand stilled in its exploration. "You grew up without parents?"

She nodded, rolling to her back, a slow blink camouflaging the emotion in her eyes.

"What happened?" he asked, watching her closely.

"My mom died when I was born. She had no relatives that I ever found."

"Katie," he breathed, not knowing what else to say, his heart instantly going out to her.

She'd never mentioned her family. So he'd assumed they weren't close. He thought maybe they lived in another part of the country, Chicago perhaps, or maybe California.

"She either didn't know, or didn't say who my father was." Kaitlin made a square shape in the air with both hands. "Unknown. That's what it says on my birth certificate. Father—unknown."

Zach's hand clenched convulsively where it rested on her hip.

"I never knew," he said. Though he realized the statement was meaningless. Of course he never knew. Then again, he'd never asked. Because he hadn't wanted to know anything about her personal life. He simply wanted to finish off their business and have her gone.

Now, he felt like a heel.

"I used to wonder who she was," Kaitlin mused softly, half to herself. "A runaway princess. An orphan. Maybe a prostitute." Then her voice grew stronger, a trace of wry humor in its depths.

"Perhaps I'm descended from a hooker and her customer. What do you suppose that means?"

Zach brushed a lock of her hair back from her forehead. "I think it means you have a vivid imagination."

"It could be true," Kaitlin insisted.

"I suppose." Since the idea didn't seem to upset her, his fingertips went back to tracing a pattern on her stomach. "I guess I'm the rouge pirate, and you're the soiled dove." He brushed his knuckles against the skin beneath her bare breast. "Just so you know. That's working for me."

She lifted a pillow and halfheartedly thwacked him in the side of the head. "Everything seems to work for you."

"Only when it comes to you." He tossed the pillow out of the way, acknowledging the words were completely true. He leaned up and gently stroked her face. "Were you adopted?"

She was silent for a long moment, while her clouded jade eyes put a hundred lonely images into his brain. He regretted the question, but he couldn't call it back.

"Foster homes," she finally told him.

The simple words made his chest thump with regret. He thought back to all the heirlooms he'd shown her. The family history. The portraits, the cemetery.

"I'm so sorry," he told her. "I can't believe I threw my castle up in your face."

"You didn't know," she repeated.

"I wish I had."

"Well, *I* wish I'd grown up in a castle." Her spunk was back, and the strength of character surprised and impressed him. "But that's the way it goes," she concluded.

"We had extra rooms and everything," he teased in an attempt to keep things light.

"Could you not have come and found me sooner?"

He sobered, completely serious. "I wish I had."

Her grin slowly faded, but not to sadness.

His own want growing, he shifted forward and kissed her lips, drawing her tenderly but fully into his arms again, feeling aroused and protective all at the same time. "Was it awful?" he had to risk asking.

"It was lonely," she whispered into the crook of his neck. Then she coughed out a laugh and arched away. "I can't believe I'm telling this to you...*you* of all people."

"What about me?" He couldn't help feeling vaguely hurt.

"You're the guy who's ruining my life."

"Huh?"

She glanced around his room and spread her arms wide. "What the hell have we done?"

"We're married," he responded.

"By *Elvis.*" She suddenly clambered out of bed.

He didn't want her to go, couldn't let her go.

"My robe?" she asked.

"Downstairs."

She swore.

"You don't have to leave," he pointed out. She could stay here, sleep here, lay here in his arms all night long.

She turned to face him, still naked, still glorious, still the most amazing person he'd ever met.

"This was a mistake," she told him in no uncertain terms.

He climbed out the opposite side of the bed to face her. "It may have made things a little more complicated," he conceded.

"A *little* more complicated?"

"Nothing needs to change."

"Everything just changed." She spotted his shirt, discarded on the floor, and scooped it up. "We never should have given into chemistry, Zach. Just so you know, this doesn't mean you have an advantage over me."

"What?" He wasn't following her logic.

"I have to call Lindsay." She glanced around the room. "She's probably downstairs. She's probably wondering where the heck I've gone."

"Lindsay's not downstairs," Zach announced with certainty.

Kaitlin pulled his big shirt over her head. "How would you know that?"

Zach made his way around the foot of the bed. "Lindsay's not coming back here tonight."

"But—" Kaitlin stilled. After a second, she seemed to correctly interpret the meaningful look in his eyes. "Really?"

"Really."

"You sure they did?"

"Oh, I'm sure." Zach had known Dylan his entire life. He'd seen the way Dylan looked at Lindsay. He'd also seen the way Lindsay looked back.

Kaitlin still seemed skeptical. "She said she wouldn't sleep with him until he admitted he was a pirate."

Zach barked out a laugh at an absurd memory. "I guess that explains it."

"Explains what?"

"The Jolly Roger flying over the pool house."

Kaitlin fought a grin and lost. "I want my ten bucks."

He moved closer, desperate to take her back into his arms. "Katie, you can have anything you want."

She gazed up at him. "I want to renovate your building. My way." Then she paused, tilting her head. "This has been a recorded message."

"I guess adding the condition that you sleep with me to seal the deal would be inappropriate?"

"And illegal."

"I'm a pirate, what the hell do I care about legal?"

She didn't answer him, but she didn't move away, either.

He curled his hands into fists to keep from touching her. "Sleep with me, Katie."

She hesitated, and he held his breath.

Her gaze darted in all directions, while her teeth trapped her bottom lip.

He was afraid to push, afraid not to.

Finally, he tossed caution to the wind, reaching out, snagging a handful of his shirt, drawing her to him and wrapping her deep in his arms. "I can't let you go yet."

Maybe tomorrow. Maybe never.

* * *

"It was the best pie I have *ever* tasted," Lindsay said to Kaitlin, her voice bubbling through the Gilby kitchen while Ginny scooped flour into a big steel bowl.

"My grandmother taught me that recipe," said Ginny, wiping her hands on a voluminous white apron that covered her red-and-white polka-dot dress. She had red-heeled pumps to match, and a spray of lace and plastic cherries was pinned into her hair as a small hat.

Kaitlin was fairly certain Ginny thought it was 1952.

"It's the chill on the lard, you know," Ginny continued her instructions, seeming to be in her element with the two younger women as baking students. "You need the temperature, the cutting, the mixing. Half in first. Like this."

"Do you refrigerate it?" asked Kaitlin, glancing from the stained recipe card to the bowl, watching Ginny's hands closely as they mixed the ingredients. She and Lindsay had been given the task of cutting and peeling apples and floating them in a bowl of cold water.

Ginny giggled. "That's the secret, girls." She lowered her voice, glancing around as if to make sure they were alone in the big Gilby kitchen. "We keep it in the wine cellar."

Lindsay grinned at Kaitlin, and Kaitlin grinned right back, thoroughly enjoying herself. Nobody had ever taught her to bake before. She'd watched a few cooking shows, and sometimes made cupcakes from a mix, but mostly she bought Sugar Bob's and she sure never had a sweet old lady walk her through a traditional family recipe.

"Best way to trap a man," said Ginny. "Feed him a good pie."

"Were you ever married?" asked Kaitlin. Ginny used the Gilby last name, but that might not mean anything. And she certainly seemed obsessed with getting men.

"Me?" Ginny scoffed. "No. Never."

"But you make such a great pie," Lindsay joked. "I would think you'd have to fight them off with a stick."

"Keep peeling," Ginny admonished her. "There's also the sex, you know."

Lindsay looked confused. "But yesterday you said we weren't supposed to—"

Ginny's sharp glare cut her off. "You didn't have sex with him, did you?"

"No, ma'am."

Kaitlin shot Lindsay an expression of disbelief.

Lindsay returned a warning squint.

"Good girl," said Ginny, smiling all over again. "That was my problem. Always slept with them, never married them."

"You had lovers?" The question jumped out of Kaitlin before she could censor it. When Ginny was young, lovers must have been something scandalous.

"Dustin Cartwell," said Ginny on a sigh, getting a faraway look in her eyes as she dreamily cut the lard and shortening into the flour mixture inside the bowl. "And Michael O'Conner. Phillip Magneson. Oh, and that Anderson boy, Charlie."

"Go, Ginny," sang Lindsay.

"Never met one I wanted to keep," said Ginny with a shake of her white-haired head. "They fart, you know. Drop their underwear on the floor. And the snoring? Don't get me started on the snoring." She added another scoop of lard. "Now, we'll be making this half into chunks the size of peas. Keeps it flaky."

Kaitlin met Lindsay's gaze again, her body shaking with suppressed laughter. Ginny was an absolute blast.

Her attention abruptly off men and sex, and back onto the baking, she let each of them cut in some of the lard, then she showed them how to sprinkle on the water, keeping everything chilled. They rolled out the dough, cut it into pie pans, mixed the apples with cinnamon, sugar and corn starch, then made a latticework top.

In the end, both Kaitlin and Lindsay slid decent-looking pies into the oven.

"You don't want to be sharing that with Zachary," Ginny warned Kaitlin. Then she paused, a flash of confusion crossing her face. "Oh, my. You married him, didn't you?"

"I did," Kaitlin admitted. And after last night, the marriage was feeling frighteningly real.

Ginny patted her on the arm. "Wish you'd come and talked with me first."

"Is there something wrong with Zach?" Kaitlin couldn't help but ask. Ginny had been alluding to Zach's lack of desirability since they arrived.

"Those Harper boys are heartbreakers," said Ginny with a disapproving click of her tongue. "Always have been, always will be."

Kaitlin had to admit, she could easily see Zach breaking hearts. He'd been darn near perfect last night. He'd driven through the dark to rescue her from a storm, then made exquisite love to her, teased her and sympathized with her. If a woman were to let herself fall for a man like that, heartbreak might well be the inevitable outcome.

Ginny turned to Lindsay. "Now, my Dylan. That one's a catch. He's wealthy, you know."

"I do have my own money," said Lindsay.

Ginny chuckled and gave a coquettish smile. "A girl can never have too much money."

Lindsay was obviously puzzled. "You don't mind me marrying your great-nephew for his money?"

Ginny looked askance. "What other reason is there?"

Lindsay's brows went up. "Love?"

"Oh, pooh, pooh." Ginny waved a dismissive hand. "Love comes and goes. A bank balance, now there's something a gal can count on."

"Your lovers didn't have money?" Kaitlin asked, fascinated by Ginny's experiences and opinions.

A sly look entered Ginny's eyes, and once again she glanced around the kitchen as if checking for eavesdroppers. "They had youth and enthusiasm. I think they wanted *my* money."

"Do you have any pictures?" asked Lindsay, obviously as interested as Kaitlin in the older woman's love life.

"Indeed, I do." Ginny wiped her hands on the big apron,

untying it from the back. Then she beckoned both women to follow her as she made her way toward the kitchen door.

In the stairwell, Kaitlin asked, "Did the other Harper men break women's hearts?"

"Every single one," Ginny confirmed with a decisive nod.

"But not their wives." Kaitlin's tone turned the statement into a question.

"Sometimes their wives, too."

"What about Sadie? Wasn't Sadie happy with Milton?"

"Milton was a fine man. He'd have made a good lover. But once they were married, Sadie, she worried all the time."

"That he was unfaithful?" asked Kaitlin.

Ginny stopped midstair and turned on her. "Oh, no. A Harper man would never be unfaithful." She turned and began climbing again.

"Then why did Sadie worry?"

"She was the groundskeeper's daughter. Oh, she pretended all right. But at her heart, she was never the mistress of the castle. That's why she wouldn't make any changes."

They came to the second floor, and Ginny led them down a wide hallway. Overhead skylights let in the sunshine, while art objects lined the shelves along the way.

"The castle is really beautiful," said Kaitlin. She wasn't sure she'd have changed anything, either.

"So was Sadie," said Ginny in a wistful voice. "Before Milton, we swam naked in the ocean and ran across the sand under the full moon."

"Do you really think he broke her heart?" Kaitlin persisted. Like Emma, Kaitlin really wanted to believe Sadie had been happy here.

"No. Not really. But sometimes she felt trapped, and sometimes she worried." Ginny swept open the double doors of a closet. She moved aside a fluffy quilt and extracted a battered shoebox, opening it to reveal a stack of photographs. "Ah, here we are. Come meet my lovers."

Nine

Zach found Kaitlin in the portrait gallery, gazing at a painting of his grandmother when she had been in her twenties.

"Hey," he said, coming up behind her. He didn't ask and didn't wait for permission before wrapping his arms around her waist, nestling her into the cradle of his body.

"Do you think she was happy?" Kaitlin asked.

"Yes."

"Did she love your grandfather?"

"As far as I could tell." He hadn't spent much time looking at the portraits over the past years, and his memory of his grandmother was that of an old woman. He'd forgotten how lovely she was. No wonder his grandfather had married her so young.

"Ginny says she felt trapped sometimes."

"I love Ginny dearly," Zach began, a warning in his tone.

There was a thread of laughter in Kaitlin's voice when she interrupted him. "She doesn't seem too crazy about you."

"But you know she's not all there, right?"

"She's a blast," Kaitlin responded. "And her memory seems very sharp."

"Well, it had to be a pretty big cage. They went to Europe at least twice a year, and spent half their time in Manhattan. You should have seen the garden parties. The governor, theatre stars, foreign diplomats."

"Okay, so it was a big cage," Kaitlin conceded.

"Come here. Let me show you something." Zach shifted his arm around her shoulders, guiding her down the gallery toward the staircase.

"Your room?" she asked.

"No. But I like the way you're thinking." He steered her down to the first floor then back through the hallways to Sadie's parlor.

"What are we doing?"

"I want to show you that she was happy."

He sat Kaitlin on the settee and retrieved an old photo album from Sadie's bookcase. Sitting next to her, he flipped through the pages until he came to one of the Harpers' famous garden parties. The pictures were black and white, slightly faded, but they showed the gardens in their glory, and the sharp-dressed upper crust of New York nibbling finger sandwiches and chatting away the afternoon.

"That's her." Zach pointed to his grandmother in a flowing dress and a silk flower-brimmed hat. Her smile was bright, and Zach's grandfather Milton had a hand tucked against the small of her back.

"She does look happy," Kaitlin was forced to admit.

"And that's a hedge, not prison bars," said Zach.

Kaitlin elbowed him in the ribs. "The bars are meta-phorical."

"The hedge is real. So were the trips to Europe."

Kaitlin flipped the page, coming to more party photos, people laughing, drinking punch, playing croquet and wandering through the rose garden. There was a band in the gazebo, and a few couples were dancing on the patio. Some of the pictures showed children playing.

"That's my father," said Zack, smiling to himself as he pointed out the five-year-old boy in shorts, a white shirt and suspenders standing next to the duck pond. He had a rock in his hand, and one of his shoes was missing. He looked as if he was seconds away from wading after the ducks.

Kaitlin chuckled softly. "Were you anything like that as a child?"

Zach rose to retrieve another album.

"Here." He let her open it and page her way through the pictures of him as a young child.

"You were adorable," she cooed, moving from his toddler pictures to preschool to Zach at five years old, digging up flower bulbs, dirt smeared across his face and clothes.

"Yeah, let's go with adorable."

"Did you get into trouble for that?"

"I would guess I did. Probably from Grandma Sadie. Those gardens were her pride and joy."

"I never had a garden," said Kaitlin, and Zach immediately felt guilty for showing her the album. He'd done it again, parading out his past and his relatives without giving a thought to the contrast with her life.

"I bet you stayed cleaner than I did," he said, making a weak attempt at a joke.

"Once I realized—" She paused, gripping the edge of the album. "Hoo. I'm not going to do that." She turned another page.

"Do what?"

"Nothing." Her attention was focused on a series of shots of the beach and a picnic.

"Katie?"

"Nothing."

He gently removed the album from her hands. "I upset you."

"No, you didn't."

"Liar."

She straightened her shoulders. "It was hard, okay."

"I know."

"No, you don't."

"You're right. I don't." He folded the book closed and set it on the table beside him. "I'm sorry I showed you the photos. It was thoughtless."

"Don't worry about it."

"What were you going to say?"

She pasted him with a look of impatience.

"I've got all night to wait," he warned her, sitting back and making a show of getting comfortable.

She clenched her jaw, looking mulish, and he prepared himself for a contest of wills.

But then her toughness disappeared, and she swallowed. Then she closed her eyes for a second. "I was going to say…"

Part of him wanted to retract the question. But another part of him wanted to know, *needed* to know what she'd gone through as a child.

"I was going to say," she repeated, sounding small and fragile, "once I realized people could give me away." Her voice cracked. "I tried to be very, very good."

Zach honestly thought his heart was going to break.

He wrapped an arm around her and drew her close. She felt so tiny in his arms, so vulnerable. He hated that she'd been alone as a child.

"I'm sorry, Katie," he whispered against her hair.

She shook her head back and forth. "It's not your fault."

He drew a deep breath. "You've been alone for a very long time."

"I'm used to it."

But she wasn't. She couldn't be. Nobody should have to get used to not having a family. Zach had lost his parents when he was twenty, and that had been devastating enough. He'd still had his grandmother, and he'd always had the Gilbys. And he'd had Aunt Ginny, who usually liked him very much.

"Look," said Kaitlin, pulling back and wiping a single tear from her cheek. "There's a full moon outside."

He twisted his head to look out the window. "Yeah?"

"You want to go skinny-dipping?" she asked.

"Yes," he answered without hesitation.

* * *

The salt water was chilly against Kaitlin's skin, but Zach's body felt deliciously warm. He held her flush against himself, her feet dangling just above the sandy bottom. Over his left shoulder, she could see the distant lights of the Gilby house. And when she turned her head the other way, she could see the Harper castle in all its glory.

The gardens were smaller than they were in the pictures, but they were still lit up at night. And an illuminated path wound its way from the edge of the garden to the sandy beach, where she and Zach had stripped off their clothes before plunging into the surf.

"Lindsay is talking about staying a few more days," Zach offered.

Kaitlin drew back to look at him. "With Dylan?" Lindsay hadn't said anything to her. Then again, she had spent most of her time at the Gilby house.

Zach's teeth flashed white under the moonlight. "I think they have worked out their differences."

"You mean Lindsay won," Kaitlin corrected. "Where's my ten dollars, by the way?"

"Dylan thinks he's the one who won."

"He totally caved."

"I don't think he cares."

"By the way, if Ginny asks, they're not having sex."

"Ohhh-kay," Zach slowly agreed.

"She'll probably ask," Kaitlin warned. "She's obsessed with Dylan's love life."

"I won't answer," Zach pledged.

"Good."

Neither Kaitlin nor Zach spoke for a few minutes. The cool waves bobbed their bodies, while the sound of the surf rushed up on the sand, punctuating the breeze that whispered through the bushes along the shoreline.

"You want to stay, too?" Zach asked softly, rocking her back and forth in his arms.

Kaitlin stilled against him, not sure what he was asking.

"With Lindsay?" he elaborated. "For a few days? You could work right from here?"

"What about you?" she asked, still wondering what he meant by the invitation. Was he asking her to stay on the island, or to stay with him?

"If you're staying?" A slow, sultry smiled curved his mouth, darkening his eyes to slate. "I'm sure not leaving."

Kaitlin's smile grew in return. "Okay."

"Yeah?"

"Yes."

He spun her in a circle, and she wrapped her legs around his waist, her hands gripping his shoulders for balance. His hold was tight under her bottom as she knifed through the water.

The moon glistened high in the sky, surrounded by layers of stars. They were the same stars that Lyndall had used to navigate his way to the island hundreds of years ago. The same stars that Sadie had gazed at as a girl and as a woman, a mother.

Zach slowed and stopped, the waves now the only motion around them. Kaitlin gazed at the lighted gardens that Sadie had so clearly loved. The woman had been the guardian of the castle, the keeper of the family's heritage. And because of her decisions, Kaitlin had been trusted with the Harper office building.

Zach nuzzled her neck.

The office building was much newer, of course. But Kaitlin couldn't help but believe the renovations would matter to Sadie. Maybe Zach was right. Maybe wholesale change wasn't such a great thing. Maybe Kaitlin had some kind of responsibility to his family.

Maybe she needed to rethink her approach.

"Zach?" she ventured.

"Hmm?" he asked, the vibration of his lips tickling the sensitized skin of her neck.

"Could you get me a copy of the Hugo Rosche plans?"

He drew back, brows going up. "Really?"

"Yes."

"Sure." He nodded, the nod growing faster. "Of course I could."

"I'm not making any promises," she warned him.

"I understand."

"I'm just going to look." She had no idea what she was going to do now. She still needed her career, which meant she needed a fantastic project for the Harper building. But maybe there was a compromise of some kind. She just didn't know.

A smile curved Zach's mouth. "No problem."

"I don't want you to get your hopes up."

"Oh, Katie." He planted a long, warm kiss on her damp mouth. He drew back, his grin wide as he smoothed her hair. "My hopes have been up for quite some time now."

She gave in to her desire for him, tipping her head and giving her lashes a few flirtatious blinks. "And what exactly are you hoping for?"

"You. Naked."

She made a show of glancing at their bodies. "I'm liking your chances."

"In my pirate's lair." He kissed her neck once more, then her jawline, her cheek, working his way to the corner of her mouth.

"Piece of advice, Zach?"

"Speed things up?" he asked hopefully, and she couldn't help but laugh.

"For future reference, that line will probably be a lot more successful if you refer to it as a castle instead of a lair."

His hand closed over her breast, peaked and sensitized in the cool, damp air.

She gasped at the sensation.

"Lair," he repeated on a growl.

"Fine. Yes. Whatever."

Three days later, Dylan's parents arrived, back from their business meetings in Chicago. And, as usual, they brought company.

Zach was happy to see them. David and Darcie were two of his favorite people in the world. After his parents died, they'd become even more important in his life. David was a brilliant businessman, while Darcie was the most loving and compassionate honorary aunt Zach could have wished for.

Still, he knew this meant the end of his interlude with Kaitlin. Dylan would never have a woman stay at the house with his parents there, and it was past time for Zach to get back to Manhattan.

"You weren't kidding about them having a few friends over," Kaitlin observed as they drove the golf cart the last quarter mile to the Gilbys' house. Music wafted from the open windows, and it was easy to see groups of people circulating on the deck.

"What are the Gilbys like?"

"David's savvy, hardworking, a great guy to go to for advice. Darcie's friendly, gregarious. You'll like her."

"What will she think of me...?" Kaitlin's voice trailed off on the half-finished question.

He put his hand over hers. "We can let her think whatever you like." He paused, but Kaitlin didn't step in and offer a suggestion. "How about a business associate and a friend?" he asked.

Kaitlin accepted with a smile.

Zach fought a shot of disappointment, but he let it slide. He didn't want people to think Kaitlin was his business associate. He wanted them to think... He paused. What? That she was his lover? His girlfriend? His wife? His hands gripped tighter on the steering wheel. He was going to have to figure it out. Not right this minute, of course. But soon.

"Lindsay will probably stay at my place for the night," he told Kaitlin. "When it's only Ginny, well, she'd never notice. But with his parents, Dylan doesn't..."

"I understand," Kaitlin said, nodding easily.

Zach hoped Lindsay would react the same way.

Then again, that was Dylan's problem. Zach's problem was figuring out where things were left with him and Kaitlin.

Would they continue seeing each other in Manhattan? He had quickly grown used to waking up with her every morning. He liked having her around for breakfast, reconnecting over dinner. Hell, he wasn't even sure he wanted to sign the damn divorce papers anymore.

Of course, that was ridiculous.

Luckily, that decision was months away.

He glanced at Kaitlin's profile, taking in her pert nose, those gorgeous green eyes, the spray of freckles that had come out in the sun. And, of course, her wild, coconut-scented auburn hair that he buried his face into every chance he got.

At the top of the driveway, he pressed the button to open the garage door, pulling the golf cart inside, unable to shake the feeling that something precious had just ended.

He stepped out and rounded the vehicle. Then he took Kaitlin's hand, leading her to the three steps and the doorway that would take them into the house and the party.

Unable to help himself, he stopped her there, cradled her face in his hands and kissed her thoroughly.

She responded, like she always did, soft lips parted, a light touch of her tongue meshing with his. Her breasts pressed up against his chest, and she came up on her toes to meet him partway. He loved that about her.

His arms tightened around her slender waist.

This wasn't goodbye, he told himself. She worked for him, with him. They'd both be in Manhattan. They would see each other at the office every day.

Hell, they were *married*. She couldn't just run off and disappear from his life. He'd find a way to keep her with him for a long time to come.

She pulled back. "You keep this up, and they're never going to believe we're business colleagues."

"We're husband and wife," he said gruffly.

She grinned and playfully swiped her index finger across the tip of his nose. "We're pretty much faking everything here, aren't we, Zach?"

He opened his mouth to protest, but she turned away, skipping up the stairs, opening the door and ending the moment.

He quickly trapped the door with his hand before it could swing shut. Music chimed from the sound system, while chattering voices spilled from the deck into the great room. All the staff members were working, impeccably dressed and serving drinks or circulating with appetizers.

Zach knew the kitchen would be a hive of activity. He also knew Ginny would be in her element, visiting with guests into the evening until she gave in to exhaustion. He saw Kaitlin heading toward Lindsay on the deck and started after her.

"Zach," came David's booming voice. "Great to see you at home, son."

"Welcome back, sir." Zach shook his hand.

"You remember Kevin O'Connor." David gestured to a fiftyish gentleman with a three-olive martini in his hand.

"Swiss International Bank," Zach acknowledged, shaking again, checking for Kaitlin out the corner of his eye.

"Kevin has a client," David began. "He's out of Hong Kong, and he's got mining interests in Canada and South America."

"I see," Zach said, dutifully focusing his attention. Mining companies were massive shippers; ore was both heavy and voluminous. And a Hong Kong client likely had access to the mainland China market. Zach's personal life would have to go on hold for a moment.

The moment turned into half an hour. A drink was put into Zach's hand, and a third man joined them, a friend of Kevin's with an interest in manufacturing.

By the time the conversation wound down, Kaitlin was nowhere to be found. Neither was Lindsay.

He managed to track down Dylan, who was with Ginny, then he was rewarded when he heard Kaitlin's voice from behind him.

"You must be enjoying the party," she offered breezily to Ginny, who was decked out in chiffon and diamonds, a folded, lace fan in her hand and her dogs at her feet in rhinestone collars.

"And who is this young lady?" Ginny asked in an imperious tone. She leaned toward Kaitlin. "Are you here with my grandson? He's a catch, you know."

Zach turned in time to see Kaitlin's surprise morph into obvious disappointment.

"I'd stay away from this one," said Ginny, tapping Zach's arm with the fan. "He's a reprobate and a heartbreaker."

Kaitlin's eyes clouded to jade.

"Auntie—" Dylan stepped in "—this is Kaitlin Saville and Lindsay Rubin."

"Pretty," Ginny acknowledged with a gracious sweep of her fan.

"Kaitlin is my architect," said Zach.

Ginny looked at him, eyes clouding with puzzlement. "Are you changing the castle? Does Sadie know?"

There was an instant and awkward silence.

Zack had been through this before, about a dozen times so far, but it never got any easier.

He gently took Ginny's hand and lowered his tone. "Aunt Ginny, do you remember that Sadie passed away?"

Ginny drew back warily. Then she gave herself a little shake. "Of *course* I remember. I meant…" Her voice trailed off.

Dylan stepped in again. "Auntie, would you like to dance?"

Ginny snapped him with her fan, seeming to recover. "I'm too old to dance. People my age are dropping like flies." Her attention turned to Lindsay. "You should dance with my grandson. He has a lot of money."

Darcie joined the circle, and Zach took the opportunity to whisk Kaitlin away.

"You okay?" he asked as they made their way out onto the deck. The sun had set, and the lights were coming on all over the grounds. The music seemed to swell louder, and the conversation grew more animated as the guests consumed martinis, wine and single malt.

"She didn't remember me at all." Sadness was clear in Kaitlin's tone as they came to the rail.

"She will," Zach promised, not sure if he was lying or not. Ginny's early memories were her best. Recent events often escaped her.

"She taught me to bake pie." Kaitlin's voice was stilted. She leaned her arms on the railing and stared out at the ocean. "Nobody ever taught me to bake before. I was starting to think…"

She paused, then tried a lukewarm smile. "I'm being silly. She's old. Of course she forgets things. You were great."

"I didn't do anything."

"How many times have you had to tell her about your grandmother?"

"A few," Zach admitted. And he was sure that previous one wouldn't be the last. He stared at the lights at his place, wishing they were down there right now.

"Kaitlin?" Ginny's voice surprised Zach. "There you are, dear." She sidled up to Kaitlin, glancing warily around them, her voice becoming conspiratorial. "I've changed my mind."

Kaitlin's smile was bright as she blinked away the telltale sheen in her eyes. "You have?"

"That nice girl, Lindsay?"

Kaitlin nodded, and Zach smiled in relief.

"I think she should sleep with Dylan."

"What?"

Ginny placed a hand on Kaitlin's arm. "Hear me out." Then she turned and gave Zach a censorious look. "Excuse us please, Zachary. The women would like to talk."

Zach held his palms up in surrender and backed away.

He circulated through the party a little, and then Dylan caught up with him outside David's study and herded him inside to where they were alone.

Dylan seemed agitated. He crossed to the small bar and poured himself a scotch. "You okay to take Lindsay down with you tonight?"

"No problem."

Dylan waggled a second, empty glass, raising his brow to Zach in question.

"Sure," Zach answered, walking farther into the room, the noise of the party fading behind him through the open door.

"I haven't told her yet," Dylan confessed, handing Zach a crystal tumbler of single malt then taking a sip from his own.

"You need my help?"

Dylan shook his head, moving to the bay window. "She'll be disappointed. At least, I hope she'll be disappointed. But she's a trouper. She really is, Zach. She's quite the little trouper." He took another sip.

Zach moved closer. "Are you okay?"

"Sure. Fine. Why?"

Zach had never seen Dylan act this way, not over a woman, not over anything. "Something going on between you and Lindsay? I mean, other than the obvious?"

"What's the obvious?"

Treading on unfamiliar ground, Zach chose his words carefully. "A physical…connection?"

"Oh, yeah. That."

"But there's more," Zach guessed.

Dylan shot him a look that questioned his sanity, but Zach had no idea how to interpret it. Was there something serious going on between Dylan and Lindsay? Had he made her angry again?

"I should warn you," said Zach, stepping into the silence. "Aunt Ginny is out there advising Lindsay to sleep with you."

Dylan stilled. *"What?"*

"I assume it's to trap you into marriage. You might want to watch your back."

"I don't think it's my back that needs watching," Dylan muttered.

"You don't seem too worried."

Dylan shrugged.

Zach watched his friend's expression carefully. "Seriously, Dylan. Is there something going on between you two?"

Dylan frowned. "I'm not saying there is."

"Are you saying there's not?"

Dylan compressed his lips. "What about you and Kaitlin?" he asked, turning the tables.

"Nothing," Zach lied, perching on the arm of an overstuffed leather chair. He wasn't ready to talk to anybody about his relationship with Kaitlin. He didn't even have it straight in his own mind yet.

"You're sleeping with her," said Dylan.

Zach shot him a pointed look. "That's just…" In fact, Zach wasn't sure exactly what it was. Somehow his physical attraction to Kaitlin, their renovation battle and their mock marriage had all meshed together in a way that was well past confusing.

"Sex?" Dylan asked bluntly.

"It's not relevant," said Zach.

"What about the renovation? Is that relevant? You haven't forgotten why she's here, have you?"

"No, I haven't forgotten why she's here."

Dylan took another drink. "So, the plan's working?"

"It's going great," Zach admitted, trying to inject some enthusiasm for how well things were working out for him on that front. "She asked for the Hugo Rosche plans. She's been using them for the past few days. And, well, I think she's getting that Grandma Sadie wasn't progressive and flamboyant. And she's figuring it out for herself, which is exactly what we wanted."

"So, your devious little scheme is coming together in spades," Dylan summed up.

"It was *your* devious little scheme."

"You approved it," Dylan noted. "You implemented it. And it looks like you'll save yourself a bundle."

"I did," Zach agreed. Too bad saving a bundle didn't seem so important anymore. Too bad he'd started to wish he *could* give Kaitlin her dream project, unlimited funds, unfettered imagination.

"I think we've heard just about enough," Lindsay's lawyer voice cut in.

Zach whirled, nearly spilling his drink.

In the study's open doorway stood Kaitlin, her face completely pale.

Lindsay's face was beet-red.

Dylan had turned to a statue.

"You—" Lindsay pointed to Dylan, anger quaking deep in her voice "—scheming little pirate-boy. You take us back to Manhattan, right this minute."

Ten

The next afternoon, Kaitlin struggled to forget the entire weekend. If she chalked up her experience on Serenity Island to yet another childish fantasy where she found a family and lived happily ever after, she could cope with the way Zach had systematically and deliberately ripped her heart out.

It wasn't real.

It had never been real.

Working from her apartment, she'd gone back to her original renovation designs, ignoring the twinges of guilt when she thought about Ginny and Sadie and what they might think of what she was doing to the Harpers' Manhattan building.

This wasn't about Sadie, nor was it about the Harper and Gilby families. This was about Kaitlin, and her career, and her ability to stand on her own two feet and take care of herself every second of every day for the rest of her life.

So despite the knowledge that Sadie was unlikely to approve of the three extra floors, the five-story lobby, the saltwater aquarium and the palm trees, those features were staying, every single one of them. And she'd added a helipad. Who knew when Dylan would want to drop in?

She'd even thought about replacing the fountains in the lobby with a two-story waterfall. In fact, she was still considering it.

It was halfway through the afternoon, and her legs were starting to cramp. She rose from her computer, crossing the living room to the kitchen, snagging her second Sugar Bob's doughnut. She knew they were becoming an addiction. But she promised herself she'd add an extra half hour at the gym every day, and she'd kick the habit completely just as soon as the Harper building renovation was complete.

A woman could only handle so many things at once. She took a big bite.

There was a rap on her door, so she ditched the doughnut in the box and tossed the box back into her cupboard, wiping the powdered sugar from her lips.

For a split second she wondered if it might be Zach. Then, just as quickly, she promised herself she wouldn't open the door if it was.

She wouldn't.

She had absolutely nothing left to say to the man.

But when she checked through the peephole, it was Lindsay standing in the hallway. Kaitlin opened the door to find her friend balancing a large Agapitos pizza box on one hand and holding a bottle of tequila in the other.

"Pepperoni and sausage," Lindsay said without preamble, walking forward as Kaitlin opened the door up wide and shifted out of the way. "I hope you have limes."

It was only three-thirty. Somewhat early to start in on margaritas, but the day was already a nutritional bust, so what the hell?

"How are you holding up?" asked Lindsay as she crossed to the small kitchen table while Kaitlin shut and latched the apartment door.

"I am absolutely fine," said Kaitlin, her determination putting a spring in her step as she squared her shoulders.

"You are a terrible liar," Lindsay countered.

That was true enough. But Kaitlin also knew that if she said something loud enough and often enough, sometimes it started to feel true.

Kaitlin headed for the fridge, reciting the words she'd rehearsed in her mind. "So it turned out to be a con. It wasn't like we didn't expect it to be one. Zach was fighting to save money. I was fighting for my career. Our positions were incompatible from the get-go." She paused, taking a moment to regroup her emotions. "Though I have to admit, I didn't expect him to be quite so good."

She tugged open the fridge door, fighting to keep her voice even, but not doing a particularly good job. "Still, I was colossally stupid to have fallen for his act. I mean, didn't you and I call it almost to the detail before we left?"

"I never thought he'd take it as far as he did," Lindsay ventured from behind her.

"I did," said Kaitlin with a decisive nod as she bent to scoop a couple of limes from the crisper drawer. "He was trying to use sex as an advantage all along."

She'd known that. And she had no idea why she'd let herself sink so far into a ridiculous fantasy. She'd figured it out, yet in four short days he had her convinced to do exactly what he'd wanted with the renovations, and she was romping wantonly in his bed every night to boot.

Stupid move.

She snagged the limes.

Yesterday she'd been angry.

This morning she'd been heartbroken.

Right now, she was more embarrassed than anything.

"What about you?" she asked Lindsay, making up her mind to quit talking about it as she closed the fridge.

"What about me?" Lindsay had perched herself on one of the stools at the small breakfast bar with the pizza box in front of her.

Kaitlin set the limes down on the countertop and pulled a long, sharp knife out of the wooden block. "What about you and Dylan?"

"There is no me and Dylan."

"There was yesterday."

Lindsay gave her blond hair a quick toss. "He's dead to me."

"I like that," Kaitlin said defiantly, slicing into a lime. It sounded so unemotional and final.

"Have you heard anything from Zach?" Lindsay asked.

Kaitlin squeezed half a lime into the blender as she shook her head. "If I see his number, I'll hang up. And if he drops by, I won't answer the door."

"What about the renovation?"

Kaitlin emphasized her words by pointing the knife tip to her computer on the dining table. "I am doing my full-blown design. I'm adding a helipad and a waterfall. It'll be fabulous. I'll probably win an award."

Lindsay flipped open the cardboard box, folding it back to reveal the gooey, fragrant pizza. "I can't believe they turned out to be such rats."

"Dead-to-us rats," Kaitlin stated, fighting to keep her emotions in check over the thought of never seeing Zach again.

Why had she let herself trust him? Did she think he'd love her, really marry her, have babies with her and turn her life into some fantasy?

She was Kaitlin Saville, penniless orphan. Things like that didn't happen to her.

Lindsay tore a bite from one of the pizza slices and popped it into her mouth. "You thought he was the one?" she ventured softly.

Suddenly exhausted, Kaitlin set down the knife. "Stupid of me, I know."

"It's not your fault."

"It's all my fault."

"He played you."

"And I let him. I encouraged him. I helped him. And now all I have left is revenge."

"Revenge can be satisfying," said Lindsay. "Especially when it's going to save your career."

"I don't want revenge," Kaitlin responded with blunt honesty, turning to squeeze the other half of the lime into the blender. "I hate revenge. I feel like I'm getting revenge against Sadie instead of Zach." She dropped the lime peel and braced herself against the countertop.

She knew she couldn't do it.

She couldn't spend Harper money on a design she knew Sadie would hate. Her laugh sounded more like a cry.

"Katie?" Lindsay was up and rounding the breakfast bar.

"I'm fine," Kaitlin sniffed. But she wasn't fine. She was about to give up her career and her future for a family that wasn't even hers.

"Don't you love it when you know you've been a jerk?" Dylan asked, cupping his hands behind his head and stretching back in the padded chair next to Zach's office window.

Zach was standing, too restless to sit down while his mind struggled to settle on a course of action.

"I mean," Dylan continued, "sometimes you're not sure. But other times, like this, you're positive you've been a complete ass."

Zach folded his arms across his chest, watching the clouds streak across the sky far away over the Jersey shore. "Are you talking about me or you?"

"I'm talking about both of us."

Zach turned. He didn't know about Dylan's behavior, but he maintained that he'd been put in an untenable position. He never set out to hurt anyone. He was only trying to do right by his company and his family.

"And what should I have done differently?" he demanded.

Dylan grinned at Zach's upset. "I don't know. Maybe you shouldn't have pretended you were married."

"I *am* married."

"I'm guessing not for long."

Zach shook his head. "She's not going to divorce me. It's her leverage."

At least he hoped Kaitlin wasn't going to divorce him yet. He wasn't ready for that.

Dylan crossed an ankle over one knee. "Conning her into scaling back the renovation was one thing. But you're not a heartless bastard, Zach. Why'd you mess with her emotions like that?"

Zach felt his anger rise. What he'd done with Kaitlin was none of Dylan's business. It was between him and Kaitlin. It was… They were…

"And what about you?" he queried, deflecting the question. "You slept with Lindsay."

"That was a simple fling."

"And what do you think I had?"

Dylan sat up straight. "I don't know, Zach. You tell me." His gaze moved meaningfully to the package of papers on the table between them.

"That's nothing," Zach denied. That was simply him being a decent human being, something which Dylan didn't seem to believe was possible.

"You put nine private investigators on the case."

"So?" Zach had wanted something fast. More men, better speed.

"So how did that benefit you?"

"It wasn't supposed to benefit me." It was meant to benefit Kaitlin, to put a smile on her face, to banish the haunted look that came into her eyes every time the subject of his family came up, which was nearly every second they were on Serenity Island.

But the effort had pretty much been a failure. Despite the high-end manpower, all he'd found of Kaitlin's heritage was a grainy old newspaper photo showing her grandparents and her mother as a young girl. The family home had burned down, killing the grandparents and destroying all of the family possessions when Kaitlin's mother was sixteen, two years before Kaitlin was born.

The picture, two names and a gravesite were all Zach had turned up.

"You still going to give them to her?" asked Dylan.

"Sure," said Zach, with a shrug, pretending it was no big deal. "Maybe I'll mail them over."

"Mail them?"

"Mail them."

"You don't want to see her in person?"

Zach bristled. "To do what? To say what? To let her yell at me again?" Truth was, he'd give anything to see Kaitlin again, even if it was only to hear her yell. But what was the point? He'd chewed up her trust and spit it out, over and over again.

"You could tell her you sold the ship."

"Big deal." So Zach had come up with seventy-five million dollars. It wasn't as if he had a choice. Kaitlin would be full steam ahead on the renovation again, and the only way he was going to get his company back was to give her the carte blanche she'd demanded. The only way to do that was to sell an asset. So he'd sold an asset. She wouldn't give him brownie points for doing that. "You think an old newspaper photo and money I had to give her all along are going to make a difference?"

"You gotta try, Zach."

"No, I don't."

"You're in love with her."

"No, I'm not."

Dylan coughed out a cold laugh and came to his feet. "You sorry son-of-a—"

"I am not in love with Kaitlin."

He liked Kaitlin. Sure, he liked Kaitlin. What was not to like?

And, yeah, he'd have stayed with her for the foreseeable future. He'd have woken up next to her for as long as she'd let him. And maybe for a few days there he'd entertained fantasies about what could happen between them long term.

But those were just fantasies. They had nothing to do with the real world.

In the real world, he and Kaitlin were adversaries. She'd wanted to save her career, and he'd wanted to keep his company intact. She'd won. He'd lost. Nothing to be done about it now but mop up after the fallout.

"I saw your face when she walked out," Dylan offered. "I've known you your whole life, Zach."

Zach turned on him. "You know *nothing*."

"You're going to lie to me? That's your next big plan?"

"I don't have a next big plan."

"Well, you'd better come up with one. Or you're going to lose Kaitlin forever."

The words felt like a stake in Zach's heart.

He didn't love Kaitlin. He couldn't love Kaitlin. It would be a disaster to love Kaitlin.

He swallowed.

"What about you?" he asked Dylan.

"I already have a plan," Dylan stated with smug satisfaction. "And I don't even love Lindsay. I'm just not ready to let her go yet."

"That's how it starts," said Zach.

Dylan's brows shot up. "And you know this because…?"

"What's your plan?" Zach countered.

Okay, maybe he did love Kaitlin just a little bit. But he'd get over it.

"I'm kidnapping Lindsay. She wanted a pirate, she's getting a pirate. Can I borrow your yacht?"

"You can't kidnap her."

"Watch me."

Zach took in the determination in Dylan's eyes. And for a second there, he wished he could simply kidnap Kaitlin. If he could get her on board his yacht, he could probably keep her there for a few days, maybe even a few weeks. By the end of it, like Lyndall, he might be able to win her over.

On the other hand, she might have him arrested. Or she might throw him overboard. Or she might decide the Harper building needed to be a hundred stories high and truly bankrupt him.

Kidnapping was not a real option.

Instead, he'd give her the money. He'd give her the news clipping and the photo. Then, like the gentleman he'd once been, he'd step out of her life forever.

* * *

Three margaritas later, Kaitlin splashed cold water on her face in the small bathroom of her apartment. She and Lindsay had started to giggle about half an hour back, but now she found herself fighting tears.

It didn't seem to matter that Zach had played her for a fool. She'd fallen in love with him, and no matter how many times she told herself it was all a lie, she couldn't stop wanting the man she'd known on Serenity Island.

She dried her face and ran a comb through her hair, gathering her frayed emotions. Much as she wished she could drink herself into oblivion today, it was time to stop wallowing in self-pity and get her equilibrium back.

Her career in New York was over. Truthfully, she might as well walk away from the Harper project altogether. What Sadie and Zach would want wouldn't do a thing to save Kaitlin's career.

At least most of her boxes were still packed.

Another tear leaked out, and she impatiently swiped it away. She told herself she was tough, and she was strong, and she was independent. And she would salvage her life or die trying.

She left the bathroom at a determined pace, rounding the bedroom door into the living room. There, her steps staggered to a stop.

Zach stood in the middle of her apartment, large as life and twice as sexy.

She was too stunned to shriek, too stunned to cry, too stunned to do anything, but let her jaw drop open.

"Hello, Kaitlin."

She still didn't have her bearings. "Huh?"

"I came to apologize."

She glanced swiftly around the apartment. "Where's Lindsay? How did you—?"

"Lindsay left with Dylan."

Kaitlin gave her head a little shake, but she wasn't delusional. That really was Zach standing there. "Why would she do that?"

"He kidnapped her," said Zach. "I wouldn't expect to see her for a few days."

"He can't do that."

"That's what I said," Zach agreed. "But I don't think those two have ever cared much about the rules."

"Lindsay's a lawyer." Of course she cared about the rules. She was passionate about the rules.

Zach seemed to ponder that fact for a few moments. "Yeah," he conceded. "Dylan may have a bit of a problem with that when he brings her back."

"Is that a joke?" Was Lindsay about to jump out of the closet?

Instead of answering, Zach took a few steps forward. Her heart rate increased. Her chest went tight. And a low buzz started in the base of her belly.

She knew she should fight the reaction, but she had no idea how to turn it off.

"He took my yacht," said Zach, moving closer still, his gaze locked with hers every step of the way.

"So you're an accessory to kidnapping?" Her shock at the sight of him was starting to wear off, replaced by amazement that he was actually standing here in front of her. She could feel herself sink reluctantly back into the fantasy.

"Dylan told me she wanted a pirate, so she was getting a pirate."

"Is that why you're here?" she asked. "To help Dylan?"

"No."

"Then why?"

"Because I have something for you."

She forced herself to go cold and demanding. "I hope it's a big check." She knew she'd given up, abandoned the renovation, but Zach didn't need to know that yet.

"As a matter of fact, it is."

"Good." She gave a decisive nod, marveling at her own ability to hold her composure. The urge to throw herself into Zach's arms grew more powerful by the second.

"Seventy-five million dollars," he told her.

It took a few seconds for his words to sink in.

"What?" She took a reflexive step back.

"I sold a ship."

"What?"

"I'm giving you seventy-five million dollars for the renovation."

Kaitlin blinked at him.

"But that's not the real reason I'm here."

For a split second, hope flared within her. But she squelched it. Zach couldn't be trusted. She'd learned that the hard way half a dozen times over.

He handed her an envelope. "I'm here to give you this. It's not much."

Watching him warily, Kaitlin lifted the flap. She slid out a laminated picture. It showed a twentysomething couple with a young, blonde girl at the beach. The caption was *Holiday Travelers Enjoy Fourth of July Celebrations.*

She didn't understand.

"Phillipe and Aimee Saville," Zach said softly, and it felt as if Kaitlin's heart stopped.

"It was the best I could do," he continued. "There was a house fire in 1983. None of their possessions were saved. But the private investigators found this in the archives of a New Jersey newspaper. The little girl is your mother."

Kaitlin was completely speechless.

Her grandparents?

Zach had found grandparents?

Zach had *looked* for her grandparents?

Her fingers reflexively tightened on the photograph, and she felt herself sway to one side.

Zach's hand closed around her shoulder, steadying her.

"I've had three margaritas," she told him, embarrassed. She ought to be completely sober for a moment like this.

"That explains why Lindsay went so quietly."

Kaitlin fought against the sensation of his touch, even as she struggled to make sense of his gesture. "How? Where?" *Why* had he done this?

"I had some people start looking last week. After you told me." His hand tightened on her shoulder. "And I couldn't stand to see the pain in your eyes."

Her throat closed tighter, and her chest burned with emotion. She had to blink back tears at his thoughtfulness. Her voice dropped to a pained whisper. "How am I supposed to hate you?"

He drew a deep breath. Then he closed his eyes for a long second. He reached out and gently smoothed her hair back from her forehead. "You're not."

His hand stayed there, resting against her hair. Her nerves tingled where he touched. Her body begged her to sway forward against him, even as her mind ordered her to hold still.

She couldn't trust him. She didn't trust him. Oh, my, how she wanted to trust him.

He stroked his way to her cheek, cupping her face, tilting his head at an angle she'd come to recognize, to love.

He was going to kiss her, just like he'd done a hundred times, maybe a thousand. His lips dipped closer, and she moistened her own. She inhaled his scent, and her body relaxed into the exquisite moment.

"You're not supposed to hate me," he repeated on a whisper. "You're supposed to love me."

Then, he paused with his lips just barely brushing hers. "Because I love you, Katie. I love you so much."

His mouth captured hers, sending joy cascading through her body. His kiss was deep, sweet and long. His arms wrapped fully around her, hauling her close, pulling her safely into the circle of his embrace.

She clung to him, molding against him, passion and joy making her feel weightless.

After long minutes, he finally drew back. "Renovate anything you want," he rasped. "I'll sell half the damn fleet if I have to. Just don't leave me again. Not ever."

"I gave up the new design," she told him.

He drew back. "What? Why?"

"Sadie wouldn't like it."

Zach stilled. "Sadie doesn't matter. The past doesn't matter. Only the future, Kaitlin. And you're the future. You're *my* future."

Kaitlin's heart soared at the thought of a future with Zach—such a loving, thoughtful man.

Her voice quavered as she spoke. "You found my grand-parents."

"I did," he acknowledged. "I know they were buried in New Jersey."

"You know where they're buried?"

"Yes."

Twin tears rolled from Kaitlin's eyes at that. "Have I mentioned that I love you?"

"No." He shook his head. "You hadn't. And I was getting worried."

"Well, I do."

"Thank goodness." He drew a deep breath, tightening his arms around her. "I told Dylan to give me an hour. Otherwise, you were getting kidnapped, too."

"You would not."

"Hell, yes, I would. One way or another, you and I are starting on a whole new generation of Harper pirates."

Kaitlin smiled at his joke, her body sighing in contentment. "Sadie would be pleased."

"Yes, she would," Zach agreed. "She'd also be gloating over the success of her scheme. In fact, I can almost hear her chuckling from here."

Kaitlin moved her hand to take another look at the picture of her grandparents. Her grandfather was tall. Her grandmother slightly rounded with light, curly hair. And her mother looked bright-eyed and happy with a shovel and pail in her hands. "I can't believe you did this."

"We can go visit their graves." He paused. "I swapped Dylan the yacht for a helicopter. It's standing by."

Kaitlin was overwhelmed by this thoughtfulness. But she wasn't anywhere near ready to leave his arms.

She molded her body to his. "Or maybe we could go in an hour or so?"

He sucked in a breath, lifting the picture from her hand and setting it safely on an end table. Then his eyes darkened, and he bent forward to kiss her thoroughly.

"Maybe in an hour or so," he agreed and scooped her up to head for her bedroom.

Epilogue

Following a month-long kidnapping, Lindsay and Dylan's wedding was held on Serenity Island, on the emerald-green lawn at the Gilby house, next to the pool. The bride was radiant, the groom ecstatic and the guests a who's who of New York City. According to Ginny, it was the biggest party the island had held since the heyday of the 1940s.

Dylan had insisted on flying the Jolly Roger, while Ginny confided gleefully to Kaitlin that since the wedding was so rushed, she wondered if Lindsay might be pregnant.

After the toasts were made, the five-tiered cake was cut and the dancing had started in the late afternoon, Zach drew Kaitlin to one side.

"There's something I need to show you," he told her quietly, tugging her inside the house and down the hallway toward the garage.

"We can't leave now," she protested, trotting on her high heels, the glossy, champagne-colored bridesmaid dress flowing around her knees.

"We'll be back in a few minutes," he assured her, opening the garage door.

"Zach," she protested.

"What?"

"Are you crazy?"

He turned and playfully kissed the tip of her nose. "Crazy for you."

"This isn't a joke." She tried to sound stern, but she didn't seem capable of getting angry with him. Since the afternoon in her apartment, and their helicopter trip to the cemetery to put roses on her grandparents' graves, she'd been almost giddy with love.

He braced his hand against the passenger side of a golf cart. "And I'm not laughing. Hop in."

"I will not hop in." She crossed her arms stubbornly over her chest. She wasn't abandoning Lindsay on her wedding day.

"Have it your way." He gently but firmly deposited her on the narrow bench seat.

"Hey!" She scrambled to get her dress organized around herself.

"There's something I really have to show you." He jumped into the driver's side and turned on the key.

Before she could escape, the cart pulled smoothly out of the garage onto the gravel driveway and the road that led down to the castle.

"I can't believe you're kidnapping me," she harrumphed.

"It is the pirate way."

"You are *not* allowed to ravish me in the middle of a wedding reception." She smoothed her dress over her knees and put her nose primly in the air.

Zach gave her a wolfish grin, and she was forced to wonder which one of them would prevail if push came to shove, and he did decide he wanted to ravish her.

They drove all the way down to the Harper property.

As they entered the castle gardens, she felt herself relax. This had quickly become one of her favorite places in the world. It was filled with such history and such happy memories.

Zach pulled to a halt in front of the family chapel, then he hopped out and came around to assist her.

She shook her head in confusion as she clambered around the awkward dress. It was made for fashion, not mobility. The bodice was tight, coming to a drop waist, while the satin skirt billowed out with crinolines, ending at knee length. "This is what you wanted to show me?" She'd been in the gardens a thousand times.

"Have patience," he told her.

"I'll have patience after the reception. Seriously, Zach. We have to get back."

But he led her by the hand to the bottom of the chapel steps.

"What are we doing?" she breathed in frustration.

A secretive smile growing on his lips, he reached into his tux jacket pocket and drew something out, holding his palm flat so that she could focus on a small heirloom ring.

It was a delicately swirled gold band, with a sapphire center, flanked by diamonds.

"I don't know how old it is," said Zach. "But I think it might have belonged to Lyndall."

"Stolen?" Kaitlin asked, glancing up.

"Let's assume not." Zach's silver eyes sparkled. He held her hand in his, stepping forward, voice going soft. "Will you marry, Katie?"

She was still confused. "I am. I did."

"I know." He smiled. "But I don't think we got it quite right the first time." Then he nodded to the old chapel. "It's traditional for Harper brides to be married right here."

Kaitlin understood, and her chest tightened with emotion. "You want to…"

"Absolutely. Marry me, Kaitlin. Do it here. Do it now. Love me when you say the vows, and promise my family you'll stay with me forever."

She blinked back the sting of tears. "Oh, Zach."

The ancient door swung open with a groan, and a preacher appeared in the doorway.

"This way," he told them softly, turning, robes rustling as he made his way to the front of the ancient church.

Zach squeezed her hand as they mounted the steps, leading her over the uneven stone floor, past worn wooden pews, to the altar that Lyndall had built for his own wedding, the very first wedding on the island.

Kaitlin swayed sideways against Zach, absorbing the feel of his strong body.

Footsteps sounded behind them, and she glanced back to see Lindsay and Dylan, still dressed for their own wedding.

"Oh, no," she moaned under her breath.

"They insisted," Zach whispered, tucking her arm into the crook of his.

As they stopped at the front of the church, one of the staff members stepped out and handed Kaitlin a bouquet.

White roses.

From Sadie's garden.

It was beyond perfect, and Kaitlin had to blink against the sting of tears.

Lindsay and Dylan took their places, and Zach wrapped an arm around Kaitlin, gathering her close for a private word. "I love you very much, Katie," he whispered.

"And I love you," she whispered back, feeling as though her heart might burst wide open.

His tone went husky as he tenderly stroked her cheek, wiping her tears with the pad of his thumb. "Then, let's take our vows and put this ring on your finger."

* * * * *

"Do you want your child back?"

"Of course I do!"

"Smile then—and get out there with me. Let the reporters have a good look at my future wife. Hold your head high. Hold my hand."

Her palm felt cool when she slipped it inside his, small, and he gave it a clench as he guided her around the corner. She walked easily beside him, but a hint of alarm still lingered in her voice. "Landon, I feel like all these people can see right through me. That they know this is a farce and that I have no clue who you are."

"Do me a favor, Beth?"

"What?"

"Act like you love me."

Dear Reader,

We've all made mistakes in our lives. Some minor. Some big.

But what about when those mistakes shape us for the rest of our lives and take the one thing we love most from us?

What if you choose the wrong husband and years later he takes away your beloved son?

And what if the only hope of getting that innocent boy back is to ask for help from the one man whom you've always thought was an enemy?

These were the kind of questions that popped through my mind as I wrote Beth and Landon's story—a story I absolutely *love*!

I mean, just imagine having to ask your sworn enemy for a favor…how difficult asking for this favor would be, how embarrassed you'd feel, and how determined and desperate you'd have to be in order to go through with it.

Now, imagine *his* side: your enemy's ex-wife desperately attempting to bargain with you, and at the same time, stirring your long dormant lust. Sounds complicated, right? And exciting!

Readers, meet Beth and Landon.

A woman who wants her son back.

A man who wants his life back.

Enemies joined by one common goal: revenge.

They're both people who think they only have vengeance in their hearts. What a lovely and thrilling surprise it would be, if they discovered they had something more…

I hope you enjoy their story!

Red

PAPER MARRIAGE PROPOSITION

BY
RED GARNIER

All the characters in this book have no existence outside the imagination of
the author, and have no relation whatsoever to anyone bearing the same name
or names. They are not even distantly inspired by any individual known or
unknown to the author, and all the incidents are pure invention.

Published in Great Britain 2011
by Mills & Boon, an imprint of Harlequin (UK) Limited,
Eton House, 18-24 Paradise Road, Richmond, Surrey TW9 1SR

© Red Garnier 2011

ISBN: 978 0 263 88324 4

51-1111

Harlequin (UK) policy is to use papers that are natural, renewable and
recyclable products and made from wood grown in sustainable forests. The
logging and manufacturing processes conform to the legal environmental
regulations of the country of origin.

Printed and bound in Spain
by Blackprint CPI, Barcelona

MILLS & BOON

You can find all Mills & Boon titles at our website
millsandboon.co.uk

> **For a limited time only**, we are offering you an
> **EXCLUSIVE 15% OFF** when you order online.
> Simply enter the code **15NOV11** at the checkout.
> But hurry, this offer ends on 30th November 2011.

PLUS, by ordering online you will receive all these extra benefits:

- Purchase new titles **1 MONTH AHEAD OF THE SHOPS.** Available in paperback and as eBooks!

- Order books from our huge backlist at a discounted price

- **Try before you buy** with Browse the Book

- Be the first to hear about exclusive offers in our eNewsletter

- Join the M&B community and discuss your favourite books with other readers

Terms and Conditions:
- Offer expires on 30th November 2011
- This offer cannot be used in conjunction with any other offer.
- Code can only be redeemed online at www.millsandboon.co.uk
- Exclusions apply
- Discount excludes delivery charge.

NOV11

Red Garnier is a fan of books, chocolate and happily ever afters. What better way to spend the day than combining all three? Traveling frequently between the United States and Mexico, Red likes to call Texas home. She'd love to hear from her readers at redgarnier@gmail.com. For more on upcoming books and current contests, please visit her website, www.redgarnier.com.

As always, with my deepest thanks to—
Krista, Charles and Shana
Thank you for making this book shine.

This book is dedicated to my flesh-and-blood hero.

One

Desperate.

Desperate was the only word to describe her at this point, the only word to justify what she was doing.

Her heart rattled in her chest, and her clammy hands shook so hard she could barely control them.

She was stepping into a man's hotel room—uninvited.

She had lied to the housekeeper to gain access, and this only after days of having groveled to this elusive stranger's secretary and attempting to bribe his chauffeur. And now, as she embarked on her first felony, Bethany Lewis expected to crack under the pressure.

Legs trembling, she shut the door behind her, pulled out a little black book and clutched it to her chest as she eased deeper into the presidential suite—uninvited.

The space was lit by soft lamplight, scented with the sweet smell of oranges. Her stomach rumbled, still starved for today's breakfast, lunch and dinner.

A small lacquered desk sat by the window. Behind it, the

satin, peach-colored drapes were gathered aside to reveal a wide balcony overlooking the city. A silver tray with chocolate-dipped strawberries, an assortment of cheeses and polished fresh fruit was laid out on a glass coffee table. Next to a single unopened envelope that read *Mr. Landon Gage*.

The name was synonymous with old money, sophistication, power. For years it had been whispered to Bethany in hate. *Landon Gage will pay for this. The Gages will rot in hell!*

But the Gages were swimming in money, and if this was hell, then Beth would take it any day against the purgatory she'd had to live through.

She navigated around the Queen Anne settee, thinking of her six-year-old's cherubic blond face as she'd last seen it, wary-eyed and fearful as she left for trial. *Mommy, you won't leave me? Promise?*

No, darling, Mommy will never leave you….

Hollowness spread in her breast at the memory. She would brave a fiery dragon. She would lie and cheat and steal if only to make those words real to her little boy.

"Mr. Gage?"

She peered beyond the slightly parted double doors that led into the bedroom. Downstairs, the children's cancer charity function was in full swing. Bethany had planned to blend in as a waitress and make her move, but the tycoon had not made an appearance yet, although it was worldwide knowledge that he was in the building. Among the waiting crowd, his name had been whispered in anticipation, and suddenly Beth couldn't stand the suspense.

On the large king bed, a glossy-leather briefcase lay open, surrounded by piles and piles of papers. A laptop hummed nearby.

"You've been following me."

Startled by the rich, deeply masculine voice, her eyes jerked to where a man exited the walk-in closet. He swiftly closed the buttons of his crisp white shirt and fixed her with a sharp, ice-cold gaze. Bethany backed into a wall. His presence was so staggering, her breath wheezed out of her.

He was taller than she'd anticipated, broad, dark and intimidating as a night demon. His body was fit and toned under the dress shirt and tailored black slacks, and the damp hair that was slicked behind his wide forehead revealed a face that was both utterly virile and sophisticated. His eyes—an old, tarnished silver color—were weary and remote, somehow empty-looking.

"I'm sorry," she said when she realized she was gaping.

He took in her physique. His gaze lingered on her hands, the nails shredded down to stubs. Beth resisted the urge to squirm and fought valiantly to stand there, dignified.

Carefully, he absorbed the knit St. John jacket and skirt she wore, loose around her waist and shoulders after she'd lost so much weight. It was one of the few quality suits she'd been able to hang on to after the divorce and one she'd chosen precisely for this occasion. But his gaze narrowed when he caught the shadows under her eyes.

Her tummy clenched. She could tell he wasn't as impressed with her as she with him.

He seized a shiny black bow from the nightstand and pinned her with a bleary look. "I could have you arrested."

Surprise skittered through her. He'd been aware of her? Hounding him for days? Hiding in corners, calling his office, begging his chauffeur, *stalking* him?

"W-why haven't you?"

Halting before a vanity table that looked ridiculously dainty next to him, he tied the bow around his collar with long, nimble fingers, meeting her gaze in the mirror. "Maybe you amuse me."

Bethany only partly listened to his words, for her mind suddenly whizzed with possibilities, and was coming to terms with the fact that Landon Gage was probably everything they said he was and more. The very bastard she needed. A bona fide, full-throttle, lean, mean son of a bitch. Yes, please, let it be.

Something had become clear to Beth. If she ever planned to be reunited with her son, she needed someone bigger, badder than her ex-husband. Someone without conscience and without fear. She needed a miracle—and when God wasn't listening, then a pact with the devil was in store.

He spun around, clearly put out by her silence. "Well, Miss…?"

"Lewis." She couldn't help it; felt a little intimidated by him, his height, the breadth of his shoulders, his palpable strength. "You don't know me," she began. "At least not personally. But you might be acquainted with my ex-husband."

"Who is?"

"Hector Halifax."

The reaction she had been expecting did not come. His expression revealed nothing, not the mildest interest, definitely not the anger she'd been striving for.

Bethany wiped one clammy hand on her jacket and eased away from the wall, still keeping a careful distance. "I hear you've been enemies for a time."

"I have many enemies. I do not sit around thinking of them all day. Now if you'll make this quick, I'm expected downstairs."

Quick.

She didn't even know where to begin. Her life was such a tangled, thorny mess, her emotions so beat up, her story so sorry she found there were few descriptors that would do it justice and no *quick* way to explain it.

When she at last spoke, the horrible words caused actual pain in her throat. "He took my son from me."

Gage slammed his laptop shut and began to shove the files into his briefcase. "Aha."

She focused on his hard profile and wondered if he'd known, suspected, that she would come to him. He seemed not in the least surprised by her visit. Then again, he looked like a man who'd seen it all.

"I need...I want him back. A six-year-old should be with his mother."

He locked his briefcase with an efficient click.

Tamping down an anger that had nothing to do with him and everything to do with her ex-husband, Beth attempted to level her voice. "We battled for him in a custody hearing. Hector's lawyers provided photographs of me having an illicit affair. Several, actually. Of me...with different men."

This time, when his eyes ventured the length of her body, she experienced the alarming sensation of having him mentally strip off her clothes. "I read the papers, Miss Lewis. You've got quite a reputation now."

He reached for his wallet on the nightstand, slipped it into his back pocket and lifted a tailored black jacket from the back of a nearby chair.

"They paint me as a Jezebel. It's a lie, Mr. Gage," she said.

Gage unapologetically started across the suite and thrust his arms into the coat sleeves.

Beth briskly followed him out of the room and down the hall and to the elevator bank. Her heart tripped when he stopped. He slammed his finger into the down arrow, then leaned back on his heels and regarded her plainly. "And how is this my problem?"

"Look." Her voice shook, and her heart was about to pop. "I have no resources to fight him or his lawyers. He made sure I received nothing. At first I thought there would be a young lawyer hungry enough to put his name out there and take a case like this with no money, but there isn't. I paid twenty dollars to a service online just so I could see what my options were."

She paused for oxygen.

"Apparently, if my circumstances change, I could petition for a custody change. I have already quit my job. Hector accused me of leaving David all day with my mother while I worked, and my mother…well, she's a little deaf. But she *loves* David, she's a *great* grandmother," she quickly defended, "and I had to work, Mr. Gage. Hector left us without money."

"I see."

His steady regard caused a burning heat to crawl up her neck and cheeks.

No doubt in her mind that she was being judged all over again, and right now, it felt as humiliating as it had in court.

The elevator arrived with a ping, and she followed him inside, inhaling deeply for courage.

And to her dismay, all she could smell the moment the doors closed and they were enclosed in such a small space was him. Clean and musky, his scent unsettled her nerves. It felt as if she had pins in her veins.

God, the man was seriously, ludicrously sexy and he smelled really, really good.

Beth shouldn't have noticed this, but she was having trouble organizing her thoughts.

Landon Gage crossed his big, strong arms and gazed with notable impatience at the blinking LED numbers, as though they couldn't reach the ballroom floor soon enough.

"I do not care about the money, I want my child," Bethany whispered, her voice soft and pleading.

No one had recognized the good, loving deeds she'd done right as a mother. No one had cared that she'd told David stories every night. No one had paid attention to how she'd been to every doctor visit, had mended every little scrape, had dried every tear. No one in court had seen her as a mother, only a whore. That is all they had wanted to see, and what they'd wanted to believe. Bethany, and men. Men she didn't know, men she'd never even seen.

How easy it was for the wealthy and powerful to lie and for others to believe them. How much had it cost Hector to doctor that evidence? A pittance to him, she was sure, compared to what he took from her.

Lost in thought, she had not realized Landon had stopped gazing at the numbers and was, instead, scrutinizing her profile as she gnawed on her lower lip. "And I repeat. How is this my problem?"

She met his gaze head-on. "You are his enemy. He despises you. He means to destroy you."

He smiled a fast, hard smile, as though he knew a secret the rest of the world didn't. "I would like to see him try once more."

"I have…" She waved the book. "This little black book. Which you could use to bring him down."

"Little black book? Like we're in high school?"

Beth flipped the pages. "Phone numbers of the people he meets with, the kind of deals he's done and with whom, reporters he's dealing with, the women." She slapped it shut with some drama. "Everything is here—everything. And I will give this book to you if you help me."

He stared fiercely at the little black book, then into her face. "And Halifax hasn't noticed this book is…in his ex-wife's hands?"

"He thinks it fell overboard the day he took me yachting."

A dangerous fire sparked in Landon's eyes; a dark, forgotten vendetta coming to life.

But the elevator jerked to a halt, and his expression eased, once again calm and controlled. "Revenge is tiring, Miss Lewis. I'm not a man who makes a living at it."

And then he swept out past the doors, stalking into the noisy, swirling ballroom, and Bethany felt her heart implode like a soda can crushed under his foot.

Music and laughter boomed. Jewels glinted under the chandelier light. Beth could see the top of his silky ebony hair as he wound through the sea of elegantly dressed people and soaring marble columns. She could see him—her one and only chance—walking away from her. And all she could think of was *no*.

Waiters twirled around with armfuls of canapés, and

Bethany methodically maneuvered around the crowd. She caught up with him by the sloshing wine fountain as he snatched up a glass.

"Mr. Gage," she began.

He didn't break stride as he tossed back the liquid. "Go home, Miss Lewis."

Beth sprinted three steps ahead of him and raised the black book with imploring hands. "Please listen to me."

He halted, set the empty glass on a passing tray, then stretched his hand out to her, palm up. "All right, let's see the goddamned book."

"No." The book went back to her chest, protected with both hands. "I'll let you see the book when you marry me," she explained.

"Pardon?"

"Please. I need my circumstances to change so I can get custody. Hector will hate the idea of you having me as a wife. He will…he will want me back. He will fear what I can tell you. And then I can bargain for my child. You can help me. And I will help you destroy him."

Something akin to disbelief lifted his brows. "You're a little thing to be full of such hate, aren't you?"

"Bethany. My name is Bethany. But you can call me Beth."

"Is that what he called you?"

Her hand fluttered in the air. "He called me *woman*, but I can't see how that matters."

The disgust on his face said it all, how romantic he thought the "pet name" to be. Bethany did not have time to explain, for he'd plunged back into the crowd. Everyone, it seemed, either came forward or waved at him. Event security spotted Landon from their posts, and their quick eyes landed immediately on Beth.

"Look, I warn you," she said, bumping her shoulder against a woman who said, "Hey!" and swiftly apologizing before sprinting back to his side. "Hector is obsessed. He believes you're out to get him and he wants to get you first. If you do not actively do something, he will tear you apart."

He stopped and frowned darkly. "I don't think you have the vaguest idea of who I am." As he bent forward, his narrowed gray eyes leveled ominously with hers, making her hackles raise. "I am ten times more powerful than Hector Halifax. He'd dance in a pink tutu if I said so."

"Prove it! Because all I can say is Hector is happier than he's ever been. He's not hurting at all."

"Landon! God, Landon, there you are."

He did not glance up at the speaker, but stared at Beth with eyes so tormented they provided a peek into the darkest pits of hell.

Her heart pounded a thousand times in only a couple of seconds.

And still he didn't speak.

"Let me make this clear, Miss Lewis." Whatever she'd seen in his eyes vanished as though a shutter had dropped. "I am not in the market for another man's leavings—nor am I in the market for a wife."

"It will only be temporary, please, my family is helpless against his, I cannot even see my son! I crawl around the streets waiting for a glimpse of him. You're the only man who hates my ex-husband as badly as I do. I *know* you hate him, I can see it in your eyes."

His lips thinned into a white, grim line.

"Landon, are you enjoying yourself? Can I bring you anything, darling?"

Not even the fluttery woman's voice, coming somewhere behind his broad shoulders, could tear those lethal silver eyes away from Beth's. He seized her chin and tipped her head back. "Perhaps I do hate him," he said silkily. "More than you will ever know."

"Landon," another voice said.

His thumb slid up from her chin to explore her trembling bottom lip. A jolt shot across her body. An avalanche of longing unlike anything she'd ever imagined crashed in her. She trembled, head to toe.

"Landon," yet another voice said, this one male.

He ground his teeth, grabbed her elbow and began dragging her through the tumult of people toward a back hall, into a little room. Slamming the door, he closeted them in shadows. Only a faint flicker of city lights was visible through a small window.

"Bethany." He seemed to struggle to grasp the last tatters of his patience. "You seem like a smart woman. I suggest you come up with another plan for yourself. I'm *not* interested."

"But you're still talking to me, aren't you?"

"In two seconds, I won't be."

She caught his arm, noting his eyes were getting a little dark, a little wild. She couldn't help but think that if she pushed a bit…if she pushed just a bit more…

"Please," she implored, her voice praising. "The public loves you. The court will want to know my new husband to believe I am respectable. They will want to know how much you make and what you do…" Aware that she was squeezing his biceps—very hard, very strong biceps—and that he'd gone rigid as if he didn't want her to, she let go. "You're an enigma, Mr. Gage. You give to charities. You…you're adored by the media."

Adored because he had been on the deep end of a tragedy. Adored because he—powerful, handsome, rich—had been shattered once, like a human being.

"The media is twisted." He leaned back on his heels and scoffed. "It is also mine. Of course it loves me."

"They fear you, but they revere you."

He glanced out the window, his brow creasing in thought. "What do you know of Hector's dealings?"

"Names. People he's bought in the press. Future plans." At the thoughtful angle of his chin, she plunged on more boldly. "I will tell you everything. Everything I know—and I promise you I know enough."

He silently weighed her words, considering. Yes! She could see that he was tempted, sorely tempted. Hope spread inside her like a winged shadow. *Help me, Landon Gage, for Christ's sake, help me.*

Because she saw in this stranger's eyes the same lost, caged fury he must see in hers. And sometimes a stranger is all you have in the world when your friends don't hang around to watch the bloodshed. When they'd picked corners and they had not picked yours.

Landon Gage would understand. Someone, at last, would reach out a hand to her. Please.

He gave a toss of his head, emphatically denying her. "Find someone else."

Stifling a rising bubble of hysteria, Beth slapped an arm across the door while fiercely clutching the book to her breastbone. "How can you do this?" she hissed through her teeth. "How can you let him get away with what he did to you? He destroyed your life. He still actively destroys it."

She could hear the furious scowl he wore in his words. "*Don't* pretend you know anything about my life."

"Oh, I know *all* about it, I even watched while he did it. He did it to me, too!"

"Listen to me very carefully, Beth." His voice dropped, low and husky but laced with the unyielding iron of his will as he bent over her, a looming shadow eating up her soul. "It has been six years. I have put the past behind me, where it belongs. I'm not consumed by rage anymore when for years all I thought of was murder. Do *not* provoke me, or I may just take it out on you."

"This is your chance, don't you see?" She was grasping at straws and she knew it. "I thought you would feel what I do. Don't you just *hate* him?"

He pried her arm aside and reached for the doorknob, but she blocked the exit, experiencing a horrible sensation of watching her last chance slipping through her fingers.

"It will be over within a year, when I have David back. Please, what does a woman need to do to convince you!"

The book crashed to the floor as Beth grabbed his jacket, rose up on tiptoe, and slammed her lips to his, giving the kiss everything she had. Her lips wildly tried coaxing his, and her eyes flew open when he twisted her around in a dizzying spin. With enough force to yank the breath out of her, he pinned her back against the wall. "Are you out of your mind?"

She shivered, felt dazed and disoriented. Her lips burned from that kiss, a kiss he had not returned, one that had devastated her nonetheless. God, his chest was steel, his hands were steel, his annoying will was steel steel steel. "What will it take to make you help me?" she asked brokenly, sagging against the wall.

"Why did you kiss me?" he demanded.

He skewered her in place with his hands and the weight of his long, impossibly hard body. Her eyes widened. Her breasts prickled. An unmistakable stiffness bit fiercely into her pelvis. Oh, *God*. Somehow, with that awkward and pitiful excuse for a kiss, he'd gotten aroused.

And Beth was so…so *shaky*. She hadn't felt this in years. Ever.

"I…"

Wet by her, his plush, gleaming lips were the most distracting thing she'd ever beheld.

His fingers tightened on her wrists and his rolling deep voice vibrated across his muscles. "I don't play games, Bethany. My sense of humor runs thin and if you raise a little red flag at me one more time, I *will* charge."

"Lan, there you are. You're up for the microphone."

He abruptly released her and Beth rubbed her sore wrists. A striking dark-headed man scrutinized them both from the doorway. Interest lit up his features and made his lips curve upward. "And who might the lady be?"

"Halifax's wife." With that disgusted statement, Landon stormed out of the room.

"I'm not his wife!" she shouted after him.

The newcomer shot her a look of incredulity, and Beth spread her trembling hands down the plackets of her jacket, futilely attempting to regroup. She snatched the book, which lay open, facedown on the floor.

"Garrett Gage," the man said with a wry smile.

She hesitated before seizing his outstretched hand. "B-Bethany. Lewis."

"Bethany, you need a drink." He handed over his glass and easily tucked her free arm into the crook of his. He patted her fondly, like they were new best friends about to share intimacies. "Talk to me, Beth. May I call you Beth?"

Two

Revenge.

Revenge on a blonde, blue-eyed, tempting little platter. Landon couldn't quite push her image aside. Elegant in her blue suit, dignified with her chin jutting out defiantly. Bethany Lewis.

With circles under her eyes.

He doubted she slept any more than he did. He cursed under his breath, telling himself he did not care whether she, too, fought demons at night.

He should have been inclined to doubt her claims. A man became suspicious after the wind was knocked out of him… *I'm leaving you for another man…*

But the story had flooded the papers. Bethany Halifax, now Lewis, had endured a dirty divorce and an even uglier custody battle.

Which Landon shouldn't give a damn about.

On his fifth glass of red and after the ordeal at the microphone, he downed the liquid slowly, forcing himself to enjoy the taste as he rested his elbows on the stone balustrade and contemplated the hotel gardens. The night had grown quiet, so that through the sound of water lapping against the edge of the hotel pool, through the sound of lonely crickets in the distance and the faded sounds of traffic even farther away in the city, he could hear his own thoughts.

Hector Halifax's woman.

Kissing Landon's lips like her life depended on it. Kissing him not subtly, but hard and fast and desperately.

It irked him immeasurably, her desperation, and he wasn't certain why. Perhaps because he knew desperation. What shallow company it was, what a lousy counselor it became.

Perhaps because despite his resistance, he'd responded to her. Why *her?* She was not even the most beautiful thing he'd ever seen, and certainly not that sexy with that man-eating fury in her gaze. But when he'd felt her coaxing lips against his, he'd experienced the strangest, most exhilarating ecstasy. With her, trapped between him and the wall, the urge to rip off that tasteful jacket and fill his hands with her, fill her mouth with his tongue, had been more than he could bear.

He should've tasted her. He hadn't felt this bothered, this turned-on, in years. He should've tasted that mobile, hungry little mouth—was it sweet? Hot?

He tensed when behind him, long sure footsteps approached, followed by his brother's voice. Garrett. The youngest, Julian John, had to be around somewhere, too. Maybe necking with a waitress.

"I'm surprised you've stuck around this long," Garrett said, propping his elbows on the weathered stone.

Landon shrugged, not annoyed so much by the crowds when he was able to escape them. "I'm waiting for her to leave."

His brother chuckled, a sound much like Landon's had been before he'd forgotten how to do it. "I admit I'm very intrigued about the contents of that little black book."

Landon remained silent. He was intrigued, too. But he was the eldest, the cool head. His mother, his brothers, depended on him to make decisions with level-headed precision, not stemming from rage.

A breeze rustled across the nearby bushes.

"I don't remember seeing such hate in someone's eyes before," Garrett said. After a charged pause, "Except maybe yours."

An old, familiar rage crawled inside Landon's stomach. He plucked a leaf from a prickly little bush, tore it in half, and tossed it aside. "If you have a point," he said flatly, "then make it."

"You know, Landon, I've been waiting for you to do something about what happened all those years ago. Mother's been waiting. Julian has been, too. You never mourned. You never got drunk. You went to work the next day, hell, you worked like a dog. You're *still* working like a dog."

"And this is the attitude you all wanted me to take? I pulled Dad's newspaper up from the ground, Garrett. I branched out online and tripled its earnings—you wanted me to get *drunk?*"

"No," he admitted, contrite. "I wanted you to do something that will balance things out. I think it's long past the time you took a hand to this. You know goddamned well you can crush him."

"Halifax?"

A glint of mischief sparked in Garrett's eyes. "Don't tell me you haven't thought about it."

"Every night."

"There you go." With a satisfied grunt, Garrett emptied his wineglass and set it aside. "Landon, come on. You're the loneliest bastard I know. We've stood by for six years watching you close yourself off. You're not even interested in women anymore. The anger is reeking off your pores, its eating you inside."

Landon rubbed two fingers up the length of his nose, his temples beginning to throb. "Back off, Garrett."

"Why not take your revenge, brother?"

He didn't know what happened. One moment he clutched his wine and the next the glass shattered on the nearest stone pillar, the shards scattering across the floor. "Because it will not bring them back!" he roared. "I can goddamned kill him and they're still. Not. Coming. Back!"

The silence that followed felt like a noose around his throat. He'd said too much, had lost control, showed his brother just how very close he was to losing it, how perilous he found each day to be. How pointless it all seemed. Power, respect, even life itself. It was all one big nothing.

Landon felt *nothing* but...hollow.

"Damn it," he muttered, cursing himself and that female for bringing thoughts of Hector Halifax to the forefront.

Landon hated thinking about it, hated remembering, the phone call late at night, all the evidence the detective had discovered. But at the same time, it haunted him. How could he have been so blind? So fooled? Chrystine had been having an affair with Halifax for several months; the detective confirmed she'd been texting and emailing and stealing out into the night to see him. Landon hadn't known of her betrayal until the day he'd buried her.

He'd felt cornered into the marriage, hadn't wanted her, but she'd been pregnant with his child and he'd done the "right" thing with every intention of making it work.

He'd failed. And he'd failed to protect that chubby little infant, who'd already learned to sit, and grin and say "Papa."

His son had died because of her.

And because of Halifax emailing in the middle of the night, demanding of Landon's wife that it was *now* or *never*. She either went to him *now* or they would *never* be together.

Chrystine had been taking medication, medication Halifax had prescribed, medication no nursing mother should have been taking and no sane person should be driving on. Halifax had known, and he'd still made the demands. Demands he knew Chrystine would follow when he'd threatened not to "prescribe" for her any longer, vowed not to see her anymore if she did not follow. The night had been stormy, dark and though Chrystine had anxiously thought *now,* she would go to him *now,* the crash had said *never.*

Neither she nor her son had taken another breath.

Landon never again felt his son's tiny, dimpled hand wrap around his finger. He'd never see him as a young boy or guide him through the painful process of becoming a man.

"I know they're gone." Concern etched in his features, Garrett reached out and firmly seized Landon's shoulder. "Maybe they're not coming back, brother, but I was hoping you would."

Bethany sat outside on a carved wooden bench next to the valet parking booth, staring at the black book on her lap. *You've brought the anger back to my brother,* Garrett Gage had said with a marveled smile. *I might even thank you.*

She was still puzzling over his words, mulling over her own situation.

Now what?

Spotting Landon Gage's burly chauffeur lounging by the hood of a black Lincoln Navigator across the street, a man who'd earned both her respect and her frustration when he had refused to be bribed or coerced into letting Bethany climb unsuspected into the back of Gage's car, she returned his knowing smile and sighed.

She'd stopped believing in fairy tales the instant she'd realized she had married a toad and no, they did not change into princes after a kiss after all. So why had she ever thought a stranger could help her? The enemy?

In his mind she was a Halifax. She'd always be a Halifax, and he must *hate* her for it.

But Gage had been damaged by Hector Halifax, and although he had gone on with his life, the death of his family had been irrevocable. Bethany could still do something, would fight as long as there was breath in her body.

She wouldn't live apart from her son.

She blinked when Landon strode out of the revolving doors, his square jaw clenched so tight she'd bet it hurt. He swept his gaze across the moonlit sidewalk and, when he spotted her, skewered her with a look. He halted only a foot away. "When?"

"When what?"

"When do you want to marry? Friday? Saturday?"

Bethany gaped at him, at this big self-possessed man with the wild gray eyes. She shook off her daze, and the words leapt off her tongue. "Friday. Tomorrow. *Now.*"

"Be in my office tomorrow. I'll have a prenup drawn." He tossed a black credit card into her lap. "I want you in an expensive dress. Buy it. Look virginal if you want to get your son back. And buy yourself a ring." When all she could do was gawk in disbelief, he pointed a finger in her direction and gave her a grim, warning look. "You get nothing, you understand? When we're through."

She rose to her feet, her nod jerky. "I want nothing but my child back. I'll find a job where I can work at home, I'll never lose him again."

His fingers curled around her bare wrist and guided her close enough for the granite strength of his body to threaten hers. He was so big Beth couldn't help but feel…tiny.

"Be sure this is what you want, Miss Lewis. By the time I'm finished with your husband there won't be anything left."

With that, he spun around, leaving her breathless with exhilaration, gratefulness, strange little flutters in her stomach.

"Mr. Gage!"

He swung back to face her, running a big tanned hand along his face. "Landon."

"Thank you, Landon."

His eyebrows drew together. "I'm not doing this for you."

"I know. Thank you, anyway."

He hesitated, then retraced his path back to her, seizing her elbow and ducking his head. "Will there be something else on the menu, Beth?"

Her lips parted, closed, parted again. "What do you mean?"

God, his face was cruel, it was so handsome. His mouth, beautiful. His eyes, entrancing. His touch…my word, his touch.

His thumb brushed against the sleeve of her jacket, giving her flutters. "I'm asking if we'll be reaching some other kind of understanding, you and I."

She clung to his gaze, drowning, seeing no land in the distance. Nothing but the determined man before her.

"What kind of understanding," she asked in an odd, cragged whisper. "I don't think I understand."

But her nipples were hard as diamonds under her jacket, begging for…something. A touch; his touch.

His expression distinctly famished, he reached up and hypnotically traced her lips with his middle finger. "I wonder…" His voice was terse and textured, and he watched her with eyes that probed into the darkest, loneliest part of her. "If you'd like to kiss me again, slowly this time. And in bed."

Oh, God.

Oh, my God.

She could see by those enlarged pupils he was visualizing this!

He curled a finger under her chin. "Are you interested? Beth?"

A shudder rippled through her. The eyes. So fierce and lonely and bright.

A needle of an image stabbed into her mind, this virile beauty, hot and hard and pushing into her, and she…oh, God, she'd die.

She'd felt the powerful, restrained force in his body when she'd kissed him; all of it, it seemed, directed at keeping from kissing her back. How would it feel to have Landon Gage unleash all that suppressed strength into her? She'd crack. She'd detonate.

She'd say no. She had to.

No was a small, hard word, and small people learned to say it the hard way. Beth had learned six years ago that the hard little word *no* would have meant the difference between happiness and despair, freedom and entrapment.

Now it had to be, couldn't be anything other than *no.*

What if he insisted?

What if he didn't?

"I think we should really stick to the original plan."

But her quiet denial, although logical and truthful, planted a small, potent little ache inside her.

His nostrils flared. He stepped back with a curt nod, and Bethany realized that the brief, tight look that passed over his face was hunger. "Good to know."

Within seconds he issued explicit orders to his chauffeur, and then he stormed back into the building—leaving Bethany clutching the little black book with one hand, and Landon Gage's corporate credit card with the other.

Three

"I can now clearly see why you haven't had a woman in ages, Lan. Maybe Julian here could teach you a thing or two about subtlety."

Landon was hunched over the boardroom table the next morning with the newest copy of the *San Antonio Daily* spread out over the surface. Ignoring Garrett, he continued circling. He did this every day. He did it before they went to print. He did it afterward. Every single day.

"I don't want a woman." Landon flipped to the next section. His red pen streaked across the sports header. "Twenty-four mistakes, Garrett, and counting. I suggest you wipe that grin off your face."

"So you just want *her,* then? Because this prenup—" Garrett waved the papers in the air "—is a bit out of the norm. Jules, if you may offer an opinion on our brother's state of mind—what do you think of the prenup? It boggles the mind that a woman would sign that thing."

In a characteristically lazy move, Julian snatched up the

proffered document. He propped a shoulder against the wall and skimmed through the terms. He said, in his usual flat tones, "Twisted and somewhat distrustful. Good, Landon. Very you."

"Thank you, Jules. This is a joining of two enemies after all."

Garrett shook his head, then navigated to the chrome bar and refilled his coffee. "You're setting yourself up for a divorce from the start, brother."

Landon's pen unerringly circled. A date wrong. A period missing. "Yes, well, this time both she and I will know it's coming."

"You forget I was there last night, Lan, and in case you didn't notice, you had her pinned to *the wall*."

Landon froze. He scowled down at the page, pen in midair.

An image of Beth *pinned to the wall,* vulnerable with her lips wet, her chest heaving against his, made Landon's chest cramp. God, he hated weakness. He took advantage of it in others and loathed it in himself. He dropped the pen, raked a hand through his hair, and blew out a breath, glowering at his nosy brother. "You know what the scorpion told the turtle when it stung its ass dead?"

Garrett sipped his coffee. "Humor me."

"It's in my nature." Landon glared. "That's what it said."

"And in English?"

"In English, Garrett," Julian interjected, "his enemy's ex-partner is now going to be Landon's wife, and he doesn't trust her."

Garrett blinked, shocked. He set the coffee down with a thump. "You were the *turtle* in that story?"

"Here we go, Mr. Gage." His assistant, Donna, strode into the room with her arms full of old newspapers. Every piece written on Halifax, every page with Bethany on it. "Some of these date back several years."

Landon moved toward the pile Donna had just set atop the

table and began spreading them out. "Unfortunately, we seem to have snitches," he told his brothers.

"Seriously?"

"Beth possibly knows their names—she hinted as much. I want to see who's been rallying for Halifax for some time." He opened the top sample, skimming for mentions of Beth. He could do this on his computer, he knew. But this was the one thing where Landon was ridiculously old-fashioned—he loved the smell, the feel and the substance of paper.

"Maybe it's in the little book?" Garrett quipped.

Landon cocked his brow at him. "And maybe Halifax is in fact an idiot? I'd have to be deranged to base my actions on the writings in a book."

"Why are you marrying her if not for the book?"

Landon was not going to tell them. He continued to skim. "Perhaps I just want a war buddy."

Garrett let out a bark of laughter. He slapped his back. "Brother, you want another kind of buddy."

Landon opted for silence.

"Whatever imbecile tracks his own dirt in a book deserves what's coming to him," Julian said in disgust.

"They deserve Landon."

His brothers laughed, and Landon shoved a sheaf of clippings at each of them. "Either get back to work or make yourselves scarce."

Garrett settled down on a chair and, eyeing him through the top of the open newspaper, said, "Mom wants to know all about her, you know."

"I'm sure she got a full report from you, Garrett. Julian," Landon said, knowing his younger brother's verbiage was almost exclusively reserved for the women, "you talked to your friend in family law?"

"He'll be here tomorrow. He's catching a red eye."

"Good. Garrett, you're sending out men to cover the engagement party this evening?"

"I got it."

Landon's attention honed in on a heading. *Halifax's Wife Caught In Illicit Affair.* A picture of Beth exiting the courtroom was followed by a long, detailed analysis of the court hearing. An awful possessiveness fisted him in its grip.

Grimly, he surveyed her picture. Something in her eyes was like a plea, an innocence.

She could be a liar, a trickster, a tease.

And, damn it, Landon still wanted her.

It was that complicated, and that simple.

Last night, as he lay in bed, remembering her, he'd sought reasons for the lust raging through him and had found none. Except that her wild, reckless kiss had promised breath to a dead man.

He was a man.

She was a woman.

He wanted her.

He'd have her.

If he had to pay her, if he had to wait, if he had to wrap Halifax by the feet and hang him upside down for Beth.

He'd have her.

All right, Beth, go get him.

Her heart pounded frantically as she at last made it to the top floor of the *San Antonio Daily*. With a fortifying breath, Beth followed Landon's laser-eyed assistant—the one who'd denied her entrance to see him a number of times—to a formidable set of massive double doors.

An unfamiliar sensation assailed her as the practical woman flung the doors open and led her inside. Landon, in a sharp suit and a killer crimson tie, came around the boardroom table to greet her. Her stomach twisted and turned as he approached. What was this? Anticipation, excitement, dread?

Landon had been called many things she could remember, but the word *gentle* hadn't been among them.

"Beth," he said.

He stared directly at her as he strode over. Framed by

spiky, dark lashes, his eyes gleamed as they raked her form. Suddenly, she couldn't breathe, he looked so sexy when he smiled at her.

"Hi, Landon," she said, shyly smiling back.

His two lawyers rose to greet her, and Beth shook their outstretched hands. She'd wanted to look respectable today; she'd worn her hair back in a tidy chignon, a dark clean business suit, and a light sheen of makeup.

She had never felt so self-conscious and wondered if he approved.

Dismissing his assistant, Landon hauled out a chair for Beth and huskily said, "Sit."

She sat.

She tugged her skirt down to her knees as the men settled around the table. One began distributing a thick file around. The prenup, she hoped. So they could get this circus started.

"All right, ma'am, if you'll kindly open the document in your hands. Mr. Gage has…"

Landon's sour-faced, white-haired lawyer trailed off in consternation when Beth flipped the document open to the last page and asked, "Do any of you have a pen?"

Two pens appeared in her immediate line of vision.

She took the blue one. Landon's chair squeaked as he leaned back; he watched her with the intensity of a diving hawk. His brow creased in displeasure when she set pen to paper.

"Read it, Beth," he said.

She glanced up at him. God, he was an extremely magnetic man. He even looked grander once one knew about his reputation, but that wasn't what made her a little awestruck. It was the air of suppressed energy about him, his relaxed posture only a guise, for she could sense the latent tension in him, his hard-bitten strength. She'd tasted it in his lips.

Those lips. Stubborn and closed like the man. She'd shivered all night pretending he'd but for a second, a millisecond, opened them and let her taste all that anger and strength he so tightly reined in.

Aware of the heat crawling up her cheeks, she lowered her face, loathing to think he'd notice she was fantasizing about him by day.

"I'm not after your money, Landon. I get nothing, you said that before. And I'm poor as a mouse. You can't possibly take anything from me that Hector hasn't yanked away already."

If he thought he could discourage her from her marriage plan, well, he didn't know how stubborn she could be.

Landon cocked his head, a panther pricked into curiosity. "Prenups are not only about money."

"Miss Lewis, if I may," White Hair rushed in, face grim over the fact that Landon didn't seem to be playing hardball enough to suit him. A formal clearing of his throat later, he folded a page. "On your wedding night you're expected to deliver a little black book with contents of a personal nature regarding Dr. Hector Halifax. And as your new lawfully wedded husband, Mr. Gage agrees to provide for you in all the ways a real husband would as long as you cease any and all association with your ex until your partnership with Mr. Gage is terminated. Any infidelity on your part would result in both the termination of this agreement and your marriage." The lawyer lifted his head to speak to her directly. "I'm afraid these terms are not negotiable."

Beth was so insulted that Landon Gage would believe the worst of her just like everyone else had, she didn't move. Eyes narrowed, Landon surveyed her reaction.

He gazed across the table at her with such a proprietary, blatantly sexual expression, the ring she'd just bought in his name and placed on her finger began to scorch.

She held his gaze, her insides in turmoil. "I was faithful to Hector for as long as we were married. I'm not who they say I am."

It took him a moment to answer, and when he did, his voice could've melted the ground under her feet. "I don't really care if you were faithful to Halifax, but I care that any woman with my name attached to hers is faithful to *me*."

Faithful to Landon Gage…

Something effervescent slid through her veins, and an awful burn arrowed down her breasts to the warmed, aching place between her thighs. She felt branded, taken in a way that didn't demand their clothes to be off, as Landon's eyes sucked her into their depths and filled her body with a horrible ache.

"This is a mock marriage, but I still can't risk making any mistakes for my son. I'm not and won't be seeing anyone, period." Her eyes narrowed as another thought occurred to her. "What about you? Will you be making the same guarantees?"

"Contrary to general beliefs, I'm not a womanizer."

"But it takes just one woman to turn your life upside down," Beth countered.

"I'm looking at her now."

His succinct words and their unmistakable meaning flooded her with mortification, but they didn't seem to have the same effect on him. Landon was utterly still; unapologetic, patient, male.

Bewildered, she pulled her attention back to the contract and inhaled once or twice, she couldn't be sure. Her heart was still doing that flipping thing fish did when they were dying.

She kept hearing two words the lawyer had mentioned: intimately acquainted. "Our arrangement is strictly a… partnership. Right?" she said.

A tomb-like silence gripped the room.

His lack of response made her edgy. She stole a peek at Landon, and the intensity in his stare made her close her legs tight under the table. Hunger glimmered in the depths of his pupils, wanting, *desire*. Deeper warmth flagged her cheeks, hot as flames. "What is it, exactly, that you're demanding of me?"

More silence. His face was as unreadable as a wall as he steepled his fingers before him. "All I demand, Beth, is your fidelity. If you want to sleep with someone—you'll sleep with me."

Oh, God, when Landon spoke that last, her skin went hot. He made it sound like a promise, a decree.

And though romance and sex were the last things on her mind right now, his ill-concealed interest stirred *her* interest and made her aware of how beautifully virile he was. His body had to be the most exquisite living sculpture she'd ever beheld. Landon filled the shoulders of his jacket, his broad, strong frame overpowering the chair. The air was so charged with his masculinity, Beth couldn't help but remember she was female.

They engaged in an unsettling staring contest. The silence was finally interrupted by the brown-haired lawyer with the glasses who jumped up to the podium, sounding a bit flustered. "Well, then. On a private addendum that is to remain under Mr. Gage's supervision, we state that after gaining custody of your child, the marriage will proceed for a short time, until the waters calm down," he argued, his tone softer than White Hair's. "And when the moment comes to part ways, Mr. Gage expects you to grant him a fast, discreet divorce in exchange for a small settlement, which you and your son can use to begin a new life."

She couldn't believe the discomfort of discussing this—her son, her economics, her future divorce—in a boardroom, and briefly she thought she'd rather her seat rear back and catapult her to the sky.

For some reason, her body pulsed with Landon's stares, with his nearness. Each quiver and tingle of awareness reminded her of every want and need and craving not appeased for years, for a lifetime.

Stopping the lawyer in midsentence, she glared at the dark, still man across the table, and firmly whispered, "I don't want your settlement. It's *you* I want, you're the only one who can hurt Hector."

He betrayed no reaction, except that, on the table, his fingers slowly curled into his palm.

"Now, in case any child results out of your union, Mr. Gage gets full custody," the lawyer said.

Shock swept through Beth. "There will not *be* a child."

Her reaction was so wild and instant, Landon threw his head back and gave a bark of laughter. The sound was such an unexpected rumble, striking such a discordant note with the rest of his composed self, it sent an uninvited jolt into her system. Outraged, she glowered. He really thought this funny?

To risk a child for a little bit of sex with the man!

"You'd take a child away from me?" Beth asked, disbelieving. "Is that any way to start a marriage? An association? A *war* team?"

His eyes danced in what seemed like mirth. "The way I see it, Beth, we start with honesty, which is more than I can say for my last marriage." He sobered almost instantly, and his shoulders lifted in a shrug. "I distrust everyone, please understand."

Her chest contracted. He could've reached inside her with those tanned, blunt hands and squeezed her heart.

Beth understood too well.

He'd lost one child, and he wouldn't lose another.

He'd been betrayed. Just like Beth had been betrayed.

And when you stopped believing in people, deep down there would always be a part of you that you would never give, that nobody could *ever* again reach.

Landon wouldn't trust Beth—but he would help her. And how, she marveled, had she enlisted such a man's aid? She knew a gift from the universe when she saw one.

And there he was, sitting across the table—beautiful and ruthless. God help her.

No, God help Hector Halifax when Landon Gage was through with him.

The thought invigorated her, exhilarated her. It could've been foreplay for the way her body responded to the idea of her new husband stomping all over Hector for all the times he'd stomped on Beth.

Relaxing in her seat, she confessed with a mischievous grin, "I'm still marrying you, Landon. Toss any more hoops you want me to jump through, but I'm still marrying you."

A flicker of admiration passed across his face. Then the awesome silver in his eyes turned molten, his jaw bunched tightly—and he appeared shockingly...eager. A strange gravity entered his voice. "How about you sign those papers now, Bethany?"

The white-haired lawyer nodded in the direction of the document. "Miss Lewis? If you please?"

Bethany.

No one ever called her that.

Trying to dismiss the fact that he'd made it sound so intimate, like Bethany were his pet name for her, Beth signed the dotted line with a flourish and pointed the end of the pen at Landon. "Mrs. Gage," she said, correcting the lawyer.

Landon's eyes flashed. For a slow heartbeat, Beth pictured him lunging across the table, hauling her to him, and feasting on the lips he'd rejected the night before.

"I'm a Gage now," she whispered.

"Not yet." Slow and sure, his lips formed the wickedest, most dangerous grin she'd ever seen. "Gentlemen, I'd like to be left alone with my fiancée."

Four

A tense silence descended as soon as the doors sealed shut with a soft *click*. Then Bethany spoke. "I think we should talk about our plan. I want Hector groveling, Landon. I want him penniless, honorless, childless and whimpering like a whipped dog."

Landon's eyebrows rose.

He gazed at her and struggled not to show the way her words affected him, stirred his deepest, darkest appetites.

He had lied to his brothers.

She was so damned cute like this, murderous and practical, she probably didn't even know it.

Yeah, Landon had lied.

He *did* want a woman, and she was in this very room with him.

Somber, he rose and started around the boardroom table. His heart pounded a slow, heavy rhythm. "He'll be humiliated," he said direly.

"Publicly, I hope."

He fisted his hands. "He'll be a babbling idiot by the time we're through with him."

Bethany clasped her hands together and grinned. "I love it!"

Some unnamable sensation exploded in his chest.

He'd never had this kind of foreplay. Promising to run over the enemy while already imagining plundering the spoils of war, in this case Bethany's nice pink mouth. But he'd thought of her awkward kiss all through a sleepless night, and in his mind he'd done what he'd wanted to from the start and had taken possession of that mouth, kissing her wildly, savagely, and he'd been mad with lust when he woke. What was it about her?

He gazed into her eyes, clear blue, specked with gold and glinting with mischief.

In the sunlit space, she appeared younger and less pre-occupied than she had last night. Her hair, tied softly behind her, framed a delicate oval face, her pale slim neck adorned by a small gold necklace. Her skin was milky and smooth, but what Landon could not get over was her mouth, and the way he could still feel it on his.

Roughly he whispered, "Did you get a dress?"

"Yes."

"White and virginal?"

"Beige. And decent." From her small leather purse, she promptly took out his credit card and a folded receipt. "Thomas is my new best friend. He told me you'd like it."

His forehead furrowed. "My chauffeur saw it?"

"I wanted opinions. I don't know your taste."

"Neither does Thomas." He took his card back, and the receipt, and felt a prick of disappointment when he couldn't succeed in brushing her fingers more than a second.

"I bought a ring, too."

He took the slim fingers she held up within his and surveyed the modest band.

Her hand curled around his and electricity rushed up his

arm. The touch flew to his head like a bomb, heating his chest, his groin.

He struggled to tame the lust coursing inside him and thumbed the rock as though it were precious and not a half carat grain of rice. He drawled with deceptive casualness, "This is from me?"

"Yes." She angled her head back and studied him while he pretended to study the small rock. He noticed loosened strands of wheat-blond hair making her look sweet and vulnerable. "I like simple things," she whispered.

"It's small…" Like she was. A small little package, full of possibilities, shining the light upon revenge.

She sighed dreamily, as though she were thinking of that, too.

All of a sudden, everything about Bethany seemed to have an erotic nature. Her silky voice. Or maybe the loose, businesslike clothes which just made a man want to know what was underneath. Or maybe it was the hunger in her eyes, her thirst for blood. Halifax's blood.

Damned if Landon didn't find that sexy.

His mouth went dry as he remembered their mouths, blending, hers moving, his tight and burning, too. Surely he was making it out to be more than what it had been.

She was too thin.

And she couldn't have been softer.

She kissed too hard.

And she couldn't have been hotter.

Who was he kidding? It had been exactly as he remembered, and it had promised breath to a dead man.

"I worried you'd change your mind today," she said, retrieving her hand.

There was something perverse about wanting to cover that smile with his lips.

He'd played honorably once. For his son. But Chrystine's treachery had left him with nothing. He didn't plan to end with nothing now, not ever again.

He regarded her steadily, crossing his arms. "Has a Gage ever given you his word before?" Halifax's woman, he thought. And now mine.

"No."

"Then what gave you reason to doubt it?"

She shrugged. "I've learned not to trust what people say."

Feeling himself smile, he signaled to his adjoining office. Trust was important to him. His brothers trusted him, his mother, his employees—and soon enough Bethany would trust him, he'd make sure of it. "We should get down to business."

"By all means." Swiftly on her feet, she clutched her purse and followed him into the wood-paneled office. "Revenge awaits."

They were smiling as they walked. Smiling, together. And suddenly the thought of living with her and not having her was intolerable, not an option.

This little Buffy the Husband Slayer was going to be his wife, and he was making her his woman. This little thing thirsty for revenge would get her deepest desire from Landon, delivered on a silver platter—Halifax on a tray with an apple in his mouth—and Landon would take his own justice one step further.

Bethany, her son, Halifax's family…

Would be Landon's.

"I'm organizing a celebration tonight at La Cantera." He moved behind his desk and derived a purely male satisfaction at the approval in her gaze. "I'm fairly certain it would help your image to be seen at a small, tasteful gathering to announce our engagement. Wouldn't you?"

She took a seat across from his and thoughtfully considered. "I agree," she then said, crossing her legs. "Yes. And when would the wedding be?"

Beautiful slim legs. Damn, what were they talking about? The wedding, right.

"Friday at city hall works for you?"

"Of course," she said, her teeth white behind her smile.

Landon had to tear his eyes away from her, as he punched the intercom button on his phone. "Donna, are my brothers available? I'd like them to come in."

"I'll get them."

It was important for his fiancée to get better acquainted with his brothers before the press flocked around them tonight. Thankfully, within minutes, his efficient assistant led both men inside. They wore their best, politest smiles.

"Donna," Landon said as he started toward Beth. "Have the car ready in three minutes."

"Right away, sir."

He shot both men a "behave" look past Beth's shoulders and then grasped her arm to lead her forward. "Bethany, you met Garrett, didn't you?"

"Yes, he seemed very nice."

"He's not." Landon brought her over to Jules. "Julian John, Bethany Lewis."

"A pleasure," drawled Julian as they shook hands.

Landon bent his head to hers. "He's not nice, either, Bethany."

She grinned.

And when that white grin reached his eyes, Landon thought: *I'm good as dead, just like Halifax.*

This isn't going so bad, Beth thought, relieved as Landon led her through the halls of the executive floor of the *San Antonio Daily* toward the elevator bank. Not so bad at all.

True, they hadn't yet discussed their plan in detail, but it didn't matter. Beth knew a lot of things about Hector. Little rocks to toss in his path. Big boulders, rather.

She couldn't wait to watch him trip.

"They're my brothers but they drive me mad. It's a chemical thing," Landon said.

As people stared in their direction from their cubicles, Beth frowned. Did they know she was marrying their boss soon? Did they know it was a farce?

"Your clothes are in the car?" Landon asked then.

She spared him a quick nervous glance. Maybe they just thought it odd to see their boss smiling down at a woman. "Yes."

"Excellent." His cool nod, combined with that same lingering, totally unexpected curl of his lips, made her return his smile. "There's apparently much speculation about you around here, Bethany," he idly commented.

She nodded, already having surmised as much. But now something else troubled her mind. "Where are we going, Landon?"

The elevator doors rolled open, and he guided her inside. "My place."

"Your place," she repeated.

"My home. Where you'll be living with me."

They stepped off the elevator and crossed the marbled lobby, and Beth was struck with curiosity about what the next couple of months living with him would be like. "It's a good idea for you to start getting settled in before the wedding. This will make our relationship more plausible."

Beth could only nod at his logic.

They rode quietly in the back of the Navigator and, twenty minutes later, arrived at the entrance to a gated community. Then passing a sprawling emerald-green golf course and sweeping estates, the car halted at another gated entry.

Beyond the forged iron gates, a two-story, gothic-inspired, gray stone-brick house loomed in view. The lawns surrounding it were perfectly manicured, lush and green.

"Wow. This is it?"

"Yes," Landon said absently, then seemed to come around from whatever he'd been reading on his phone and met her questioning blue gaze. "You expected different?"

She shrugged. "An apartment, maybe."

"You forget." He opened his hand; a beautiful, long-fingered, tanned hand that for some reason made her skin pebble. "I used to have a family."

A family, yes.

He'd had a family he could not recover no matter what he did.

Her chest gained a thousand pounds at the sad thought. No matter how hopeless her situation had seemed lately, Bethany couldn't begin to imagine the pain of losing a loved one so abruptly.

"I'm sorry," she said quietly.

She followed him from the car and up the steps to the arched entrance.

They'd died in an accident—his wife and child. One rainy night.

One rainy night when Hector Halifax had been leaving Bethany with her newborn in her arms to meet with Landon's wife.

Eyeing his stoic, sculpture-like appearance through the corner of her eye, Beth wondered what else Landon knew. What he didn't know.

As they entered the spacious limestone-floored house, Beth noticed two huge mastiffs near the darkened fireplace. They rose up on their wide black paws when spotting Landon, tails starting to wag as they padded over.

"Mask and Brindle," Landon crisply said. She supposed the fawn-colored, two-hundred-pound beast with the black face was Mask, and the striped, black-and-brown, two-hundred-pound beast was Brindle.

She took a step back as they approached to sniff her, swallowing back a gasp when she bumped into Landon's solid chest behind her.

Dogs!

And she thought this would be easy?

Landon steadied her, his hands on her upper arms, his voice in her ear. "They don't bite."

A shiver that had nothing to do with fear skittered up her spine. "Oh."

"Sit."

The dogs sat. Their tongues were a mile long and dangled lazily while they waited to do more of Landon's bidding.

"See?"

He still had not let go of her. She angled her head just a fraction, and their noses almost bumped. "A dog bit me when I was little," she confessed, for some reason thinking it appropriate to whisper. As though she were in a church or a library. "I've had a healthy respect for them ever since."

"Yet you still married one?" He smiled.

"I married a snake—it's an entirely different species."

When he continued to smile that almost-there smile, she could almost feel it against her lips. At this close distance, Beth spotted the darker silver rim around his irises spreading like smoke across his eyes. Her knees went weak. He really was gorgeous.

Was he seducing her? God, it was working. His touch, his voice, the heat in his eyes.

"These two are a bit heavy to roll over," he said quietly, clenching her shoulders a bit, "but you can ask them to shake your hand if you'd like."

"Later," she said, blushing because she began to see a little complication. This man had an effect on her. A huge effect. He didn't even have to kiss her for that. His presence was an open, blatant call to all things feminine inside her which she shouldn't, for the love of God, embrace right now.

"Good doggies," she said, staying clear of the intimidating pair while at the same time putting distance between her and Landon.

After commanding, "Release"—a word which sent the dogs plopping back down before the fireplace—he led her up the sweeping limestone staircase.

The bedroom they entered at the far end of the hall was spacious, sparsely furnished, decorated in a black-and-white palette that went heavy on the black and sparse on the white. A guest room, she supposed.

But a string of unexpected words popped into her head.

"If you want to sleep with someone, you'll sleep with me."

Her stomach twisted as though she'd just taken a plunge on a roller coaster, and she had trouble shaking off the thought of sharing that very big bed with the very big man standing to her right.

There was no denying there had been some serious vibes going on between the two of them back in the conference room. But Beth had to concentrate on what was important: getting David back.

Her life was a mess and she'd taken fretting to a whole new art form. She didn't need more worries.

Hopefully, Landon wasn't getting any bed-sharing ideas.

She peered up at his hard profile. Of course he wasn't. Landon was in it for the little black book, and for what she could tell him about Hector.

He'd entered the room first and pulled off his jacket as she followed. "This is your room." His jacket fell with a thud atop a corner chair. "Unless you want to sleep in mine."

She wasn't sure if he was kidding or not and didn't have time to decide. "I'll keep this one, thank you."

His white cotton shirt pulled attractively across his shoulders as he calmly held out his hand. "The book? Do you mind if I have a look now?"

"Yes, I do mind, actually."

He wiggled his fingers. "Come on. Give it over, Bethany."

She frowned. "I said you could read it when you married me, didn't I?"

His eyes sparkled in amusement. "We're more than halfway there—the sooner I see what that bastard's after the sooner I can skin his ass on a platter."

The thought of Hector laid out like a dead pig on a tray was too lovely to deny. It brought butterflies to her stomach. "All right, but only the first two pages. You can read the rest after the wedding."

She waited for Thomas to bring up her suitcase, then extracted the black book from the outside zippered compartment. "Okay, so let's talk about our plan. I want Hector to be left with nothing. Absolutely nothing."

Landon's lips twitched, and when she noticed she felt herself respond. Damn, how did he do that? Every time he smiled she found herself smiling back like a dope.

After handing over the black leather book, she followed Landon's stealthy movements as he hauled a chair out from behind a desk and sat. He calmly paged through it.

"So why did you marry him?" he asked.

"I was young and pregnant." Beth plopped down on the edge of the bed, suddenly uncomfortable in her skirt and jacket. "And all right, yes, stupid."

He flipped to the second page and didn't raise his head, his hard, aquiline profile unreadable.

"I used to wonder why he'd want to marry me," she admitted with a shrug. "I felt so flattered. He would call every day and ask to see me. Then I guess he saw what a good daughter I was to my parents. He wanted an obedient, biddable wife—like all men desperate to feel powerful want someone meek."

Landon looked up, and when his lips smiled and did that eat-your-heart-out thing *again,* she felt a strange elated sensation.

"You were biddable, Beth? What happened?"

She burst out laughing. "Oh, stop it."

"Did you ever let him medicate you, Beth?"

She frowned at the question, at the hard edge in the word "medicate". There had been times when Hector had diagnosed her "problems"; she needed to grow up, and get serious, and act like his wife. Apparently, he hadn't had any pills for Beth's ailments. "Hector specializes in chronic pain—and nothing of mine ever ached except my pride."

And now she'd grown up, hadn't she? Now she'd put all her efforts into acting like someone's wife—*Landon's*.

His finger slid down a page, and he read a name out loud. "Joseph Kennar. He's one of our reporters."

"He's bought."

Landon appeared anything but surprised. "Everyone's for sale unfortunately." He continued reading, his eyes sharp as the point of a knife on the page. "Macy Jennings. Another one of our reporters."

"Also bought." Then she added, with a bit of disgust at herself because she could not, for the life of her, explain why she told him all this. "Hector would do anything to ensure he had the best reputation. He wanted to treat anyone that was rich and powerful, and keeping his name clean in the media guaranteed this. But I suspect Hector did more with Macy than just exchange money and favors."

"And you let him?"

She let him? Had she? Just so he left her alone? "Well I…I guess I ignored him. I thought that…for David I would tolerate it." God. Stupid stupid stupid. What would Landon think of her?

"But then?"

He seemed so inordinately interested in her that she was grateful his head was still bent over the book. Otherwise, his questions and his unyielding attention would be too much. Still, she felt so stupid over what she'd tolerated.

"But then I couldn't do it even for my baby," she admitted. There. All right, that wasn't bad, that she had finally found her courage and left the sleaze. She'd sold David on the "new adventure" he and Mommy would take, and he'd been excited.

She seized the nearby pillow and clutched it to her chest, suddenly needing to hold on to something. Every time she thought of David her stomach lurched as if she'd been poisoned.

"I left Hector a year ago and took David with me, and I found a job at a flower shop. Hector made contact weeks later. He apologized, said he wanted me back, but all I wanted was to be free. Of him. I filed for divorce and when he found out, he ranted and threatened, said I wouldn't see a dime. He was right, I didn't. But I was still happy. Just me and David and Mom. But then he filed for custody."

"He struck where it most hurt," Landon said, slapping the book shut with a deafening sound.

He'd read only two pages. As she'd asked him to. And something about that, the respect for her wishes in that action, made the walls inside her crack a fraction.

Wow. An honorable man. Who'd have known she'd ever see one of those?

"He *did* strike where it most hurt." Beth closed her eyes briefly as the pain sliced her anew. "He tore me apart. I couldn't even explain or say goodbye to my own son."

And what is my baby doing now? Who hugs him instead of me? And when will I be able to hold him again?

"Hector will be furious when he learns we've married," she admitted, struggling not to shiver.

Landon leaned back in his chair and canted his head, his lips thinning in distaste. "Let the man stew for a bit, Beth. Wonder what we're concocting."

But suddenly it struck her that more than angry, Hector would probably be annoyed. He treated patients with chronic pain and he'd always felt above them—like *he* would never feel the kind of pain his patients did. But Beth knew that he did. His wounds were internal; and they had festered.

His entire adult life, he'd seemed irked by the knowledge that there was someone better in this city, someone he couldn't touch.

Someone the "love of his life" had chosen over him.

Hector had never recovered from that blow.

"I've never seen someone hate as powerfully as he hates you," she admitted, and a wave of embarrassment washed over her.

She should've done something before. Sooner. She should've run with her son the moment he was born.

Hector had married Beth, and for a time she'd believed he cared. But in mere months she'd realized the truth. She'd been the means to make another woman jealous. Hector had been crazy about Landon's wife, feverishly wanting what he couldn't have and loathing the man who had ruined his chances with her. Chrystine would've married him if Landon hadn't been the better man. And Beth had never seen a man so hell-bent on ruining someone for being honest, richer, better, like Hector had.

"He was in love with my wife," Landon said noncommittally as he crossed his arms, a neutral expression on his face.

"I'd say more like obsessed. He didn't seduce her out of love, Landon. He seduced her to humiliate you."

"You're right, Beth."

The words, steely and loaded with the promise of vengeance, whirled like a storm inside the room.

Beth felt it inside her, like one would feel a death wish, fury, hunger.

She had never understood this hatred of Hector's—until now that it ate at her, demanded some sort of retribution, that she take a hand at justice once and for all.

Hector had lied about her. He'd taken *David!*

He'd turned her into a sick person who only thought of revenge. She'd never been this vicious but the thought of hurting her ex-husband held so much appeal she felt flutters of evil, cruel excitement at the mere prospect. At night, her fantasies weren't girlish or even romantic anymore. At night, she felt so angry, so frustrated, she imagined how good she'd feel once she'd clawed the bastard's eyes out.

Did Landon feel this, too?

Would he stop at nothing, like her, until they'd ended up the winners?

Her pulse hitched when he pushed his chair back and rose with the ease of a wild cat. A large, stealthy wild cat who'd insisted that if she wanted to sleep with someone, she'd sleep with *him*.

"You're certain you're up for tonight?" he asked. "The press can be exhausting and so can my mother."

She wrinkled her nose. It was a miracle a powerful creature like Landon had even had a mother. That he'd been vulnerable once. And oh, yes, she'd been born for tonight, she was more than ready for it. "Believe me, so can mine be."

His brows flew up in genuine interest. "What did you tell yours?"

"That I finally found a white knight." When he didn't smile at her stupid joke, Beth sobered up and hugged the pillow tighter. "I told her I was marrying a man who would help me get David back. She was ecstatic. And you? Your mother?"

"I mentioned she should prepare to welcome my new wife. She was stunned speechless after my announcement, which is unusual for my mother."

"But she knows this is temporary?"

He didn't seem in the least bit concerned, and gave a nonchalant lift of his shoulders. "I didn't go into details, but she'll know where I'm coming from when she realizes who you are."

"Were," she corrected, watching him head for the door. "I'm reinventing myself now."

His interest clearly piqued, he turned around and crossed his arms over his broad chest, stretching the material of his shirt. "Who do you want to be now?"

"Me. Bethany. Whoever I was before Hector Halifax put his filthy hands on me."

For the first time in many many years, she felt hopeful, and as she drank in the brooding dark image of Landon, she wondered if he even realized this gift he gave her without meaning to.

She could smell him in the room, cologne and soap, and the scent was oddly reassuring. A surge of warmth, divine and wicked, began to pump in her bloodstream. His neck was tanned and thick, and his hands were wide, large, the fingers long and blunt. She had always been fascinated by men's hands, and his were so very virile.

"Have I said thank you?" she asked, her voice strangely thick.

He was silent for a moment, then, his voice equally terse, "Wait until you get your kid back."

Her temperature spiked. He was frightening, so powerful, so male, that Bethany had to remind herself he was on her side.

"Landon," she said before he could exit, "would you mind if I invited David to the celebration tonight? I'd like to invite my son."

"I don't mind."

"But what if he comes with him?"

"Halifax?" Landon leaned negligently against the door frame as he contemplated, unruffled like only powerful, self-possessed men could be. "He wouldn't dare."

"But if he does? You will be civil, won't you? I wouldn't want David to be exposed to any violence."

With an amused, wolfish quirk of his lips, he shook his dark head. "Beth, I'm posting a dozen reporters around the premises so they can capture me ogling over you. Believe me, I'm not announcing to the world what we'll be doing." Did he just wink at her? "Don't fret. They'll think we make love, not war."

Five

Make love.

Was there even room for making love when you were at war?

The nervousness welling inside her made her breathless as they drove to the engagement party.

Landon sat behind the wheel of his sporty blue-and-tan Maserati, tearing through the highway while Beth replayed the phone call she'd just made in her head.

She hadn't expected David to answer; he was too young and was observed too closely for that. But to the nanny who'd picked up in his stead, Beth had explained about her engagement party and how much she'd love for David to be there. Beth prayed that the kindnesses she had shown this young woman in the past would be repaid now.

Say you're taking him out, she'd thought as she'd given her the hotel address, *take him out for a walk, and let me see my son tonight.*

She considered the possibility of Anna mentioning her call

to Hector and shuddered. No. The next time she hoped to see her ex-husband was in court.

Facing her *and* Landon.

Landon studied her in the dark interior of the car. She shuddered again, this time, in pure feminine awareness. She'd never known she could respond to a man like this.

He wasn't even doing anything, for the most part kept his eyes on the highway, but she was somehow inhumanly aware of his presence and his occasional straying gaze—her own gaze felt magnetized to it. His darkened eyes said more than they should as he quietly watched her.

In his eyes, she saw vengeance, justice and something just as dark, just as dangerous she dare not put a name to.

"Relax, Beth," he said, his voice, although mild, powerful and commanding as it cut through the silence. "Trust me a little. By the time he loses his pride, his word, his company and his child, Hector Halifax will have no idea what hit him."

But it was Beth who felt struck an hour later, while their petite celebration was underway in the sprawling gardens of the prestigious La Cantera Golf Resort. And Beth knew exactly what hit her.

The sight of the looming figure blocking her entry to the hotel lobby.

She'd thought it proper to rush inside a moment and check her makeup and hair before the press took their pictures. She had to look sharp, smart—respectable. Show the world that no, she wasn't a slut, and she wasn't the clouds-for-brain careless mother Hector had painted her for, either.

She'd been eager to discover if David had come.

But she didn't see her boy. She didn't even make it to the ladies room.

Instead, she found Hector.

Correction: Hector found her.

Her blood froze. She felt his presence at five feet like an open assault on her person, there was such antipathy in the air.

He just stood there, blond and blue-eyed in the cool, calm

moonlight. People always used to think he was her brother. But no. He was a monster. A polite, cold-hearted monster.

He'd taken things from her he shouldn't have taken, abused her in mental and emotional ways she should never have allowed, trampled her innocence, her self-respect. *Do you know how to do anything except stand there looking pretty, Beth? Are you goddamned stupid?*

Bethany had sucked it up, because that is what her mother had taught her to do. "Beth, if your father didn't like the eggs, I'd suck it up and make him new ones. Suck it up, baby, I didn't raise whiners in this house."

Except with Hector it wasn't the eggs. It was how Beth ran the house with a free hand, how she put their child in danger if he licked his hands and ate germs from the supermarket cart. It was everything about Beth.

Her father had been strict and her mother had sucked it up. But her mother had received love and praise from her husband, too, while Beth had received nothing. Months after a lavish wedding and a hopeful "I take thee," Beth had found herself a shell of a person, glancing at women out in the street and envying how carefree they looked, how independent.

Beth had forgotten how to laugh for her kid.

By the day she packed her and David's bags and left Hector, she'd spent months building up her self-esteem, gathering the remains of what had once been a person and trying to become someone again. A mother.

Even *that* he'd taken away from her.

Now they faced each other, and she wasn't sure who appeared more stunned. They'd spotted each other in the same instant. His mouth parted. She expected something would come out of it, but for a moment nothing did.

He took in her appearance—the dress Landon had provided at the last minute. Elegant and midnight blue, it made her skin seem smooth as porcelain and her eyes more electric.

Her heart beat one, two, three times.

Hector's doctorly face—the one he used to persuade his

patients to do whatever he told them to because he, in fact, was a god—failed him. His mouth clamped shut and color rushed up to his face, as though the sight of her—alive and looking well—infuriated him. He took a step.

"You're marrying Gage." The sneer lashed at her like a whip crack, and she hated that she instinctively flinched, panicked into immobility.

"You're marrying Gage and you expect me to let you see our son? Why did you call him? You're forbidden to talk to him. You're forbidden to see him, or have you forgotten?"

Confrontation. God, she hated this.

Not here, *not here.*

Beth glanced around the patio, and when she saw nothing but shadows, her chest constricted with foreboding.

No one was within hearing range, unless she screamed.

But with reporters here?

She didn't want to. She hadn't screamed the time she'd found a hairy tarantula in her kitchen, and she wouldn't scream now.

Oh, God, taking in the sight of his boyish, pretty face, she couldn't believe she could be disgusted by any living being so much. Not even cockroaches.

In the space of six years, this man had managed to turn a healthy human being into a puddle of fear, a nobody, a robot, and even now as she stared at him, she felt that fear, that anger, that despair that he had her son with him and she didn't.

He had everything.

But she had Landon.

Struggling to tame her emotions at that thought, she eased back a step, but that only made him move forward. Hector seethed with palpable anger, while fury and hurt churned inside her belly. *He took my little boy from me.* Her voice sharpened. "David is as much my son as he is yours." How dare Anna tell him she'd called? How dare he take David away from her? How dare they?

"And you're not seeing him again, I'll make sure of that!"

Blasted by the frigidness of his words, she could do nothing as he caught her elbow before she could run and yanked her forward, his serpent's hiss thrust into her ear.

"If you ever, ever, tell Gage anything about me or my practice…"

With a breath-clogging twist, Beth wrenched free and cried mutinously, "What? What are you going to do?"

"You don't want to know, Beth, but I assure you, you'll wish you hadn't opened your mouth to speak."

A gust of wind lashed at her, kicking up strands of her hair. She pushed them back and glanced around one more time, frantically now, unable to help wishing Landon could see her. Hell, she almost wished his dogs were here, flanking her. She'd never thought she'd be so happy to see two beasts like that near her person before, but the relief she felt thinking of the bodily harm they could inflict on Hector made her suddenly love that pair.

"If you put a hand on David," she warned with renewed courage, her nails biting into her hands as she clenched her fists.

"I don't need to put a hand on him to hurt him and you know it. I'll just tell him the truth about his mother and see how he likes it."

"Lies, all lies!" Nearly bursting with rage, Beth edged backward, wanting to flee.

"I'm not alone now, Hector," she said, sucking in a calming breath. His eyes flared slightly and Beth remembered Hector saying how much he'd relish destroying the Gages. Well, she wouldn't let him! "Landon is much more powerful than you are," she informed him proudly. "And he won't rest until David's back where he belongs."

She didn't know if Hector believed her, but in her panic-ridden thoughts, she prayed he did and put a cork on his threats already. This didn't have to get so bloody. For David's sake, in fact, she wished she could come to a satisfying arrangement in the most quiet way possible—but she knew her new husband deserved better. He deserved his revenge.

And she was so starved for Hector's blood, she wanted him to get it.

"You're mine, Beth." Hector hissed out the poisonous words. "I'm here, right here." He knocked his head with his knuckles, hard. "You're weak, and I've got you, I *control* you, and I will have you again, you will come crawling back to me, mark my words."

With that, Hector spun around and walked away. Her eyes burned as she watched his retreating back until everything in her line of vision became a blur. The encounter left her limp. She fell in a pool of her own skirts, and sat back against the wall of the building.

"God," she shakily gasped, suddenly covering her face in her hands. How could a person you hated so much have given you the thing you most loved in the world?

"Say, Gordon, where did my daughter run off to?"

"Landon," he said to his new mother-in-law, a chirpy, sunny woman with a confused, tremulous smile. "And I'll find her, Mrs. Lewis, give me a moment."

The woman appeared bemused as to what he'd said and nodded twice. She really *was* deaf.

Depositing her with Beth's father, who currently got acquainted with Julian John, Landon scoured the gardens and opted to check the least trafficked entry to the lobby. The press was getting restless. They wanted their money shot and the success of their plan depended on Landon to deliver.

He found her lying on the ground by the side of the long building. He spotted the midnight blue skirts of her dress first pooled all around her, her hair covering her profile as she mumbled angrily to herself.

He halted in his tracks. "Bethany?"

Her head snapped back. "Landon." The breath *whooshed* out of her.

He felt a sliver of dread at the sight of her pale face, as pale as the moonlight, her eyes as round as the moon but dark and terrified.

"What are you doing?" he asked uneasily, stalking forward and dropping on his haunches.

Bethany craned her neck back to meet his gaze. Her smile lacked conviction. "Hey," she said in a quavery voice, then she sighed and rubbed her face with unsteady hands. "I was feeling miserable all by myself."

Landon was at a loss. He knew how to deal with his mother—a blunt, forthright woman who'd borne three sons and had survived a husband who'd put any alpha to shame. But Beth…she was so rigid and so wound up, fighting so hard to stand when her life had crumpled around her, he just didn't know what to say to her. He couldn't explain how easily he understood this, understood that she was looking for herself, for her strength, while at the same time searching desperately for a light at the end of the tunnel.

He reached out and covered one milky white hand with his, awkwardly at first, shocked by his body's instant reaction to such a simple touch. "You okay?"

Hell, it had been too long since he touched anyone. Too long since he'd wanted to make this sort of contact, this contact he enjoyed making with Beth. Her shoulders sagged as she gripped his fingers, and a jolt of her scent made his nostrils flare. Lemons. God, she smelled so good he found himself leaning closer for another whiff.

"Hector was just here," she said, squeezing his hand.

His hackles raised, every muscle in his body clenching. "Where?"

Beth sighed drearily while thoughts of Halifax slammed into Landon's mind, one after the other. Halifax being seen by the press…Halifax meeting in secret with Beth, swiftly and efficiently ruining the new, respectable image Landon planned for his fiancée.

His grip tightened so hard Beth winced. "Beth, where?"

"He's gone, I think."

He released her. But a swift, overwhelming anger surged inside him like a tidal wave, and his mind clamored for him to do some serious damage to that weasel. Halifax could spoil everything. He could ruin their pretend engagement, make the press believe she was still a treacherous Jezebel and that now she'd found a new target: Landon.

It was a hard sell, but not impossible.

Nothing was impossible for a twisted mind like Halifax's. Christ, the man begged for it. And Landon was aching to give him what he deserved. Not here, not tonight, but the bastard had had it coming for a long, long time, and now the clock was ticking. Tick, tock, tick, tock.

The man had the balls to waltz into his engagement party and exchange words with his bride—just like he'd had the balls years ago to sleep with his wife.

Landon breathed out through his nose, attempting to focus, control his rage. Belatedly he noticed Beth's bewilderment and felt his gut clench.

Searching for something to say other than the twisted things he wanted to do to the man, he gently stroked the top of her shiny blonde head with his hand, curving his palm around her skull and drawing her gaze to his. He had to do something, say something to comfort her. "Here I thought you'd met my mother." He felt his lips curl upward.

She made a sound, like a laugh, then regarded him as if he'd just become a giant scorpion. "Landon, maybe this wasn't such a good idea. Us...marrying..."

He shot her a get-serious look, then seized her chin in one hand and searched her gaze. A wrenching sensation slammed into his midsection. "Maybe I underestimated you," he murmured. "You have feelings for him."

"I have hate!"

"Then *use* it! Hang on to it, Bethany. Your hate will feed mine. You want me to be ruthless, don't you?"

"Yes."

"You want me to have no heart? To trample him to the ground?"

"Yes."

"Do you want your child back?"

"Of course I do!"

"Smile then—and get out there with me. Let the reporters have a good look at my future wife." He helped her to her feet, gritting his teeth as he felt his body respond when her breasts brushed against his chest on her way up.

She wiped at her face and straightened her shoulders, amazing him with how easily she composed herself. "I'm sorry, I'm not usually so emotional."

"Hold your head high."

"Okay."

"Hold my hand."

Her palm felt cool when she slipped it inside his, and he gave it a squeeze as he guided her around the corner. She walked easily beside him, but a hint of alarm still lingered in her voice. "Landon, I feel like all these people can see right through me. That they know this is a farce and that I have no clue who you are. I mean, do you like sports? Do you take your coffee black or—?"

"I like sports. And I like strong coffee."

"I have mine with milk, two Splendas and cream."

"Do me a favor, Beth?"

"What?"

"Just act like you love me."

Six

Blinding camera lights exploded as they approached.

Beth put all her efforts into her smile and struggled to remember *why* she needed to fool all of these people. *Look fabulous, Beth, look besotted, ecstatic,* she thought, *so ecstatic a judge won't resist granting custody of David to such a dazzling couple.*

Landon was greeting the press in a congenial tone when a brazen reporter elbowed himself forward, mike in hand. "Miss Lewis—how does your ex-husband feel about the wedding?"

Beth had not been prepared for that question. She and Landon had reviewed some facts in the car when she'd asked him for instructions on dealing with the press, and he'd said, "Whatever you do, don't lie. Twist the truth however you want, but don't lie, not to them. One lie will take your credibility, and then you'll never get it back."

Very admirable and smart of him. But now she glanced

worriedly at Landon and saw that he smiled at the group, an arrogant lilt of his lips that made his eyes turn to ice.

"If the good doctor's smart about it, he'll wish us well," he said, and with a nod, signaled to another reporter in a move that granted him the next question.

"Miss Lewis, how did you two meet?"

She spoke quickly, grateful at how easy the answer came. "We met at a benefit. Just one peek at this man and I was done for." Landon smiled at her, and her stomach tumbled.

"Mr. Gage, after so many years a widowed bachelor, why marry now?"

Landon's sudden frown indicated he thought the questioner may, just may, be a little bit stupid.

After allowing this reaction to sink in among the reporters, he spread an arm out toward Beth. "Take a good look at her, gentlemen, and tell me what healthy red-blooded American male wouldn't be honored to have this woman at their side?"

Hoots and a "Right on, Landon!" spread across the group, and a few other questions came up, to which he and Beth easily responded. Did he think she was beautiful? When she was young, she'd been thought beautiful by boys. But now? After Hector?

A few other questions came her way, and Beth tried to keep the mood light and happy, following Landon's cue and wry jokes. Then Landon nodded at a young man she'd heard was a famous celebrity/social-scene blogger.

"Any hints on where you'll be honeymooning?" the man asked.

"Somewhere quiet," Landon replied with a cool smile, and another round of flashes exploded.

"Mrs. Gage, how do you feel about the wedding?"

This time the microphone was held out to Landon's mother, who stood a few feet behind them, and Beth's spirits sunk. Her future mother-in-law would hate her. What woman who witnessed their son being dragged to war wouldn't?

They'd been introduced just hours ago and Beth had felt like the proverbial bug under the woman's silver-handled loupe. But Mrs. Gage had class, and she said with a regal tilt of her head, "I'm thrilled to have another woman in the family. We haven't had much time to talk, but I can already tell Beth and I have a lot in common."

Like what? Landon? Beth wondered.

A reporter next turned to Garrett. "How about you, Garrett, any thoughts on your new sister-in-law?"

Garrett made a mischievous face that sparked up an attractive glint in his eye. "Regret that Lan saw her first."

The reporters laughed, and Beth jumped in, suddenly inspired. "Actually, *I* spotted him first."

Landon smiled at her, pulled her close to his side, and her stomach went crazy again. Within moments, Landon waved the press off, insisting they end the session. "Last shot, guys."

"How about a kiss from the couple."

He ignored the suggestion and let them take another round of pictures, still holding her, but only lightly.

"Kiss her, Mr. Gage," another reporter encouraged.

He smiled sharply, and swiftly handed her a glass of champagne—and they drank to more flashes.

Though they both continued to smile, something sizzled between them.

Beth heard a chorus of requests begin and hated how silly, how *predictable,* how absurd it was to be asked to kiss someone you really had no reason to be kissing.

The chorus rose to a crescendo all of a sudden, deafening her clamoring heartbeat. "Kiss her! Kiss her! Kiss her!"

Her color rose as Landon took her champagne flute and set it aside. "Well, Beth."

It was inevitable.

"If there are any doubts left, we might as well dispel them."

Of course, she should take one for the team, do this for David…

The pressure of his fingers on her back brought her one step closer to him. Their eyes met. He smiled down at her, but his gaze held a warning. A request to comply.

His eyes were heat and flames; black coals burning. *It's all for show, all for show*—Beth recited the thought like a mantra—*sliding your hand into his, your legs turning to syrup, not remembering why you're here, it's all for show.*

She suppressed a tremble as he ducked his head, still smiling.

She wanted to smile like him, but couldn't. It was an act, it had to be, how she parted her lips and waited for his mouth. He breathed in her ear. "Easy."

She wanted to melt.

The way he concentrated on her mouth made her go hot.

Their lips touched. His brushed over hers at first, a wistful, feathery touch that sent her control careening down a precipice she feared she'd never recover. She held her breath until her lungs burned and found her fingers digging into his shoulders.

He didn't have to put his hands, warm and strong, on the sides of her face as he kissed her.

He didn't have to smell like he did, or brush her lips so exquisitely.

He didn't have to slide his tongue inside, but he did.

Desire hit her like a cannon blast, making her legs tremble. She gripped him harder and he slanted his head, in command as his mouth closed over hers, taking hers, leading. Wow, he deserved an Oscar. She believed that kiss to be as real as the reporters believed it, as real as her skyrocketing pulse. It wasn't a messy kiss, it was soft, long and warm, and it was heartbreaking.

Because she'd wanted it since the moment she'd seen him come to her rescue after the Hector debacle. She'd wanted it since he'd helped her to her feet, his body a fortress of strength and warmth. She'd wanted it since the first reporter suggested they kiss and he'd pretended ignorance.

God, maybe she'd wanted it forever.

He didn't end the kiss abruptly, but quietly, his mouth lingering over hers, as though still not ready to detach, their breaths mingling as, inch by inch, he drew back. She almost moaned, her lips burned, her body burned, the heights of need to which he'd sent her unimaginable.

Slowly, Landon adjusted their stance, shifting so that she covered his hardness with her rear.

Noticing she was flustered, he waved a commanding hand at the press. "Enough. That's enough pictures tonight."

The flashes stopped. Photographers stepped back a few paces, but Landon didn't allow Beth the same luxury; his big hand rested on her hip proprietarily. His fingers bit into her skin, keeping her against him.

When the reporters dispersed, Beth wiggled free, avoiding his gaze, then snatched another champagne glass and went behind the safety of a twisting oak. Cloaked in shadows, she slumped against the tree trunk and blinked into the darkness.

How could a man kiss like that? She'd felt stroked all over, indecently stroked. She'd never been so aware of having such sensitive, eager nipples.

She kept telling herself that having sex with him would be a bad idea, a risky venture, one where if she ended up pregnant, he'd take her child just like Hector had. But even as her mind raced with protests, the other side of her brain already formulated a list of ways to avoid pregnancy while bringing their passion to fruition.

Damn. How was she supposed to say no to a guy who kissed like a volcanic avalanche?

She exhaled a breath she'd been holding, tightened her hold on her glass. She felt…helpless. Resented having to give him any kisses. It had been difficult last night at the hotel in her awkward attempts to enlist him, and it had been more so now that they'd been watched. She didn't want to know his taste and now, well, now she'd never be able to forget it.

"You handled yourself well."

Startled, she spotted her mother-in-law a few feet away. The woman wore an emerald green dress and a string of pearls, and her smile beamed with approval.

In the face of all that dignity and Texan charm, Beth forced herself to straighten, smoothing her hands along her hips. "I'm not new to the newspaper scene. It's just nice to be treated with respect for a change."

A chilly breeze sent the skirts of their dresses fluttering. "Then let me give you a piece of advice, Beth." She jerked her chin in the press's direction. "You win those people's hearts, and you win the world."

Beth narrowed her eyes, confused by this bit of wisdom. She'd been swept into Landon's golden, glittering world of silk and velvet and music tonight—and they were lies, all lies, all for one purpose only.

Didn't the woman know?

"Landon's already doing that," she then replied, cautiously. "Winning their hearts and the world."

She gazed out at the gardens that led to the parking lot. They were vast and beautiful but they were shrouded in darkness. Dark and beckoning like Landon.

Past her shoulder, she spotted him, polite and easy as he talked to some of the reporters. He was such a solid, dynamic man, every time she saw him she found herself holding her breath.

"Why you, I wonder."

That comment snapped Beth around. There wasn't antagonism in her voice but genuine curiosity glimmered in her soft gray eyes.

"Me?"

"Well…" A jeweled hand fluttered in the air. "He's been a bachelor for six years, and a lot of women have tried to get him. Why you?"

"I don't want him, Mrs. Gage, and he doesn't want me. We just happen to want the same thing."

Spying on Landon once more, she watched him sip his drink as he assessed his surroundings.

"Maybe that's why…" she added, to herself.

The woman huffed. "My son doesn't need anyone to take down any man."

Beth nodded, then thought of the little black book, of their prenup, their upcoming marriage. There was more at stake for her than for him. Why did he agree to marry her? Because he hates him, too, she thought. Her stomach contracted at the thought of all that Landon had lost because of Hector. "We won't last," she said out loud, unable to take her eyes off her betrothed.

Hector criticized the press, but Landon respected them and was clearly admired in return. Hector had hated that about him. Landon needed only to stand there, be cordial, treat them like human beings, not bend to them or try desperately to be liked by them, and they adored him. Whereas Hector used to bribe them.

"Have you met Kate?" Eleanor's voice filtered through her thoughts.

Beth spotted a young redhead heading in their direction. She radiated so much energy, she could've been a little sun. Her lopsided smile had troublemaker written all over it.

Beth liked her instantly.

"I'm the caterer," Kate said, offering a tray. "And you're Beth. Hi, Beth."

"Kate is also a friend of the family." The affection in her mother-in-law's words was also visible in her gracefully aged face.

"*Almost* family," Kate corrected as she picked up an hors d'oeuvre from her own tray. She winked conspiratorially at Beth. "I'm going to marry Julian. Poor guy doesn't know it yet."

Beth glanced in Julian's direction, but her gaze never reached him. Her eyes snagged on Garrett, who watched Kate as she tasted her creation.

"Umm. Delicious, if I do say so myself," Kate said, and smiling, licked her fingers before a riveted Garrett.

She was playing a game, Beth realized. A game of jealousy. Kate waved at Garrett, smiling to him, and Beth could see the expression in Garrett's face, tight with displeasure and heated with lust.

She thought about warning her of playing games with these men, with a Gage, but then bit back the thought. For wasn't she in league with a Gage? And weren't they, too, playing a game? Kissing, for crying out loud. With tongues. There absolutely had to be no more kissing—her son was at stake. Her entire future!

"Why are you all being so nice to me?" she asked Kate when her mother-in-law became engaged with another couple, for Kate seemed like someone who spoke the blunt, unfiltered truth. Honestly, if she were Landon's mother and a strange woman had asked him to marry her in a week, for any reason, she'd want to smack both the woman and her son.

But Kate patted her shoulder. "We're nice because you're *good* for Lan."

"Me? See, now you have no idea what you're saying."

She'd proposed a bloody game of revenge—she'd become some sort of vengeful witch. Courtesy of some sleazy bastard.

Kate propped a shoulder against the oak tree. "The truth is the last few years have been painful for the family, seeing Landon like he's been." Beth's gaze drifted to the tall, breathtaking man currently dismissing the reporters. "He's always been the head, and when he's so quiet, so…unfeeling, well, there's tension, you know? All he did was work and work and work, and that's not healthy."

Both women's gazes were drawn to him. Landon turned his head to look at Beth, and as they stared, the corner of his lips twitched. She saw a glimmer of victory in his eyes, shining with satisfaction, as he slowly lifted his champagne glass to her in celebration. The press had bought it. The kiss, the engagement. They'd bought it.

Beth smiled back at him, lifting her own glass in a distant toast.

Partners in crime.

God, she loved having him on her side!

He loved the way she kept scouting the crowd for him.

Hell, he loved the way she kept trying not to smile at him.

And the way she'd melted, like pudding, when she'd kissed him.

"You do realize you're smiling. Right, Lan?"

Landon tore his gaze from Beth and drained the last of his champagne flute. He'd been smiling? Like some idiot? He hadn't realized. His mind had been spinning all night, plotting, planning. There was still no unleashing of his anger, and then the lust that had come afterward, with Beth's kiss. "Halifax was here," he told Garrett.

"What—tonight?"

"Son of a bitch talked to Beth."

"Can you trust her, Landon?"

Landon stole another glance at her, one of many this evening. He needed to think with his head.

"I should post someone on her."

"What about that detective who brought you all the dish on Chrystine and Halifax?"

"Is he still the best?"

"I think so, yes." Garrett's eyes, black as coals from their father's side, narrowed thoughtfully. "Why would you want someone on her tail?"

Landon frowned into his glass, surprised to find it empty. "My own peace of mind."

"You don't think Halifax sent her to you, do you? How far can his fury run?"

He couldn't take his eyes off her, so pretty as she talked

animatedly with Kate. "If it runs as far as mine then there's no telling what he'll do."

Garrett propped his shiny Italian leather boots up on a stone bench. "You can still back out, Lan. You haven't married her yet."

Yes, he could. He didn't need Beth to ruin Halifax, he knew that. But somehow, the desire for revenge just wasn't as fierce without her.

He remembered how pale she'd been moments ago, how frightened, and the thought of her getting hurt made him grit his molars. "Halifax could be more dangerous than we think."

"True." Garrett shrugged. "Then again, I still can't see why that guy hates you so much."

"Because he wanted Chrystine... They were fooling around after she had the baby—remember all those emails the detective printed out for me? Hell, Garrett, I still can't believe Beth was married to that scumbag."

His son had died because of that bastard. Because of his selfish demands that Chrystine meet him the night of one of the worst storms on record.

The loss of that bright-eyed baby boy had almost killed Landon. No parent should have to feel it, no man, no animal, no innocent woman who'd do anything for her son.

"While I go poking into his business, I need to know Bethany's safe. If she's being followed, where she goes, what she eats."

"Has it occurred to you she and Halifax might be out to ruin you together? She may still be loyal to him. In the end, Chrystine was."

Landon pondered those words. But to compare Bethany with his first wife was unfair. Chrystine had been a social-climbing, self-centered princess, and Landon had known what she wanted from him from the start—his money, and the power his name would grant her. He hadn't planned to give her either—until she got pregnant. And to a man like him, marriage had been the only option.

Bethany, on the other hand, just wanted her kid back.

"She's my fiancée now, Garrett, and in a few days, my wife. Not his," he growled then.

His chest swelled with unexpected possessiveness at the thought.

Tonight she'd stood tall, and Landon felt damned proud of the way she'd held up during the photo session.

She'd smiled, she'd acted with class and style, and the kiss she'd delivered had been so scorching, so real, she'd left him hot and bothered and eager to stake his claim on her once and for all.

In the quiet moonlight as she chatted with Kate, Beth's face had lost its paleness and her cheeks now glowed a soft pink. She looked so pretty he worried it would…haunt him.

"You're determined to go through with the wedding."

"Yes," he said, emphatic.

"Why?"

He'd asked himself a dozen times. Why did he want to marry her?

Because she made him want revenge…because he never tired of staring into her blue, blue eyes…because there was something about Bethany, plain and simple as he'd thought she was, that just got to him. And every minute was getting to him more.

"She deserves better than this, Garrett," he said, honestly. Better than loneliness, lies and Halifax.

Across a handful of shoulders, he watched Bethany push a wheaten strand of hair behind her ear… "Christ, she's so sexy." He dropped his head back in exasperation, closing his eyes for a second. "She'll be sleeping sixteen steps away from my bedroom door starting tonight—I doubt I'll sleep an hour."

Garrett burst out laughing, then pounded Landon's back with one hand. "So, what are you going to do about it?" he asked.

Patience, Landon thought. Cold showers and more patience.

"You've never romanced a single woman in your life. They all came to you, just like Beth did."

"Obviously, Bethany's different." She didn't want him. Did she? She needed time.

She was a woman rediscovering herself, taking her first steady steps to seize the things she wanted. And Landon needed, had to make sure, that those steps lead her to *him*.

He caught her watching from afar, her eyes shining with excitement. Then she gave him one of those shy, we've-got-them smiles.

Slowly, he returned it. While he did, his heart boomed loudly, his blood stirred, and his mind was pulled in all kinds of directions which led to the same end.

Beth, in bed, with Landon.

"You know what I think?" Garrett offered, though God knows Landon hadn't asked for his opinion. "I think you're falling."

Landon grimly shook his head.

"You're falling."

He tipped his glass up to his lips, but when no liquid came forth, he snatched a new glass from a passing waiter. "Negative, little brother. I'm merely interested."

He thought of the torment of romancing her, night after night, watching her defenses crack, one by one, and his insides turned to fire. Yes. He'd do it gradually, so methodically she wouldn't even realize how fiercely he wanted her....

"You're not seducing her already, and that's not like you. Why isn't she in your bed? I'm telling you. You're falling."

"Garrett?"

Garrett continued to nod direly. "Falling big-time, bro."

"Shut up, moron."

But his brother had a point here, a very valid point.

If he wasn't careful, he was going to fall for his own fake wife before he'd even bedded her.

Seven

Score one point for the avengers.

And zero for the pig.

Beth was humming the next morning, she was so pleased about last night.

She hummed during her shower, she hummed as she brushed her hair, she hummed as she selected the shoes she would wear—a pair of classic Mary Janes—and mentally planned all the test recipes she would be posting on Kate's new website.

Kate had mentioned wanting to expand her catering business, create a blog, menus, an online site. Last night Beth had asked Landon to borrow one of his computers and had delved into the task with the sight of being able to do something from home, when she regained custody of David.

So Beth had stayed up late last night, inspired and invigorated, because things were changing.

More than just her residence had changed.

Beth was different. She was taking charge of her life—she was getting David back.

And this time, she was going to keep him forever.

Landon, however, was not humming when she spotted him downstairs. He was on the phone, his tone crisp.

"In an hour. At the office. Right. I want him on the job starting today."

He hung up. Beth said, "Good morning."

She went to the coffeemaker on the buffet table, scooping grounds into a basket. Then assessed him from the corner of her eye as she waited for the coffee to start trickling.

He looked so sharp. In a black suit and tie, clean-shaven, his dark hair still damp from a recent shower and slicked back to reveal his hard-boned face. Lord, he was striking. But this morning...brooding somehow.

His hands were thrust inside his pockets, but Beth wasn't fooled by the casualness of that pose. Upon further inspection, she realized his expression was positively morose.

Puzzled, she took a seat at a small round game table, and Landon surveyed her with slitted eyes. What was up with him today?

"Did I miss something?" she asked, frowning.

He made a noncommittal sound, as though whatever he'd been about to say couldn't quite be said, and shook his head like the situation was dire.

His expression made Beth's unease increase tenfold. *"What?"*

"Who told Halifax of the engagement party? You?"

Her hands began to shake so hard, she set down her coffee mug before she spilled it all over herself. Something tumultuous charged the air. Landon looked...enraged. "I called David, remember? You said I could invite him."

"And who did you speak to? Hector?"

She frowned in consternation and her stomach churned uncomfortably. "Anna, the housekeeper. She's become a nanny to him, I think. Why? Why do you have that look on your face?"

He reached for the sofa, then flung a newspaper for her to see. "The picture today in every newspaper except the *Daily* is not ours. It's of Halifax."

Beth gasped as she spotted Hector's loathed face staring back at her from the black and white picture. "No!"

The headline was even more disgusting than Hector.

Gage and Lewis engaged in illicit affair long before wedding date...

"Yeah," he said, tightly, and slammed his fist into the table. "Hell, yeah."

Panic bubbled up inside her. "God! You're the owner of a newspaper, can't you do something?"

"Beth, it wasn't just the *Daily* covering the party, it was the *Houston Chronicle*, the *Dallas Morning News*, even the *Enquirer*, for God's sake."

"And that is my fault, how?" Beth pushed her chair back, the outrage that swept her so intense her voice trembled. "I'm sorry it didn't go as we planned but that certainly wasn't me. And you full well know we're not—you and I are not having... having sex."

His pointed stare and the way it slowly raked up and down her body made her nipples bead so wickedly under her buttoned shirt she wanted to hide. "No, Beth, you and I are not having sex yet."

Her blood bubbled in her veins. What did he mean by *yet?* "Landon, it was a mistake to call David. I see that now. But he's just a little boy. All I wanted was to see him."

But Landon rammed a finger to his temple and made a twisting motion. "Emotions make us sloppy, Beth. You need a cool head."

"How can I when my son is with that monster!"

Crossing the distance between them, he seized her shoulders and leveled their gazes, as if that alone could make her see the problem through his glimmering silver eyes. "Precisely why you can't risk our position." God, his stunning features were so much more amazing up close, she could barely decipher his words. "You can't attempt to see David anymore, not until I say so—I can't have you saying or doing the wrong thing around Halifax. It could compromise everything. Understand me?"

"I understand."

He released her. "All right," he relented, dropping his arms. "So not a word to Halifax unless our lawyer is present—agreed, Bethany?"

"Why on earth are you snapping at me, I'm on your side!"

"Just stay away from Halifax from now on." He grabbed the newspapers scattered throughout and rammed them into his briefcase before locking it shut. "I've got to go."

"You forgot this one." She glowered down at the paper as though she could destroy it with one glare. God, it was so not what they'd planned, she wanted to hit someone. "What are we supposed to do now?" she asked him as he took the paper from her. Their fingers brushed and sent a disquieting little tingle through her arm.

The kiss. Oh God, she'd almost mated with him right there in front of everybody, and for nothing. For more lies, more and more lies from Hector.

Landon started for the foyer, all angry power and dark predatory steps. "We do what we planned to do. We're getting married."

The front door slammed shut.

For Beth, the next few days were busy.

They consisted of overseeing the run of the household along with the housekeeper, Martha; working on her and Kate's project; worrying about David and cursing that loathed, cheating, bribing snake Hector; wondering what Landon was doing and when he would get home and if he would smile at her; then back to Kate and Beth's project.

Her new friend was thrilled to have Beth help with her catering business. She'd used the word "brilliant" to qualify Beth's Gourmet for Kids idea; fancy recipes for kids like stacked chicken fingers over a bed of fries. Just knowing Kate thought the idea could work, and that if it did, Beth would be able to do it from home, thrilled her.

She'd asked Kate if they could offer recipes on the site for free and make money offering advertising, and Kate had given her carte blanche on it.

The website was still under construction, but Beth was pouring all of her creativity into the design down to every last detail, even making sure that while a customer navigated the site, a cute little carrot appeared rather than a mouse arrow.

And Landon. Well, that man was enough to keep a woman on her toes. He drilled Beth about Hector, more determined than ever to find out the skeletons in that beast's closet. Beth had, by some miracle of nature, been able to resist handing over the black book yet. Just to make sure that he had enough incentive to marry her.

It was hard not to yearn for his company when he went to work, though. He was a greedy Monopoly player, a ruthless chess player, and he loved to steal her out at night for a ride in one of the cars from his collection. He drove well beyond the speed limit at midnight when there was little traffic.

Her traitorous heart leapt every time he walked into a room and flashed her that smile of his and called her Bethany. Oh, he was suave, that one was.

Did Hector think he won after bribing the press after their engagement party? Ha! That would not be the case with the judge. *Not this time, pig.*

She grinned at her reflection and tried that out loud. "Not this time, pig!"

Yes, it felt awesome.

It was past evening now. The eve of their wedding.

Landon was still at the *Daily* as usual, and Beth stood before a vanity and oval mirror in her simple silken wedding dress.

Why she'd thought it important to try it on again, she didn't dare dwell on.

The dress was sexier than she remembered, she thought as she critically studied herself. It hugged her body in an enticing way. The cut, though demure, somehow still managed to be modern and attractive, and the flattering cream color made her sort of...

"Stunning."

She stiffened at the male voice, then caught sight of Landon's piercing regard in the mirror's reflection. The color crawled up her cheeks. "It's bad luck for the groom to see the bride in her wedding dress," she said.

Nothing moved. Time, the world, had paused when Landon arrived.

Swallowing awkwardly, Beth turned and shrugged. "But I guess we're getting divorced, so..."

He remained motionless, a sentinel blocking the door.

His eyes glowed. So, so slowly, they wandered over her body, head to toe, and they glimmered with such heat they scorched every inch of her they covered.

The form-fitting dress with the high neckline suddenly felt as transparent as a spider's web.

She bit her lip, unable to stifle the shudder that coursed through her. "It feels glued—" she pulled at the satin on her hips "—to my skin." All of a sudden.

"The only thing glued to your skin are my eyes." His voice was husky, and Beth's thighs liquefied. Ducking her head, she unclipped her hair and used it to create a waterfall so he couldn't see her blush.

His words...hurt. The way he looked at her. Hurt.

Maybe because she was starting to admire and respect him. And because he was amazing and sexy and kissable and staring at her with those bedroom eyes all the time, and she couldn't stand it.

Her insides knotted, and she closed her eyes and covered

her face with her hands, smothering a groan. "Can you please get out of here, Landon? You're making me nervous."

She kept her eyes shut and strained her ears to hear him leave. Hopefully, he'd close the door behind him, too. But for a charged moment nothing in the room seemed to move.

Her heart stopped when she heard a footstep, and a second, and a third. To her alarm, they were coming in her direction. Suddenly, Landon stood too close. His familiar scent penetrated her lungs, making them want to explode.

His arms, strong and hard, slowly slid around her waist. A fluttery, hopeful sensation danced inside her and she couldn't quite quell it. He murmured her name over the top of her head as he drew her to his strong body.

Feeling naked and vulnerable in his arms, she dropped her hands to his shoulders—in a poor, poor effort to push him away—but didn't dare open her eyes.

What was he doing?

Why had he stared at her as if she were naked?

God, what was he *doing?*

"Look at me," he said.

She bit her trembling lower lip and quietly refused to.

His hand slid languorously up her spine, and his fingers caressed the bare skin on her back as he huskily murmured, "Look at me, Beth…"

She felt the gentle cup of his hand on the back of her head, drawing her forward until his lips were a breath away.

"…and tell me you don't want this."

He covered her lips with his. She stiffened at the contact, trying to fight it, but his lips felt plush and warm, and when the wet silk of his tongue swept into her mouth, she was lost. Lost in the moment, in a kiss that was profound with yearning and rough with hunger, a kiss that was shattering and devastating and beautiful, a kiss from a man she wanted and feared and admired.

An unfamiliar desperation rose inside her, the need to experience this closeness with someone staggering in intensity, making her not only respond but do so with hot, ardent abandon. Whoever he was, whatever he was, he was suddenly more crucial than air, and her every defense against him fled. Her fingers bit into his shoulders and her mouth began to move frantically under his.

"More," he rasped, and slanted his head, "Give me more."

A moan rushed out of her, muffled by his mouth as their lips dissolved in a hungry, wild exploration. He tasted of coffee. Smelled like a man. His hands greedily roamed her sides, along her back, clutching and kneading even while pressing her against him.

Eager to investigate every plane, ridge, angle of his body, she let her hands venture up his back and curled her fingers around his thick nape. His arms tightened around her and he groaned into her mouth. He was so aroused! She could feel it, the thundering in his chest against her breast, the sharp shudder that rushed through him as he deepened the kiss and ground his need against her in slow, suggestive moves of his hips.

Rather than fill her with fear, the stab of his broad, unyielding hardness sent a flood of warmth across her body, and the muscles of her tummy clenched with need.

In the darkness of this bedroom and very late at night, she'd wondered if he spent sleepless nights like she had, thinking of him. If he was haunted by the kiss they'd shared before the press. And if he'd both been waiting for and wanting a new one. But it was insane!

Squirming, she pushed him away and gasped for air. He pulled back, and her chest heaved crazily, and her lips tingled with the sweet moisture of his mouth.

He cupped her face between both his hands and focused on her eyes with a heavy-lidded gaze. "I won't apologize," he said, a warning.

Dizzied, Beth had trouble pulling away, couldn't seem to find her grounding. She found herself clinging to his collar with her fists. "Why? Why did you kiss me?"

There were no reporters now, no priest demanding he kiss the bride, no need to kiss her at all. She'd done the same to him that first night, but she'd been desperate. What about him?

He didn't answer. Instead, he gently pried her cramped fingers from his shirt, set her arms at her sides with a brotherly pat, and smiled a devil's smile from the door. "Good night, Bethany."

He could still taste her.

It amused him. It annoyed him. It made him feel *starved*.

Across the room, Landon watched the blonde, blue-eyed vision in a cream wedding dress mingle among the well-dressed crowd and colorful blur of dancers.

They'd planned a small celebration—nothing too posh. Bethany had asked for simple and simple was what Bethany got.

Lush white casablancas populated his home today. They were accompanied by music, candles and a promising buffet. A buffet that couldn't possibly satisfy Landon's hunger. No, nothing could appease this hunger. This aching, growing void for more.

The tension between them had been building during the week. Like a fire stoked with their plotting, their glances, their smiles. Landon was known as a patient man, but his body didn't listen to patience tonight.

He thrummed with desire. Had strained against his pants all through the ride to city hall. He'd watched her loose honeyed hair brush against her shoulders, her small, pert breasts rise and fall under her form-fitting dress.

It would have taken nothing to lean over and kiss her again. This time touch her, caress her soft skin, wrap his hands around her hair.

But she wasn't ready. Last night she'd pushed him away. And Landon would wait. So she trusted him, respected him. Wanted him bad enough to come to him.

His wife…

The tantalizing thought made him groan low in his throat. Did she moan when she made love? Did the thought of being legally bound to him play with her libido the same way it did with his? He closed his eyes and exhaled a ragged breath, attempting to forget the way her mouth had tasted, of apples and pears.

With effort, he pushed away from the limestone column in the foyer and made his way back into the party, watching Kate and Bethany chat. Her dress molded to her slender body, and the sight drove him up the wall.

Bethany spotted him, said something to Kate, then both women, Kate with her tray which she seemed hard-pressed to set down, and Beth with a smile, began coming forward.

People circulated around the living room and the small dance floor, but the noise of them went distant, unimportant somehow.

Because Beth and Kate were coming over.

His pulse went haywire.

Someone slapped his back and stopped him in his tracks. "I noticed you haven't kissed the bride," Julian said.

Garrett was with him, and the three men stood watching the women wind their way across.

"And why is that?" This from Garrett. "Last time you celebrated this very wedding, you gave us all quite a viewing, Lan."

Landon's pulse jumped as it always did when Bethany stared at him with those big bright eyes. He lowered his voice so she couldn't hear him. "It's about time I kissed her in private."

"I'm kinda put out you haven't tasted my spinach rolls," Kate said to Julian when they arrived, extending the tray.

But it was Garrett who instantly snatched one up, made an obliging sound and tasted it. Landon had seen Kate in ponytails—she was the closest to a little sister the Gages had—but it was Garrett who got five stars for sticking by her side when she grew breasts and a penchant for trouble. Poor Garrett.

"Well?" Kate prodded. "Good?"

Garrett said something, but Landon didn't hear. He hungrily studied Bethany's mouth. Her fragrance wafted into his lungs. Sweet and female, creating havoc with his insides. He didn't know what it was about her. Something intrinsic in her, the sexual siren mixed with the fierceness of a mother cougar and the calm of an angel.

"There's more where that came from," Kate said. "And there's dancing, too. You guys have heard of that, haven't you? Something people do to have fun?"

Garrett muttered something to her, yanked the tray away and shoved it into a waiter's hands, and dragged her to the dance floor. Julian took his exit cue when no one spoke a word. Bethany remained, uneasy on her feet, tucking her hair behind her ears.

Landon stepped closer, and before she could turn to leave, he reached out and seized her wrist. His voice sounded gruff even to his own ears.

"Do you want to dance?"

Oh, God, he was so sexy.

The offer—the low timbre of his voice and the rough way he'd asked her—sent a flock of winged creatures loose inside Beth.

She nodded before she realized what she was doing and allowed Landon to lead her past Kate, past Garrett, past their families, past their friends.

They'd organized only a small celebration, had already smiled for pictures for the press. Beth had met some of Landon's Harvard friends, business colleagues. They'd done everything but dance. In fact, they'd done everything but act like a newly married couple.

Until now.

Her heart felt like a restless rabbit as they reached the farthest corner of the dance floor. Whomp whomp whomp.

This was probably just for show but the excitement

swimming inside her was all too real. God, what was she going to do?

She felt his hands splay on her back and took a deep, ragged breath. The music flared and Landon drew her into the circle of his arms. The memory of the way he'd kissed her last night, the way the sight of her in this very dress had made him lose his normally sharp mind, made her stomach clench.

Striving to keep calm, she set her hands lightly on his wide shoulders and searched for chat topics in her brain but couldn't find any except one. Suddenly, that reckless kiss they'd shared had become the proverbial white elephant in the room.

The tension crackled between them, and her nerves felt like electrical wires. "You kissed me."

His eyes flashed. He tightened his hold around her, and her traitorous body molded against his lean, hard length. "I remember you kissing me back."

His rumbling voice, so near, sent little tingles racing up and down her spine, and she didn't want them to.

In a sleek black suit and silver tie, Landon was so arresting it took an enormous effort for Beth to focus on the matter at hand. Focus on anything but the rightness of being in her mock husband's arms, with those piercing thick-lashed eyes on her face.

"Landon, I wanted to speak to you about the hearing," she said.

"Beth, I don't want to talk about this now."

"But I do. I was going to bring it up tomorrow after you'd read the book but we might as well discuss it here. The sooner we get David back, the sooner we can get divorced, right?"

She just didn't trust herself not to do something stupid while married to him. Enduring his proximity every day, knowing he was near every single sleepless night, was the slowest, most painful kind of physical torture she'd ever known.

She couldn't take this much longer.

She licked her lips in nervousness. "The book's upstairs—

you could probably read it in a few hours. How soon could we schedule a hearing?"

His face was indecipherable, but the firmness of his arms around her gave her the sensation of being both trapped and protected. "We need to be married for a while before I request one. And before I do, I need to make sure we'll win. I hate to say this, but you can't afford to lose again, Bethany."

She met Kate's curious gaze as she danced by with Garrett, smiled a little at her, then sighed. "It's just that every day that goes by I fear I'm losing him. What if he doesn't want me anymore? What if it's too late?"

"Your son loves you. How could he not?"

The words touched something hidden inside of her, places she dare not get into for fear of crying. She forced herself to face him. "What if he stops? What if he feels I abandoned him, what if he's told I'm a monster and he believes it? I know I can't see him but just the sight of him, to see him smile at me, that's all I want. Just to know that he...that he's still my little boy."

The tenderness in his eyes loosened a ribbon of sadness inside of her. "You feel like you disappointed him," he murmured, stroking his splayed hands up her bare back.

His warm, soothing caresses made her throat clog with emotion. "I probably did."

"You feel like you should've seen it coming, should have protected him?"

His hair had grown longer, and the silky raven black tips curled playfully at his collar. Suddenly, disturbingly, she reached upward and delved her hands into the thick silken mass. He stiffened. His hands halted. His chest vibrated as though he'd held back a groan.

Slowly, they started moving again, to the music.

She was mesmerized by the depth in his eyes, the stormy understanding, and suddenly she knew he wasn't just talking about her, not anymore. She lowered her voice, so that none of the nearby dancing couples overheard.

"You couldn't have known, either, Landon. Accidents happen."

He pulled her closer, and a muscle worked taut at the back of his jaw as he clenched it. "I could've stopped her, Beth, I heard the door, I knew there was nothing between us, I suspected she wasn't well."

She didn't realize she tenderly stroked his jaw until she heard him breathe in, deep, as though trying to collect himself. Collect her scent.

Her nipples pricked at that sensual thought.

With a low groan, Landon turned his face into her hand and brushed his lips against the inside of her palm. "So, no, to your former question. It's not too late for you," he murmured.

His eyes held that same smoldering admiration she'd seen all week, and it made her gaze rush away and her hand return to his shoulder.

He looked hungry and compassionate and strong. Strong enough to hang on to. He was utterly gorgeous, this big bad husband of hers. Which had been creating some big bad problems for Beth.

She ached to kiss him, slide her fingers up the thick tendons at his neck, bury her face against his throat and just smell him.

"Let's not talk about it anymore," she said, quietly, then forced herself to listen to the haunting tune playing while a knot of tension continued growing in her stomach.

"You're right, let's not," he agreed.

She heard the rustle of silk as he slid his hand up her back. Her pulse quickened as his thumb grazed the bare skin.

"You enjoy...dancing?" she asked, starting to pant.

His lazy smile could disarm a regiment. "I would if you'd start moving with me."

She laughed and swayed a little more, allowing him to press her close enough to be aware of every beautiful, hard part of him. He smelled male, clean. Delicious.

His hands shifted trajectory, sliding down her back, long fingers making goose bumps prick across her bare arms.

"Mother and Kate are staying over tonight," he murmured as he studied her with scorching eyes. The deliberate brush of his fingers against the start of her buttocks made her catch her breath. "They don't want to drive at such a late hour to Alamo Heights. I'm afraid you're going to have to share my room tonight."

Her breath hitched in her lungs. The thought of being near him was hell. She feared she could resist anything, anyone, but him. *Don't don't* don't *make me lose myself, Landon.*

"What about the other room down the hall, the one—"

"That's my son's room. And it's off-limits."

His son's room. Her heart stuttered, then her eyes widened in realization. So he didn't know. He didn't know, couldn't speak that way about his son if he knew.

Pain knifed through her at the thought of knowing something so vile about his past that he didn't. He must believe that Chrystine and Hector's affair had started after he and Chrystine got married. Beth had once supposed the same, until the day she'd confronted Hector and had learned that he and the woman he was sleeping with apparently went back for years.

She loathed to think Landon didn't know that Chrystine and Hector had fooled around together before Landon even met her, and that when she ended up pregnant, Landon hadn't been the only possible father.

He'd only been the most convenient one for her purposes.

Something wrenched painfully inside her stomach at the thought of telling him. She could tell him, yes. That his first wife had been an incredible actress and a very convincing liar. But why open that wound? Why hurt him like that when he'd been wonderful to her?

God, she needed a drink. A whole lot of drinks. A margarita, a martini.

Unaware of why she'd stiffened, Landon eased his hold

around her a fraction. "Relax, Bethany. I'm not going to hurt you."

She shuddered, and for one brief moment, let her eyes drift shut and her stiffness melt away into his strength. "I know."

And Beth wasn't going to hurt him, either. Not this man. Not now, and not with this truth.

Eight

Overall, he'd say the wedding was a success.

The reporters had taken shots, most of his friends had departed, and now only family remained, lounging on the twin sofas inside the book-lined study.

Beth was on her fourth glass of champagne. Landon had consumed double that amount. She smiled now as though happy, smiling like…well, he didn't know what. But her smile was so pretty it made his lips curve, too.

"I'm thinking of something silver…" Beth's mother, Helen, said.

Everyone made their guesses, and Landon watched his wife pick the cranberries from the nut and dried fruit mix.

Note to self: she likes cranberries.

He kept wondering things, like if she slept with socks or not, if her soap smelled like she did, if she sighed when she made love, or moaned, or whimpered. He wondered if she was ticklish, and if the faraway look that sometimes shadowed her eyes was due to missing David.

He'd not wanted anything like this for years.

Unbelievable, that suddenly he was up for revenge, he was up for sex, up for seduction. Now every morning he awakened with a charge of anticipation, knowing that a woman would be under this roof with him, soon in his bed, a woman so wound up he knew she needed this as badly as he did.

"Landon, your turn."

He lifted his gaze to Kate. "My turn for…?"

"Twenty questions."

Beth's smile faded as she considered him expectantly, and a fierce tangle of desire and emotion kept getting bottled up inside him. He couldn't understand this irrational pull she had on him, but tonight he was tired of pushing against it. He scraped his chin with his thumb and forefinger, unable to think of anything.

"Something blue," he said at last.

His mother sipped her tea while his brothers started guessing, and smiling. Landon shook and shook his head. And Beth was…there were no words to describe her. That form-fitting dress looked delicious on her. He wanted to use his lips to pry it off, his teeth…

Inch by inch, the blood seemed to leave her face as he approached her, a sudden clatter of claps and cheers goading him forward. His heartbeat vibrated like thunder in his body. She inched back, buried in the sofa cushions, as he advanced.

Bending down, Landon seized her delicate chin and forced her to meet his smoldering stare. She'd been averting her gaze. Now he knew why—her eyes were welling with it. She feared this, them, the hunger between them.

"What do you think you're doing?" she murmured as he reached out to seize a handful of soft, honeyed hair. The tendrils slid like silk as they sifted between his fingers. God, he wanted to learn everything about this woman, wanted her to look at him like his mother had looked at his father before he'd died, with love and knowledge and unity.

She caught her breath when he ducked his head and, as he spoke, grazed the curved top of one ear. "My wife's eyes are blue, aren't they?"

Gently, he palmed the back of her head and dragged his mouth to cover hers. With a slight pressure of his lips, she opened, and something inside him snapped when her taste flooded him. Warm, sweet. His body went crazy for more, so he tightened his hold and let his tongue take a deep foray into her mouth. Cheers erupted around them. He had to stop, damn, he really did, but she'd just put her arms around his neck and slanted her head a bit, and, Jesus, if they'd been alone he would be tearing at her clothes, he wanted this so much.

Prolonging the moment, he deepened the kiss for just a couple of seconds longer, wanting to see if he could taste her sweet anger, hatred, passion and need inside of her. Maybe she could taste it inside of him. He tasted it all, tasted more than that. Dreams, martinis, cranberries, desire.

"I want you, Bethany," he said as he tore away and growled into her ear. "As much as I want to nail Halifax to the ground, that's how hard I want you."

He eased back, and Beth blinked up at him like she'd been ravaged without her will, and as if he'd been the bastard who'd done it. A burning need to touch her, kiss every part of her, swam through his veins. Her hair tumbled past her shoulders, her eyes were heavy and sleepy and brimming with need.

She hadn't pushed him away, and that alone knifed him with satisfaction and the need for more.

The cheers morphed into comments from his brothers, but Landon's sole attention was focused on Beth.

She seemed troubled, battling the sparks, what had been building between them. Her hands shook as she pushed herself to a stand. "I think I'm going to bed."

Landon didn't plan to remain here, being baited by his brothers, questioned by the mothers, or ribbed by Kate. He swept her up in his arms. "Good idea."

* * *

"Landon Gage, you did not just do that."

Because there was no brown bag she could cover her face with, Beth had to pretend she had hallucinated the stupefied stares of their family members as Landon carried her up the stairs. Like freaking Rhett Butler!

His steps were purposeful as he reached the landing, his jaw determined. "I think I did."

The dogs trailed close at his heels. She squirmed, worried that her poor grasp on reality was slipping. His kisses just got better and better and her breasts tingled like her lips did. "Landon, put me down."

"You're drunk, Beth."

"And?"

"And I'm going to take disgusting advantage of that." He kicked the door shut behind him and set her on her feet. Her legs felt wobbly, the room spun a little. "You have one minute to get in that bed, Bethany Gage. I'm going to kiss you senseless."

"Ha!" was all she could say. Her hands trembled as she got busy plucking at her earrings, slipping off her shoes, stealing covert glances at him as he removed his jacket, whipped off his belt. Their movements were rushed, even her awkward ones. *Rushed.*

"I can't imagine what they're all thinking!" she burst out, reaching to her side to unzip her dress. "They're going to imagine we're upstairs, doing…that."

The dogs whined out in the hall.

Landon kicked off his shoes and quickly unzipped. Bethany blinked as he pulled off his pants. He had long, hair-dusted, muscular legs and thick thighs and calves and… He was a dream. A little girl's fantasy of a prince and a little girl's fantasy of the villain, all in one man.

She couldn't do this, couldn't bear to see him. He was dreaming if he was going to kiss her senseless again. He already had, and she already feared she was losing herself in her daily fantasies of this man.

Storming into the bathroom and closet, she washed her face, slipped into the T-shirt she used as pajamas that someone—probably Martha—had brought from her room, and then she jumped on the bed, quickly sliding under the covers.

She would not look at him, and for a few seconds, she actually succeeded. She had to cool down her jets, get herself calm and in control.

But she felt strange, a little wicked, like she had stolen a moment with her husband and that fact alone made her naughty. She turned just as he shrugged off his shirt. His chest held her mesmerized, made her lungs stop working. She'd never thought a man could be so beautiful and so virile at the same time.

She swallowed at the sight of all that bronzed flesh, the rippling muscles as he yanked the shirt off his wrists.

"I don't feel married," she blurted. "Do you?" This felt more like having an affair with the sexy town bad boy who also happened to have millions.

"Like I said, you're drunk, Beth."

She rolled to her side, giving him her back, forcing herself to stop staring at his body. "The first time I married, I cried on my wedding night," she said, because she figured talking would distract her. She didn't feel like crying now, though, she actually felt…kind of tingly and very weird.

"I'm sorry."

She swallowed. "I guess it was the moment I realized all those little romantic ideas in my head—that's all they were. Ideas, not reality."

She heard the drapes snap shut with a yank. "The first time I was married I got stone drunk."

She whipped around to face him at that. "Why?"

"Perhaps I felt cornered."

He climbed into bed in his boxers. The mattress squeaked. Her heart did something else entirely; it seemed to vault. He was practically naked under the covers, and within inches of her.

His scent wafted to her nostrils, and the butterflies in her stomach jumped and twisted as her lungs fought for air. "Cornered twice into marriage," she said, flipping around once again, hating the pulsing sensation between her legs. "I left a light on in the bathroom—it's the only way I can sleep."

He edged closer. The heat of his body singed her backside. He set a big calloused hand on her waist, and her breasts felt suddenly painful and heavy. "What are you afraid of?" he urged.

"Hector." *You.* "I slept alone most of my married life. I would lie in bed and pray he wouldn't come in, even though I felt so lonely sometimes."

His hand on her waist squeezed gently, almost possessively, and she was shocked that other parts of her body were jealous for his touch. "You don't have to sleep alone tonight."

"I love David." She shut her eyes tightly, fighting the magnetic force that seemed to be urging her to turn around and run her tongue all over his silken skin. "I think I wanted to love his father, but he makes it so difficult." *And I don't want to love* you.

His thighs brushed the back of hers as he began spooning her. "Beth, you don't have to sleep alone tonight…"

She bolted upright and wiggled to the edge of the bed. But all her muddled brain could seem to wrap itself securely around was the mind-numbing, exquisite fact of sharing a bed with the one man in the world who could make her feel like a wanton. "Please tell me you're wearing something more decent to bed," she said, more like a plea. Why was he not odious? Why was he actually…likable? And sexy?

Sitting up, he glanced down at his mouthwatering chest and then frowned. "I don't feel like wearing anything." He met her gaze, then engulfed her shoulders in his hands and urged her closer. "Beth, I can feel how lonely you are, maybe that is why I want you. Will you understand what it's been like for me?"

She couldn't do this, open herself up like a present, then have his male expectations get a big bad whack of disappointment. She couldn't tear off the bandage, open the scars left by her past, no matter how sexy her husband. Hector had said she was frigid, and she feared, because he'd had a lover and had loved another woman, that he was probably right. "Landon, thank you...for helping me, but I don't think..."

He pulled a wad of his hair and groaned in frustration. "Bethany, I swear to God if you say thank you one more time..."

The dogs scratched the door.

"Aww, hell."

He stormed across to let the dogs inside and Beth heard them plop down on the carpet while Landon swiftly locked the door.

An excited, head-tingling sensation swept through her at the thought of being "trapped" with him.

Beth feigned sleep so Landon would stay on his side of the bed, and lying still in her pajamas while tucked in his sweet-smelling bed, she cursed herself for being ten times a fool when the mattress creaked and he slid in behind her. Of course nothing would stop this man from getting what he wanted. He grasped her waist and dragged her to him, and it took all her effort not to whimper.

She should have demanded another room, she knew, but there were guests in the house, and all would be occupied except one that belonged to his memories.

"Beth," he murmured, an erotic, decadent rasp in her eager little ear. He nibbled her earlobe, the full length of his granite-hard front pressing against her back. Her blood warmed like lava, melting her down to her bones. He was all flesh and muscle against her backside, except for those cotton trunks. Something hot and hard pressed between her buttocks, while his bare thighs grazed against hers as he slid his hand up her hip, under her shirt. She mewed softly.

A dog whined.

"Shut up, Mask." His hand slid up her abdomen, and Beth felt something unfurl inside her like a ribbon. Longing. Wanting. "Bethany," he roughly pleaded.

The sheet slid down her body as he slowly pried it down to her ankles. Beth had an urge to grab it back to her chest but then he'd know she was awake. She lay utterly still, felt his eyes caress her where his hand slid the T-shirt higher and higher. He cupped her buttock in his other hand, over her silken panties. She almost jolted when he groaned as though he were in terrible pain.

The dog whined again.

"Ah, hell." He left her, flung the door open. "Out, guys."

She heard them pad outside, then waited in anticipation, cold without the sheet and his body.

He came back to the bed and spooned her again, tighter this time. He devoured her shoulder with his hungry mouth, again cupped her buttocks in his hand. "I can hear you breathe, Bethany. You're not asleep, you're nowhere even near asleep."

She fought to control her breathing but felt drunk with his scent, with the wanting spreading through her. This was such a bad idea…sleeping together…after days wondering and thinking about him and wanting to stay away….

He stroked the edge of her panties and tugged. "Can I take these off, hmm, can I take these off, Beth? I'll kiss you and touch you…that's all I'll do tonight, only what you want me to."

She closed her eyes tighter. His hunger made her feel so special, that she had to remind herself he had been in mourning, was known to be a solitary man, maybe felt lonely. He probably wanted to take something from Hector. It wasn't her he wanted—he just wanted sex.

But tonight's unexpected kiss came back vivid in her mind, and when he slid his hand to cup one aching breast, a sound escaped her.

"Ahaaaa—" he drew out the sound, lacing it with pleasure "—you want me?"

She made a sleepy sound, murmured, "Sooo tired," and rolled onto her stomach. He came with her, his mouth a moist flame ravaging her nape. "It's been a long time for me, Beth. I won't pretend I don't want this. You."

He didn't stop touching her. He seemed to be memorizing her curves, seemed to have gone wild, like an animal, a caveman, as his hands traced her sides up and down, his hips rocking seductively against hers. "Turn around and kiss me again, Beth."

His body heat singed her back, and she could barely keep from moaning when he ground harder against her, tightening his hold on her hips, dragging his tongue up her neck. Her toes curled, and her sex rippled with wanting.

"Landon," she breathed. She forced herself to lay stiff as a board, but what he was doing felt entirely too good. She went lax, grabbed the pillow in front of her and moaned as he burrowed a hand under her body and pinched one nipple. "Oh." She arched back instinctively, and then nearly screamed in delight when he circled it with his thumb.

"Kiss me, Beth."

"I…" She turned around to face him, breathing hard. "I can't feel my tongue."

"God, you're so sexy all uninhibited like this, give it to me." Sweeping down, he closed his mouth over hers and gently suckled her tongue into his warm mouth. She felt that, goodness, she did. He tasted of champagne and her dizzied senses swam like frantic fishes in all kinds of directions as she let herself get even more drunk on her husband's intoxicating flavor.

She twisted her tongue around him and trailed her fingers over his chest before she remembered why this couldn't be. "Oh, no, we shouldn't—Landon, don't." Bolting upright and pushing him away, she smoothed her T-shirt with awkward, trembling hands. "I'm sorry. I can't. Not after the papers I signed."

He looked at her for a moment, then gave a long exhale. "I'm not losing another child. If you get pregnant, I want it."

Regret thickened her voice as she attempted to recover the sheets, needing something to clutch instead of the gorgeous man before her. "I'm not giving away a baby of mine, not even to you—I won't risk it. Excuse me but you're sitting on the sheets."

He cursed and drew her so close, embraced her so tight her breasts were crushed against his chest and her hands had to release the sheets she'd been trying to hang on to for sanity.

"Stop thinking so much and just feel for a minute," he growled, then smoothed his hands along her hair, and murmured, "It's all right, I'm not going to hurt you. I'm going to pleasure you, Bethany, I'm going to make you forget every man in your life but *me*."

Her insides disintegrated at that passionate vow. The need to kiss him, be with him, became so acute, she wanted to weep and scream in frustration. She wanted to say, *to hell with it!* and give her husband a wedding present no husband in his right mind ever forgets.

But he wasn't truly her husband, and she couldn't bear to repeat her mistakes, set herself up for heartache again. She'd been an innocent when she'd married Hector, but now she knew better.

She wiggled free of his hold and succeeded in pulling a part of the covers back over herself, as though they were the Berlin Wall itself—probably barely enough to keep a man like him away. Her voice, though she tried to keep it steady, broke in the end. "The black book is in the top nightstand drawer. I'm sure that's what you want to read tonight, being that you married me for it."

For a long, wretched minute, he didn't speak or breathe or move. Then her heart wept when he grabbed the book from the nightstand, carried it outside and shut the door behind him.

Nine

He'd gone through the headache thing with his first wife. Landon knew a willing woman when he saw one, and unfortunately, Bethany wasn't it.

Grim-faced behind his massive office desk, he waved the black book he was showing to his brothers. "The key to my success."

He handed it over, every single word he'd read in it seared into his mind.

Leaning back in his chair, he watched them sift through the pages, first Garrett with a thoughtful frown, then Julian John with raised eyebrows.

"One would think your disposition would change after last night," Garrett mulled out loud.

"I spent my wedding night reading that little gem there, not with my wife."

There was a bleak silence as Garrett digested this.

"Now why on earth would you do something so stupid?"

"She doesn't want me, Garrett."

"You're joking, right?"

"This is not something to joke about."

"She doesn't…desire you?" The words hung in the air, and they were so painful to hear, Landon found himself gritting his teeth. "I don't believe it."

"Believe it."

Julian glanced up from the book, raising both eyebrows. "Every woman wants you. You had girlfriends before you even had your first bike."

"Why wouldn't Beth want you?" Garrett demanded.

That was the worst question of them all. Landon remembered last night. How her nipples had pricked under his fingers. How her body had molded against his. He'd planned to give her no choice, make her beg for it.

He couldn't.

He didn't want her like this.

He wanted Beth willing—he wanted her to give him everything.

"Two names." He stuck out two fingers, pushing Beth from his thoughts. "Macy Jennings and Joseph Kennar. They're bought."

"No way."

"Yes way." He glared. "Apparently, Halifax sends them ten thousand dollar deposits every couple of months to ensure good press coverage on his 'miracle' treatments. We need to find a way to monitor their calls and hopefully get some solid evidence of their involvement. Plus it will help us determine what Hector is up to."

Garrett rolled up his shirt and made a note on the inside of his arm. "All right. Done. Can't wait to can those suckers when we're done with them."

"Right. And there's another interesting name near the last pages. You see it?" Landon pointed to the book Julian kept sifting through.

Julian's brown brow raised. "Miguel Gomez?"

Landon nodded affirmatively. "That same one. Miguel

Gomez a.k.a. el Milagro. He's known for smuggling pharmaceuticals out of Mexico and to the States."

"Ahh, so the plot thickens…" Garrett said juicily, steepling his fingers. "The black book hath spoken."

"It has, indeed." Landon pulled out a sheaf of papers from the top folder of his stack and passed them to Garrett. "The insurance company's already halted some of Halifax's payments. There have been allegations of him duplicating claims, and they're thinking of suing."

Garrett skimmed. "Health care fraud. How fun. That shouldn't be too hard to prove."

"It shouldn't be." Landon's gaze shifted from one brother to the other while they both surveyed the info. "Now, if one of you gentlemen could arrange an interview with one of his assistants? The head nurse, maybe? We need her to talk, and we need her to talk dirty."

"I'm sure Jules will have them crying mercy in a minute."

With a cocksure smile, Julian dropped the book back on the desktop and folded his arms. "Of course."

Landon nodded. "Tomorrow would be good. Hell, today would be even better." He remembered his wife's frustration over not seeing her son, and fresh determination surged through him. "I'm meeting with our lawyer at two, I need to fill him in on this development. Halifax's been keeping the child away from her, and Beth's anxious to see him. We need to move fast. I want to prove the good doctor isn't fit company for an ape, much less a little boy. It would be easy to accomplish if we get the nurse to testify against him—as a character witness."

"Consider it done," Julian said with the assurance all Gages were known for.

"Halifax wants Beth back, Landon, you know he does."

The quiet words struck a chord, and for a moment, Landon felt them reverberate in his body.

Frowning at the thought of her ever even considering to so much as talk to Halifax, he gazed at today's headlines scattered over his desk.

Surprise Wedding!
Millionaire Magnate Back at the Altar.
Love in the Era of Money.

He was pleased there wasn't hostility in any of the articles—crucial for her to get David back. But then there was that other article that irked Landon beyond normal. It contained the picture of one sick man ominously holding up his forefinger.

Halifax: "It's not over 'til it's over!"

"Did Garrett tell you Mom invited your wife to the range today?"

Surprised, he glanced up at his youngest brother. Julian rarely kidded around. "To the shooting range? Mom?"

"Yep. And Beth."

Landon couldn't help it. He threw his head back and laughed. The image of Beth, bloodthirsty and hungover, holding a rifle in those sweet little hands. Damn, it was funny. "Right. Well, then." He shook his head in disbelief and then flicked on his monitor, determined to get to work.

"Figured out how to romance your wife yet?" Garrett asked.

Landon busily scribbled a thought on a legal pad before him. *Help her find something to do from home. Buy her cranberries.* "Focusing on Halifax now."

A snort from his brother. "Nothing stirs a woman's libido like talking about an ex."

Landon ignored the bait and waved them off. "Whatever. Just get out of here."

He had things to do.

A business to run, a man to destroy, a child to recover and a woman to woo....

"See my dear? Now, after holding a gun and firing that haystack clean off the line, don't you realize we can do anything?"

Two weeks later, Beth found herself in the shooting range again.

Squinting her eyes under the glowing sun as a shock of adrenaline rushed through her veins, she lowered her rifle and drew in a calming breath. She'd started to adore her mother-in-law and their weekly visits to the shooting range. "Well, I didn't quite hit it just yet, Eleanor."

"Oh, but twenty or thirty more tries, we both know that haystack is dead."

Within three seconds, Eleanor aimed her rifle, shot and reloaded.

"Landon's my eldest."

She shot and reloaded.

"He's been alone too long."

She shot and reloaded.

"I hope that doesn't impair his ability to interact with a woman."

She shot. Then lowered her rifle to give Beth a turn.

Beth aimed, lips pursed with effort, her hands weighed by the long, sleek weapon. "He's very nice, Mrs. Gage."

"Nice." She humphed. "I don't think he'd like to be called that by you."

"Well, we're not staying married forever," Beth said, peering through the hole as she sighted one fat haystack. "This was a mutual understanding. Spurred by our mutual hate for the same man."

"Yes yes yes. But I saw the way my son looked at you. And I saw no hate in those eyes." Even through a set of thick goggles, Beth felt Eleanor's dark eyes scrutinize her profile, as though all the answers to the woman's questions were written on Beth's cheek. "And when you look at him, I see no hate in yours, either. Nor indifference, for that matter. I'm an old goat, and I know a couple of things when I see them."

Beth blushed, gritted her teeth and pressed her finger into the trigger. Pop! The bullet flew—Lord knows where it landed. It did not hit a single target.

"Your mother and I chatted yesterday." Eleanor winked at Beth before she aimed once more, rendered positively feral by those goggles and with that secretive smile she wore. "We're playing canasta today. And…other games. Games like matchmaking my son with her daughter. Isn't that fun?"

Beth's eyebrows furrowed as she watched the woman take a perfect shot. Bam! "If your matchmaking is as good as your shooting," Beth grumbled, "then no, it's not going to be fun at all."

This would not do.

Matchmaking among mothers, the last thing Beth needed at this point. Specifically, because her husband seemed to be the sexiest thing walking the planet. And because apparently Beth wasn't as frigid as her ex-husband had led her to believe.

The frustration of waiting for a hearing had been riding on her nerves. Every day when Landon arrived from work Beth asked the same question over dinner: Do we have a hearing yet?

I'm on it, he'd say.

She was beginning to wonder if they would ever reach that day. And in the meantime she was suffering, totally, wretchedly suffering. True, Kate's website launch so far had been a moderate success. A few inquiries in the form of emails had already trickled in, and on a burst of inspiration, Kate and Beth had decided to add a "Share your Recipe" section to the website. But even those fun plans and little satisfactions failed to quell the internal turmoil in her.

Landon Gage had her sleeping in her bed alone at night for the past two weeks imagining things like sliding into his bed and smoothing her hands up his chest and into his hair and…

Shaking off the thoughts, Beth stormed into his room when she heard him come into the house. "Landon, our mothers are playing canasta."

"And?"

Her heart tripped—in a white buttoned shirt, without a

belt and in his black slacks, Landon looked rumpled, ruffled, gorgeous. "And…and, and I think they're conspiring against us."

"In what sense?"

Bethany watched wide-eyed as he began to unbutton his shirt, then couldn't remember what she planned to say. When she did, she realized she sounded ridiculous. As if there was the remote possibility that either of them would fall, which there wasn't. No matter how much matchmaking. Was there? "Oh, forget it. How was your day?"

"Tiring." And in that instant, a thought teased her: *What if he were really my husband? What if he'd come home from work and David would jump on him like his dogs did and he'd smile and rumple his hair…*

Landon produced something from his pockets. "Here. I brought you something."

She stared in interest down at a book. It was a cookbook, and even better, it was one she'd never read before. Her chest squeezed as she stroked her fingers along the glossy surface. It was such a nice gesture on his part. A gesture which told her he didn't mind finding his kitchen in a mess while she explored new recipes. And which told her, in a way, that at least a couple of minutes today, he'd thought about her, too. "Thank you, I don't know what to say. Thanks from me and… thanks from Catering, Canapés and Curry."

"Nice name. I'm guessing you came up with it since Kate had failed to find one for over a year?"

She nodded, still so touched she felt stroked all over.

Landon crossed the room toward her, and Beth nervously licked her lips when he raised one bronzed big hand to cup her cheek. His thumb, gentle and warm, wiped a smudge of dirt off the tip of her nose. "You went shooting today?"

That touch alone felt like an electric current that started in her nose and ended with a jolt in Beth's toes. "Y-yes. I love it. I always feel so…powerful."

Her cheeks flamed as he disappeared into his bathroom,

turned on the shower, then came back out and pulled his unbuttoned shirt out of his pants. Her gaze felt glued to his, she couldn't seem to pull free of his quiet stare.

"Your mother insinuated that my mom and she think… They're trying to get us together. They're crazy. A marriage based on nothing but common hatred," she said.

He nodded indulgently, all bronzed skin and gleaming muscles as he shrugged off the garment, and his hands went to his pants. Beth watched, wide-eyed, as he began to unzip. Her breasts tingled. A prick of awareness danced across her skin.

"What else do we have in common other than Hector, I mean…" She trailed off when he stripped to his underwear. Her lungs closed off all air.

He stood before her for a moment, as sexy and comfortable in his skin as an underwear model, while a prominent bulge pushed against the stark white cotton of his trunks. Even down there, Landon Gage was bigger than Hector.

He was more man, more everything.

In other words, too much for Beth.

She became aware of how fast her chest heaved when he gave her a sardonic smile. "Are you staying here and watching or are you letting me take a bath?"

Beth stumbled back a step, a trembling hand reaching for the doorknob. "I'm leaving."

"Close the door, Beth."

She turned to go, but then spun around. "Landon…"

He kicked off his trunks, his back to her, and when she saw his nakedness all of her blood seemed to rush to the center of her being, where it gathered into a burning pool of desire. Her breath left her completely, and the book slid from her fingers and landed with a thud on the floor.

Landon's buttocks were so muscled, they clenched as he stepped out of his underwear—every small and large muscle of his body taut and rock-like under his skin. He glanced past his shoulder. "Yeah?"

She shook her head to clear her thoughts. But oh. *Oooh.* She'd been wondering for days, had been aching for a peek of him, she was so bad, and suddenly this was so embarrassing.

"I'm no good at this. Landon, I…" She clung to the door handle behind her, her knuckles white as she squeezed it for support. "I'm sorry about our wedding night. My life was shattered when I left him," she hurriedly whispered, "and I know that I will be leaving you and I really want to…be prepared, you know? I guess I just worry if I make others believe it, a part of me will believe it, too, and I don't want to, it's not *real*. Nothing's real to me but David."

He reached into the bathroom for a towel, and wrapped it easily around his narrow hips. "But we expect nothing." Even half covered she could hardly think. His chest was so beautiful, all of him making her mouth water, especially the smoldering proposal in his eyes. "I don't expect anything from you, Beth, nor you from me, except to trample Hector. Neither of us is hoping the other will love us like we love or be with us forever."

"But our mothers hope."

He started forward. "Mothers will always hope."

He caught her shoulders and she squeaked and flattened back against the door. "No, please no, no kissing!"

He let his arms drop at his sides and cursed low in his throat as he squeezed his eyes shut. "Fine." He stepped away, jaw clenched taut. "Fine. If you change your mind, you let me know."

"Landon, are you angry?"

He didn't answer.

"Landon!"

"I'm not angry, Beth, just get out of my room." He grabbed the cookbook and shoved it into her chest before he stalked away.

"Wait…" she called him, and he turned at the bathroom door. Their gazes locked.

He was dark and tall and looking very much a husband,

while she stood there by the opposite door, with a new dress she'd bought on sale that he hadn't even noticed, a huge knot in her stomach and a horrible sense of loss. She clutched the book to her chest. "It's not you, it's me."

"No," he said, tersely. "It's him."

He closed the bathroom door, and for a minute, Beth stood there frozen and confused. Then she charged into her room, tossed herself on the bed and buried her face under the pillow. She screamed into the down, a scream of total and wretched frustration.

What had he meant by that? If Landon thought this had anything to do with Hector, he was *wrong*.

It was David who worried her, David who kept her locked in her room at night, David and how he deserved a stable future, not living through another heartbreaking divorce.

She clenched her eyes shut and tried to shut down the images that tormented her.

Landon in the shower. *Naked*. Landon naked with all that thick muscle. Landon giving her a mere book and making her feel like he'd given her a piece of the moon.

She groaned. She went under, yanked the covers up to her head and tried not to think of his hot kisses, his surprising smiles, his penetrating stares.

Impossible. Vivid, mushy and sweaty thoughts of her husband made her hot, and squirmy, and it made her ashamed.

She couldn't do this. Sure, she could do *this*—pretend marriage. But she couldn't do the rest.

Her and Landon's relationship was just a convenient business arrangement that would open beautiful possibilities for her future—her son, specifically.

But even as she reminded herself to keep Landon's and her expectations in line, in her mind she pictured being coiled so tightly around Landon neither of them could breathe.

Beth! she chastised herself. *Remember what happens when they want what you can't give. What happens when you let yourself fall in love with a man who doesn't really want or need you.*

Sighing, she rolled to her side, and an ache settled around her chest as she thought of David. She closed her eyes and imagined him sleeping, always cherubic—like her very own angel. And she prayed he dreamt of gumdrops and licorice sticks, of puppies and kittens, of anything but the hell going on between his mother and father. "Good night, David. Sleep tight."

Beth knew for sure that she would not.

Because just down the hall in his big room, in his big shower, bare-chested and most definitely alone, was Landon.

Ten

The weeks passed, each day loaded with a strange mix of companionship and charged pauses, growing friendship and stolen touches, talk of revenge and looks that were heated with longing.

This morning Beth had a strange hole inside her. She couldn't take his kindness any longer—it made her feel weak and hopeful and besotted, when all she wanted was to feel angry and abused again and concentrate on what most mattered to her.

"Where are we going?" she asked, tearing her eyes away from the scenery and meeting his sharp silver gaze.

Landon lounged in the backseat of the Navigator this Saturday morning, carefree and relaxed in tan slacks and a white polo, but his gaze shone with interesting secrets. One corner of his lips kicked up a notch. "I've arranged for you to see David."

Beth's every muscle jerked at that, and her heart went bonkers in her chest. "You have? How? When?"

"I spoke to a mother of one of his school friends. He's over for a play date today and I thought—"

"You did not!" she gasped, then covered her mouth with trembling hands. *"Ohmigod!"*

"Breathe, Beth," he said, leaning forward in his seat, his eyes crinkling at the sides. "It's a bit risky. We're violating the custody arrangement, but we're compensating your friend with a generous amount in exchange for her silence—and nobody will know as long as David understands he needs to keep quiet. Do you think we can pull this off?"

Her chest moved. "Yes, God, yes! David and I have been keeping secrets from his father for forever—he'll never tell!"

It depressed her to think that David was too old for his years, but it was true. Ever since he was three, he'd seemed to notice how easily his father angered. He'd loathed the fact that every time his dad felt displeased he'd issue a silent treatment that made both David and Beth want to hide.

But how had Landon managed to set this up? Her mind whizzed with questions, but they all ended with one simple fact, one unerring truth: no matter why, or where, or how Landon had managed to schedule a meeting with her son, the only important thing was that he *had*.

She would see her son today.

She felt so big all of a sudden it was a wonder she fit inside the car.

As they rounded a corner, Beth's attention became riveted on a familiar redbrick house. The fenced front lawn was green and trimmed, and a set of bicycles were tossed over on their sides in the driveway. She spotted two kids playing by the rosebushes and her heart soared at the sight of the blond little boy—*her* little boy. She almost heard music in the background, could practically see his aura shine like an angel's.

Barely a second after the car halted, Beth shoved the door open and ran across the asphalt to the fence. "David!" she

shouted, as she entered the yard and closed the gate behind her.

He pivoted instantly, a baseball in his hand. "Mom?"

His fingers tightened around the ball, but he didn't run to
her. He stayed frozen in place, in loose jeans and a striped
T-shirt. He eyed his good friend Jonas first, as if asking for
his permission, but all Jonas did was stick his hand out for the
ball.

"Sweetie, oh, darling baby," Beth choked as she dropped
to her knees and stretched out her arms. "I've missed you so
much."

He crashed into her and Beth's eyes welled up as they
clutched each other. He smelled of shampoo and grass and
little boy, and for a moment Beth inhaled as much as she
could.

When her pulse calmed, she began asking him what he'd
been doing, reminded him his father could not know about this
if they wanted to be together again, and then she remembered
Landon, now leaning against the car, and she seized David's
little hand and rose to face her husband. The sun made his dark
hair gleam and glazed his tanned skin like warmed honey.

His expression was inscrutable, but there was emotion in
his eyes. The silver in them had intensified to a sharp polished
metal.

She brought David over to the fence. "Landon, this is my
son, David. David, this is Mr. Gage."

Landon's son would be his age, she realized. Had he wanted
to be a dad? He seemed to be ruthlessly suppressing the urge
to go back into the car.

"Is he my new daddy?" David asked, blinking.

Her motherly instinct didn't take long to kick in. Beth
quickly began to arrange his shirt, comb his hair, and out of
habit, checked his temperature. "He's mommy's special friend,
my love. And he's doing everything he can to bring you home
with us. With me. Do you want that?"

"Yeah," he admitted.

Both man and boy continued regarding each other warily. Landon with a hand in his pocket, the other restless at his side.

David kicked the grass. "Does he like horses?"

Smiling because that's just the thing that her David, the animal lover, would say, she hugged him again. Tight. Had he grown? He'd grown an inch, she was sure of it! "He has two big dogs," she told him excitedly. "They're as big as lions. You would like them."

"Jonas's mother said you would come. I didn't believe her but I wanted you to. She said I could make you something and I made you this." From the back pocket of his jeans, he retrieved a paper and gradually unfolded it to show her a drawing of spaceships and stars that read, "David+Mom."

"Oh, my! Well, there, Commander, that is one dangerous aircraft, and is that big heart mine?"

He nodded, his grin already showing a missing tooth. Beth thought of how they would play astronauts and cowboys and anything else they could conjure when they got back together. She'd deepen her voice to sound like the villain so David could trap her and be the hero.

She rumpled his hair and stole a peek back at the house to find Mary Wilson standing by the kitchen window with little Jonas now at her side, watching their reunion with a smile.

Beth nodded at her and mouthed, "Thank you."

As though having at last convinced his legs to move, Landon approached the fence, still so quiet. He reached over the top of the pickets. "Hi, David." He offered his knuckled fist, as Beth supposed he might do with his brothers, and said, "If you bump it, it means we're friends."

David frowned, not easily sold. "Can I see your dogs?"

Landon didn't seem to know what to say. He kept staring down at her son with a mixture of confusion and pain.

Beth blurted, "You can ride them like ponies if you'd like to!"

That did it. Her son's entire face changed from wariness to full adoration. "Okay."

And he lifted his balled little hand and bumped it against Landon's big one.

"Thank you."

Minutes after leaving David, Beth's excitement had dimmed and morphed into a fuzzy, warm flutter as Thomas drove them home. She felt like hugging Landon but instead fidgeted with the pearl button on the lapel of her shirt. David's drawing was neatly stashed inside her purse. David's scent, his smiles, every word he'd said, had been tucked away inside her, too. Her heart threatened to burst.

"He seemed happy to see you," Landon said, his eyes glimmering with pride.

"Yes." Beth felt her chest contract, remembering how David's face had lit like a sunbeam when she'd told him they'd be together soon. When? he'd asked, again and again. When...

A lump gathered in her throat. Even after such a wonderful day, tonight there would still be an injustice in the fact that someone else would be tucking her son into bed.

Beth realized with a start that Landon's thigh and her own pressed together, that they were sitting too close, and that it would be rude to slide away. So she tried not to notice how thick his thigh was. How hard.

She felt she needed to say something but didn't know where to begin, or how to organize her thoughts. Her armor had been stripped away; she trembled with emotion, excitement and something else. He smelled so good up close, like the wind. Like a man.

Landon gazed out the window. He looked terribly big and terribly lonely. All her walls against him, all her reservations, seemed to have morphed fully into all these awed and inspired feelings of admiration and respect and desire. God, what was she supposed to do with these?

"Your son…" she began.

"Nathan," he corrected.

"Nathan. He'd be around David's age?"

He nodded.

Should she have brought up this subject? It seemed to be the one on his mind, but speaking of the boy without telling Landon what she knew proved difficult. "This must've been hard for you."

He signaled at her, and let his eyes sweep meaningfully over her. "Not particularly. You seem very happy, Bethany."

Her cheeks heated up, and she averted her face. "It's not easy being a parent. You never imagine you could care so much."

He made a sound, like a snort. "And yet the instant you hear that wail and stare into their eyes, they've got you."

"They do!" she agreed.

They shared smiles, and the comfortable quiet between them morphed into something smoldering and sensual.

"You know," Landon said, so softly she felt the whisper in the interior of the car like a tangible caress. "I still don't know when you got me, Beth." He cocked his head and regarded her with the eyes of a man who knew too much. "Maybe when you came spitting fire—asking for my help. Or maybe when I see you looking at me the way you do."

Flooded with mortification, Beth raised a halting hand and lowered her face. "Landon, don't."

He reached out and cupped her shoulder, grazing her arm with his thumb. "Don't what?"

The heat radiating from his body made her squirm. The ache inside her continued opening, like a ravenous animal, turning her desire into pain. "Don't talk to me like this." *Yes, please do, tell me if you care, too.*

No, he mustn't!

He leaned back negligently and studied her with impressive calm. The sunlight streaming through the window cast playful shadows on his profile. "But you like it when I talk to you like this."

She struggled against a barrage of emotion. She did like it, she loved it, but she shook her head fast, still not ready to admit anything.

Landon Gage wasn't a pillar she could lean on tomorrow, wouldn't be a steady presence in her life. There were just these few...moments. With him. Dangerous moments, crowded with dangerous thoughts.

"I don't...want to."

"Now you're blushing."

"Because you're flirting."

"Flirting." A sprinkle of laughter danced across his eyes. "I'm being honest with my wife."

She raised her eyes to his. "Then can you honestly tell me you're not trying to seduce me?"

He offered no argument for a moment, but then said, in a voice that broached no argument, "If I were trying to seduce you, you'd be right here." Meaningfully, he patted his lap, and her eyes hurt at the image of the prominent bulge between his parted thighs. "You'd be right here, right now. And I wouldn't be sleeping alone tonight—nor would you."

She tried reining in her jumbled thoughts, but couldn't seem to get past the words "seduce" and "you'd be right here." "Then you're just playing some sort of game?" Her voice came out unsteady.

He shook his head. "I'm definitely not playing."

"Then what?" she persisted. "What's this about? What is it that you want from me?"

"You really want to know what I want?"

"I want to know what you want, yes!"

"Your trust, Beth. Before you give me anything else, I want your *trust*."

They engaged in a brief staring contest, Landon's eyes scalding, Beth struggling to tame the wild impulse to put her lips on his beautiful stern ones.

Stricken by the realization that Landon always brought out the lonely, impulsive teenager in her, she lost the staring contest and glanced down at her purse on her lap. "What makes you think I don't trust you?"

"Do you?"

She opened her mouth to say yes, yes, she did, despite not wanting to, when Thomas interrupted. "Sir, I've got orders to drive you to the office right away."

"First we drop off Bethany."

Beth frowned, inched a bit farther away, hoping distance between them would give her distance from emotions, too. "Something important at the office?"

"Not really." He shifted in his seat, his legs opening wider now that he had more space.

"If you'd pardon me, sir." Thomas cleared his throat and caught her gaze in the rearview mirror. "It's Mr. Gage's birthday today, Mrs. Gage. The office always celebrates despite his say in the matter."

Beth gaped in stunned surprise. "It's your birthday."

His birthday. Her husband's birthday.

Oh, wow. She must be the worst wife in the history of the world.

She hadn't known...

She hadn't known about his birthday.

But she tried to reassure herself, telling herself, in her mind, that she knew Landon in ways others didn't.

She knew that his loyalty was steadfast and not easily given, knew that he'd done right by his first wife and generally right by everyone around him. She knew that he was quiet and thoughtful but knew how to laugh, and that his smiles—unlike Hector's—were real and reached his eyes.

Pursing her lips in determination, she opened the window. "Thomas, I'll be accompanying my husband."

Landon didn't protest.

He glanced out at the cityscape as though it didn't matter, but his fingers began to drum over his thigh.

Ten minutes later, when they arrived at the top floor of the *San Antonio Daily*, the noise was deafening. Eighty people circulated in the office space, if not more. Balloons had been hung from the ceiling. Computer screens held birthday greetings and songs were blaring from speakers. People wore funny hats.

It warmed Beth to witness this, to know that Landon was so respected his people would do this for him. It made her proud to walk next to him.

"Goodness, your people love you," she exclaimed, wide-eyed.

He cocked one sleek eyebrow. "Surprised?"

"Amazed," she admitted, and impulsively reached up to smooth back a strand of dark hair that had fallen on his forehead. "But not in the least bit surprised."

This seemed to please him, and his grip tightened on her elbow as he guided her across the hall.

Of course, his brothers were present, too. Situated right in the center of it all. Julian John uncorked the champagne, pouring the liquid into dozens of glasses, then took a swig directly from the bottle and kept it to himself. Clad all in black, which suited his dark good looks, Garrett was fighting with Kate over who got to wear the silly hat she kept planting over his head. Beth doubted Kate was catering, but she was there because she was practically family to the Gages, had grown up in their household when her father, the Gages' bodyguard, had been killed in the line of duty.

Landon greeted everyone by name and introduced Beth as his wife, and he put his arm around her. Beth felt shy and self-conscious, but when the partygoers returned to their mingling and Landon focused on her, holding her lightly against him, all her awkwardness melted under a creamy swirl of excitement.

"This is a really nice party," she whispered, touching his arm briefly as she said this.

The candidness in Landon's gaze affected her almost as

much as the whisper of his fingertip trailing along her jaw. "It's even nicer with you in it."

A shiver raced through her, impossible to suppress.

God, what was happening between them?

Neither seemed to stop touching each other, neither seemed to stop staring, to want to put distance between them or be anywhere else but near.

Before she made a fool of herself, Beth told her husband the sweets buffet called to her and managed a smooth escape, leaving Landon with his mother.

"Never seen him smile like today," an older woman hovering by the candy, who'd been introduced as Julian's assistant, told Beth. "Mr. Landon, I mean. And all the girls and I agree it's because of *you*."

Landon smiling...

Because of *her*?

The thought moved her so powerfully Beth couldn't speak through the ball of emotion in her throat. Because Landon Gage not only made her happy sometimes, too, but he also made her ache. Ache for him. For more.

She picked through the sweets and popped a handful of dried cranberries into her mouth, but they did little to appease the building urge to scan the room and find him.

She wanted him.

Admired him.

Loved his attitude, his strength, his dynamism. Loved his eyes, his face, even the way he scowled. She loved his... She loved all of him.

Oh, God, love, she thought with a wrenching in her stomach.

She loathed to think that *this* was how it felt—the helpless, excited, burning and frightened sensation she got every time she saw and thought about and stood near Landon.

"Blow it, brother!" Garrett cheered as they surrounded him near the three-tiered cake and the pair of flaming candles that boasted the big blue number 33.

Chuckling softly while shaking his head, Landon positioned

himself at the end of the long table. That flattering white polo shirt really suited him, Beth thought dreamily from afar. He had such a thick, bronzed neck, his shoulders so hard—

"Beth!" Kate called her. "Get over there next to Lan for a picture. He won't bite you." She stuck her tongue out and held up the camera. "Not that I can say the same for the cake."

Landon trapped her gaze from across the room. Was it caring she saw in his incredible eyes?

Weak-kneed, Beth started walking over, her heart pounding like a drum. At that very moment, Kate's guarantee of him not biting didn't reassure her. A gleam of possessiveness glimmered in Landon's eyes, and the mine-mine-mine! they seemed to echo set the tips of her breasts on fire where they pressed against her top.

He watched her advance. The way his attention homed in on her made her blood simmer. If they'd been anywhere else, anywhere else but in a roomful of people, Beth didn't know what they'd be doing. No, that was a lie. She had a pretty good idea of what they'd be doing, what they could be doing—like regular husbands and wives.

"Come on, brother, make a wish!"

Landon bent forward, and as his eyes met Beth's over the candles, a slow smile spread on his lips and made her thighs turn liquid. Desire wound around her like a vine, bringing with it a world of emotions she couldn't suppress. Love…

They weren't normal husband and wife, but they were more than Beth had ever been with her ex-husband. More connected than Beth had ever imagined feeling to another living thing. The candles smoked as he blew them out all at once. Crazily, she wondered what on earth a man who had everything could wish for. And it struck her.

He wished for me.

The thought was irresistible. Her hands clenched at her sides, and she could almost hear the last weak little barrier inside her crumpling.

And maybe all my life I've been wishing for him.

* * *

Something accompanied them home.

Something searing and undeniable. Electricity leapt from him to her, her to him, charging Beth's nerve endings as they entered the quiet house.

They took the stairs side by side.

Expectation tickled inside of her as she reached her bedroom door.

She half hoped Landon would draw up behind her, half expected for him to turn her around and claim a heated kiss.

He didn't.

Startled when he said good-night, Beth heard his footsteps, muffled on the carpet as he made his way down the hall.

With an awful disappointment, she slipped into her spacious lonely bedroom, then surveyed the contents of her closet.

She had to do something, wouldn't forgive herself if his kind actions went unrewarded, if her wanting continued to be unappeased. She wasn't sure where this determination, this courage or this desperate want had come from; she only knew she needed her husband. She needed to show him her loyalties were with him, her gratitude, her respect and desire. Her trust.

Were with him.

Dragging in a breath, she eased into a little number she'd never worn before, and then without thinking about it too much, quietly made her way to Landon's bedroom.

The door stood partway open.

Her blood rushed so fast and heady in her veins it deafened her to the single word she spoke. "Landon."

His head shot up at the sound of his name.

They stared in the quiet, sizing each other up. Beth in the threshold to his bedroom, Landon in bed with the covers to his waist, bare-chested and bronzed, already with a book in his hands.

Her eyes hurt, he was so compelling. Hard, bulging muscles stretched taut across his broad shoulders. She could see his biceps and the defined bands of his abs before they disappeared under the crisp white sheets.

Nervously, she wet her lips and forced herself to shut the door behind her. "Did you have a nice birthday?"

Clenching his jaw, Landon set his reading material aside. "Thank you, yes. Did you need anything?"

His clipped tone hinted that he wanted her to go, and for three long heartbeats, Beth considered it.

But she remained, struggling for the words. *Love me.*

Landon waited in silence, then let out a sigh. "Bethany, I'm hanging by a thread in more ways than you can imagine. If it's nothing urgent, I suggest you go back to your room now."

She did not know what to say. She'd been so insistent they keep a healthy distance, she now realized it would be a struggle to let him know that things…had changed. Everything. Had changed.

Breathing deeply, she brought her hand to the tie of her silk robe around her neck and fiddled with it. "I'd like to sleep here," she said.

Frowning, Landon sat up, looking all gorgeous and puzzled and frustrated. "Is there something wrong with your bed?"

Don't say no, please don't send me away.

She'd never seduced a man, and the thought of being rejected made her cheeks heat up and her legs want to aim in another direction.

"It's empty."

With a low groan, he banged the back of his head against the headrest and closed his eyes. "Ah, Beth. How can I say this…" His Adam's apple bobbed as he swallowed.

"Please don't turn me away."

A tremor spread through her as she waited, clenching the fabric from her nightgown in her hands.

If he denied her, she'd be devastated. Devastated.

Landon cursed under his breath and rolled to the other side of the bed. "Let me put on something, all right? And we can talk."

Mute, Beth gaped at his gorgeous body as he eased out of bed, the ripple of muscle down his back as he plunged into his pajama bottoms. She gazed longingly at the covers, wanted to slip inside them, where Landon had been naked just now. His sheets would be warm, but she didn't know if they were welcoming.

"What is it, exactly, that you want from me," he growled as he strode over wearing loose cotton sleep pants, haphazardly tied.

She bit her lower lip in uncertainty. "Kiss me good-night?" That was as close as she got to asking him to take her, and apparently he didn't believe his ears.

He stared in wonder, his expression revealing he still didn't seem to know what to make of this visit.

"Not like a friend or a partner—like a husband," she amended.

Understanding made his eyes flash.

He clenched his jaw so tight, a muscle jumped in the back, then he plunged both his hands into her hair and set his forehead on hers. "Do you want to be kissed by your husband?" he hissed.

"Yes." She linked her hands behind his head and shuddered in expectation. "Please."

He shut his eyes, let go a breath, and didn't do anything for a long, long time.

Rolling his head against hers, he made a low, hungry sound. "Now tell me," he said slowly, roughly, his voice ragged with desire, "you want your husband to make love to you, too."

She didn't answer for what felt like a year.

It was a dream, it had to be, but Beth felt too slim and warm to be a figment of his imagination. Landon had a desperate urge to get close to her. Closer. To feel her body around his, penetrate its depths, fill them with his essence.

He'd never gone without sex so long, but now it wasn't sex he craved, it was mating with his wife, finding that union, that closeness. Searching her, finding her secrets, delving into the darkest parts of her, allowing her access to his.

He didn't know what would happen if he kissed her. He didn't know if he could *stop*.

She'd asked for a kiss, but Landon wanted her to want more, want it all.

He bent his head when she didn't respond and watched her reaction as he grazed her lips.

She trembled against him. "Landon," she moaned weakly and the way she uttered his name catapulted his need to alarming levels.

His heart pounded. *Stop stop stop, you idiot, you're losing control.*

But she wanted him. She was here, she was asking for it.

"Do you, Beth?"

An anticipatory groan rumbled up from his chest as he whisked her lips again, holding his breath at the tantalizing contact. "Do you want me…Landon…to make love to you?"

He moved his lips over hers, gently attempting to coax them apart. Her hands tightened at his nape as he slid his hands up her back and held her against him. He gave himself a minute to savor the rightness of her body against his, the difference in their forms, and deepened the contact when she opened a little.

"I won't stop," he rasped, seizing her plush bottom lip between both of his. "I'm going to touch you, and lick you, and strip you down to your skin, and I won't stop until morning."

When she shifted in his arms just slightly, giving him the impression she wanted him even closer, he lost control and slid out his tongue to taste. Once. Side to side, his tongue traced the entry of her lips. "Say it," he whispered. "Say the words to me."

"Yes," she breathed.

His tenuous hold on his control threatened to snap when her lips parted, and her warm, damp tongue curled seductively around his. The coy caress destroyed him. Patience, measure, reason fled. Need flared in his body like a rising tide of lava, and a hunger pent up for years surfaced with a vengeance. He crushed her to him and opened his mouth wide, kissing her like only a man too starved or too desperate could. His initial sampling became a feast. A claiming. His claiming.

He growled when her lips moved with the same frantic eagerness as his, and still he demanded more. He drank of her, letting the sweetness and the honey and the taste of her flood his mouth in a flavor so intoxicating it made his head spin. He'd underestimated the power of her. The temptress in disguise with the worried eyes and the heart of a lion that had driven him insane for weeks.

She moaned into his mouth, and desire ricocheted within the walls of his body, painful in its force. The prenup, the fake wedding, it all vanished from his thoughts. He could only think of his bed. With this woman in it.

He tore his mouth free and slipped his hands around to cup her tight, round bottom, then dragged her flat against him, letting her feel the painful length of his erection straining against the fabric.

He gazed into her surprised eyes, curling his hands to get a handful of soft, willing flesh as he covered her mouth again. They moaned in unison.

He opened his lips over hers, drinking what she gave him, demanding more. He'd thought she was a vision. He'd thought she was a dream. And he couldn't stop kissing her, touching her, thrusting his tongue inside her depths to taste her. Hot. So hot. So sweet.

He added teeth to the kiss, biting, nibbling at her, and when she tightened her arms around his neck, he thought his chest would implode.

"Landon," she said in a reverent whisper as her mouth trailed down his chest, quick and hungry. No, voracious. Landon felt dizzy as she peppered warm, moist kisses on his heated flesh and stroked her fingers down the muscles of his abdomen.

Yes, he thought as the blood stormed through his body, *yes yes* yes.

His every muscle taut with need, he guided her back and urged her down on the bed. She fell there, her skin luminous in the moonlight, every shadow dancing over her body making it clear her nightgown was sheer.

His erection pushed even harder, ready to rip through his pants. "Did you come to my room to seduce me?" He trembled knowing the answer, and leaned over her waiting female body, watching her nod slowly, almost hesitantly.

"Yes."

She came up to her knees and reached out for his drawstring. But Landon planted a hand on her tummy and forced her onto her back again, in lust, in agony. "Ladies first." He couldn't understand his own words. His breathing had morphed into something haggard.

With slow, barely steady hands, he tugged the ends of the ribbons that held her nightgown together. One by one the bows came undone.

"Show me what's mine," he said, softly.

Her eyes darkened with hunger as she raised her shaky hands to her throat, keeping the garment closed. Then the fabric slid down one shoulder, then lower, exposing the round globes of her breasts, her flat stomach, and then...

He swallowed the aching lump in his throat. "Put it aside," he said gruffly.

Every rustle of fabric was audible through the silence—until every inch of her was revealed to him.

His body throbbed painfully but he hesitated before lying over her, unsure of what his hands would do, knowing how he could lose his mind touching her. She had gotten to him. He had wanted her the first day when she came to ask for help, had wanted her every night when he woke up in a wrenching, unfulfilled sweat produced by dreams so vivid and erotic he would remember them even by day. He'd been fantasizing about a family with her, a real family.

He would never let her go.

He grabbed her wrists gently between his hands and guided her arms up over her head, pinning her there, so he could see her in the dim lighting.

She gazed up at him, her eyes shining with need and want.

Holding her wrists trapped in one hand, he slid the other between her heaving breasts, past her navel, to caress the silky curls at the apex of her thighs. "Been waiting to touch you." He stroked the glistening folds with one finger, then inserted it into her tight sheath and she gasped and arched back in pleasure. "I need to see, Beth…your face…hear the sounds you make."

Her eyes drifted shut as he inserted a second finger, her face twisting into a grimace of pleasure. "Please," she said, and tears laced her voice. "Touch me."

"Where? Where, Beth baby? Here?" Releasing her wrists, he cupped one breast and roughly scraped his thumb across the pebbled nipple, pleased when she vaulted up to his hand.

Her voice shook. "Everywhere."

She looked so damned beautiful, still shy somehow. And beautiful.

His heart beat so hard he thought he'd crack a rib, and inside of him, a painful need began to squeeze his gut. Two wives. One had betrayed him to Halifax. And this one…his little Buffy. He couldn't even think of her betraying him, couldn't fathom how it would feel.

"Beth," he huskily prodded, seizing her hand and guiding it under the elastic of his pants. "That's for you." He twirled his tongue across the tip of one breast, breathing hard as she enveloped his erection. He pitched his hips deeper into her palm. "To pleasure you." Growling, he turned his head to lick the other breast, suckling it into his mouth. "To show you how much I want you."

"I want you, too. I want you so much, Landon."

The words, what he craved and so much more when she

combined it with a flutter of her fingers against the length of his aching hardness, undid him. He'd let down his walls, had let her inside, and he trembled with the force of his desire.

He closed his eyes, tangled his fingers into her hair, and kissed her, really kissed her.

She was his, would never again belong to anyone else—every breath she took, the plea in her eyes, the delicate nectar sliding along his fingers as he dipped the middle one between her legs, it all confirmed she was Landon's.

He threw himself into that kiss.

Her need for Landon consumed her, her hand sliding out from stroking that mouthwatering hardness to now claw all over his back as she pressed closer and kissed him deeper. She couldn't remember wanting a man so much, wanting anything so much.

She gasped when he tore free.

With burning silver eyes, Landon ran his fingertip gently over her trembling lip. His velvety voice sent her into pulsing, surging bliss. "Is this my present, wife?" He stroked her lips and bent his dark head, kissing them gently. "These lips?"

Fevered for his touch, she closed her eyes and purred, having never been spoken to so erotically. "Yes."

She could smell him all around her—cologne and cleanness and desire. He grazed her lips and she felt an incredible rise of sensation and need. The sound, weak, was hers as his hand slid down her back, to grab her buttocks and press her against his hot hard length.

"Are you my present, Beth? Your breasts? Your body?" he whispered fiercely and gathered her closer against him, his weight bearing her down on the bed. He covered her mouth before she could say yes.

She sagged and clung to him as his strong, supple tongue made a path into her mouth. Scalding hot and sweet, he swirled it around hers. Her thighs went liquid as she felt his teeth behind his lips, gently biting her flesh.

She moaned, kissing him back, kissing his throat, his shoulders, her nails biting into his back.

"Need to see…" he murmured against her temple.

He stretched his arm out and flicked the other lamp on. The room burst with even more bright light. Beth gasped and covered her breasts with her hands, crossing her legs, feeling much more vulnerable, totally revealed.

Landon shifted back to take in her image, his lids half-mast across his eyes. "Remove your hands."

Her stomach jumped in her body, her skin on fire, her veins thrumming with heat. "Don't look."

"Remove your hands, Bethany."

"Oh, please," she whispered, knowing she would not be able to resist him.

He grasped her wrists and urged her arms aside, her breasts bared for his eyes. His eyes smoldered at the sight of the creamy globes with the puckered areolas. "You've been hiding from me for weeks. I won't let you hide anymore."

She flushed red, reaching to where her nightgown lay discarded somewhere over the bed, but his hands covered the mounds. "Oh," she gasped.

She sucked in a breath when his thumbs swiped across the nipples.

"Beth, I've wanted to see…" With the heel of his palm, he lifted it to his mouth as he ducked his head. "These lovely babies…" He brushed his lips back and forth. "From the moment I met you." He latched on to one and she shivered. He wrapped his arms around her waist and drew her against his chest. "We make good war, Bethany… Do you love with the same passion you hate?"

She bit her lower lip and clutched the back of his head, her voice a squeak. "No."

"I don't believe you, little wife, I don't believe you one bit."

She shut her eyes. A burst of passion overruled her, greater than hate, greater than anything.

He reached between their bodies to pull the drawstring of his pants open, his arms fully extending as he positioned himself over her once more. He was naked now. As naked as she.

What Landon revealed made her eyes widen and her mouth flood for a taste. His penis strained, enormous and powerful.

"Don't be frightened." He cupped the back of her head and held her imprisoned for his descending lips. She responded to his kiss, drowning in a sea of ecstasy, loving how his arousal rubbed against her stomach. She was swept into a tide of lust as he gently rocked it against her.

A need for him, for feeling him buried into her depths, built and clenched inside her womb.

Her hands roamed and savored the silk of his skin under her fingers, his form solid and heavy and smooth, his jaw deliciously abrading her skin as he nuzzled her breasts. Simple, unadultered lust. It was just that. But it felt like more, like it was everything. A deluge of sensations assailed her.

"I've pictured you like this so many times, Bethany." He reached between her legs and his touch slipped and slid into her. "I pictured you wet...as wet as this. Soaked for me."

She was lost in his eyes, their warmth swirling around her. She surged upward, clutching his shoulders, and scraped her cheeks like a cat against the faint stubble of beard along his jaw.

"Landon." Her fingers then trailed down the furring of dark hair on his chest. His mouth was a flame racing through her skin. Every groan of his surged in her blood like a drug, intoxicating her.

His tone slid like a rasp of silk, low and seductive. "My beautiful wife."

Twisting her head on the pillows, she caught him closer to her, bringing his prominent erection to nestle between her thighs. She parted her legs—a perfect fit. "Please."

He started leaving her, and her limbs clenched around him in panic. "No!"

"Shh. I'm merely getting a condom."

She released him, flustered. "Oh." She stole a glimpse of his rigid stomach, his hair-dusted thighs and calves as he bit the foil packet and tore it open with his teeth. He slid the protection on, and she had never seen anything sexier than Landon's hands, covering his erection. "What?" he persisted with gentle firmness.

She shuddered, pierced with rapture as he sat on the edge of the bed. "Thank you—for remembering about that."

He dragged her over his lap, his hands guiding her legs around his hips. He impaled her slowly, completely, and groaned. His lips locked around her risen nipples and suckled. She bucked as pleasure shot through her. He blew and licked at the peaks, killing her softly. Heat spread through her body, unfurling like ribbons. She heard her moans, their bodies slapping in rhythm. His cheeks were flaming hot, Beth's body perspiring and quivering like a strained bow.

She'd never known anything could be like this, this togetherness existed, this passion, this need and this hunger.

His hips arched into hers hard. Over and over again. His hands guided her own movements, bouncing her against him. Faster, deeper, with more purpose.

Her body ruled, screamed, opened and closed around him. The burn intensified, the clench in her womb unbearable.

Her cry came first, but the sound he made was greater, so sexy, so low, torn from his chest as he shuddered.

And in that instant it was just him and her, no war, no one else, but Beth and Landon.

Eleven

He wanted to see her.

One night, one long board meeting, three phone calls, one conference call and two coffees later, Landon Gage wanted to see his wife in the middle of the morning.

Holy God, he'd never felt like this. Superhuman, all powerful, complete.

In the six years before her he'd needed nothing but himself. Now it was early morning, and he stood in his office by the sunlit window, remembering how he'd woken up with a warm, snuggly Beth less than four hours ago. His body hungered still, an animal awakened and demanding to take every need and craving not appeased for years. He wanted her again—right now.

But he would not be satisfied with just her body. He wanted something else.

The family he'd been robbed of.

Her trust, her respect, hell, her *love*.

He wanted it.

He'd watched her hair, thick and lustrous, tumble past her shoulders as she lay asleep, and he'd memorized her lips, wet and plump and desirable, and his face had tightened with pent-up need as he stood in his Boss suit, dressed for work and unwilling to leave.

She'd stirred in bed like a sleepy kitten and stretched out her arms above her head, her breasts peeping out from under the covers. He'd never seen anything so beautiful. He wanted to bend over and gently take the pink peaks of her nipples and suckle her, but instead he sat next to her and placed a hand on her hips, caressing her.

"Rough night?" he asked, huskily. He caught her scent in the sheets, mingled with his, and he felt light-headed.

Beth made a sultry sound and rolled to her side to face him. Her smile was endless, her cheeks flushed. "I still think I dreamed it. You?" Her voice was throaty with sleep—he liked it.

The urge to taste her again rippled in his insides. He bent, smelling her, inhaling her, a sensation he recognized as anticipation heating his blood and groin as he kissed her lips. "I've got to go."

She pulled him to her. A prickle of excitement tightened every inch of his body as their mouths tangled, so he kissed her harder. But his thoughts intruded, tormenting his insides. Halifax must be taken care of….

He set himself free. "I've got to go," he repeated, more sternly.

She sat up with a frown, glancing at the clock. "What time is it?"

"Seven-thirty."

He watched her tie the ribbon of her wrinkled gown, and his body screamed for him to rip off his tie and jump back in bed with her.

He forced himself to take several steps to the door. "I pride myself in being the first at the office. I'm late as it is."

Her eyes twinkled with laughter. "So everyone will know you spent last night in bed with me, then."

Only I'll know, he thought. *And I'll know it all day.*

Lust vibrated inside him at the thought, tightening his legs, his groin, as he watched her walk over on those amazing bare legs. "You're my wife," he said, gutturally. "From this moment on, you sleep in my bed."

Instead of protesting, she nodded slowly, which only served to heighten his desire to alarming levels. They'd trusted each other completely, no walls, no deceit. She'd told him things, about how she'd wanted him, and he'd told her things, too.

"Maybe you should stay awhile," she said in a wispy voice, fingering his collar. "And I'll make you breakfast, Landon."

Court hearing, he thought as he gazed fixedly at her soft, delicious mouth. *Need to schedule the court hearing. Then Beth leaves and I go back to the way I was before. No! I won't allow it. She's mine—she's staying with me.* Me.

God, but she was caring and warm and giving. He could stay with her all morning.

But he didn't. He hadn't.

He'd exerted every ounce of willpower, told her to go buy something for court and had made it to the office on time before his brothers. On time to his meetings, to give Beth what she wanted. Her son.

He'd never been so determined to nail Halifax before—as though that one action would make his every unknown dream come true.

From 9:00 a.m. to 11:00 a.m., Landon had closeted himself with his lawyers and brothers to review the evidence they had on Halifax so far. Mason, the attorney at family law, assured him that with the taped confession Julian had wheedled out of Hector's head nurse, the odds were on their side. Not to mention, the staggering evidence of health fraud stacking up on Hector's back. The man was embezzling pharmaceuticals with the help of a wanted Mexican smuggler. He was robbing health insurance companies by duplicating claims, and prescribing expensive, dangerous medications the patients didn't really need.

The guy was a con man, a liar and a fraud with an M.D.

Once they'd finished their discussion and wrapped up their plans, Landon attempted to delve back into work, but kept thinking about the tousled siren he'd left this morning in bed.

He wanted to feel confident about the hearing, but too much rode on that one day, one decision, to find any ease for the stiff muscles in his back. He felt tense, primed like a prized fighting bull—and damned hot at the thought of being with his wife again.

He wanted to see her. Smack in the middle of the day, he wanted to see his wife.

He picked up the phone and dialed the house, but when Martha mentioned Bethany had gone out with Thomas to the mall, he rang for his assistant.

"Donna, I'm taking an early lunch with my wife. Reroute all my calls."

In the midst of a shopping frenzy, Beth opened the dressing-room door. "Miss, would you happen to have this in—"

Landon's Hermès tie stood an inch from her nose and Beth squeaked and covered herself as if she were naked. She stumbled back. "What are you doing here? Get out!"

"Relax." He stepped inside, shut the door and leaned back on his heels, forehead furrowed as he regarded the skirt and jacket she'd tried on. "Drop your hands, let me see."

Beth dropped her hands, wanting to pull a bag over her face, she felt so red. She forced herself to remain still as his eyes traveled her, lingering in indecent places. The suit was about as secretarial as they came, but she could've been stark naked for the way his eyes regarded her. "Good." He met her gaze with a sarcastic tilt of his lips. "For a woman twice your age, perhaps."

"I need to look respectable for court," she reminded him.

"You can look both young and respectable." Suddenly, he was deeper into the room, prying through the choices that hung to the side. With the bright overhead lights, his face was perfectly clear. Bronze, chiseled, he was a Greek god.

"Can I help you with any sizes?" The saleslady peeped through the shuttered door.

He straightened as though the woman had been speaking to him. He flung the door open and Beth heard a startled gasp. "Yes. Bring my wife something elegant, expensive and unique. Not too showy, well-cut..." He turned his attention to Beth. "Your size?"

"Six."

"Six it is. Anything else, sir?"

He studied the lingerie piled on the corner chair—white—which she had discreetly brought over to try on.

"And lingerie," he added, watching Beth's reaction as he lifted a plain cotton panty up to his line of vision. "Something feminine and smaller than this."

Bethany could find no place to hide, with all the mirrors in the room. She saw four Landons—his back—his profile—his front. All of the sights were quite mesmerizing. His fingers touching the panty was the sexiest thing she'd ever seen.

Landon plopped down on the sole chair and folded his arms behind his head as the woman came in with an assortment of clothes. Beth dared not look at the prices, but the fabrics were exquisite, the cuts sublime.

All it took was a man in Hugo Boss to say, "Bring something nice," and suddenly, voilà, Chanel was on the rack.

"Akris," the saleslady said of a cream dress with a boat-cut shoulder. "You won't want to take it off. Like second skin, very flattering on." She turned to Landon. "And—" She pulled out bra after bra, panty after panty, of the most decadent lace imaginable. "For your wife."

"Leave them here."

She did, and then asked if Beth needed help with the Akris

dress. "It's difficult to button in the back," she explained. "Rows and rows of buttons."

Landon had opened a magazine among a stack on a small table and pretended to be riveted. The saleslady proceeded to help Beth out of the jacket and skirt so she could get into the dress. "I'm used to the men hardly even looking. They've seen everything," she muttered into Beth's ear.

"Yes, but mine is—"

"Gorgeous, darling, oh, goodness, the ladies outside are just waiting to have an eyeful."

Beth frowned. *Oh, were they?* She pretended nonchalance as the woman slipped the Akris dress on and began to work button after button, and when Beth turned, Landon's hot, appreciative gaze hit her like a blast.

"Well," the lady said, patting her back, "what do you think?"

Beth caught her reflection; she looked good, the dress fitting beautifully and making her seem even curvier than she actually was—which in her case was a good thing.

But the opinion both women waited for did not come.

For the longest time, Landon said nothing. Then gruffly, "Leave us, please."

He set the magazine down, and Beth's heart began to thump wildly as the saleslady departed. The dress detailed everything—the soft mounds of her breasts, the peaked nipples, her hips.

"Do you like it, Landon?"

She needed to hear his opinion now, because his gaze made her mind pull this way and that, and her stomach kept fluttering.

He reached out to her waist, inspecting the texture, his features hard with concentration as he considered. He fondled a breast, pushed the mound high in his hand and rubbed gently. "Why did you marry him?"

His touch and all that it caused inside her made it difficult to speak. "I told you. I was young. And pregnant. And stupid—"

As she spoke, he looped his fingers through the gold belt around her waist and drew her toward him. As their hips met, their lips met, and she felt him respond, growing harder against her, groaning as he kissed her.

When he stopped, he let out a breath of frustration, and released her. But he did not step back, continued caging her in with his body. He reached around her and plucked open a button, then another. "Why him?"

She reached behind her and tried closing the opening, but his hand was already there, stroking downward. She watched his face contort in hunger. Felt his jealousy, how it was eating at him, burned in his eyes. "He...he did something nice for me. I thought that meant he was a nice person, and I was too young to know better."

He undid a couple more buttons. His big hands trapped her buttocks in each. He kneaded the flesh. "Me buying you clothes is nice. Isn't it?"

"Yes, you—you buy me nice clothes, thank you."

"And yet I'm still the bastard who will help you sink him." His erection scraped against her pelvis and he held her there, his prisoner, and bent his head to let the tip of his tongue dip into her cleavage.

The hot wet heat of his tongue made a sound rise to her throat, a sound of agony. "Yes."

He gripped her bottom tighter and hoisted her up in the air, forcing her legs around him, forcing her to cling as he braced her back against the wall. He caught her earlobe between his teeth, making her toes start to tingle as he nibbled.

She flushed all over. "Landon, don't."

His mouth teased her, approaching hers, retreating then coming closer once again. She shuddered as he pressed into her. Her nails dug into his shoulders.

"Do you see that bit of red over there?" He jerked his head toward the hangers that held all the wicked lingerie.

"Yes."

He touched her cheek with three fingers, stroking downward

so sensually she could burst. "I want to know it's under this dress."

"Landon, I don't…"

"Say, 'Yes, Landon'—that's all I want you to say. No one will know. Only me and you. Our own personal little revenge over Halifax." When he moved her arms up high over her head and lowered his head he added, "Let's go out tonight, you and me, Beth."

"You're asking me on a date," she panted, breathless and yet struggling to get free. "Won't our mamas love that."

"I don't care about our mamas. What do you say?"

A laugh escaped her and he broke into a grin, chuckling with her. Her husband. Her wonderful, strong, thirty-three year old husband. On a date.

"Yes."

He kissed her lightly on the forehead before he released her. "You better be ready for me."

But he'd worked Beth so well she thought perhaps her husband should be the one who should be ready for her.

He sent her home with an Akris dress and one very sexy red lingerie set and a mind that whirled and whirled with memories of what they'd almost done in a Neiman Marcus dressing room.

For the rest of the afternoon, she delved into the new "Share Your Recipe" section of the catering website. When the phone rang, she didn't think twice about answering. She lifted it from the desk with a happy "Yes?"

"Outside Maggiano's restaurant at the RIM shopping center. Meet me there in twenty minutes—or you can forget about David."

Halifax hung up.

Twelve

Fear had a strange beat. It slowed down everything—the time, the way Beth's mind processed things. It slowed down everything except her heartbeat. Beth couldn't let Thomas drive her to the restaurant, so she asked for the Navigator, saying she wanted to see her mother, hating to have to lie but too frightened not to.

She made it there in seventeen minutes, but the fear, the gut-wrenching fear, made it seem like years.

These were seventeen minutes of torture where she imagined the worst—David being shipped off somewhere, out of her reach, her touch, forever.

Whatever you do, don't fall apart, Bethany.

Outside the Italian restaurant, under the shadow of a green tent, Hector lit a cigarette, the tip glowing as he watched her shut the car door and come over.

Heavy clouds gathered above, promising a heavy rain. A family of four exited the restaurant, their cheerful chatter contrasting with the silence with which Hector greeted her.

Beth waited for him to speak first, keenly aware of his potential for violence. But for endless minutes he merely smoked his cigarette and looked her slowly up and down as though he could see Landon's fingertips and brands on her body.

It struck Beth how in six years married to him, she'd never experienced an ounce of the happiness, the connection, she'd felt with Landon in a matter of weeks. How sad that she hadn't known this before, hadn't known that things didn't need to be stale, that things could be better than boring and actually be wonderful.

"You've been talking to Gage," Hector drawled in a hard, insulting voice, putting out his cigarette with his boot. "He's been poking around my business—what did you tell him, Beth?"

She loathed to discover the fear she'd once had of him was still present, crawling up her spine and ready to immobilize her. It was followed with animosity, and hate, so much hate she began to tremble.

"Well, he is my husband. And we do talk, Hector." It had been a long, long time since she'd spoken to him so firmly.

His eyes became slits, as he gave her the most chilling, most frightening smile. "Your little game has gone on long enough. I say it's time we put a stop to it, don't you? Your mouth has been flapping open for weeks and Beth?" He pitched his voice lower. *"I don't like it."*

Bubbles of hysteria rose to her throat, and she had to swallow before speaking. "The game has only just begun," she said, fighting to sound confident. "I've told him things, Hector. But I've still got to tell him how you medicated his wife until she couldn't even think straight!"

His eyes widened, and he took a threatening step forward. "You wouldn't dare."

"Oh, I dare all right!" She took a step back—and Hector another step forward. "He's on to you, Hector. He knows what you are!"

He manacled her wrist in one hand, his tobacco breath blasting across her face. "One more word out of you and your little husband—"

"You can't hurt him!" she spat, anger and frustration sharpening her voice as she squirmed to free herself. She wanted to shrink from his gaze, his lashing words, his beastly touch. "You've tried for years and you can't touch him!"

His expression contorted into a terrifying sneer. His nails bit into her skin. "Oh, I can hurt him. I'll tear Gage apart if you take me to court, Beth."

She laughed cynically. "Right. Like *you* can destroy a Gage."

Smiling that Lucifer-like smile, he released her. Beth rubbed her wrist as he lighted another cigarette, took a drag, then flicked it down on the ground, and stepped on it. "You're a Lewis." He blew the smoke into her face. "A little nobody. As easily crushed…as this. And Gage…he's scrupulous and it will get him killed. That's no way to win a war, Beth. You'll never get David. Ever."

Her breath grew choppy. Fear and fury whirled and churned in her belly. How could you spend years and years of your life with a rat? How could you bear it?

And Landon. What would he do when she told him about this? He'd warned her not to see him, talk to Hector, but he didn't understand this bastard had her *child!*

"Why do you want him?" she screamed, gripping her purse tight to her chest to keep from flinging it at him. "You hardly paid attention to him. Why do you want him?"

"Because you do." His face was a mask of rage, and his words poison. "Oh, I may have eventually given him back to you, after you learned your lesson of what happens when you leave me. But not after Gage, oh, no, never after Gage. Unless…" Hector snagged her elbow and immediately the space between them disappeared as he stepped forward. "Unless you divorce him and come back to me."

Somewhere in the depths of her panic, she found her courage. She yanked her arm free, and said, "Go to hell."

But he moved fast and he seized her by the arm. This time he cut off her circulation. "Look behind you, Beth. Do you see my blue Lexus parked by the oaks?"

Woodenly, Beth turned, his grip spreading a biting pain up her arm. She saw him. David. His little face pressed against the glass, tears streaming down his cheeks.

Panic choked her.

"David!" she cried, and started for him without thought. Hector yanked her back by both arms and wheeled her around to face him.

He pressed his face inhumanly close, so that when he spoke, she could feel his loathsome lips moving against her own pursed ones. "The only way you can see him and touch him and kiss him is if you return to me. If you return to my bed."

Beth didn't know how she managed, only knew that she had to leave, now, before this became a public spectacle.

She spat into his face, wrenched free, and ran, her breath soughing out of her chest like a hunted animal's. She flung herself against the side of the Lexus and tried yanking open the door, but it didn't budge. "Mommy!" she heard David wail from the inside, frightened, and her heart broke when she heard the muffled cry coming over and over like a litany.

Tears flowed down her cheeks as she fought with the door. She was crying—crying for him, for her, for every mother.

Helpless to get him out, she put her hand against the window and spread it wide and spoke as loudly as she could. "David, I'm going to be with you soon, I promise! I *promise!*"

And then, before she could notice that David had also spread his palm open on his side of the window, fitting the shape of his small hand into hers, Hector had revved up the engine and sped off with a screech of tires.

Taking her son, her baby, with him once more.

* * *

Landon jotted down notes on the legal pad on his desk, then typed the data into his computer. His intercom buzzed, and Donna's voice burst through the speaker.

"Mr. Gage, Detective Harris here to see you."

"Show him in."

His office doors swung open. Harris was a little man with an unremarkable face and a keen eye—the perfect spy. He sat and pulled out a sheaf of papers, matching Landon's brisk manner. "Your wife was out and about today," he said.

Landon's answering smile was brief, cool, as he lifted another file to skim through. "I know. I was with her this morning."

"Well, she seemed to be in a rush to make an appointment this afternoon."

Landon's movements halted. She'd gone out?

When the man remained silent, Landon shot him an impatient look over the top of the report he'd been reading. "And she went where?" Landon set the report aside, and the little man shifted when he gave him his undivided attention.

"To meet Hector Halifax."

Harris dropped the pictures on his desk and Landon's chest muscles froze until he couldn't breathe. He smiled thinly, but inside he experienced something he hadn't felt before. Not in six years. Not ever. He thought he was going to get *sick*. "She went to see Halifax?"

"Indeed."

An instinct to protect her, grab her close to him and never let anyone, much less a rat like Halifax hurt her, warred with the need to grab her little neck and shake some common freaking sense into her.

Why? Why, Bethany, damn it, why?

He gritted his molars in anger. "You must be mistaken," he said.

But Harris rarely was, and signaled at the photographs. "I'm sorry, Mr. Gage. But the pictures speak for themselves."

Landon glared down at them at first, still stunned by the fact that Beth had met Halifax today...

Today, of all days, when they'd at last been granted a hearing date. What she'd done was both reckless and stupid, and finding out this way only poked at the ghosts of a dark, bleak past Landon had long ago tucked away.

Forcing his hand to keep steady, he inspected the pictures on his desk, one by one. This was the second time the man across his desk had brought him this kind of news. The first time, it had enraged him. And now...

His heart stopped at the sight of her in the photographs—the sight of her betraying him.

They were touching... Halifax was touching her... Beth was letting him. His lips were... My God, they were against hers. What was this? What in the hell was *this?*

"Did you witness this yourself?" he demanded.

"I had some blind spots, sir, as I lingered inside the restaurant. But the times they were together, they were close. As you can see."

Landon saw.

Outside, life continued. The office noise. The ringing phones. He set the last picture down and bent his head, his voice rough as tree bark. "What time?"

"This afternoon. 4:30 p.m."

He squeezed his eyes shut against the emotions that assailed him. The thought of the bastard touching her, of Beth standing there while he held her delicate arms, Beth meekly waiting for the kiss to deepen, made Landon want to tear open a wall.

There had been signals, warning bells. Telling him not to trust, not to *want* her. Landon had ignored them, every last one of them. Her meeting Halifax during their engagement party—her resistance to sleeping with Landon.

He hadn't understood why, but he'd forged ahead, first out of revenge perhaps, then out of sheer blind need, pretending he could build something with Beth, something that lasted, something that through the hate and anger and revenge shone special.

Could he have imagined whatever had been growing between them? Could he be that blind? That stupid?

Or had Beth simply thought to sweet-talk Halifax into relinquishing custody?

But Halifax would use this evidence against her.

Growling in frustration, Landon scraped a rough hand down his face, then he and the detective exchanged a glance that spoke volumes. "Did my wife leave with him?" Landon asked.

"No. When I exited the restaurant, she was getting into her own car."

But not before they'd *kissed!*

Rage stiffened his muscles, gripped his throat, made it hard to speak. Beth's pretty profile in the photo blurred as his vision went red. Halifax. Once again, the bastard thought he could take his wife away from him.

And Beth had gone to him. Despite Landon's warnings, despite how delicate the situation was.

She'd run to the enemy and cast Landon into a role he'd sworn never to be cast in ever again: the fool.

Beth was waiting in the living room, listening to the patter of rain while the dogs slept by the dark fireplace, when she heard Landon's car pull up in the driveway.

After chewing most of her nails off wondering how to describe her encounter with Hector, she felt so glad to see Landon walk through that door, his hair wet, rivulets sliding down his jaw, tiredly dropping a portfolio at his feet, that she flung herself against him and eagerly pressed her mouth to his. "Thank God you're home!"

Stiff and unresponsive, Landon set her aside and commanded the dogs to back off.

Stunned, Beth watched him carry his portfolio over to the desk where he kept his agenda. He set it down on the surface with a thump. "Do you have anything you wish to tell me, Beth?"

He trapped her gaze, and her already-wrung heart seemed to die a sudden death.

She sensed something was wrong.

All around Landon—her husband, her lover, her new best friend—was a wall, emitting a signal to stay away.

The romantic fantasies she'd been entertaining, the ones of kissing him and loving him before she confessed she'd seen Hector, were destroyed by this harsh reality.

Landon was as closed to her as she'd ever seen him.

Tight-lipped, he retrieved a folder from the inside of the leather case. With an impenetrable look in his eyes, he went to the small bar and prepared a drink. "Cat got your tongue?" he prodded, file in one hand as he poured with the other.

"What's wrong with you…?" Beth asked, confused and wide-eyed. "And what's with the file?"

As he brushed past her, he put the folder in her hand. He fell into the chair behind a small desk with his drink in hand, and said, "Open it."

Beth's hands trembled as she obeyed.

It wasn't the tone he'd used, icy with contempt, or the way he held himself unapproachable as he sat there that unnerved her. It was the look in his eyes.

He knew.

"Recognize the woman in those photographs, dear wife?"

She stared at them and almost keeled over.

The images were staggering, images of her and Hector, speaking and arguing and *kissing*. The bile rose to her throat as she tossed the photos aside. "It's not how it looks, Landon."

Landon smiled, deceptively. Beth opened her mouth to explain more but was dazzled by the gleam of his eyes, stormy with something raw and masculine. Storming with *jealousy*.

Beth could almost hear the trust between them shattering like glass.

Oh, God, what had she done?

"I promise you, Landon, it's not how it looks." With legs that felt ready to buckle, she approached the desk one step at a time and struggled to find the words. But the words seemed to tumble one after the other, fighting to come forth. "He insisted on seeing me, and I needed to know what he wanted. I didn't…kiss him. He forced me. He… Landon, I didn't kiss him."

All expression left his face, but his eyes blazed hot enough to incinerate her. "And what did he want? Huh, Beth? You?"

It hurt to speak. "Yes," she said tightly. *But I'd rather die.*

Lightning struck outside. Rain slammed against the windows, and the howl of the wind echoed in the household. Like the night Landon's first wife died, the night Hector abandoned Beth to meet her; the weather was just as tempestuous and volatile tonight.

Beth felt a worse kind of storm brewing inside her. Fury. It came with a vengeance, overpowering her. She leapt forward as though she'd just been unleashed from captivity and pushed her finger into Landon's chest as he leapt to his feet, too. "How dare you spy on me, how dare you! I did nothing wrong. I'm not…I'm not Chrystine! My baby is with that beast. How can you expect me to not do anything?"

He caught her finger in his hand. "I told you to stay away from him, Beth!"

Her chin jerked up in defiance. "I'm a mother and I'd do anything for my child! What about you, huh? Are you even *helping* me? Or do you conveniently find obstacles in order to keep me around to slake your lust?"

He scoffed. "Slake my lust, that's what you call it?"

"That's what it is! What else would I call it?"

"I didn't slake my lust with you last night, Beth. I made love to you. Love, damn you!"

"Well, excuse me if it doesn't feel like it!" she lied.

Making a sound of frustration, he flung her hand aside as if she'd singed him and drained his glass in one long gulp.

Breathless with fury and emotion, Beth cradled her finger to her chest with one hand, hating that it tingled after he'd grasped it, and when he remained quiet, she shook her head.

"I'm your revenge, Landon, why don't you just admit it!" she cried. "Tit for tat. A wife for a wife."

He'd been so insistent about getting her in bed, she just knew it was his personal war against Hector.

She heard a faint click outside and saw a sudden flash of light then...thunder.

Landon moved far away from her, to the opposite side of the room. He put a hand up to the window as he watched it rain. A strange gravity entered his voice. "Then the joke's on me."

The tension thickened between them, black like tar in an equally black silence.

The clock ticked under the staircase.

She gazed at his wide broad back. She was so angry and at the same time so in love her throat hurt. Inside she felt dark, dark and lost. She was paralyzed, shattering in panic. Because she loved him. And suddenly it felt like he would never return that love.

"Why did you let him touch you, Beth. Do you miss his touch? Do you want it?" he asked raggedly.

"No!" She gasped, aghast that he would think it.

"You rejected mine all this time because it was him you wanted? Did you pretend I was him last night? When you came for me did you—"

"Stop it, stop it!"

His head fell forward, against the window, and he shook his head ruefully. "Why don't you *trust* me?" he hissed.

"I do, Landon, I *do*. I was frightened. I had to know my son was okay. I was helpless all my life, standing like a good little wife by his side. I don't want to be that person anymore!"

He whipped around and pointed a finger. "You're not his wife anymore, Beth, you're mine. My wife!" he thundered.

"I *know* that!" she shouted back.

"Then aren't I entitled to know my wife is meeting my mortal enemy? I vowed to protect you, Bethany—you and your son. My God! That man, that bastard takes my first wife, and he thinks he can take my second?"

She sucked in a gust of air, for the first time realizing that he'd not only been concerned for her safety, but he was terribly jealous, too. And he was speaking of her as a real wife. Touched in places no one in her life but Landon had ever touched before, she lowered her voice. "I'm all right," she said, so vaguely she wondered if he'd heard her. "And I'm not going anywhere."

He met that with silence.

Dark, emotionless silence.

"I didn't kiss him," she repeated, her voice threatening to crack. Landon's face was twisted in torment, and Beth felt twisted on the inside. "Hector wanted me to...to go back to him. I froze when I saw David in the car, watching us, but I swear to you when Hector pulled me close I shut my mouth tight and I—"

Landon growled so angrily, so deeply, so possessively, she fell quiet.

The wind rattled the window casements. Beth shook with the urge to set things right, but she didn't know how. "I spat at him," she continued, after a moment. "It felt amazing, it did... until he drove away with David."

She made a choked sound at the memory and put her arms around herself.

Revenge had been so simple once. Now Landon thought her a liar, as vile as Halifax, as vile as Chrystine had been, and the thought of being compared to them in his mind distressed her.

"I didn't kiss him," she insisted, staring down at the floor when looking into his accusing eyes became unbearable. "Please believe me."

"Those pictures, Beth—" his voice was low, weary "—could

be used against us at court if he ever finds them. He painted you as a Jezebel once—he'll do it again."

She gathered her fortitude and met his gaze. "I don't care what anyone thinks as long as you believe me."

Watching her, he plunged his hands into his pants pockets as though he didn't know what to do with them. "What we need is to convince the judge you're a good woman, Beth."

She made a distressed sound and flung her hands up in the air. "He threatened me! He grabbed me! I yanked away when I could. What was I supposed to do!"

"I'm going to *goddamned kill him*."

Stunned by the words, Beth blinked.

Landon cursed and approached, the concern and anger etched across his face making her hope soar. "Did he hurt you?" he demanded.

Beth held her breath as his hands briskly sailed down the front buttons of her shirt, unbuttoning and parting the material, then she gasped when he shoved the material down her shoulders and arms until it dangled from one of her wrists.

Dying with lust, she stood meek as Landon frowned and studied her, skimmed his fingers along her throat, the tops of her arms, her elbows. The skin was unmarked. He expelled a relieved breath and met her gaze, a look of male awareness settling in his eyes.

When he cursed low in his throat and left her standing there, struggling to rearrange her clothes, she'd never felt so cold, so abandoned and rejected.

"I had a child once," he began, his ragged words gaining force as he turned around, "and if you cared for yours as much as you say you do, you'd have played it safe and *stayed away* from Hector Halifax, Bethany."

"He wasn't even your son, Landon!" she screamed, out of her wits with fury over his accusations, his blindness. Didn't he know, damn him? Couldn't he see she was achingly, painfully in love with him? She hadn't kissed Hector. All she wanted, needed, was Landon's support tonight, not his accusations.

The tomb-like silence that followed her cry shattered when Landon spoke.

His timbre was dangerously, warningly soft. "What did you just say?"

Beth lowered her voice. "He was Hector's son. He wasn't yours."

His hands balled and his arms trembled and then, *then* he made a low, terrible sound that tore through her like a knife cut.

That's when it struck her. When the horrible words she'd said dawned on her. What she'd said, how she'd said it, angrily, meant to hurt him.

"Landon, I'm sorry, I—" When she reached out for him, he cursed and stepped aside, giving her his back. "Landon, I didn't mean it like this. It's just that Hector demanded a DNA test before he and Chrystine ran away. I saw the results. He's the father. They fooled around for years, he and Chrystine. They loved making each other jealous. They married us to spite each other off, Landon. Chrystine loved to rub it in Hector's nose how she was able to snag you when you were the best catch—"

His smile grew chillier, and he began to laugh, holding up a hand to stop her. "Don't. Say anymore."

Stopped by that cynical sound, Beth helplessly stood a few feet away, and the ground under her feet had never felt so perilous. What had she done?

Her throat was so clogged she barely heard her own voice, which sounded strangled when she spoke. "I realize I should've told you before, about your son."

"You knew, all this time. You knew about my son and you let me think…you let me talk to you about him…you—"

"It makes no difference!" she cried.

He roared and slammed his chest with one fist. "It makes a difference to *me!*"

He'd still been holding his drink in his other hand, and a slosh of whiskey splashed onto the carpet. Cursing, Landon drained what was left and set the empty glass on the desk, then he stared into its depths.

She considered how she'd take it if someone came up to her and told her David wasn't her son. How she'd feel if *Landon*, a man whose respect she wanted, had told her this news in the same way Beth had told him.

She shrunk inside her skin, feeling so small.

"I'm sorry, Landon," she said, her voice small, too.

Her eyes welled up for the second time today. She was afraid the tears wouldn't stop until morning.

She didn't know where she found the courage to speak. "Where d-do we stand now? With us? With...David?"

He wouldn't tear his gaze off that empty glass. "I said I'd get you your son back. And I will."

And us?

She couldn't ask it again—somewhere deep down, she knew. Could hear the word "divorce" as clearly as she heard the thunder.

They'd become each other's enemies.

Thirteen

"Pretend you love me well and hard or by God this will blow up in our faces!"

Landon hissed the words into her ear, and a hot shiver raced down Beth's spine. Her nerves were stretched taut in a combination of anticipation and fear.

This was the day she'd been waiting for.

Her heart pounded a nervous beat as she gazed around the space they'd been appointed. The courtroom was exactly the one in her earlier trial: impersonal and cold.

The judge's seat above them loomed empty while their lawyer busily shuffled his notes. His name was Mason Dawson, a young, ruthless attorney already reaping the benefits of his killer reputation. He had assured Beth and Landon every time they met that he didn't lose.

Beth prayed his winning streak wouldn't end with her.

Hector's lawyer, on the other hand, sat at the table on the opposite side, stealing glances at her wristwatch. It was a smart choice to have a woman represent him—someone female to soften his image.

Beth's parents, Mrs. Gage, Garrett, Julian John, Kate and even Thomas had settled themselves in the benches.

But what Beth was most aware of, with every atom, cell and fiber in her body, was the man at the table beside her.

Landon fairly reeked of fury. He stood tall and solid to her right, a tower of testosterone that pricked her body with awareness.

She couldn't help but think of the Akris dress she wore, the underwear she wore beneath. Would Landon even attempt to discover if she'd worn the red lingerie like he'd told her to?

God, she was lovesick. Or just sick.

"He's late," their lawyer muttered to them.

Just then, the doors burst open, and Hector appeared.

He looked like a man who'd just had an encounter with a rabid lion and had barely come out of it on his feet.

He stumbled forward, a dark coffee stain on his olive green coat. His hair was rumpled, his face streaked with dirt as though he'd tripped in a mud puddle.

He whipped off his coat as he went to his table, his cheeks flushed with two bright red flags. His lawyer, concerned, immediately rose, and he bit out, "I'm fine! Just an inconvenience." He glared in Landon's direction.

Beth frowned, her eyes sailing to his inscrutable profile.

Had Landon somehow planned Hector's…inconvenience?

The object of her wondering edged closer to her, and the back of his long fingers grazed her knuckles, the contact as sudden as it was exquisite. Landon prolonged that touch, and finally snatched up her hand in his.

Her knees turned to jelly, and a lump of emotion lodged in her throat. She could cry. She knew he held her hand for appearances, pretense, and yet she squeezed and curled her fingers through his and held on to him like a lifeline.

His breath stirred the hair on top of her head, and when she trembled slightly, he laced his fingers tighter through hers. His voice softened. "Relax. Look confident."

Beth tried. This was not the moment to get emotional, to dwell on the past horrible weeks. But she couldn't stop weeping inside.

There was no removing that sensation, that horrible sensation of having been hanged. Stabbed in the chest. Or shot.

She'd hurt him in the worst possible way, and now Landon hated her.

She stiffened when the judge appeared in a swish of robes. He was a bald man with a beard, a determined set to his jaw, and clear eyes.

"Ladies and gentlemen, this court is now in session. The Honorable Judge Prescott presiding. All rise."

Beth's mind whirled with images of David's toothy grin, memories of how his face had been streaked with tears the last time she'd seen him, and her heart felt ready to implode. She may have nothing, she realized, straightening her spine, but she fought for everything.

When she stood up, she met Halifax's sparkling blue gaze—icy cold. She made her own expression glacial.

Together, her parents and Landon's group crowded the two front rows on their side. They presented a united front, a respectable family. Standing so close and so proud, the Gages emitted that same power Landon did.

But…why was that not reassuring?

Because without Landon's respect, Beth felt apart, not one of them. Because without Landon's interest in her, the caring way he'd protected her before, she felt…fraudulent.

Like Hector.

"Your Honor," Mason began in a crisp opening statement. "I stand before you today on behalf of my clients, Landon and Bethany Gage, with a petition for full custody of David Halifax. Landon Gage has been an upstanding citizen of this community for the past thirty-three years. His wife, Bethany

Gage, has been outrageously accused in the past—and has suffered a great injustice. A mother. Robbed of the opportunity to give love and affection and participate in the raising of her son."

A dramatic pause ensued while Mason raked the courtroom with his eyes, continuing only when convinced everyone's focus lay on him.

"I beg you to consider today, who is the better custodian? A father who's suspected of fraud, a father whose very nature of work keeps him long hours at the office, such as Dr. Hector Halifax? Or a solid, upstanding couple, a well-respected businessman and a dedicated mother whose guidance is indispensable to a young child David's age?"

He allowed the question to linger before he resumed his seat in dramatic silence, and Hector's lawyer opened her own statement with a receding chuckle.

"Your Honor, Dr. Hector Halifax's reputation is pristine. His entire life he's been dedicated to the well-being of others, especially his own son. Should a man be punished for loving and protecting his child from his mother's neglect? Should a man who has nurtured and cared for young David during the past year be discriminated against for being a single parent?" She glared at Bethany. "Considering the petitioner's numerous love affairs while she was married to my client, I doubt her marriage to Mr. Gage will even last long."

The petitioner, in this case Beth and Landon, was the first to call up a witness. Beth.

She took a series of measured steps to the stand, inhumanly aware of the sexy lingerie that hugged her body under the dress. She sat and concentrated on inhaling, in and out, in and out. But for the way she truly felt, she could've been naked and strapped to an electric chair.

"Mrs. Gage, how long were you married to Hector Halifax?"

Beth focused on Mason's striped tie. That lone, harmless tie was the only spot she would allow herself to focus on.

"Almost seven years."

"Were you happy during those seven years, Mrs. Gage?"

She wrung her hands. "I was happy when our son was born."

Mason thoughtfully paced the floor before her. Playing the game she supposed all lawyers played, he allowed her heart to beat three times before he spoke again. "Were you happy during the remainder of those years?"

"No."

Mason swung round to face her fully. "No. You weren't happy married to Hector Halifax." He approached, his expression as intent as his voice. "Can you tell the court why you were unhappy?"

Skewered under not only Mason's sharp brown gaze, but also a dozen others, Beth struggled to find a starting point.

"Did he physically abuse you, Mrs. Gage?" Mason leaned back on his heels and waited. "Was he unfaithful?"

She seized her cue, almost leaping. "Yes. He was unfaithful."

Mason stole a brief glance in the judge's direction. "Hector Halifax was unfaithful to you. When did you decide to leave him?"

"When I realized he'd loved another woman all the time he'd been married to me. And when I realized I didn't love him anymore, maybe never really had."

"How did Hector take it? Your separation?"

Aware of Hector's eyes burning holes through the top of her head, she wouldn't give him the satisfaction of looking at him.

"We had several failed attempts to separate, but he persuaded me to stay. I was only successful when David turned six. Over a year ago."

"Did his method of persuading you to remain married include blackmail, Mrs. Gage? Perhaps…in the way of these pictures? Presented to court during your first hearing?"

Beth spotted a wad of pictures in Mason's hands, and the

humiliation she felt threatened to overwhelmed her. Just to think of Landon seeing those pictures of her in different men's embraces, even if they were fake, made her stomach roil. "Yes, that did play a part. And of course, he threatened to take David away."

"Your Honor, may I present for evidence both the pictures *and* lab report which concludes these photographs have been tampered with?"

The judge received the stack of pictures and the lab paper Mason produced and reviewed them in tense silence. Beth squirmed in her seat, part of her wishing she'd had such a kick-butt lawyer on her side the last time she'd been in court, and another part dreading what came next. Hector's lawyer looked so pale and pissed Beth was sure she was going to be that woman's lunch.

Mason continued the interrogation, his questions expertly phrased in ways that shed light on the good, caring mother she was. A loving wife who hadn't been properly appreciated by her first husband.

Her nervousness escalated when the topic led to the new man in her life. Landon. To speak of Landon and Hector in the same conversation almost felt like blasphemy.

Beth struggled to put up a brave front, an image of a new family, but in the deepest, darkest part of her, she knew what she said was a lie every bit as bad as those Halifax loved making. She didn't offer a wonderful new family and a new father to David—she offered only herself and her love.

Suddenly, it didn't feel like enough next to the Gages.

It didn't feel like enough next to the protection, the safety Landon represented.

Everything he'd promised he'd do for Beth, he had. Whatever the verdict, Landon Gage had come through for Beth.

He'd gotten her a new hearing.

And what had *she* done for *him?*

Her throat felt crowded with unspoken words and remorse for how she'd hurt him. She hadn't been his wife who'd betrayed him, who'd abandoned him one rainy night, but she felt like she was—because she'd opened his eyes and he loathed her for it.

Her spirits plummeted when Mason finished off his questioning, and now the other lawyer's turn came up. Beth braced herself for the attack. The female lawyer's eyes glimmered as she approached, not even bothering to hide the fact that she enjoyed every second of Beth's anxiety.

"Mrs. Gage, tell me one thing," the smooth-talking woman began. "Why did you marry Landon Gage? Was it because you needed to clean up your image? Or because of his money?"

Mason slammed a hand down. "Objection, Your Honor!"

"Objection sustained."

"Your Honor," the defense argued, adding a winning smile to drive her point home, "her motivations for the marriage are dubious, at best, especially so soon after her divorce from Mr. Halifax. I insist Mrs. Gage give us a direct answer to a direct question. Why did you marry Mr. Gage?"

Beth waited for someone to object, her dread escalating.

No one objected.

"I'll allow it," the judge conceded, sighing. "Answer the question."

Frantic, her eyes searched a pair of familiar gray ones across the room. The instant her gaze locked with Landon's, her chest exploded with emotion. "I love him," she said, lowering her face as the words, so true and so audible, trickled into her own ears.

"Mrs. Gage, please speak up, we couldn't—"

"I love him. I love Landon."

Landon stiffened as though the truth had been a lie, the confession a slap.

Peering at him through her lashes, Beth's hopes of forgiveness were pulverized. His jaw hardened, and his eyes flashed with accusation. The look in his eyes destroyed her confidence. *Pretend you love me well and hard or by God this'll blow up in our faces,* he'd said.

He thought she was pretending!

"You say you love your husband, and yet my client mentions you've been speaking of a reconciliation?"

Her stomach felt so cramped she thought she'd vomit. "There's no reconciliation."

"Mrs. Gage…" Hector's lawyer lifted a shiny flat object in her hand. She lengthened the moment until the curiosity to discover what she held up for inspection ate at Beth on the inside—like the attorney surely intended it to. "When was this picture taken? Contrary to your attorney's claims on the former pictures, this one is fully authentic, is it not?"

Her entire world, her entire perfect world which consisted of her enjoying a lifetime of full and complete custody of David, seemed to crumple as she gazed down at the photograph. Somehow, these people had managed to produce a new set of photographs from the meeting at Maggiano's. God! How many of these vulgar folks had been watching them? How many cowards had stood there, snapping pictures while her life fell apart, and done nothing to help her?

Outraged, Beth scrutinized the close-up of Hector's lips a breath away from hers. Landon had known this would occur. He'd warned her. He'd told her not to go, and one morning over coffee, she'd agreed.

Then she'd gone to meet that stinking rat Halifax anyway.

And guess what? Landon had been right, and Beth had been utterly *wrong*.

Flustered and blushing a disturbing shade of red, Beth met the woman's hard stare head-on. "Hector called and said I wouldn't be able to see my son if I didn't meet him. You can check the phone records."

"As a matter of fact, I have. Wasn't that you calling from Mr. Gage's home the afternoon of your engagement party?"

"I was calling my son!" Beth burst out, then quickly caught herself and pursed her lips.

Calm. She had to stay *calm*.

The questioning continued; and each lashing sentence pounded her like a sledgehammer. Had she committed infidelities as well? Did she have proof of this supposed infidelity her first husband had committed? Had she written this love note? A love note! A lie, a prefabricated piece of evidence, like those Hector loved to produce.

Beth, upon a silent glare from Mason, limited her answers now to yes and no. Most were no. No, no infidelities, no love note, no reconciliation, until the lawyer tired and allowed Mason to call his next witness.

Landon took the stand.

It seemed that even time stood still in a show of appreciation for his lithe, powerful walk. Beth observed him as she resumed her place at the table, inwardly wanting to sigh. Every sharp plane of his face fascinated her; the arrogant slant of his nose, the raw power in his jaw and the dark shadow across it. She would not look at his thick, fat, plump, delicious mouth, or she would never be able to concentrate.

Mason kept his interrogation brief, but Beth perked up in interest when Hector's lawyer approached to question Landon. If someone could put that hateful woman in her place, it might as well be him.

"Mr. Gage, do you have children?"

His hard, sinewy muscles rippled as he folded his long arms over his chest. He leaned back with such a look of calm that could make even Hector's glares look less chilling. "No."

"Have you ever had children?"

Beth's chest muscles tightened at the knife-edged question. Landon, expressionless, allowed the attorney to wait for a moment before he answered her. "I had a son."

"And where is your son now, Mr. Gage?"

My God, was the woman even human? Beth was furious on Landon's behalf and trembled with the impulse to charge up there and tear the attorney's eyeballs out. No one could know how painful it was to Landon to speak of this boy, except Beth.

"He passed away when he was ten months old," Landon tersely replied.

The judge's expression broke with empathy as he regarded Landon.

"Tell me, Mr. Gage. Is David your son?" the attorney asked.

"He's my wife's son."

"And my client's son?"

"Correct."

The lawyer paced thoughtfully. "When did you meet your wife?"

Landon told them when. She asked, not without a hint of sarcasm, "A confirmed bachelor for so long, with your choice of women, why marry one with such a 'reputation'?"

Mason lifted the pen he used to make notes. "Objection, Your Honor, she's slandering my client."

"Sustained."

The perturbing laugh the woman released only made Beth's fury escalate. "I must rephrase. Mr. Gage, why did you marry Bethany Halifax?"

Mason flew to his feet this time, slamming down a hand. "Objection, Your Honor! Mrs. Gage is insulted by the deliberate use of her old name and I must ask that it be stricken from the record."

"Sustained," the judge conceded.

Now, the opposing attorney set her jaw in determination and walked so close to Landon, Beth had to angle to the side to see his face. "Do you love your wife, Mr. Gage?"

Landon's gaze flicked to hers. He lowered his voice to a rough whisper, and although he wore an expression of cold indifference, his eyes gleamed with intensity as he stared at Beth. "Yes."

If Beth had just been torpedoed, the impact would have been less than that single word.

"How do you feel about this picture, Mr. Gage?"

A shadow crossed Landon's eyes as he inspected the

photograph she showed him—no doubt the same disgusting, humiliating photograph she'd shown to Beth. "Enraged," Landon said, his low, silken voice laced with a threat.

"Why does it enrage you?"

"Because Halifax exploits the fact that my wife loves her child—and will go to any lengths to blackmail and hurt her."

The lawyer seemed vaguely amused as though she couldn't fathom where Landon got such an idea, then asked plainly, "Do you hate Hector Halifax, Mr. Gage?"

The question hung in the air for a tense moment. Sirens wailed inside Beth's head, a warning.

"Do you admit, Mr. Gage, that *you* hate Hector Halifax and would do anything to hurt him? Would go to *any lengths* to ruin him?"

Silence.

Beth held her breath until her lungs burned, mentally willing him to deny this accusation. If he didn't, they would be doomed. But then she knew Landon, and she knew that Landon Gage did not lie....

Then a hard, murderous word resounded in the room, spoken without apology or hesitation. "Yes." Mason cursed quietly at Beth's side, while Landon continued. "I hate Halifax. And I *will* ruin him."

Hector's attorney smiled in victory, then waved an arm out as though that were that. "No more questions, Your Honor."

The second day of the hearing, Landon again held Beth's hand.

His grip was warm and strong, offering much-needed support as they watched Hector take the stand. While she put every effort into reining back her nervousness and her bleak thoughts of the day ahead, Landon looked eerily calm today.

The men had been locked in Landon's study all through last night, and it seemed that whatever last minute evidence

Landon had provided made the lawyer conspiratorially tell Beth this morning, "It's in the bag."

Beth had no idea what the men planned to accomplish today, but as the hearing got underway, when Hector's head nurse and primary character witness was being questioned, Beth prayed they had a plan.

Because the head nurse somehow managed to make it sound like the bastard was on his merry way to being canonized.

"He's been a good father, completely dedicated to providing for his son…" the head nurse was saying. A tidy woman, she had clear skin, little makeup, a bun at her nape that did not have so much as a hair out of place. Her hands remained clasped over her lap as she spoke.

Mason didn't seem impressed.

"Dr. Halifax provides his son with what, exactly?" he asked her, addressing the court first, then the woman. "Money? Or time, love and comfort, as his mother did?"

The head nurse bit her lower lip.

"Your Honor," Mason then said, when the woman didn't answer, "may I submit for evidence this recording of the witness speaking."

Before Beth could register what happened, a small tape recorder played, and the nurse's eyes went huge as a voice remarkably like hers rang out.

Oh, yes, he's horrible in that respect. He's cheap with money, cheap with praise, cheap with everything. We have photocopies of patient records and submit them twice for insurance payment. All I do is change the patient's name…

Murmurs erupted in the courtroom. Astounded whispers.

Patients are so paranoid, it's so laughable. If the doctor tells them there's a miracle drug that will cure all their troubles, most will jump in without question—they're addicted to the medical marijuana the doctor's supplying. It's such good stuff, do you want a little hit?

The courtroom whispers escalated to shocked voices.

"Tell me, Miss Sanchez," Mason broke in in a booming voice. "Is that you speaking?"

"Objection on the grounds of irrelevance, Your Honor!" Hector's lawyer cried, hands on the table.

"Overruled," the judge said. "Sit down, counselor."

Landon gave Beth a reassuring hand-squeeze as the nurse shifted uncomfortably in her seat, a bug under the microscope. Her eyes sought out Julian John's in the benches, and Beth puzzled to see her brother-in-law shoot the woman a winning, you're-screwed smile. The kind of smile the cat would give the mouse. "Yes. It's my voice," she admitted, shooting daggers at Julian, who didn't seem to mind at all.

"Is that you speaking about Dr. Halifax?"

"I...yes."

"Is that you referring to Dr. Halifax committing insurance fraud in order to 'provide' for his lavish lifestyle while negligent of his child?"

"Uh, well—"

"Is that you *admitting* to Dr. Halifax's numerous *illegal* activities, in which you've played a part?"

"But I was only—"

"Is that you, Miss Sanchez, speaking from first-hand knowledge about Dr. Halifax being engaged in *medical malpractice* and the *illegal* prescription of *medical marijuana?*"

She lowered her face as though she wanted to bury it under her sweater. "Yes."

Mason allowed the answer to echo in the room until it faded into a charged quiet. Then, curtly, with a pleased nod, he said, "No more questions, Your Honor."

When Hector was called up to the stand, the air of the courtroom became charged with hostility. His own lawyer interrogated him first, asking him questions about his son, making suggestions that hinted at his being a loving father when Beth knew that was not the case at all! How could she have ever married him? How could she have thought that whatever childish infatuation she'd felt for him could be love? What she felt for Landon defied even comparison—an ocean compared to a grain of sand.

When Mason got to have his go at the man, he had a take-no-prisoners expression on his face. He lifted a piece of paper for all to see. The court, the judge and then the witness.

"Is this your email, Dr. Halifax?"

Hector didn't so much as glance at the page. "Possibly."

"Yes or no, Dr. Halifax. Did you write this email to a patient of yours, Chrystine Gage?"

"Yes," Hector tightly conceded.

"And is this you, Doctor, threatening not to hand out any more prescriptions to your patient unless she did what you commanded?"

"I was merely—"

"Is it or is it not you, *threatening* a patient?"

"Yes," he ground, through clenched teeth.

Mason shook his head in bleak disapproval. "What drug was your patient on?"

"I don't remember."

"Your Honor." Mason produced a new piece of evidence. "We have a prescription from Dr. Halifax made out to Chrystine Gage two days before her death for a drug called Clonazepam.

"Isn't Clonazepam prescribed not only as an anti-anxiety medication, but also as a sleeping pill?"

Hector was silent.

"Isn't it risky for a patient to drive under the influence?"

Hector still didn't respond.

"The witness will answer the counselor," the judge commanded.

"Yes, the drug can be used as a sleeping pill!" Hector grumbled. "Driving is not recommended while using it."

"And yet that is *precisely* what you were demanding your patient do—that she drive to a lonely parking lot in the middle of the night to meet you. That is what your patient ultimately did, resulting in the crash that killed her and her young boy. You *killed* a ten-month-old baby, Dr. Halifax. You *killed* a mother and her child—what's there to recommend you for taking care of your own child?"

"Objection, Your Honor!"

"Overruled. The witness's comment on this is relevant. *Answer.*"

Hector scowled at Beth, the blatant fury in his gaze palpable as a tornado.

He began shaking, visibly shaking in his seat, and burst out, *"You."* He trained his finger like a gun on Beth's forehead, and his mocking tone felt like shards of glass scraping down her skin. "You're worse than I am! Who do you think you are, you little tramp?"

"Silence!" The judge hammered.

Hector's face contorted as he stood, his stormy, furious blue eyes tempting Beth to curl herself into a ball. "You think you can come here and humiliate me?"

"Counselor! You will silence your witness or I'll hold you both in contempt!" Furious now, blue veins stuck out on Judge Prescott's neck.

Hector fell quiet, chastised and displeased, but Mason wasn't yet done with him.

The little black book came up for showing. In the book were Hector's contact numbers for Miguel Gomez, the man who smuggled the illegal marijuana Hector had been sticking to his patients. Also in the book were the numbers of several bribed members of the press who'd promptly been fired not only by the *Daily*, but from the competition as soon as their questionable activities had been reported. Stumbling over his denials, Hector ended up, unwillingly, admitting to all the allegations Mason presented.

By the time he left the stand, her ex-husband looked like an unstable madman, unfit for being a doctor or a parent, while Landon sat quietly beside her, the epitome of the somber businessman.

Scrambling to get back the upper hand, Halifax's lawyer called up the last witness. The entire case now hinged on the nanny.

Anna took the stand, and once she settled in the seat, she made eye contact with Beth.

Hector's lawyer interrogated her on Hector's parenting. Anna answered the questions easily at first, but she kept glancing at Beth, as though waging some sort of silent battle inside herself. Her answers seemed to be limited to "yes" and "no," but she spoke them as though they were wrenched and squeezed out of her by force.

When it was Mason's turn, he first asked her basic questions about her role in raising David. He seemed to barely be getting warmed up when her eyes scanned the room, took in the sight of Landon's family, then returned to Beth, and she blurted, "I can't do this," in a wild and frantic voice.

Like a predator spotting his prey's weakness, Mason jumped at her. "What is it you can't do? Continue working for Dr. Halifax? Continue allowing this injustice—"

"All of it. I can't do it anymore!" Her eyes welled up, and her voice broke as she continued, slightly calmer, "They promised…I'd live well for the rest of my life. As a token of appreciation from the doctor, if I testified. The nanny who testified previously is no longer working at the home. She took the money they gave her to testify last time, and now there's just me. I've been promised a good education for my son, you see. He's almost David's age…" She trailed off and swallowed, as though the next words proved difficult to say.

"But I can't bear to watch this anymore. The child shouldn't be punished like he has been. David needs his *mother*. There's only so much a nanny can give him, and he gets none of it from the doctor. The boy needs his *mother*."

Tears pricked Beth's eyes, and she quickly delved into her bag in search of her tissues. She hadn't expected the nanny to come through for her like this, but then maybe, just maybe, there were more good, decent people in this world than bad ones.

Whispers spread across the room. Hector jumped to his feet and called the nanny a liar, and the judge moved his hammer as he demanded silence.

During recess, Beth wiped the moisture from her cheeks and sat with Landon on a small bench out in the hall. "I'm sorry," she said, clenching her damp tissue in her fist. "That must have been difficult for you. Talking about Chrystine and…"

"Nathan." Landon's timbre dropped to a rough whisper. "His name was Nathan."

The pressure mounted in her chest. She nodded. Nathan.

Imagine Landon as a father. He'd be such a great father. Great brother. Great husband. Oh, God, would he ever trust her again? He was a just man but she suspected he wasn't a forgiving one.

Feeling faint and pale, Beth smiled exhaustedly at him. "You talked to Anna, didn't you?"

"We made sure the court knew what a scumbag Hector is, but we didn't talk to her, Beth. That was all your doing. Clearly she respects you."

The words, somehow, seemed a compliment.

She hesitated, then edged closer, desperate to again reach places she'd reached in him before. "Do you think we'll win?"

He continued absently staring at the crowded hall before them. "We'll win."

She wanted to say something, but felt emotionally drained. Still, she attempted something light and funny, even though she didn't feel like laughing. "Lucky you, you'll be getting rid of me soon."

He turned to her then, and the lack of emotion in his eyes frightened her. His empty smile in no way warmed her. "Not soon enough."

Still stunned minutes later, Beth couldn't even hear through the noise of her blood rushing as they went back inside. The judge resumed his seat and began speaking. He mentioned foreseeing Hector having to answer some severe new accusations in the short future.

Beth heard the fateful words only barely, still struggled to swallow the sour dose of truth Landon had given her. *He couldn't wait to get rid of her.*

"Custody awarded to the petitioners…effective immediately…"

The verdict gradually sunk into her thoughts. She saw the judge rise to leave and Hector's stunned reaction. She noticed Landon shaking Mason's hand. Beth blinked, swayed as she rose to her feet.

Had they won?

So fast? She'd waited months and had expected her misery to last days and days, and now they'd *won?*

The rest happened in a flurry of movement. Being hugged by the Gages, by her mother, her father, by everyone but Landon.

Outside, after a wait that felt eternal, Beth squinted as she watched a car pull over, and David stepped out, running toward her with a grin and another drawing. She glanced at Anna, who smiled at them both from the bottom steps of the courthouse.

"Anna, thank you," she murmured under her breath, then quickly started for her son. God, was she *dreaming?* She wanted to sing and cry and dance.

"Mom! Mom, I made us a drawing!" He didn't kiss or hug her but immediately showed the paper to her and pointed at the figures drawn. "You, me and dog man. See!"

Beth's stomach clenched. The gigantic brown dog he'd drawn covered nearly half the page, and the rest of the picture contained David, Beth and Landon, holding hands while straddling the monster dog. "But sweetie, dog man …" *Won't be around for long.*

She fell quiet when Landon walked up beside her. "Dog man is taller in person," she improvised, flustered as she straightened. Her mom's sad, sympathetic look made a lump grow in her throat. Why was it when you made one dream come true, another fell apart?

Landon remained at her side, and all she became aware of was the fact that he didn't touch her. "Home?" he asked.

Temporary home, Beth thought, already pained to expose David to Landon's household. He couldn't get too settled in, could he?

Beth seized David's hand and tried a smile that didn't quite make it. "We're ready." God, that tiny hand inside of hers felt so right.

Ducking his head to meet David eye to eye, Landon bumped fists with her son, both of them smiling and doing it naturally this time. "You can sleep in Nathan's room," he told the child.

The generous offer only made Beth's misery complete. For she, better than anyone, knew how zealously Landon had guarded that room. Before he'd known the truth about his baby.

Thomas opened the car door, and the three of them climbed inside, David excited, Landon quiet and Beth torn between excitement and despair, on their way to a make-believe home.

She and David hugged all the way.

Fourteen

The house was silent tonight.

Four months had passed, and every day of living with a fake family had been silent, wretched torture.

Landon stared out the window, not really seeing the manicured lawns outside. He was in his room, alone. Just him and the divorce papers. His bedroom had never felt so empty. The furniture couldn't fill the space. Nothing could fill the vast feeling of loss and emptiness.

Mask and Brindle, who'd taken to sleeping with David now, were down the hall in the boy's room.

And Beth…

He didn't know where she was. What she was doing. They barely spoke a word to each other. He knew she worked long hours at the computer during the day, and that she waited by the window when David arrived from school. He knew she slept with the door halfway open to hear anything amiss in David's room at night.

He knew that sometimes, when tired, she spoke in her

dreams. And he knew that most of those times, she spoke his name. He'd also heard her cry once. Soft sniffles at midnight, coming from her room, making him toss in his empty bed wondering why she cried. He didn't hold his breath thinking it was him she cried for.

They'd been with him for four months now, four months and twenty nine days. Living with them felt like living with a ticking time bomb.

It was impossible to explain to Garrett, who'd been asking questions, or to anyone, what he'd been feeling all this time, seeing Beth every day, seeing her son frolicking out in the gardens during the afternoon. Her son, who was the same age Nathan would've been.

Longing didn't hold a candle to the emotions that bombarded him. Now his every muscle was taut with tension, tension which could find no relief, no kind of comfort. Because the tension that most gnawed at his gut stretched between Beth and him—and it was always home as long as she was.

He had to get rid of them, both of them.

He had known, from the moment he'd seen her in his hotel room, that she attracted him. He was a man accustomed to analyzing before acting, and he'd believed he'd somehow be able to remain immune to Beth's effect on him.

He hadn't.

Just as he hadn't predicted how badly he wanted to make things right for her. Even in ways he hadn't been able to make them right for himself.

No matter what she'd done to him, no matter that she'd lied and betrayed him, Landon had given her his word. She would have her son back at any cost, and Landon would have Halifax's head.

It had been four months and twenty nine days. Why had he not celebrated his victory over Halifax yet?

Because she's still here.

Landon wrenched off his tie, shoving it into his pants pocket. Halifax didn't deserve to be walking on the same planet Beth and her son were. And therefore, he would not. He was answering to a hell of a lot more charges now and would probably spend the rest of his life behind bars. Not only had the insurance companies sued him for millions the man in all likelihood did not have, but the District Attorney had charged him with distribution of illegal substances, and criminally negligent *manslaughter*. His situation was bleak.

As bleak as…Landon's bedroom.

"Damn it," he cursed. Before he knew what he did, he removed his coat, rolled the cuffs of his shirt, yanked the door open, and scoured the house for his wife.

She'd tried talking to him several times, always uneasily, but the intense sting of betrayal he felt kept building inside of him, and it left no room for listening to Beth. No room for coddling her. No room for anything except waiting to recover whatever life he'd had before her, and forget he'd ever married her.

He found the door to her bedroom partway open. Something tightened inside him as he pushed it wider and gazed into the dimly lit room. "Beth? Can we talk?"

Beth sat at the vanity, brushing her hair as though the act calmed her, and stopped when she heard him. She spun around on the upholstered ottoman with wide unblinking eyes, her mouth slightly parted. The picture of Halifax leaning in unbearably close to those pretty pink lips came back to Landon, making him want to rip down the drapes and toss them out the window.

He wanted to grab her shoulders and shake her, take her, but instead his hands curled in on themselves, clenching tight at his sides.

"I thought you were at dinner with your brothers," Beth said.

"They were irritating me, so I left them to irritate each other." He propped a shoulder against the door frame, struggling to steady his heartbeat. He'd been inventing dinners all week—anything to stay away from home. From her. But tonight was different. "I merely wanted to see if you were all right."

Her smile held a hint of sadness. "So now you're talking to me."

He did not deny his lack of attention. How could he? He didn't want to see her, couldn't stand eating with her, could barely keep on living in the same house with her without going insane. Holding her little hand in his at court had been painful. Hearing her say she loved him with the same mouth she'd both kissed and lied to him had been among the most painfully mocking things in his entire goddamned life.

She rose to her feet in an easy, effortless move that made her body sway under the loose pastel green robe she wore. "Landon, about what I said at court—"

"I didn't come here to talk about what you said," he interrupted.

The hurt that came to her eyes made him want to charge across and do something to erase it. But she quickly wiped her expression clean, and he quickly dashed the thought of doing anything for her except what he'd promised he would and had already accomplished. Getting her son back.

Made visibly nervous by his visit, since he'd been doing a damned fine job of staying away from her room for weeks, Beth chewed her lower lip. "What did you come up here to talk about, then?"

I wanted to look at you one last time.

"I came to let you know…" His blood swirled. After the brutal feel of his own exposure at court, admitting to a room full of people what he had not admitted even to himself, every atom, cell and nerve in his body vibrated with yearning for her. Every night, every day. He had to leave, now, before he regretted it. He clamped his teeth and shook his head, frustrated with himself. "Forget it."

He spun around, but she called his name.

"Landon!"

He stiffened, and his head came up a bit, but he didn't

turn until several slow, painful seconds passed. He faced her once more, not wanting to notice how her hair fell in a golden waterfall past her shoulders, framing her delicate face, not wanting to think that she looked vulnerable and beautiful and ready for bed.

"It's about the divorce, isn't it," she said.

Something cracked inside, but he'd be dead before he showed it. He nodded. "I wanted to say goodbye."

The next day started easily enough, ordinarily enough, except for the yellow folder Beth found on her nightstand. Landon must have gotten close to leave it there during the night, and her stomach tumbled realizing she must have slept through it.

So…

It was indeed goodbye.

During the morning she felt numb. Couldn't bring herself to open it. But she knew what it was. She accompanied Thomas to drop David at school, then she called her mother to let her know they'd be coming over today and staying for a week or two, until she could rent the small one-bedroom house at Crownridge she'd spotted.

David would miss the dogs. Between packing for them both and stealing sidelong glances at the envelope, Beth scoured through the dog books in Landon's study in search of the right breed for them. Maybe a little dog, which wouldn't bark and disturb the neighbors. She pored over the books, and stopped at: Old English Mastiffs.

Her insides wrenched as she read the description. *So.* This was why Landon didn't have a Doberman, or a German Shepherd. Mastiffs were loyal to the death. And it struck her how, above anything else, her husband valued loyalty, and how Beth had disappointed him.

She and David moved out that afternoon, before Landon returned from work, but even then, she didn't dare open the envelope.

She found herself staring at it the next morning, torn between finding out its contents or setting it on fire in the kitchen stove.

"Your father says Hector's going to get a life sentence, and there's really nothing he can do about it but serve it. Beth! Are you listening to me? I don't appreciate seeing you moping, Bethy. We really must do something about it."

Beth sat at the small old breakfast table—the envelope next to her plate. Outside, cars drove by. But no. No black Navigator or blue Maserati pulled over in front of Mom's home. Probably, there never would be.

She sipped her coffee, wondering what to do, wondering if she'd always been such a coward, when her mother's frequent, worried glances prodded her to speak. "I heard you," she said at last, sighing. "Hector's getting at least thirty years. I'm sorry, Mother, but I'm not pretending to be surprised. The man had gotten away with it for too long."

"Speak louder, Bethy, I'm not wearing my hearing aid. And stop looking at those papers and open them, for heaven's sake. Here. Take this knife."

Okay, then.

Opening them now.

Beth's hand trembled as she sliced into the top folded edge, her pulse jumping in fear. "We agreed on this, you know," she said, to the kitchen in general. But had they agreed on kissing each other senseless? On telling each other secrets, fears, opening themselves up for heartbreak?

The memory of Landon telling her—*Before you give me anything else, Beth, I want your trust*—made her eyes start to burn. He'd given her his own trust, clearly. And she'd proved it a mistake.

"Well? Are those divorce papers?"

"Yes." Beth clutched them to her chest as though they were a declaration of love, while in her mind she imagined ripping, stomping on or losing them. Landon thought this was it, then? That she'd just take the papers and not be allowed an explanation? Not allowed a formal goodbye other than that brief, angry visit he'd paid her room last night? "Mom, can I borrow Dad's car for a bit?" Beth said, loudly enough for her mother to hear.

"Oh yes yes, of course!"

She fell deep into thought as she drove, the envelope her only passenger.

Now with her business up and running, she could find a place—nearby, in the same school district. And buy a car. She could start over as she'd always wanted to. Her and David, against the world.

But not before she saw Landon.

Dread coiled around her throat as she was led into his office. Then, coming around the desk in all his glory was Landon Gage. His was a face she would not see every day again, a voice she would not hear again. Here was a man who wanted to get rid of her.

On tenterhooks, Beth lowered herself on to the chair across the desk from his. "I thought I'd personally bring you these," she said, then cleared her throat and slightly raised the envelope to his attention.

"Not necessary." His timbre was about as inanimate as a lamp.

Beth bit her lip, then, trembling, set the papers on his desk. "I also thought you'd want this back." The small diamond on her finger flashed as she twisted off the ring.

She laid it over the envelope with a tiny but deafening "click".

Neither could bear to look at it.

Landon reclined in his seat and clasped his hands behind his head, his eyes slowly raking her body. "How are you? How's David?"

She smiled, tremulously, and wondered how she could even manage it. *Just as you managed to sign the divorce papers, Beth.* Very grudgingly.

"Happy. David's happy. Landon…thank you. You did as you promised and you were so good to me." So good for me…

She counted the prizes hanging behind his wall, recognitions of him as a newspaper genius, and tried to calm down. Once, when she was little, she'd shattered her tiniest, most prized crystal figurine into what seemed like a hundred little pieces. It was a swan her mother had given her, and she had treasured it. But no matter how much she prayed, the figurine was beyond repair, the shards so tiny they only cut and cut at her fingers when she tried to mend it. Was that the case with Landon? She could wish and pray and want but she would only cut herself more. He didn't look at her with warmth. He looked at her not like a husband, but an enemy. They. *They* were beyond repair. But she had to try.

"If that's all…" He shuffled some papers—and Beth got the message clearly, even though he spoke again in interest. "Kate tells me you're officially a partner in her business."

She waited for him to say more, something about them, words welling in her throat. No. She should not do this. She would divorce him and she would bury her past and start a new life for herself. But she did not want a divorce. She wanted, needed forgiveness. Her own and his. And love. It still thickened her veins, danced in her thoughts and in her heart. Her nerves quivered. Inside, she screamed. *Love me back. Have pity on me and hold me…like before…like when you loved me with your body….*

"Business, yes. We're doing great with online advertising on our recipe section."

"Good. Very good, Bethany."

"Landon, why are we doing this?" she blurted. "Why won't you listen to me?"

One eyebrow lifted, as though he could not for the life of him have heard correctly. "We had an agreement. We've fulfilled both our ends."

"So what happened between us…? We're to pretend it never happened at all?"

"Beth," he said with a significant pause, and she could see him grapple for words. "I expect…things of my wife."

He left them unsaid, the things he wanted.

His voice dropped a decibel, became a terse, quiet confession. "Is it wrong that I expect you to be loyal and truthful with me?"

Beth gulped as she watched him rise, eager to dismiss her. She leapt to her feet. "What if I was trying to protect you? What if you have me all wrong? I'm not who you think I am, Landon! If you'd only let me show you…"

He went rigid when she sailed around the desk.

"Bethany—" He caught her shoulders, but didn't push her away. "We were a bad idea. I thought I could live with it, knowing you were Halifax's first, but I can't. I can't stand the idea. I can't stand the idea of you…lying to me."

"I can't stand it either, but I can't change the past, please understand. I just didn't want to *hurt* you."

Frantically, she slid her palm up his shirt, his chest solid, hot through the cotton. She could feel every sinew of muscle underneath. Deep, forgotten places inside her clenched. "Landon, please."

"Beth, what are you playing at?" His voice grew husky. Desire trembled there. His hand on her back began to squeeze her, began to want and feel and knead.

She pressed closer, a little in agony, seeking ease for the horrible burn growing inside her. "Last night I saw you… I thought my husband came to get his good-night kiss."

He groaned. Images of his sculpted body began to tease and tantalize her. Him in nakedness, the male form in all its glory, chiseled like a statue but warmer. Just one time—they'd been together just one time—and it haunted her. She pressed her legs together and tried to breathe slowly. But the images remained. Clearer, more vivid. They were memories. Of when he'd been inside her. Of him biting at her breasts. Of her nails sinking into his back. Of that consuming passion they had shared.

He pressed her back against the window, caging her in with his body. "Damn you."

He swept down—but stopped a hairbreadth away. Opening her mouth, she flicked her tongue out to lick the firm flesh of his lips. Explosions of colors. Mouths melding. Skin, heat, ecstasy. "Is this wrong?" she taunted. She draped a leg around his thigh and flattened herself against his chest, her breasts crushed against his ribs, her tummy to his. "How can this be wrong?"

"I don't…" His hand fisted in her hair and he opened his mouth, giving her the mist of his breath. She waited for that kiss, the searing kiss that would put everything behind them. It didn't come. "Want you anymore," he huskily murmured, the graze of his lips across hers so bare and fleeting she mewled with a protest for more.

His hold tightened on her hair before he released her. "Goodbye, Miss Lewis."

Fifteen

Landon prowled the city, simmering with pent-up need, anger and despair. He couldn't bear to go home. It felt empty, the house, his room, his bed. Beth was gone, and the relief he'd assumed he'd feel with her departure wasn't coming.

He couldn't stop thinking about her, what she'd said about a ten-month-old baby. How she'd looked in his office, desperate as that first day, this time desperate for something Landon could no longer give her.

He drove along the highway, and before he knew where he headed, Landon stopped by Mission Park cemetery. His son's gravestone; he'd visited only once before years ago. Why now? Why was he back here at this place that held his most haunting memories?

Because he's my son.

He gazed down at the lettering, engraved in the granite headstone. Nathaniel Gage.

He's not your son, he's Hector's…

To hear his own wife say it had been a blow, but once the

words registered, he'd felt more than anger, more than despair. He'd felt betrayed and played and violated.

They'd won at court—but the satisfaction of winning hadn't accompanied the success. Landon had lost. Because it was just the kind of cruel twist of fate that Landon should love something of his enemy's. It was just the kind of cruel twist of fate that even knowing Nathan was not his son, and belonged to the bastard, Landon still loved him.

Nathaniel was a Gage.

He stroked a hand over the curved top of the gravestone. He didn't understand. He never would. One second his attention was elsewhere, and when he'd looked back his wife and kid were gone. The accident had revealed her treachery. Phone calls, emails, letters. Years betraying him behind his back. But never had he imagined it had dated to before. Before Landon had met her, before he'd married her.

To think how she'd snagged him, young and in his prime, pretending he was the father of her unborn child. For the length of their short marriage Landon had been faithful, making an effort, for her, for Nathaniel. And all that time, she'd been seeing Hector.

His son would've been thirsty for life.

And Chrystine's treachery robbed him of it.

But now, even now, when he'd taken everything of Halifax's, his practice, his respect and his freedom, Landon could not enjoy the victory. He could not go back to the way he was before. He loved that son, wanted him as his, and the path of revenge had opened up a whole new wanting for him.

He wanted Bethany—the son she and Halifax had. That, too, he wanted. Because it was hers.

Yes, a cruel twist of fate it was. To love the two things that had first belonged to the enemy.

A bouquet of flowers appeared out of nowhere—white roses suddenly laid there, over the grave, tied by a sleek white ribbon. Landon glanced past his shoulder to confirm his suspicions, and sighed.

He wasn't alone. Comfortably clad in a flowery dress and a pair of maroon cowboy boots, his mother nailed the Texan matron look down to a tee.

"What are you doing here?"

"I come here every week. Why wouldn't I visit my grandson?" Her weathered hand stroked the name, and Landon lowered his face, said softly, "He's not mine, Mother."

She didn't jerk at the news, only regarded him with that impenetrable coolness of hers. "You were always the one ready to make the tough decisions for the family. And I think you're so used to making them, you can't believe anything can be good and simple anymore."

"Nothing in my life has ever been good or simple."

"But it is. Bethany fell in love with you. And you with her. Good. And simple."

Landon didn't respond, fought not to think of her, remember the ways her lips curled into all kinds of mischievous or shy or soft smiles.

He tossed a twig into the air. "I'm not sure she loves me. I'm not even sure what was real and what wasn't."

"I know what you were fighting for, Landon. You've never been vindictive. You've always done the honorable thing. You weren't fighting for revenge, you were fighting for a family. The family you deserve. A woman touched your heart, even when you didn't want her to, and you were fighting for her. Are you going to quit now? When you're so far ahead in the game?"

He remembered her. Her dense lashes had glittered with tears. She'd annihilated his mind and senses. How could she have filtered through his defenses?

Because he'd seen her uniqueness and he'd let her.

And she'd let him in, as well.

And he knew then that he would have no other family.

But the one he'd already claimed before the world as his.

Exactly one month after moving in with her parents, Beth wiped a hand across her moistened brow and sighed in satisfaction as she gazed across her new one-bedroom home. Only five closed boxes remained, stacked neatly to one side of the small foyer, but compared to the forty loaded monsters she'd started with, what remained was nothing.

Easily tackled in an hour, if not less.

Sighing, she opened the front door to check if any boxes remained out on the porch and frowned when she spotted a small one.

The plain brown box sat meekly on her doorstep, just over the new rug that read "Welcome."

Beth didn't remember having seen it there before.

Confusion mingled with curiosity as she shook the box. Something thudded inside. "What the…" Her hands flew to open the package.

A brand-new little black book. That's exactly what she discovered.

A brand-spanking-new little black book exactly like the one that had once brought her and Landon together. Halifax was in jail and wouldn't ever bother her or David. So why this sense of nervousness at the sight of the new book? And where, God, where, did this strange excitement come from?

Because it reminds you of the day you met Landon…

Her throat filled up with emotion at the bittersweet memory, and, carefully, afraid of what she'd find, or maybe more afraid of what she wouldn't find, Beth opened the book to page one.

Her pulse shot up. There, inside, on the first page, lay a note, written in Landon's handwriting. She read the note once, failing to go back for a second read when her eyes blurred. It was a silly note, from a man who'd always criticized anyone for writing his sins in a little black book. And now he was writing one of his.

Landon Gage is a fool, it read.

Eyes stinging, Beth looked up and saw him as a big dark blur. Him. He was there, standing there, his presence warm as a sun. He stood on the steps of her new home, looking clean and manly and slightly rumpled without a tie.

Beth blinked, feeling like a thousand angels were sweeping her off her feet, but it was only one man. Just one man, a prince to her.

A frisson of expectation went through her as she waited for him to say something, *please* say something, because she seemed to have lost the ability to speak.

He leaned against the front porch balustrade, under the shade, watching her somberly. "Hi."

Stifling a tremor that rushed from the top of her head down to the tips of her toes, Beth clutched the book to her body, still unable to believe he stood here, in the flesh, at her doorstep. "Hi, Landon."

God, she'd missed the sight of Landon Gage. She felt it proper to say something, but her mouth felt like a prison for all the words she wanted to say and couldn't.

She drank up his image as if she were seeing him for the very first time, examining the fit of his clean tailored slacks and button-down shirt, remembering the lean, hard body underneath. He'd cut his hair, and he looked very young and very handsome.

With a halfhearted smile, Landon took a step closer. "There's this man I need you to exact revenge upon. An imbecile who was about to make the biggest mistake of his life," he said direly.

His voice did things to her, awakened her body so that her senses swam. Flutters invaded her, whizzing in her chest, her stomach, her head. "So that's what the book is for," she said.

"It's for revenge, Bethany." Landon's forehead creased as he took yet another step closer. "He's undeserving, this man. Extremely undeserving. And I can think of no one else who could torture him as well as you."

"Torture him?" Her temperature jacked up another degree.

He gave a slight nod. "Uh-huh. I need you to stare him in

the face, every day, so he remembers what he almost let another man take away from him. I need you to be ruthless, to have absolutely no mercy on him, and above all, I want you to make him pay. It's a matter of revenge, Beth. And this man…" The determination in his eyes arrested her. "This man is begging for it."

She didn't laugh. She could tell by the tension in him, in his face, that it cost him his pride and ego and everything he valued to say it.

Oh, God, Landon was begging for *her.*

Her palms itched to touch him but instead she wrapped her arms around herself, unsure of how to verbalize her sentiments. Sentiments in the lines of: *I love you, yes yes yes, amen to whatever you're proposing!*

Should she invite him inside? She wanted to. But the house was still a mess, and her pride smarted at the mere thought of Landon discovering that she'd be living with only the bare necessities. Then she realized that in a faded T-shirt, shorts and sandals, she wasn't much of an improvement over her small, plain home.

"Sounds like a good plan." She remained in place at the doorway, unsure of what to do next. Her heart pounded a mile a minute and she still struggled to catch her breath. "But there's one problem."

He went rigid. He surveyed the empty lots that flanked her house, where in the future she'd have neighbors. "A problem," he said. His jaw squared, and when the wind blew in her direction, it brought his clean scent of soap with it.

She hauled in a good lungful of him, unable to stop a shudder. "A big problem." She stepped out into the porch. Closer to him.

His eyebrows slanted over his eyes, and wearing that worried frown, Landon Gage looked adorable. He pinched the bridge of his nose as though trying to stifle a headache. "What kind of problem?"

Beth could barely speak, the emotions rising inside her too powerful to rein back. "That I have no more hate left."

She canted her face to his, and the feelings of passion and need she felt for him overflowed her. Heat spread across her midsection while a swirl of desire took form in his glinting silver eyes.

"I have only one feeling lately, apart from sadness, and I have so much of it I don't know what to do with it."

The features of his face went taut with emotion as he took one more step, the final step. The one that brought him so close she could feel his breath, his heat, inhale his scent. "What is it that you feel, Beth?" He stood only inches from her, tall and dark and patient and so male she felt coy and shy.

She wanted to touch him, wanted to so much, but for the moment lacked the courage. "Like I said, I don't know what to do with it."

It was Landon who couldn't seem to help himself any longer. Pain streaked through his face, tightening his features as he moved. He framed her cheeks with his hands, his fingertips caressing her temples. "I love you, Mrs. Gage." His chest expanded under his shirt as he inhaled and set his forehead on hers. "I love you and I want you to tell me you feel this for me, that you love me, only me."

Her body responded to his evocative words, to his calling her by his name. Her blood bubbled in her veins. A head-tingling sensation swept through her and it made her faint.

He wanted her; he was here for her. And Beth wasn't going to make him beg.

Never, not for a moment in the past months, had she been confused about this. Him. And the fact that she wanted to be with him. She'd dreamt every night over the past lonely weeks, waiting, praying, that Landon would come to terms with the specialness of what they had together. That he'd love her more than her pride and realize Beth was not Chrystine.

Beth loved him. Had been spoiled for any other man but Landon.

She'd settle for nothing less than him.

"I meant what I said in court, Landon." She took his jaw in her hands, her eyelids fluttering as she rose on tiptoe to brush his lips with hers. *"I love you."*

Her soft kiss seemed to take him by surprise, and it took him a moment to take action, but then he released a low, rough groan. He encircled her waist and kissed the breath out of her, his hands wandering her curves, gripping her tight against him.

He exhaled as though he'd been holding his breath for too long. "God, Bethany." He leaned in again, this time taking her mouth slowly and deeply, savoring her taste, allowing her to savor his, then he took her hands between both of his. "I'm sorry," he murmured huskily against her. "I'm sorry for being such a fool."

"I'm sorry for not telling you about Nathan."

"I'm sorry you ever married that bastard, Beth, and that I almost let him take you away from me."

"And I'm sorry I ever met him! But then, maybe…" A thought struck her, and it was so funny, she smiled. "But then he brought us together, didn't he, Landon?"

Amusement lightened his expression, and a fingertip came up to still her lips. "The only good thing he did in his sorry-ass life. Beth, I need you. I need my wife. Marry me again. For real this time. No hidden agendas. Just two people who want to spend the rest of their lives together."

Beth grabbed his shoulders and kissed him, kissed him hard and felt him respond to her with fierce hunger, and her breath shortened until she panted. "Our first marriage was realer than anything in my life. I didn't want to get divorced."

Out of his back pockets, Landon yanked out a roll of papers and without ceremony tore them up, scattering the snow-like pieces across the porch. "Then we won't."

"Were those the—"

"Divorce papers? They were before I ripped them." He

signaled toward the house, his eyes alight with mischief. "Want some help moving out?"

"Oh, God, I just moved in."

"Show me around then?"

She laughed. "I know what you want, Mr. Gage." She gestured him into the house and kissed him again. "The mattress will arrive later," she murmured seductively.

He kicked the door shut and imprisoned her against him, her breasts crushed against his chest, her buttocks in his big massaging hands. "We don't need a mattress." He spoke huskily against her. "All we need to start again is this." He pulled out another roll of papers from behind him. "I'm sure you'll enjoy burning this prenup. We'll have another one drawn."

"So we can discuss intimacy with your lawyers? No, thank you!"

"So we can discuss my millions and millions and how much you want."

Frowning, Beth seized the prenup and ripped it in two, because trust begot trust, and she wanted to start with lots of it. "I just want you, because you're you, and not for any other reason."

He broke into a smile and squeezed her hard. "Damn, Beth, that's about the sexiest thing I've ever heard."

"Wait until I tell you about the little red number I was wearing at court."

He swept down and seized her lips with his, and he kissed her with hunger and heat, stroked the sides of her body while he raked his teeth down her neck, over her shoulder, pulled her faded T-shirt down to reveal her flesh and swirl his tongue against her collarbone. "I don't care about the red number. I care about what's beneath it. About this. My wife, and how fast I can get you naked."

Clinging to him, she kissed him for all the times she hadn't kissed him. "I'm all yours, Gage."

* * * * *